P9-BIU-223

"I have walked in Kraggen-cor, a bygone Realm of might;
but its light is gone, and dread now stalks the halls."

Brega, Bekki's son
January 18, 4E2019

CONTENTS

SYNOPSIS

This is the second part of The Silver Call.

The first part, *Trek to Kraggen-cor,* told of how the hearts of Peregrin Fairhill and Cotton Buckleburr, two of the Wee Folk—the Warrows—were stirred to excitement as rare visitors, a Man and two Dwarves, came on a mission to Sir Tuckerby's Warren in Woody Hollow in the Boskydells. Perry, the present curator of the Warren, was asked to show the visitors his copy of *The Unfinished Diary of Sir Tuckerby Underbank and His Accounting of the Winter War,* a chronicle more commonly known as *The Raven Book.*

The Dwarves were seeking to glean from the *'Book* whatever detail it held of Kraggen-cor, the ancient undermountain homeland their ancestors had fled more than a thousand years earlier when the dreaded Gargon was inadvertently set free. But the Gargon had been slain during the Winter War, and the Dwarves now sought once again to take possession of their ancestral Realm.

But Kraggen-cor remained infested with *Spaunen*—evil maggot-folk that had begun once more to raid and pillage nearby steads, and to slay the innocent.

Enraged, the Dwarves planned to invade Kraggen-cor to root out the evil; but their knowledge of their ancient homeland was fragmentary at best. However, 231 years in the past, during the Winter War, four heroes—a Man, an Elf, a Dwarf, and a Warrow—had passed through Kraggen-cor from Dusk-Door to Dawn-Gate, and their tale was recorded in *The Raven Book.* Hence, to increase their knowledge of the ways in Kraggen-cor and thus improve their odds in the coming struggle with the Spawn, the two Dwarf visitors, Anval and Borin Ironfist, guided by the Man, Lord Kian, had come to the Boskydells to read the account for themselves.

The Raven Book did indeed contain the tale of the Four

Who Strode Through Kraggen-cor, but the story was of marginal help to the visitors. Oh, the tale did yield valuable information, telling that the condition of the two known ways into Kraggen-cor would make the invasion most difficult: On one side of the Grimwall Mountains, the western entrance—the Dusk-Door—may have been broken and buried under tons of rubble by a hideous Kraken living in a black lake warding the portal. And on the opposite side of the Grimwall, the eastern entrance—the Dawn-Gate—appeared all but impossible to invade because the drawbridge over the Great Deep had been burned by the four heroes during their escape more than two centuries agone; and to try to win over that virtually bottomless chasm in the face of an enemy army seemed an insuperable task. Yet, although the visitors had learned of the chief difficulties they would initially face in the invasion, *The Raven Book* had not given them what they sought: step-by-step knowledge of the heroes' trek through Kraggen-cor—knowledge needed to wage a War upon familiar ground.

On learning of this need, Perry showed the visitors a scroll said to have been recorded years after the Winter War by one of the four heroes—Brega the Dwarf. The scroll detailed the path the heroes had taken on their perilous journey through the undermountain Realm. Anval and Borin authenticated the scroll, for they saw that it contained secret Dwarven marks; further, they vouched for its accuracy, saying that the Dwarves have a special gift: once they have trodden a path, it is within them always.

But Dwarves must actually tread a path in order to master it; they are no better or worse than others at memorization. And the Brega Path was long and complex; and for Anval or Borin to have to memorize it for the Dwarves to invade Kraggen-cor would take months—time the Dwarves could ill afford; for the strength of the Spawn had continued to grow, and each night they extended the range of their murderous raids.

Yet all was not lost, for with Cotton's help, Perry had been studying the scroll, and he had committed the path to memory; and as a stripling, Perry had always wanted to be caught up in an adventure, and at last an adventure had come to him. Hence, even though Perry felt unprepared to accept the role suddenly thrust upon him, the buccan nevertheless volun-

teered to go with Anval and Borin and Lord Kian to rendezvous with the Dwarf Army and guide them along the Brega
Path.

Impelled by friendship and loyalty, Cotton, too, answered
the call to adventure.

Thus, Perry, Cotton, Anval, Borin, and Lord Kian all set
forth upon a long journey to Landover Road Ford to meet the
Dwarf Army, even then on the march from Mineholt North
toward Kraggen-cor.

During their journey the two Warrows, under Lord Kian's
tutelage, began training at swords, for they would need to
defend themselves should they become caught in battle.

Weeks later, having overcome time, distance, flood, land-
slide, and hunger, the five comrades rendezvoused with the
Army.

Durek, King of the Dwarves, held a War council, and
meager though it was, all the information gleaned from the
journey to the Boskydells was reviewed. During the Council,
Cotton revealed that he, too, held the steps of the Brega Path
within his memory, thus could also serve as a guide. Hence,
full of unknowns, two strike plans were settled upon: The
first called for the Dwarven Army, with Cotton as their
Brega-Path guide, to cross the mountains and march to the
Dusk-Door, where they hoped somehow to avoid or defeat
the Krakenward, if there; to remove any rubble under which
the Door might be buried; and to enter Kraggen-cor via that
portal if it would open. But, because the Dusk-Door may
have been broken during the Winter War, and because the
arcane hinges could only be repaired from the inside, a
second strike plan, coordinated with the first, was called for:
here, a squad of seven persons, including Perry as the Brega-
Path guide, was to journey to the Dawn-Gate, somehow cross
the Great Deep, and if possible penetrate undetected through
the Swarm of maggot-folk and traverse the full length of
Kraggen-cor to the inside of the Dusk-Door to make repairs if
needed—if the Gatemasters in the Squad had the knowledge
to do so.

Following these two uncertain courses, the Army marched
away toward the Dusk-Door while the squad embarked for
the Dawn-Gate.

Perry and the Squad rafted down the Argon River toward

their goal, at last settling in at a riverside campsite to wait for time to pass in order to match schedules with the Army. While encamped they were attacked by a Hlōk-led band of Rūcks and nearly overwhelmed. Yet in the nick of time the Squad was rescued by Ursor the Baeran, a giant of a Man, by Shannon Silverleaf, an Elf, and by Shannon's Elven Company. Even so, two of the Squad's Gatemasters were lost to the mission: Tobin's leg was broken, and Barak was slain. Hence, but one Gatemaster, Delk, remained to perhaps repair the possibly broken hinges when and if the Squad ever reached them. Yet it was decided that the mission must go forth, even though the loss of Tobin and Barak was a severe blow. It was also decided that Shannon and Ursor would join the quest, once again making the Squad seven strong.

Meanwhile, on their own mission, Cotton and the Army had marched into a mountain blizzard and had been trapped for days. Yet, after an exhausting dig-out, followed by a long forced march, they arrived at last at the Dusk-Door. And all the while, Cotton had borne with him a small silver horn: the Horn of Narok—the Horn of the Death War—a token deeply feared by the Dwarves, for it was a relic of Dwarven legend, a legend foretelling of a great unknown sorrow to befall the Dwarves.

Indeed the Door was covered by a huge mound of rubble, and the work to remove it began. But at sundown the Krakenward attacked, devastating the ranks of the workers. After a desperate all-night struggle, by axe and sword and Atalar blade, and fire and hammer and drill, and water and stone, the Army at last defeated the Madûk, breaking the dam and draining the black lake and casting huge stones down upon the Monster. Even so, the creature had buried the Door under even more rubble, placing the rendezvous with the Squad and the entire invasion plan in grim jeopardy.

But as the tale continues, we return to the river camp where the Squad even now prepares to set forth for the Dawn-Gate, to set forth upon their dire mission to penetrate the lightless, Spawn-filled length of Kraggen-cor in a desperate bid to reach the hinges inside the distant Dusk-Door.

CHAPTER 1

THE GREAT DEEP

Perry was awakened at dawn by Delk, who had the last watch. Before joining the others for breakfast, the Warrow retrieved Bane from the log beside him; the Elven-blade had been embedded in the bark point down, the long-knife left standing upright through the night as a silent sentinel for all the company to see. And as each member of the Squad had taken his ward tour, he had kept a close eye on the sword, watching for the flickering blue flame that would gleam from the blade-jewel if *Spaunen* drew near.

Shannon Silverleaf, whose turn at guard had come after Perry's, had been especially interested in the blade, and had plucked it out and held it with reverence. "This was crafted long ago in the Realm of Duellin, a bygone Land of Atala," the Elf had said to Perry after long study, "and the way of its making is lost. This blade speaks of the Elden Days, when it was one of many weapons fashioned to engage the evil forces of the Great Enemy, Gyphon—the High Vûlk. In a way, we are fighting Him still, for it is He who bred the Rucha, Loka, and Ogruthi—as well as other evil beings—in Neddra, in the Untargarda. My forefathers in the House of Aurinor made these blades to fight that spawn.

"Alas, though many of these poniards were forged in those Elden Days, few remain in Mithgar, and fewer still are yet in use—most lie in rest in ancient graves or upon dusty tombs." Silverleaf had then flourished the blade. "But this pick still serves. I think the name for this edge, Bane, is well chosen, and one which imparts honor to the weapon. This is a great token to carry into Black Drimmen-deeve, and it bodes well

1

for our mission.'' The Elf then had plunged its point back into the log and replaced Perry at guard.

But now it was dawn, and any maggot-folk abroad would have taken cover from the coming Sun, so Perry sheathed Bane and hunkered down for the morning meal.

"Enjoy your hot tea," said Kian, "for there'll be no fires after this one until our mission is done; this is the last pot we'll brew til then. But we'll not be without tea for long: Today we start overland. At sunrise on the sixth day hence we should be entering Dawn-Gate. At midnight of the ninth day we should see Durek with Cotton and my brother, Rand, enter the Dusk-Door with the Army right behind. Then, after another day or three and many dead Spawn, we will at last build us a fire and enjoy some more hot brew."

"It will give me much pleasure removing the uninvited Wrg 'guests' from our upcoming tea party," grunted giant Ursor, and the others nodded and smiled grimly.

Soon breakfast was finished, and all the spare supplies were cached. The Sun had risen, and it was time to go. Delk quenched the fire, and all shouldered their packs. Perry took one last look at the Great River Argon in the direction the blazing funeral raft had swept. "Farewell, Barak," he whispered, and turned to join the others.

They started west over the land, walking in single file: Lord Kian led the way, the young Man armored in mail and a plain iron-and-leather helm, and armed with his silver-handled bow and arrows, and a sword and dagger; behind Kian marched Anval, the Dwarf warrior mail-shirted, iron-helmed, axe-armed; Ursor the Baeran came next, wearing a dark-brown boiled-leather breastplate and carrying his great black mace; Perry was silveron-mailed under his shirt, with Bane and a dagger at his belt, and on his head he wore a simple steel-and-leather helmet; lithe Shannon Silverleaf strode next, without armor but armed with a longbow and arrows and a knife the length of Bane; Borin and Delk brought up the rear, these two Dwarves each armed and armored like Anval, with axes and helms and black-iron mail. All wore green or grey or brown travelling clothes that blended with earth and stone, leaf and branch; and they bore packs containing the needed tools, food, and other supplies for their mission; each carried a leather water bottle at his hip. Their bedrolls and cloaks were fastened in rolls on top of the packs. Thus did they trek in file toward Kraggen-cor, leaving the Argon behind.

Soon the Seven emerged from the river-border forest and came to the wold, a treeless rolling plain that slowly rose up toward the far mountains. Occasionally a thicket stood barren in the winter Sun, and heather and gorse grew on the land. The slopes were gentle and the growth was low, and so they walked in a line straight to the west; only now and then would they make a detour to pass around an outcropping or a tangle of briars or other minor hindrance. Only twice did they come to major obstructions: The first was a deep, wide ravine across their path, running out of the northwest and down to the southeast. They clambered down one steep side and into the wooded bottom where a wide stream bubbled and danced through mossy rocks; the company took the opportunity to replenish their canteens in its clear, sparkling depths. Crossing over, they scrambled up the other side and back out onto the wold. The second obstacle was a minor bluff that jumped up out of the land to steeply bar the way. They walked north three miles before finding a cut that they could walk up through to pass beyond this high rampart.

The second day was much like the first: Even though it was mid-November, the day stayed mild and the air was calm, and so the trek was made in good weather. The course the comrades took was over gentle land, and they made good time. The wold continued to rise slowly as they marched westward toward the mountains.

That evening the Seven bedded down on the lee slope of a hill, sheltered from the light vesper breeze by a massive rock outcropping. Perry sorely missed the cheery campfire, though the Moon waxed overhead, shedding enough light to see out upon the open wold.

That night Perry was awakened by Anval, who pressed a finger to the Warrow's lips and whispered, "Bane glimmers." Perry looked in silence and saw that the guardian blade had a faint blue glint that dimly flickered deep within the rune-jewel.

All the company was now awake, crouched in the shadows of the outcropping, each facing outward, scanning the moonlit land, weapons drawn, senses alert. Shannon Silverleaf whispered to Kian and then silently withdrew and made his way noiselessly to the crest of the hill, where his keener sight and sharper hearing could be used to advantage.

Perry knelt without breathing for long intervals, straining his own hearing to detect the enemy, but he neither heard nor saw movement. Bane had been resheathed so that its werelight would not shine across the wold to give them away, but occasionally Perry would carefully draw it but a small way—an inch or so—cupping his hand to shield the glimmer, checking the faint blue flame. The flicker persisted for about an hour but slowly died away until once more Bane shone only with pale moonlight, the distant danger past.

And then Shannon came back down. "Though I saw nothing," he said quietly, "I felt the presence of evil to the south, toward Darda Galion. Mayhap my kindred will soon engage the foul despoilers on the borders of that abandoned forest."

The following day they marched swiftly across the uplands, and the wold continued to rise. They could now see the mountains, and before them was the Quadran, four peaks taller than the rest; and one of the four towered above the other three. "That is mighty Rávenor," answered Borin to a question from Perry, "the greatest Mountain in the known ranges. Even from here you can see that it looms over the others. My people call it the Hammer because of the sudden storms that maul its slopes, to the ill of those caught in its blasts." Borin gazed with admiration at its dull red sides. "Even though it now houses Squam, still I am eager to walk the halls and chambers within. And when we have routed the foul foe, and cleaned their stench from the stone, we shall make it into a mighty homeland as of old."

The next day the companions entered a low range of foothills that jutted out across the way. In the lead, Lord Kian struck for an old footway in the north of the spur, and soon they were on a narrow path wending up through the hill-chain. As they climbed to the ridge, low on the horizon far to the south they could see a darkling green. "Look," said Perry, pointing, an unspoken question in his eyes.

"That is Darda Galion, the Larkenwald," Shannon informed the buccan, "the last true home of the Lian here in

Mithgar. Most have now ridden the Twilight Ride, but a few of us remain, scattered to the four winds, living in other forests with our kindred, the Dylvana, while Darda Galion lies empty.''

"Lord Kian told us he thought the Larkenwald was deserted,'' said Perry, looking southward at the shaded green far away.

"Yes, it is so,'' responded Shannon with regret, "we no longer dwell there. Many left in the ancient days when the *Vani-lērihha*—the Silverlarks—disappeared. Others fled when once more the power of Gron arose and the *Draedan*—the Gargon—was loosed. Still more went when the Mistress—Dara Faeon—rode the Twilight Path to plead with Adon for succor. And when she was gone, the light seemed to go out of the forest. After the Winter War, many followed her to Adonar, while others lingered in Mithgar, not ready to ride to the High One's Lands. Even Coron Eiron was unready to follow her, and dwelt yet a while in Mithgar among the mortal Lands. But he grew weary of living without her brightness and now is gone too. And when all the Lian had gone from the Eldwood forest, the Dylvana, too, went away, crossing the Argon to come into Darda Erynian and the Greatwood to live with their brethren. And then Darda Galion stood empty.''

Perry stopped, pausing a moment, gazing in sadness at the now-empty realm. Then he turned and hurried to catch up with Shannon. As they tramped onward, Perry remarked, "Lord Kian said that travellers at times catch a glimpse of movement in the forest—as if Elves were still there. And I see that the green *holds dusk,* as of a Land in twilight, though the Sun yet rides the day.''

"Ah yes, the trees do now hold the foredark, for again my kindred are there. We learned that Rucha and Loka—Gyphon *Spaunen*—were stirring in Black Drimmen-deeve,'' said Shannon grimly, "and raiding south through the Larkenwald. A company of us returned, to bar the way and stop their passage through Darda Galion. But there are many companies of them, and we are but one, and thus the foul despoilers yet win through, though now we give them pause.''

"How came Ursor, a Man, to be with a company of Elves?'' asked Perry.

"Ah," replied Shannon, "that is a mystery: One night, we beset a company of *Rûpt,* and in the midst of battle, there he appeared, swinging that black iron mace with great effect. He has been with us ever since; his woodcraft nearly equals an Elf's. He talks seldom of his past, but this we now know: He was hunting *Spaunen* alone, wreaking vengeance for his wife and child, slain on a journey to far Valon. Before joining us he would lie in wait for a Ruch or three to become separated from their bands, and then he would strike. He also set snares and deadfalls and spiked pits on the paths Rucha and Loka alone travelled. Now that he is with us, he need no longer wait for mischance on the part of just one or two *Rûpt,* as you have seen, he attacks with us in fury to lay many victims by the heels. He says his revenge now goes swifter."

Perry looked ahead at the big Man and almost pitied the maggot-folk. Then something that had been nagging at the back of his mind sprang to the fore, and Perry called, "Ursor, wait!" And the Warrow rushed to catch up with the Baeran.

As the two of them strode side by side, Perry said, "Ursor, I just now remembered, your kinsman Baru, warden of the Crestan Pass, and his three sons send greetings. Baru says that all is well at home. He also trusts that your vengeance against the 'Wrg' goes to your satisfaction."

The Squad tramped onward in silence, two of the buccan's strides matching one of the Baeran's. Finally Ursor replied, "Thank you, Wee One. Long has it been since I've had word from my kith."

The Seven marched swiftly along the path and came through the hillpass and started down the far slopes. Spread out before them was a great tilt of land trapped between the eastern spur they had just crossed and the Grimwall Mountains on the western side. The slope rose up to the west and into the flanks of the Quadran: Rávenor, Aggarath, Ghatan, and Uchan. These four mountains were known to Man as Stormhelm, Grimspire, Loftcrag, and Greytower, and to Elves as Coron, Aevor, Chagor, and Gralon. Each held stone of a different hue: ruddy Stormhelm, sable Grimspire, azurine Loftcrag, ashen Greytower. Beneath this quartet of mighty peaks was delved Kraggen-cor; and cupped within their embrace was a wide, cambered valley: the Pitch.

When the slant came into view, the company paused, and

the Dwarves eagerly crowded forward to see down into the land. With a wide sweep of hand, Lord Kian gestured at the great acclivity hemmed by the mountains. "There lies the land the Dwarves call Baralan," he said to Perry, "and the Elves name Falanith; it is the Pitch." Kian then pointed toward the upward end of the long slant. "And up there at the far brim and looking down upon this slope is our next goal: Dawn-Gate. On the morrow we march to the portal, in sunlight. But now evening draws nigh, and we must camp away from this path, for its sign shows that heavy-shod feet have marched by recently: Yrm boot, I think. It would not do to be discovered by a chance patrol."

The Seven moved out of the path and to the cover of a thicket in a swale on the slope. The Sun had dropped beyond the mountains, and they made camp in the deep shadows of the peaks.

That night, early in Kian's watch, Perry was awakened by Delk to see Bane's blade-jewel flickering again with a cobalt gleam. As before, Perry slipped the blade into its sheath so that the blue light would not be seen by the enemy. Periodically he would shield it with a cupped hand and draw it an inch or two, then slide it back into the scabbard to hide its luminance. This time the light slowly grew to a strong blue flame that ran along the blade, and they heard heavy boots stamping up the path, and armor jingling. The waxing Moon was over half full, and the companions watched as a large company of maggot-folk tramped up the path and passed in the night. And within his bosom Perry's heart hammered as if it were a caged bird wild to escape.

Slowly the flame subsided as the danger marched away, until it was but a faint glimmer. Slowly, too, did Perry return to calmness, and then only by pushing aside all thought of maggot-folk and sinking deep within his memories of Woody Hollow and The Root and the sound of Holly quietly humming as she tended her flower garden.

Twice more that night the flame flickered lightly within the jewel of the Elven-blade, but the Seven saw no other Spawn.

The next morning, in early sunlight, the Squad started on the last leg of their overland journey. They came down out of the hillspur and headed west up the long Pitch. As the Seven moved onto the slope, the margins became steeper on the sides of the valley, and here and there they were covered with runs of birch and fir trees; and heather and furze grew on the land. Down below, the comrades could see a sparkling stream dashing down out of the vale: it was the Quadrill, a river fed by many mountain streams to grow wide on its run through Darda Galion, where it was joined by the Cellener and the Rothro to flow onward and come at last to the Argon.

In the early afternoon the Seven moved deeply into the Pitch, flanked on three sides by mountains. Perry could see to the north end, where a glittering rill cascaded in many falls down from the snows of Stormhelm. The stream and the path it fell beside were named the Quadran Run; the pathway led up over Quadran Pass to come down in the land called Rell. "How close are we to Durek's Army and Cotton and your brother Rand?" Perry asked Lord Kian, peering at the snow-bound pass.

"If my reckoning is right and nothing has delayed their course, the Army should now be coming to the Dusk-Door. And we are two days of swift march from here to that portal—if we could cross through yon blocked gap and then follow the Old Way. But, Perry, could you fly like an eagle, you are but forty miles, or so, over the mountain from there." Lord Kian looked down at the Waerling. "Of course, we cannot soar like the hawk, but must instead go to ground like the badger, for the route we follow is under the mountain, with many twists and turns—six and forty miles by your Brega Path."

On they marched until they came to the Quadmere, a clear, blue lakelet less than a mile from the east portal, Dawn-Gate. They went down the sward to the cold water to replenish their canteens. Anval, Borin, and Delk looked upon the still mere with a sense of wonder, for there began the realm of Kraggen-cor. On the far side of the azure pool a stone embankment fell sheer into the water; up on the level top of that shore stood a broken pillar, like a maimed finger pointing at the sky: it was a Realmstone, marking this place as being a Dwarvenholt. And runes upon the stone bade all who desired, to drink deep of the pure cold water from the depths of Châk-alon, the Dwarves' name for this quiet tarn.

Lord Kian's eyes swept the flanks of the mountain, and

then his look became fell. "There, I think. There lies the Dawn-Gate," he said in a grim voice, and he pointed up the slope.

Perry's heart jumped to his mouth, for there before him, high up on the west wing of the Pitch, stood their destination: like a gaping black wound, the east entrance into Kraggen-cor yawned mute, a dark and forbidding portal into a Spawn-filled maze. His heart thudded and his hands shook, and a thrill of fear coursed through him, for with the coming of the early morning Sun on the morrow, they would begin their desperate dash through this black hole to the far Dusk-Door. And he would be their guide, for it was his task to lead them without flaw on the tortuous way to that distant goal; and the full responsibility of his role now began to crush down on him.

Perry tore his eyes away from the black hole and let his gaze follow the broken stonework of an ancient wide roadway winding down from the entrance and into the valley below, where it was lost among the heather and gorse on the west side of the lake. But try as he might to not look, his vision was drawn again and again to that jet-black slot, and each time he looked his heart flopped over and he drew in his breath.

Ursor leaned down and said in a low voice that only Perry could hear, "Don't worry, Wee One; once we start we'll be too busy to think about it." Perry gave the large, understanding Man a flicker of a smile but said nought in return.

Lord Kian chose a thick grove of pine trees for the Squad to camp in that night. The wood stood high on the slope a mile north of the Dawn-Gate. He reasoned that Yrm forces would issue out of the gate and go east and south toward Darda Galion—away from the chosen coppice—and that any returning forces would come from that way too. Hence, well before daylight faded, the Seven were comfortably ensconced among the whin and pine, hidden from prying eyes.

As they lay in the evergreens, Perry became aware of the distant gurge of a great churn of tumbling water, and when he asked about it, Delk replied, "It is Durek's Wheel, the Vorvor." But the Dwarf did not say on, for night had fallen upon the Spawn-laden land, and they spoke no more.

Darkness overspread the valley, and shortly they saw Hlōk-led Rūcks, bearing torches, issue out of the gate. And once again Perry's heart quickened its pace. Amid the clangor of armor and weaponry, a force was assembled, and then it marched away to the east along the old, broken road. Sentries were left guarding the portal, and guttering torchlight shone forth out of the cavern. And for an hour or two the only movement was that of Rūck guards shuffling around or slouching beside the entrance.

The silvery Moon overhead cast a pale radiance down into the valley and upon the mountainsides. By its light the companions continued to watch the entrance.

A time passed, and then, tramping up out of the vale, came a company of *Spaunen* bearing bales of unknown goods; whether they carried meat, grain, bolts of cloth, or other kinds of loot and plunder, the Seven could not tell, for they were too far removed from the Gate to see the nature of the freight. The Rūcken company bore the burdens into the cavern, disappearing from view.

Another long while passed, and Perry fell asleep watching. When he was awakened, several hours had elapsed, for the Moon had set beyond the mountains. The buccan had been roused by Ursor and cautioned to quietness; a squad of torch-bearing maggot-folk had marched out of the gate and had turned north! They were coming toward the hiding place!

In ragged ranks, the maggot-folk tramped right at the pine grove; and the Seven flattened themselves, peering from concealment, hardly daring to breathe. Carefully, quietly, all but Perry took a weapon in hand, preparing for battle. The Warrow found his palms were wet with tension, and he wiped his hand on his breeks ere taking hold of his sword. But though Perry grasped Bane's hilt, he did not draw the long-knife, for he knew its werelight blazed, hidden by the scabbard. And the comrades lay in wait as the Spawn came onward.

Closer drew the maggot-folk, and now Perry could hear them speaking, but he could not make out what was being said; they were still too far away. As they came on, he found that although he could discern the individual voices and words, he could not understand their meaning at all; the words were harsh, somehow foul-sounding, as if made up of acrimonious snarls and discordant curses and grating oaths.

There were guttural growls and slobbering drool sounds. The Spawn were speaking in Slûk, an argot first spoken by the Hlôks; but long ago in Neddra, Gyphon had declared it a common language for all of Spawndom.

Perry shuddered at the sound of this festering tongue, but otherwise lay still as the Rûcks tramped along an unseen path, only to turn and march past the grove and away to the north, toward the Quadran Run.

About an hour before dawn, the *Spaunen* patrol returned from the north, scuttling in haste to be in the Gate before the Sun rose. This time, though, there were more maggot-folk in the group. When they scurried near the grove, Perry was surprised to realize that he could now understand what was being said: they were no longer using the Slûk but instead were mouthing words in a polyglot akin to Pellarion, the Common Tongue of Mithgar, a polyglot often used by Hlôks when they did not want their words to be well understood by their underlings, the Rûcks:

"Gorbash's scummy company brought in a lot of loot tonight," whined one of the Hlôks as they scrambled across the slope. "Maybe Gnar'll be pleased and lay off the whip."

"Not rat-mouth Gnar," snarled another. "That big pusbag ain't pleased with nothin' these nights. Ever since them bloody-handed Elves started cuttin' down his Nibs's minions, he ain't been pleased."

"I hear there's another whole company missing, overdue by three days—Gushdug's bunch."

"Blast that rotskull Gushdug! If you ain't lyin' that means stinkthroat Gnar'll be layin' about with his cat-o'-tails more than ever; I'll ram this iron bar up his snot if he cracks those thongs my way. It's bad enough he had me and my bunch guarding this side of that stupid path over the scabby mountain, when he knows that slime-nose Stoog's gang alone is plenty; and they can watch from shelter, whereas we can't, burn their gob-covered hides. And Gnar deliberately left me there in the cold two extra weeks after the snows closed the way. I'll rip his throat out if he even looks sideways at me."

"You, Crotbone? Ha! You've got a big mouth, maggot brain. I know you: you'll be groveling in the dirt at his stinkin' feet like the rest of us when we report in, lickin' his boots and calling him 'O Mighty One,' and all the time, just like the rest of us, you'll be wishing you could catch him from behind down in a dark hole alone, without Goth and Mog watchdogging him, then . . ."

Perry heard no more, for they had moved beyond earshot.

As the rising Sun glanced over the horizon, Delk rubbed face blackener on Perry's cheeks and forehead and directed him to put some on his hands. The other members of the company were also darkening their hands and faces and checking each other for light spots. "Remember," Delk warned Perry, "when we are hiding, do not look directly at a Grg—your eyes will catch the torchlight and shine at him like two hot coals, and we will be discovered. Look to one side, or shield your eyes tightly with your hand and look through the cracks of your fingers; especially keep those jewel-like Utruni eyes of yours covered, Waeran, for they will glow like sapphires. Also, lest its light give us away, it would be better to keep Bane sheathed unless there is no other choice."

Perry nodded and rubbed a bit more of the sooty salve on Delk's exposed cheek. Satisfied, Perry stepped back and looked around at the others, seeing darkened faces and smudged hands. "My, what a ragtag bunch," he declared. "I'd always envisioned warriors as being bright and shining, but here we stand, the 'Secret Seven,' as motley a crowd as you'd ever ask to see." Perry at first just smiled, but the more he gazed at his companions the funnier it seemed. And suddenly he broke out in quiet laughter, and he could not seem to stop. And the others stared at him amazed, and still he laughed. And then its infectious quality caught Shannon, and he began chuckling too. Soon all had joined in, looking at each other's besmudged features and finding them comical.

"Well, my wee Waldan," growled Ursor with a grin, "I hope you don't get to giggling down in the Wrg pits; we'll be dis-covered for certes, all of us sitting around in a circle laughing our fool heads off." Again the company broke into hushed laughter.

"I never thought I would set forth on a sneak mission with a group of court jesters," growled Delk. "Yet, mayhap it is a new way of outwitting the foul Grg: I doubt that japes and buffoonery have ever been used against thieving Squam before. If we meet any, we will just fall on our prats, and while they are screaming in merriment, blinded with tears of joy, we will slip away and pop open the Dusken Door and bring in the Army for an encore.''

Lord Kian laughed quietly with the others, but he knew that their fey mood concealed a tension within, for they were about to set forth on a dire mission, and as is the wont of warriors everywhere in every age, rude jests are bandied about before sallying into an ordeal. Aye, Kian laughed too, yet a grim look crept o'er his features . . . and then: ''Let us go now,'' he said, squinting at the half-risen Sun, and all smiles vanished. ''By the time we get there the light will be shining full into the East Hall.''

They started off down the slope and toward the gate. Perry's heart was racing, for they were about to step out of the kettle and into the coals. He mentally reviewed what he had told the others countless times during the overland journey about what to expect in the way of halls and chambers, especially on their initial penetration through Dawn-Gate. They had closely studied the map and reviewed every applicable bit of knowledge and lore known to Perry, Anval, Borin, and Delk. And now the Warrow nearly had to bite his tongue to keep from repeating it aloud as an outlet to relieve the enormous pressure growing within him as they strode cross-slope toward the Gate.

And then they were there.

Cautiously, bow fitted with arrow, Kian peered around one of the great gateposts and down the sunlit hall: it was empty. At the young Lord's signal, each of the comrades in turn stepped across the entryway and crept in past the great doors, torn from their hinges ages agone and flung down on the stone floor, where they still lay. Standing in the shadows, the Seven could see before them a huge room delved out of the stone, with a single outlet two hundred yards away leading down a corridor. The direct rays of the Sun shone through the Gate and struck the farthermost wall just to the right of that distant portal yawning darkly at the remote end of the chamber, that corridor which led down into the interior of Kraggencor. In rapid file, the Squad hastened across the room—the

East Hall—keeping to the south side and out of the direct
sunlight so that their own shadows were not cast down the far
passageway to betray them.

The Dwarves looked around in wonder, for at last they had
come into their ancient homeland. Perry saw little, for he was
busy counting paces, and when they reached the distant outlet
and the broad road that led down toward the Great Deep, he
was relieved to find that his measure reasonably agreed with
that of Brega's of long ago.

They entered the corridor and sidled along the south wall,
which was deepest in shadow. The farther they went, the darker
it got, but their eyes adjusted to the dim light reaching down
the passageway. Down a gentle slope they crept, another
furlong or so, stepping quietly, down from Gate Level toward
First Neath. And the light continued to fade as they went,
but ahead there began to glimmer the dim flicker of far-off
torchlight. The Seven edged to the limit of the corridor and
paused ere creeping out upon a landing at the top of a short
flight of wide stairs; the steps led down to the Broad Shelf.

The Shelf in turn came to an abrupt end, scissured by the
Great Deep, black and yawning, the ebon gape splitting out
of the high rock walls to jag across the expansive stone floor
and bar the way. Beyond the mighty fissure the wide stone
floor continued, lit by guttering torches, and on farther the
Squad could see the beginnings of the vast Mustering
Chamber—the War Hall—receding beyond the flickering light
into impenetrable blackness, the distant ceiling supported by
four rows of giant Dragon Pillars marching away into the vast
dark. Across the Great Deep a spidery rope bridge with
wooden footboards was suspended. The span was narrow;
those using it would have to cross the wide gulf in single file.
It was anchored on the near side by two huge iron rings on
iron posts driven into the stone; and it was held on the far
side by a winch set far back from the lip of the rift—the
winch a remnant of the ancient drawbridge destroyed in the
Winter War. Guarding the hoist on the distant side were two
Rūcks, squatting on the stone floor, casting knucklebones
and muttering curses at each other.

Lord Kian motioned Shannon Silverleaf forward. "Can
you fell the Rukh on the left with an arrow from here?" Kian
whispered.

Shannon eyed the distance; it was a far shot. "It would be surer from the bottom of the steps." He motioned downward into the shadows.

Lord Kian gave a curt nod, and signalling the others to remain, the Man and the Elf crept down the broad stairway. At the bottom, Kian knelt to one knee while Shannon stood straight, and each drew his bow to the full. The Rūcks continued their quarrel, unaware of their danger; one, enraged at the turn of the dice, jumped up with a snarling oath and clouted the other behind the ear. The second Ruck kicked out at the first and with a curse sprang to his feet, and they both drew their scimitars, bent on murder. But before they could close with one another in battle, *Th-thunn!* two arrows were loosed and sped hissing through the air to lodge deeply into the Rūcks. One fell instantly dead, pierced through the heart. The other stared in astonishment at the point emerging from his stomach, but ere he could draw breath to scream, *Th-thock!* two more arrows thudded into him, and he pitched forward on his face, dead before striking the stone floor.

Perry and Delk dashed down the steps, with Anval, Borin, and Ursor right behind. "Now!" barked Kian. "Across the bridge. Hurry!" But Shannon, in the lead, had just stepped onto the span when out of the first side tunnel on the left came tramping a Hlōk-led company of Rūcks. It was the change of the guard.

For an instant in time, the Rūcks stopped, frozen in amazement at the sight of these intruders. Then, with snarls of rage, the maggot-folk leapt forward, scimitars raised.

"Wait!" Kian called to his companions. "There are too many of them to meet on the open floor. We'll make our stand on this side of the bridge where they can only come at us one at a time. Ursor, to the bridge. Anval, Borin, flank Ursor. Shannon, with your bow stand thwartwise to the span from me; we'll catch them in our cross-fire. Perry, Delk, take those who get past the first rank. Yield no quarter."

Across the bridge charged the maggot-folk, the span bouncing and swaying under their rushing feet. On they came, right into Ursor's devastating mace, and Anval's and Borin's lethal axes, and the first to fall was the Hlōk leader.

His heart hammering, Perry had drawn Bane, and its blue flame blazed; the Warrow and Delk stood ready, but as of yet no Spawn had won past the front rank. Kian's bow hummed as arrow after arrow hissed into the Rūcks at the rear, and Shannon's aim was just as deadly, the bolts slashing into the foe from right and left.

The Rucks were single file on the narrow bridge and jammed closely together; those in the fore fell screeching into the Deep, hurled there by mace or axe, while those in the rear plummeted into the black depths with quarrels through them. Many in the span center turned to flee, elbowing, pushing, wildly clawing, jolting into each other and shoving one another off in their mad bid to escape; yet some at the distant end regained the far side only to be dropped by deadly arrows before they could reach the sanctuary of the far tunnels.

But one fleeing Rūck ran to the windlass, where he grabbed up a mallet and with a wild swing knocked the brake-wedge loose just as an arrow sprang full from his chest and he fell dead. Yet the winch was free and spinning as the anchor ropes ran loose. And the bridge, now held only at one end by the large iron rings, rucketted down to crash into the side of the abyss, and the remaining Spawn fell screaming to their doom. And Perry's blood ran chill as he unwillingly listened in frozen horror to the shrieks and wails of the plunging Rūcks—screams that dwindled and faded, to be lost at last in the black silence as the maggot-folk plummeted beyond hearing down into the dreadful depths.

A quick check showed that none of the Seven had received so much as a minor wound, though there was a long scimitar scar on Ursor's leather breastplate. Albeit free from injury and successful in battle, still the Squad may have lost the campaign, for they had yet to cross the gulf; and the span was down, dangling from the iron rings on the near side, creaking and swinging slowly like a great long pendulum as it hung down the sheer undercut wall of the Deep.

"Did any of the Rutcha escape to warn the others?" asked Ursor. "I could not tell, for I was busy at the fore."

"I think not," answered Shannon, gesturing toward the many dead on the far shelf. "Our arrows dropped all who tried to flee."

"Though none escaped," declared Kian, "we must be across and gone ere any more come. If that was the changing of the guard, we have at most six or eight hours—likely less—before others arrive.''

They went to the lip of the gulf and searched for a way across. The chasm was wide: the far rim at the narrowest point was some fifty feet away, and in many places the width exceeded one hundred feet.

Anval, Borin, and Delk unhooded three Dwarf-lanterns, and with Perry they lay on their stomachs on the lip of the rift and examined the depths for as far as the light shone. They could see the bridge dangling down the wall, swaying slowly, but they found no way to span the abyss, for below the undercut the sides were smooth and sheer, dropping straight for as far as the eye could see, vanishing into the unguessable depths beyond. Perry quailed at the sight of the endless fall, and pushed back from the rim.

Finding no way to cross down below, the buccan and the Dwarves strode out to the sides where the great ebon crack disappeared into the stone walls of the mountain, but the rift was even wider at those points. Lord Kian, Shannon, and Ursor spoke quietly together and eyed the distance to the winch; they saw that it was covered with a grapnel-shelter, whose rounded edges and turned-under sides were cunningly contrived to resist hooks; in any event, the cast was a long one to carry a rope of any consequence The rest of the far-side shelf was barren and smooth, flattened ages agone by Dwarven adze and stone chisel to resist invaders' grapnels.

"Our mission has failed before it ever got properly under way," groaned Perry in despair. "We are stopped here at the Great Deep. All of our hopes and plans have fallen into its black depths just as the burning Gargon fell long ago."

"Speak not the name of the Dread needlessly''—Shannon's voice held a sharp edge—"for it portends evil in Black Drimmen-deeve. And do not despair too soon, for I believe our Drimm friends will yet show us the way."

"*Kruk!*" spat Anval. "We cannot throw a hook to cross over, and we cannot go around the ends, and we cannot climb down and across. Borin, it will be slow, yet all that is left to us is a climb up and over on the roof."

"Roof? Climb?" asked Perry, looking upward, dumfounded. "How can we cross over on the roof? It must be eighty or a hundred feet up to there, and we are not flies to walk upside down on that stone ceiling. Do you propose an enchantment, a miracle?''

"Nay," growled Borin, rummaging in his pack, "not a miracle, nor spell, but this instead." From his pack Borin extracted a leather harness laden with crafted metal snap-rings and thin-bladed spikes, each spike with an eyelet on the side of the thick end; also affixed to the belting were many different-sized, small, irregular iron cubes, each hollowed out by a hole through the center.

"What is that?" asked Perry, puzzled.

"A climbing harness," replied Borin.

"And what are those things fastened to it?" Perry pointed to the metal objects.

"Rock-nails. Rings. Jams," answered Borin, unfastening one each of the three types of devices and handing them to the Warrow, who held them in the lantern light to examine them closely. Borin spoke on: "Heed: with the nail, you drive the spike into a thin crevice in the stone, then snap a ring through the eyelet; one of several leather straps is then clipped between the climbing harness and the ring. You haul yourself up and along as you go, suspended by strap on a trail of driven rock-nails and attached rings. When you come to a place where the crevices are wider, you wedge a proper-sized jam in place, slipping a snap-ring through the hole, using it instead of a nail.''

Borin turned to Lord Kian. "I will make the climb, and once across I will let myself down; and then we will fix a rope over the Great Dēop for the rest to use; or we will haul the bridge back up, and all can stride above the dark depths on its broad span.''

Perry examined the devices while Borin prepared himself for the climb, putting on the tackle, buckling the cross straps of the harness and cinching tight the wide belt burdened with the rings, nails, and jams. The Dwarf also attached hanks of rope to the belt; and he tied a small hammer by a thong to his wrist.

"Here," rasped Anval, fastening a thick leather pad to the hammer face, "it will deaden the sound of each strike." Borin nodded but said nought, for his gaze was sweeping up and across the roof.

"It is a long reach," growled Borin to his brother as they

surveyed the intended route. "Should I need more climbware, I will drop a line to you." Anval merely grunted in reply.

The Ironfists selected a place to start, and Perry gave Borin back the nail, jam, and ring. The Dwarf reached up high on the wall beside the stairs and with muffled blows drove the rock-nail into a thin crack; then began the perilous climb.

Quickly, Borin drove nail after nail into the stone, clipping and adjusting an appropriate harness anchor strap to each new nail as he went, unclipping the hindmost strap and retrieving the free snap-ring as he left each embedded nail behind; and up like a fly he clambered. At times there were handholds, and he did not use the rock-nails as he ascended. At other times, however, long still study was needed before he drove a nail or wedged a jam and moved onward. At last he topped the wall and started across the ceiling, the Dwarf now totally dependent upon the leather belting, rings, nails, jams, and harness. Perry was glad that it was not he who had to climb so high and dangle like a Yule decoration, and he was amazed by Borin's ability. "How surely he goes," breathed the Warrow, looking up, knowing that were their places exchanged he would be frozen with fear.

"Aye," answered Delk. "Borin is accounted a master stone climber—even among the Châkka."

"You speak as if all Dwarves climb like that," said Perry.

"Aye," responded Delk, "for the inside of a Mountain needs climbing more than its outside ever does. And the Châkka have been climbing Mountains since we and they were created—yet we more often climb within the living stone than without. Even so, mayhap Borin is the best of us all."

Once again Perry turned his sight toward the Dwarf above. Yet Borin's progress had slowed markedly, for he was now on the most difficult, the most hazardous reach.

Bit by bit, the Dwarf inched across the ceiling as precious time eked beyond recall into the past. And Perry fretted that the climb had already taken too long, and that more time would be spent ere the task came to an end; for the buccan knew that at any moment a Rücken band could swarm into the War Hall. These thoughts were on Lord Kian's mind too, for the young Man said to Shannon, "It is now that Borin is most vulnerable to Yrm arrow; if *Spaunen* come, we must slay any archers first." Perry's heart sank at these dismaying words, and his eyes once again turned to the exposed climber.

And up above, the Dwarf crept onward as the sands of time ran swiftly down.

Hours later, it seemed, Borin, now well out over the chasm, called down to the companions below, pitching his voice so that it would not carry into the caverns to be heard by hostile ears: *"Ziggurt!"*

"What did he say?" asked Perry.

"Ziggurt," replied Delk. "It is óne of the many Châk words describing the condition of rock. Borin says the roof stone where he is, is *ziggurt.* That means it is not completely sound; perhaps when the Great Dēop first split upward, reaching into the Mountain from below, the stone was stressed so."

"Does that mean it's going to fall?" asked the Warrow, yielding back.

"Nay," Delk assured him. *"Ziggurt* is not rotten stone, yet it may give way, but only if stressed more. *Ziggurt* means that the rock is crazed, that it has many small cracks and large, and fissures running widely through it. The rock is untrustworthy for bearing weight: small chunks may fall if pulled upon; large slabs can shatter down if stressed just so. No, *ziggurt* does not mean weak stone; it can be very strong and stand forever. But long careful study is necessary beforehand when working the stone, to prevent mishap. Yet *ziggurt* is more than I have just told you. Pah! The Common Tongue is not suited to any better description than that; it is not capable of shading the meanings of stone as is the Châk Speech."

"Time, Delk?" asked Kian. "There is the rub: you have said that time is needed to work *ziggurt* rock to prevent mishap; yet I deem that our time is nigh gone. Other Yrm patrols will come, and we must be away ere then with no trace of our passage remaining. If Gnar suspects that his enemies are within these caverns, he will turn out all of his forces to search for us. And we do not want a *Spaunen* Swarm hunting through the halls, seeking our party. No, our only hope to help Durek is to win through without alerting the entire Yrm army." In a muted voice, Kian called up to Borin, "Can you go on?"

"It is *ziggurt* for as far as the eye can see," Borin called back down, waving a hand across the gulf and toward the Mustering Chamber. "But I must try, though it will be a gamble, for the way is obscured by soot from the time the ancient bridge burned, and long study is needed, yet we have not the time. I must chance a hasty crossing."

"Wait!" softly called Shannon, cupping his hands about his mouth so that his voice would reach the Dwarf above. "There is this: if you can lower a rope to me, I can swing across—if the stone and iron rock-nails will bear my weight." The Elf looked at Lord Kian. "Except for Perry, I am the least heavy, and you cannot risk him on this scheme." Lord Kian nodded his assent.

Borin hammered in another rock-nail, and then like a swaying spider strand a thin, strong line came snaking and swinging down out of the overhead gloom. Borin had tied his hammer to the end to give the rope a pendulum weight, and he swung it as he payed it out. Shannon nimbly caught the line on one of the long arcs, and as soon as Borin called down that all was ready, the Elf gave the company a rakish grin and sprang off the edge of the Deep.

Shannon's first long swing was not far enough, and he rose to the end of his arc, seemed to pause, and then hurtled back across the yawning gulf. On the second swing he pumped hard over the bottomless pit and carried farther still, though it was not yet enough. On the third pass he almost gained the far lip of the chasm, but not quite.

Only Borin, clenched against the ceiling by the short anchor straps, did not see the Elf come closer and closer with each plunge; instead, the Dwarf kept his eye riveted to the rock-nail. The swings were placing heavy stress on the eyeletted spike, and Borin intensely watched the crevice the nail blade was driven into. On the third arc, a stone chip flaked from the crack: the nail was coming loose! Quickly, Borin jammed his right forearm up into a large *ziggurt* cleft and made a fist, wedging his clenched hand tightly in the rift; he wrapped the loose end of the pendulum rope around his left arm and forcefully gripped it. No sooner had the Dwarf caught hold than the nail tore loose, and the weight of the plummeting Elf jolted through Borin's arms and shoulders.

Silverleaf was swinging back from the far lip when he felt the rope give then catch again, and the jar nearly shook his grip loose, the line slipping in his grasp ere he caught tight. His grip firm again, he continued his arc and pumped hard on the next plunge across.

Borin strained desperately to hold on, gritting his teeth and closing his eyes with the effort, his great arm and shoulder muscles cracking with the stress, for he was the anchoring link between the stone overhead and the taut rope to the Elf hurtling the abyss below. The greatest strain came when Shannon hurtled through the bottom of the arc, and Borin strove to hold on: his right fist, jammed in the crack, felt as if the bones in his hand were breaking, and the rope wrapped around his left arm seemed as if it were cutting through the elbow, and his shoulders felt as if his arms were being plucked from the sockets. Yet grimly he held on as Shannon hurled up in a rising arc out of the depths and to the far lip. The Elf cast loose from the line and plunged forward to the stone, falling with a roll and then springing nimbly to his feet.

Aloft, Borin gave a grunt of relief, and, dangling by the leather straps between his climbing harness and the embedded rock-nails, he extracted his skinned-knuckled hand from the jam-crack and massaged his shoulders, neck, and arms. After a moment, he began coiling the pendulum rope, drawing it upward into the shadows, preparatory to starting back the way he had come.

Shannon called for a hammer and a rock-nail, and they were tossed over the abyss to him; the Elf drove the spike into a thin chink in the floor. At Silverleaf's command, Perry attached his soft and pliable ancient Elven-rope to a grapnel and threw it across to the Elf, who then wedged a tine of the hook into the eyelet of the nail, while the other end of the line was anchored to one of the iron post rings. At a gesture from Shannon, huge Ursor swung hand over hand and joined the Elf; though he was a giant, the Baeran was deft and graceful.

Perry gasped at Ursor's deed, for the line was so slender and the Man so huge, and the Warrow feared that the rope would snap; but it was Elven-made, and Silverleaf had known that it would hold ten like Ursor.

Again Perry caught his breath and gritted his teeth in fear for a companion's safety, for Lord Kian clambered down into the black abyss on the dangling bridge; while it swayed and jolted against the sheer wall, the Man hauled the far loose ends of the anchor ropes up out of the darkness and secured a light line to them. That done, he then climbed back up and out, bringing the line with him. Once out, he used another of their grapnels to pitch the slender cord over to Ursor, who fetched the heavy anchor ropes up to the far side where he and Shannon ran them onto the ancient winch. Then, with a grinding clatter of gears, Ursor began hoisting the bridge up out of the chasm, back toward its original position.

Up on the ceiling, Borin had worked his way to a place where, once again, he was above the Broad Shelf. Fixing a jam and ring in a crack, the Dwarf payed out a line; and slipping it through the snap-ring, he used the rope to free-rappel to the wide stone floor. With a flip of the wrist, he pulled the free end of the line through the ring above to come piling down. And as Anval coiled the rope, Borin removed the tackle with the remainder of the rock-nails and jams and snap rings and restored them all to his pack along with his ropes. As Borin closed his backpack, Ursor finished his task at the hoist: the bridge was once again in position, with the brake wedge in place. All the extra lines were untied and repacked. Then the rest of the Seven queued up to cross the gulf.

When Perry's turn came he clutched the hand ropes with all his might, for the Great Deep fell sheer and bottomless below him, and a cold chill rose up around him from out of its depths. He felt that the bouncing bridge would collapse again, and its swaying frightened him. He had been amazed at how casually Lord Kian had climbed down the bridge when it was dangling free and swinging beneath the undercut. He also felt that Ursor's hand-over-hand trip above the yawning chasm had taken unimaginable bravery and dexterity. And Borin up on the ceiling, hanging by narrow straps from small iron cubes or thin iron blades driven into crevices, or Shannon swinging by a slender line over those dreadful depths, well, it was all quite beyond Perry's courage and skill to do.

And now he was having trouble just putting one foot in front of another on a bouncing, swaying, narrow rope-and-board span above an endless fall into a gaping, black depth; and in his mind's eye he once again saw the Rūcks plunging to their doom. *Hey! This won't do,* he thought, *now don't you freeze in fear out here; after what all the others did, you've just got to cross over this awful black pit.* And cross it he did, trembling and clutching, but moving ahead all the time. He was greatly relieved when he stumbled onto the other side, nearly falling to his knees when his feet came off the bounding span and met the hard, unyielding stone.

Last to cross was Delk, who strolled over as if the narrow bridge were a broad highway.

After retrieving the arrows from the dead Rūcks, the Seven dragged the corpses to the lip and flung them into the Deep, pitching the Rūck weapons after. Perry threw a fallen torch into the gulf, and as it fell, a smoldering spark caught, and it burst into flame; and Perry watched its guttering light as it tumbled end over end. His sight followed it for what seemed to be an endless time as it slowly became a tiny speck of luminance plummeting down and down, until it disappeared; whether it plunged beyond an outcropping to be seen no more, or fell at last into a stream at the bottom, or blew out, or simply became too small to see, Perry could not tell. He shuddered at the awful depths involved, unable to imagine their limits and not wanting to know. Again he drew back from the edge in fear.

With one last sweeping look, Lord Kian saw that all overt evidence of the battle was gone. "I think no one will discover that we were here. Even the blood is cleaned up well enough so that only close inspection will show that any was spilled. The Spawn simply will be presented with the mystery of a missing company, and some guards that disappeared. Gnar may think that they deserted. The main evidence of our passage lies in the unguessed depths of the Great Deep."

"Not all," grunted Borin. "The rock-nails and jams are in place on the wall and roof. But they are small and dark and should go unnoticed. Even if discovered, mayhap the Squam will think them an old dead end, for they go nowhere."

"Let us be gone, then," declared Lord Kian, "for we can

do no more here, and we must away ere we are discovered.
— Perry."

With the Warrow in the lead next to Anval, they started at
a jog trot toward the black gape of the second tunnel on the
right. Dwarf-lanterns were slightly unhooded and cast narrow
phosphorescent beams to dimly light the way. The Seven
entered the dark passage and started up the first of several
flights of stairs that would lead to the Hall of the Gravenarch.
Suddenly Shannon hissed, "*Quiet!* Shield the lights. *Rûpt*
below." The Elf's sharper hearing had detected the tramp of
Rücken boots.

The lanterns were hooded and the company stood quietly,
poised on the steps. Down at the entrance of the corridor,
they saw reflected torchlight flicker by, and they heard the
heavy tread of Spawn heading for the bridge. The companions had started just in time; it had taken seven full hours to
get from Dawn-Gate to these steps, but fortunately for the
Squad the band of maggot-folk now tramping to the bridge
had come too late to thwart this initial thrust.

After the *Spaunen* passed, the companions started up the
stairway once again, coming quickly to the top and continuing down the passageway. They ignored the side corridors
and went on for nearly a mile and a half, climbing six flights
of steps separated by long stretches of level cavern. They
came to the base of the seventh flight, but the way was barred
by large blocks of broken stone amid piles of rubble. "It is as
I feared," said Perry. "*The Raven Book* tells that the roof
collapsed when Brega sundered the keystone of the Gravenarch
and nearly lost his life. We must now attempt to find a way
up to the Sixth Rise above Gate Level and come to a place
where I again recognize the way. In this search a Dwarf
should lead."

Delk Steelshank was chosen to go first, for in his youth he
had apprenticed to a Tunnelmaster before he finally turned to
the craft of gatemaking. He studied Perry's map with Anval
and Borin, and then led them down two flights of steps to the
first westbound tunnel; they strode along it for a half mile,
coming to a corridor to the right with steps bearing upward.
They climbed up the flight, and a level cross-passage bored
away in both directions. Ahead they could see another flight
of stairs going on up. They mounted these, then went ahead

and up another flight. "Here, we are on the Sixth Rise, and near to the point where we were blocked," announced Delk, and Anval and Borin grunted in agreement. "Now it is merely a matter of closing the course to come to the other side of the blockage—or of coming upon something Friend Perry can reconcile with the Brega Path."

"Hsst!" shushed Shannon, whose keen hearing again proved sharper than that of Dwarf, Man, or Warrow. "I hear another company of *Rûpt*. They tramp nigh."

The comrades looked back down the way they had come and could see the faint flicker of far-off torchlight bearing in their direction.

"This way—quickly," whispered Delk, and they bolted down a side corridor curving 'round to the east and south. Quietly they went, as swiftly as they could, the faint glow of their lanterns showing the way. They came to an opening on their left. They were about to pass it by when more torchlight could be seen ahead of them. "We have no choice," hissed Delk. "There are Squam before us and Squam behind. Into this room."

Hurriedly, they stepped into a narrow, long chamber. A great pile of fallen stone blocked most of the room, ramping upward from the center to the unseen, distant wall, and there was no way out except the one door they had come through. They were trapped!

The Seven ranged themselves along the near wall as the boots tramped closer. The Dwarf-lanterns were closed and the room plunged into darkness. All weapons save Bane were drawn and readied. They could now see the torchlight flickering up the passage and through the broken door.

Tramp! Tramp! The Spawn came onward.

Perry's heart thudded, and he grasped Bane's hilt, preparing to draw the blade should the maggot-folk come through the door.

Tramp! Tramp! They were now close enough for the Seven to hear the snarling and cursing in the Rūcken ranks.

Tramp! Tramp! Perry steeled himself.

And then the *Spaunen* marched by the door and headed on up the passage.

Perry discovered that he had been holding his breath, and he let it out in a sigh of relief. But in alarm he immediately caught it again as from the corridor there came a great cursing and shouting: the Rūcken band going up the passage had met the band coming down, and they jostled and jolted and elbowed one another as they passed. Then the second band, still grumbling, marched past the room where the Seven were hiding.

When the tramp of *Spaunen* boot became but a faint echo, Perry slid shakily down the wall and sat on the floor. That had been entirely too close. They had narrowly escaped being caught between Rūcken forces, and their mission had nearly ended after it had just begun. Perry's hands trembled and his breath seemed to whistle hoarsely in and out of his throat. But none of the others said anything and did not seem to notice.

Soon Delk cracked the hood of his lantern, and a faint glow lit up the ruined room. They sat awhile without speaking.

Perry was taking a careful sip of water when he noted a portion of a dark rune-mark on the side wall, hidden by rubble. Picking up the lantern, he stepped over to look at the ebon glyph. It was neither Common nor Elvish but, rather, it was Dwarvish. The buccan pushed some of the shattered rubble away from the top of the pile, revealing the whole of the runes written in some black ichor, now dried: ᚠᚱᚢᚴᚴᛁ

Perry looked on for a moment, puzzled. These glyphs were familiar. They were in *The Raven Book* somewhere. The Warrow frowned in concentration. It was . . . it was . . . "Hoy!" Perry exclaimed, "This is Braggi's Rune! I know where we are!"

CHAPTER 2

FLIGHT UNDER THE MOUNTAIN

Perry's announcement brought Lord Kian to his feet. The Man stepped to the wall and took a Brega-Path map from his jerkin and spread it on the floor before the Warrow. "Where?" asked Kian. Perry squatted and adjusted the lantern to illuminate the chart as all the comrades gathered 'round.

"Right here!" proclaimed the buccan jubilantly, stabbing his forefinger to the map. "This room is the Hall of the Gravenarch, Braggi's Stand. See? Here is Braggi's Rune." Perry touched a glyph on the wall beside him, then gestured about. "And this rubble around us, it is where the ceiling collapsed when Brega broke the keystone." Perry peered through the dimness at what could be seen of the extent of the room. "Somewhere should be sign of Braggi's ancient battle: broken weapons, shattered armor, the long-dead remains of the combatants; but I guess it is now buried 'neath the fallen rock."

The Warrow looked 'round at the faces of the other members of the company, eerily shadowed by the lantern on the floor. "Yonder, under that wreckage, lies the eastern hall-door," he continued, "and beyond it lie the blocked stairs where we were turned aside by the fallen stone. We've come a long way to be standing only a couple-hundred paces from where we started."

"Aye. I knew we had come nearly full circle," grunted Delk, and Anval and Borin nodded silently in agreement, "but the foul Squam drew my attention elsewhere."

"Since now you know where we stand, Perry, it must mean we can set forth," growled Borin.

"Yes," replied Perry, "for here we are past all the fallen

28

rock, and once more we are upon the Brega Path. Our way to Dusk-Door lies there.'' Perry pointed to the broken portal and through to the hallway they had fled.

In two strides Ursor stepped to the door and cautiously looked out into the corridor, then turned to the comrades. ''The way is clear,'' he rumbled.

''Then let us go forth at once,'' urged Lord Kian. ''Crossing the Great Deep, finding our way to this Rise, and eluding the Yrm has caused great delay, precious time we can ill afford.''

The Seven stepped out through the portal and took the left-hand way, travelling the Brega Path in reverse. Swiftly they went south through the passage and soon came to the Great Chamber, a huge room in the Drimmen-deeve. They peered out of the corridor and into the vast delving. No Rūcken torchlight was seen; the chamber was dark and empty. ''To the right,'' whispered Perry, ''across the wide floor and out the passage at the west end, nearly one-half mile away.''

In haste they sped across the stone floor to the far west end and sallied into the passageway there—and none too soon, for as they entered the shaft, Shannon, bringing up the rear, again whispered, *''Hsst!* The lanterns.'' The lamps were quickly shuttered. As the companions stood in blackness, far behind them in the huge chamber a *Rûpt* company bearing burning brands marched out of the south corridor, across the wide floor, and entered the north passage. When the torchlight disappeared, the Seven resumed their trek.

The corridor gently sloped downward as they went. The way before them was broad and swift, and there were no side passages. Perry knew that this would be one of the most dangerous traverses along the Brega Path: over the next five miles this passage had no side corridors to bolt into should Spawn come. But in this passage Perry unsheathed his Elven sword. ''Here I will carry Bane in the open,'' the Warrow declared, ''to warn of approaching maggot-folk if its blaze grows.'' The blade-jewel flickered a faint blue, telling of distant danger. And the companions strode on.

Quickly they marched, and the road gently curved right and left and right again as they walked downward. They trod between vertical walls beneath an arched roof. Occasionally they saw runes carved along the passageway but took no time to examine the glyphs for their message. Again the corridor curved left. As Delk had informed Perry some time back, Dwarves often shaped a natural passage into a delved road, and this corridor with its many gentle curves seemed to be one of those. Brega had called this path the Upward Way, but of course to the Seven it was a downward way, for Brega had gone in the opposite direction.

At last they came to another huge cavern. "This is the Rest Chamber, so named by Brega because of the stone blocks like seats scattered across the floor," said Perry, pointing at one of the square-cut giant stones. "Yet I think we should not pause here, for our goal is distant and our need to press on is urgent. Yon lies our course: to the west side and out we go. Ahead, about seven miles hence, is a chamber where we may rest."

Again they resumed the trek, and soon passed out of the room and back into a corridor. Perry spoke once more: "From here on we will have side fissures and passageways to hide in should *Spaunen* come; but by the same token, there are more places from which maggot-folk might fall upon us. So stay ready." Bane's rune-jewel still flickered faintly, but the danger was too distant to concern them, and they marched secure in that knowledge.

This time the corridor was less delved, more like a natural cavern: though the floor was smooth, the walls and ceiling were but lightly worked by Dwarf tool and had a rough look. The broad shaft continued to wind downward, and there were many lateral splits cleaving off into the darkness.

They marched down to the west for nearly three more hours, coming at last to the chamber foretold of by Perry. "Brega called this the Broad Hall," stated the Warrow, "but I say it is a dining hall, for I am hungry—and weary. Lord Kian, I suggest we eat and rest. It has been a long day, though I don't know exactly how far we've come nor what time it is."

"We have walked nearly sixteen miles in the caverns," declared Delk, "fourteen on the Brega Path and two to bypass the fallen stone at the Hall of the Gravenarch." Anval and Borin nodded their agreement, for the distances and directions were emblazoned in their Dwarf memories.

"Though I am not certain," rumbled Ursor, "I think the day outside has fled, and the Moon rides the eventide. It is my guess that it is now near the mid of night."

"It is two hours beyond midnight, and the Moon sinks low in the west," corrected Shannon with a certainty the others did not doubt, for though days, weeks, months, and even years seem to mean little to Elves, and they appear to note only the seasons, still they know at any moment where stand the Sun, Moon, and stars.

"Well, no wonder I'm hungry and tired," sighed Perry.

"So are we all," agreed Lord Kian. "Perry is right. Here we will eat, drink, and rest. We stand the same order of watch as before. Bane shall be our silent sentinel."

Perry hungrily consumed three crue bicuits and drank a small amount of water; on their next long march they should reach the "safe" stream that flowed through the Bottom Chamber, seventeen miles to the west, but til they did, water was to be conserved. The Warrow then plumped his pack into a pillow and, settling back, fell instantly into slumber. Bane, leaning against a block of stone, softly glinted, whispering of far-off enemies.

Four hours later, Ursor awakened Perry for his turn at guard. Again, to stay awake, the Warrow slowly paced back and forth in the dim light cast by the barely cracked Dwarf-lantern. He watched Bane, but it changed not. Finally, his tour over, he went to rouse Shannon Silverleaf.

The Elf sat quietly with his back against a wall, and his tilted eyes glittered in the lantern light, for the sleep of Elves is strange and wholly different from that of Dwarf, Man, or Warrow—if indeed Elves sleep a genuine sleep at all. It is said that in their Lands twilight rules, and the days pass not, and slumber never visits. Legend would have it that some mortals have become ensnared in this timeless existence. Yet these legends of Lands where time's hands stand still, these legends would seem to fly in the face of the Elves' "knowing" where stand the Sun, Moon, and stars. On the other hand, many would say that Elves' "power" over time *proves* that they live in twilight and sleep not. Still, it is recorded in *The Raven Book* that Lord Gildor said that though Elves could go for many days without true slumber, even they must sleep at last.

But when Perry approached the resting Elf, Silverleaf stood ere the Warrow came nigh and indicated to the buccan that he should sleep.

In all, the company had rested for some eight hours when Delk finally roused the others. They ate a quick meal and sipped water, and then they struck out once more. Perry continued to carry Bane unsheathed, and still the faint blue flame spoke only of distant danger.

The farther west they went the less finished the passageway became. Now they occasionally came upon splits and fissures in the floor; most could be stepped over, but at times Perry had to spring across, though none of the others did, being taller than the wee buccan. At one point they passed a broad tunnel merging from the right. Its worn floor bespoke heavy travel throughout the ages, yet whether it was smoothed by Rücken feet or by the Dwarves before, they could not tell. The timeworn track continued on in the passage the Seven followed, and once again their speed was considerable.

They had gone this way for a time when Perry noted that Bane's jewel was beginning to glitter more strongly; but whether the danger was before them, or overtaking from behind, or coming from the side, they knew not. "Ahead lies the Round Chamber," announced Perry. "It has many entrances and exits to hide us. It is not far. Let us make for it."

Swiftly they strode forward at a pace set by the Warrow. Bane's flame continued to grow. Finally they came to the gallery Perry had spoken of: it was another huge room, as most of the chambers in Kraggen-cor seemed to be; this one was circular, and there were many portals along its perimeter, some delved, some natural clefts. The chamber was empty, but Bane's blade-jewel now glittered brightly. "We know not which way the danger comes," said Kian, "but chances are it will issue from one of the delved ways and leave by another. Let us choose one of these unworked cracks to slip into to remain undetected. Perry, be prepared to sheath Bane's blue light."

The Seven found a natural fissure with undisturbed dust carpeting its level floor; they slipped into the cleft and waited

with lanterns tightly hooded. Bane's glow grew to a cobalt
flame that ran along the bitter edge, and Perry sheathed the
blade. The Squad could see torchlight bobbing up the south
passage they had just come from: the danger had been overtaking them from behind. A large company of Rūcks jog-
trotted out of the tunnel and into the great, round room. They
loped to the center of the huge chamber. A command was
snarled by the Hlōk leader, and the company halted. Another
command, and the Rūcks broke from their ragged ranks
and flopped to the stone floor. They were staying.

Lord Kian drew back from the cleft entrance and turned to
the companions he could now dimly see by reflected torchlight. Before Kian could speak softly, Borin stepped out of
the darkness at the back of the split and motioned Kian to
him. "This crack is a dead end," the Dwarf whispered. "We
cannot get out."

They watched the Rūcks for six taut yet somehow dreary
hours. During that time the maggot-folk had quarreled, cursed,
and snarled; several fights had broken out among them, only
to be stopped by the raging Hlōk lashing the squabbling
Rūcks and anyone nearby with a great, cracking whip. The
maggot-folk had gluttonously eaten a grisly meal of some
unknown flesh: hunkered down, slobbering and drooling, and
throwing splintered bones into the darkness beyond the torchlight after cracking them open and tonguing out the marrow.
At last, however, the Spawn had finished their gruesome
repast and then had resumed quarreling and cursing, casting
lots, shoving one another, bickering.

"This is awful," whispered Perry to Lord Kian. "We have
got to get out of here. We've lost too many hours as it is, and
we must be on our way. Can't we slip through the shadows
and out the far north door?"

Lord Kian, sitting on the floor with his back to the wall,
grimly shook his head. "Look closely," he breathed, "they
are athwart all our paths, both to the west and around the
chamber to the east and north. We have no choice but to wait
them out."

Another hour went by; then there was a great hubbub in the
chamber as a second Hlōk-led, torch-bearing company of
Rūcks loped through one of the west portals and into the vast

room, halting aflank the first band. "Where've you been, Plooshgnak, you slime?" snarled the first Hlōk, cracking his whip. "We've been stuck here waiting for your snot-wart hides too long. I ought to run some maggot holes into your stinking guts with a hot iron."

"Aw, shut your snag trap, Boshlub," snarled the Hlōk leader of the second band. "We're not the last: Gushmot's not here, blast his pus-rot teeth."

The two Hlōks were cursing each other and arguing violently when, moments later, a third company of Rūcks galloped into the chamber. The Hlōk leader of this band seemed enraged with the other two quarreling Hlōks. *"Ngash batang lûktah glog graktal doosh spturrskrank azg!"* he howled in the foul, harsh Slûk tongue. *"Gnar skrike!"* At mention of Gnar's name, Plooshgnak kicked a seated Rūck, and Boshlub cracked his whip onto the back of another and snarled orders. The first two Rūck companies fell into ragged ranks, jostling and elbowing and grumbling. With a crack of Boshlub's lash, all the Rūcks loped out through the northeast corridor. And the Round Chamber was left in dark silence.

After a moment, Perry unsheathed Bane. The blue light coldly flamed from the jewel and down the blade, but as the Seven watched, it grew dimmer. "Let's go now," urged Perry, "before any more maggot-folk come to this way station."

A glance around the great room revealed only utter blackness; no light of torch could be seen flickering through any portal. The Seven eased open the hoods of their Dwarf-lanterns a bit, to let narrow shafts of radiance illuminate the way. Swiftly the companions crossed to the north tunnel and entered the passage.

The way became narrow in places, and at times chasms bore off to the right or left, and the company would walk along the shelved precipices. Fissures opened to either side, and Perry continued to make the choices dictated by Brega's instructions. The Warrow had found no surprises in the path, for the Brega Scroll was accurate and detailed. Yet though he had not been surprised, he was astounded by the sizes of the chambers they had passed through: the East Hall at Dawn-Gate had been two hundred yards in length, two hundred in width; the Mustering Hall at the Deep was a mile long and

half that wide—according to Brega, who had seen its extent
by the light of raging flames as the drawbridge over the Great
Deep burned by Elf-set fire; the Great Chamber was a half-
mile long and a quarter-mile wide. Enormous, the rooms
were enormous. And the number of halls, tunnels, fissures,
cracks, and additional passages leading away to other reaches
of Drimmen-deeve indicated that the delvings of Kraggen-cor
were intricate beyond imagination, for what the comrades had
seen was incredibly complex and colossal—and they had seen
but a minuscule portion of the whole.

Again the way sloped downward, and wide cracks appeared in the floor. Now Perry had to leap over three- and
four-foot-wide crevices; considerable jumps for one who was
only three and a half feet tall. The Squad came to a narrow
shelf on the face of a precipice; a chasm yawned bottomless
to their right. They edged for scores of paces along the wall
above the rift before coming again to a wide ledge. The
chasm narrowed as they walked onward, and soon they were
once again striding through an arched tunnel.

They had walked, leapt, scrambled, and sidled for three
hours since leaving the Round Chamber, covering some six
miles. At last they came to the Grate Room, a small round
chamber to the north side of the main passage. Behind them
the cavern split four ways: the left-hand way was wide and
led down; the two middle ways were narrow and twisting—
one up, one down; and the right-hand way was the one
whence they had just come down. Before them the passage
ran on downward, heading for the still-distant Dusk-Door.

"We are yet one and twenty miles from our goal," announced Perry, "but I think we must rest and eat before
going on. Let us tarry in the Grate Room for a while."

Lord Kian and the others agreed; they were indeed weary,
for hiding in a crevice from squabbling Rücks had been
nearly as tiresome as would running from a pursuing *Spaunen*
Swarm. "Take care not to step onto the old grillework,"
cautioned Perry as they stepped through the door, "for it is
corroded and may crumble, and you would fall into the shaft
it covers, said by *The Raven Book* to be in the center of the
chamber floor."

The room they entered was perhaps twenty feet square with
a low ceiling—certainly the smallest chamber they had seen

in Kraggen-cor. Centered in the room, a huge rust-stained chain dangled down from a narrow, grate-covered square shaft set in the ceiling, and passed through a like grate placed in the floor, the mighty links appearing out of the constricting blackness above and disappearing into the darkness of the strait shaft below. Avoiding the rust-worn grille covering the ebon hole, Perry, along with the others, flung his pack down to be rid of the burden. He took some crue, and leaned back against his soft bedroll and sighed. After a bit he asked, "What is the hour, Shannon?"

"It is nearly the middle of the night," answered the Elf. "We have just eight and forty hours before Durek tries the Door."

"Two full days," stated Kian. "One to get there, and one to work on the Door. It is well that at Durek's Council we put aside a day in our plan to account for delay, for we have used it, and used it all. Now let us hope we meet with no further mischance, else we will not arrive in time to aid Durek."

Borin snorted in exasperation, "Had we come to the Round Chamber just a quarter hour sooner we would not have been forced to sit in that dark crack for seven hours listening to stupid Úkhs bicker. May such mishaps elude us in the future."

"Ah, but there is the rub," smiled Shannon. "Perhaps all mishaps, accidents, or calamities could be avoided if only we knew when, where, or how they were to come about. Then we simply could be at a place a moment earlier or later or not at all; or we could change the how of things by moving the rock that otherwise would be stumbled over; or we could turn the blade a different way so that a finger would not be nicked; or we could do a multitude of other things to avoid all problems. But alas! it is not ours to know the morrow, and so only reasonable steps can be taken to turn aside misfortune. Of course, if we did know the future, life would be safe—but unspeakably dull."

"Mayhap the next time there will not be so many Grg," growled Delk, running his thumb along the blade of his axe, "and we can solve the problem with a few quick strokes, disposing of the evidence in nearby cracks and crevices." Anval and Borin grunted in agreement.

"Let us rest an hour or so," suggested Lord Kian, whose thoughts were focused on their mission, "then press on west-

erly toward Dusk-Door. While we tarry, we will again use
Bane as an early beacon of danger.''

At the mention of Bane, Perry sat up, startled: he had
unconsciously sheathed the sword when he had taken off his
pack. Quickly he pulled the blade free—and its jewel was
silently shrieking, *Spawn!* the cobalt blaze blasting throughout the room as all the company started up. At that same
moment the stone door of the chamber swung wide, and a
torch-bearing Rūck poked his head through the opening and
looked in upon the Squad. *''Waugh!''* he squalled and jumped
backwards and fled down the western passageway.

Lord Kian sprang to the portal and looked along the corridor. ''The foe is upon us!'' he barked, swiftly stepping to his
pack. ''We must fly from here!''

The Seven scooped up their weapons and packs and bolted
through the door. They could hear the Rūck skreeking and
see the bobbing firebrand as he ran to meet the distant
torchlight coming up the west way. Kian quickly turned and
scanned the four eastern passages. ''There! See! Torchlight
also comes down the corridor from the Round Chamber!''

Once again they were caught between Rūcken forces;
this time, though, the Seven had been detected. There were
three ways left to flee.

''Swift!'' barked Kian, ''is there any reason why we should
not take the left-hand way? It is wider and we can go faster.''
He looked at each of the companions, and they said nothing.
''So be it! Delk, you lead, for again we must leave the Brega
Path. Let us fly!''

They sprang into the left-hand tunnel and fled downward
along the sloping floor; deeper they went under the mountain.
The way was broad, but there were no side passages, and so
they had no choice but to flee onward.

They had run but a short way when from behind they heard
a raucous horncall, its blat echoed down the passage after
them. There was an answering call, as if one *Rûpt* force were
signalling the other. Perry felt like a hunted fox, with braying
horns and snarling dogs driving after him.

As they ran, Perry became aware of an unwholesome odor
hanging faintly on the air. ''Lord Kian,'' he panted, ''I just
remembered. *The Raven Book.* Gildor. When the Deevewalkers
came through Kraggen-cor, Gildor said he did not like this

left-hand way, for it had the smell of a great viper pit, and so
they turned back and instead took the other of his two choices.
Now I smell something, something unpleasant—as if we are
running toward a foul place.''

"We cannot turn back, or even aside yet," rasped Kian,
"for surely the Yrm are now on our trail, and there have been
no side passages."

On they scrambled, downward, ever downward, down to
the very roots of the mountain and beyond, and Perry felt as
if he could hear the burden of the stone groaning above. At
last they came to a cross-junction: The main path went straight,
but within one hundred feet the corridor plunged under water.
The fissure to the right bore upward. The crack to the left had
a level floor. Neither the fissure nor the crack showed any
sign of being delved. Delk turned down the left way. "It
bears westward, where lies the Door," he stated, and onward
they fled.

The crack under the mountain twisted, turned, rose, and
plunged. Perry lost all sense of direction, and he felt as if
they had been fleeing for hours. A wide ravine had been
following along on their right, bordering their way from the
moment they had entered this tunnel; up from its depths rose
the churning sound of tumbling water. On they ran along this
rough path, scrambling up ledges, leaping wide cracks, si-
dling along narrow shelves, sliding down rock-strewn slopes.
Behind, they could hear horn blats, at times faint, at other
times loud and echoing. Bane continued to blaze with a bright
blue flame. Shannon estimated that the *Spaunen* were no
more than a half mile behind, and gaining.

They had fled for more than five hours, covering just nine
miles, for the way was difficult, when at last they came to
another junction in the cavern; it was only the second one
they had encountered since their flight began. At this junction
the water ravine ran on straight, but there was no footpath to
follow; a cross-shaft confronted them: the right-hand tunnel
passed over the ravine on a natural stone arch and ran on
upward, disappearing around a curve; the left-hand way ran
straight and down a gentle slope. Again Delk chose the
left-hand passage. "It turns back towards the Brega Path,"
he said simply.

Though it was not an arched, smooth corridor, the chosen

way was delved, for the walls and floor bore the marks of chisels, picks, and mattocks. "This is an old mine shaft," grunted Anval as he scurried over a large boulder blocking the way, "one delved deeper than any I have ever known; and from the smell, something was uncovered that would have better remained buried." All the time they had been running, the foetid odor hanging on the air had become stronger; each of the companions was now aware of the stench, though none knew what it was. But, odor or not, along the shaft they scrambled, for Rūcken horns were sounding and faint torchlight could be seen shuttering down the passageway behind them: the maggot-folk were drawing nearer.

The Seven fled down this shaft for something under an hour, going some four miles on a downward but more or less straight course. Abruptly the delved shaft narrowed, becoming a slot only wide enough to travel single file. In the notch the malodor became almost overwhelming, causing Perry to gag and catch his breath; he did not want to come into this stink, but the Spawn gaining behind left him no choice.

As they edged along the cleft, Delk exclaimed, "Starsilver! Look! See the ore vein! This delving is a silveron shaft!"

Perry could see the soft glimmer of silvery metal twinkling in the lantern light and running on ahead. And even though they were being pursued, the Dwarves paused long enough to reach out and touch the precious lode, for they had never before seen silveron in its native state. This was the wealth of Kraggen-cor; in only two other places in Mithgar was silveron known to exist.

Suddenly they came to what had been the last extent of the silveron shaft; but they could see that the end wall had been burst through from the far side: the stone was splintered as if some enormous force had blasted into the delf from beyond the wall.

They clambered over the shards of rock and came into a carven chamber. This room was the source of the foul reek, but they could see nothing to cause the stench; it was as if the fetor exuded from the very stone itself.

The chamber was long and rectangular; its far end was lost beyond the shadows. In the center was a raised stone slab, a huge block with a smooth top and carvings on the side. Here, too, were scrawled serpentine signs. Shannon Silverleaf held up a lantern and quickly scanned the glyphs. They writhed across the stone and looked somehow evil and foul, recorded in a long-lost tongue; yet the Elf was skilled at runes and rapidly deciphered the words: " *'Thuuth Uthor.'* Ai!" Shannon sucked in a gasp of air. "This is the Lost Prison. The *Draedan*'s Lair. No wonder the stone is imbued with a foul reek, for here, trapped for ages, was the Dread of Drimmendeeve—the Gargon—trapped til the Drimma were deceived by Modru's vile gramarye and delved too deeply and set the *Draedan* free."

"Trapped?" exclaimed Kian. "Trapped in this chamber? Is there no way out?"

All the lanterns were opened wide, and light sprang to the far end and filled the room. No archways were discerned, no black tunnel mouths gaped in the walls; only smooth stone, blank and stern, could be seen. No outlet, no portal of escape stood open before them, and behind, a horn blared loudly and they could hear the slap of running Rūcken feet.

CHAPTER 3

THE WORDS OF BARAK

"Quickly, Ursor, Anval, to the cleft!" barked Kian. "Borin, Delk, flank them. Let no Spawn through. If we are trapped, then let it cost them dear to pluck us forth."

Ursor sprang to the notch, shifting to one side, with Borin warding his flank. Anval leapt thwartwise the notch from Ursor, Delk at hand. Shannon and Kian quickly stepped to the third rank, and Perry took a place at Shannon's side. They could see torchlight wavering down the slot, and suddenly a Rück burst forth from the breach, to be felled by Ursor's great black mace. A second Spawn came on the heels of the first, and Anval's axe clove him from helm to breastplate. A third Rück Ursor crushed, and a fourth. The next Rück threw down his iron bar and turned to flee but was pushed shrieking and gibbering into the chamber by those behind who did not yet know that anything was amiss, and Anval smote him and the next with his blade. The maggot-folk finally stopped coming in as enough of those in the front ranks at last turned and shoved back through the press in the notch.

A time passed, and the Seven could hear the *Spaunen* snarling and cursing, but the Slûk speech was being used, and so the comrades did not understand what was being said. For a moment it became still, and then a spate of black-shafted Rücken arrows hissed through the cleft to strike the far chamber wall and splinter on the stone. Then there came a great shout from the maggot-folk and a rush of booted feet: they were mounting a charge. One leapt in, only to be dropped by Ursor's mace. Three more hurtled through and were slain by Anval, Borin, and Delk. More charged forward

41

but stumbled over the dead bodies of the slain Rūcks and were themselves dispatched. Once more the Rūcks withdrew.

Just as it had been at the rope bridge over the Great Deep, the Spawn could only come at the Seven single file, and thus the *Rûpt* could not bring their great numbers to bear to their advantage. No Rūck had yet reached the third rank of the defenders. Four warders alone could hold off an entire Rūcken army, especially since the comrades flung the dead *Spaunen* one atop another to clog the entrance, forming a grisly but effective barricade.

An hour went by, and again the maggot-folk charged. Once more the defenders slew all that entered. This time the second rank killed but one Rūck; all the others were slain by Ursor and Anval. The bulwark of dead Spawn grew higher.

Borin and Delk then stepped to the first rank, relieving Ursor and Anval, who stepped back. Lord Kian and Shannon took over the second file. Perry, who had yet to engage the foe, felt useless, but he realized that in this battle the others were larger and more effective than a Warrow would be.

But it was not only a sense of uselessness that disturbed the buccan: most of all, Perry felt a deep sense of guilt over the turn of events. "Lord Kian," the Warrow quietly declared, "I have failed you and my other comrades here; I have failed Durek and all those with him; and I have failed myself." At the Man's questioning look, the buccan continued: "Back at the Grate Room I did not keep Bane in the open, and we were discovered. Our mission is in dire jeopardy, and I am to blame."

"Perry, Friend Perry," sighed Lord Kian, "had Bane been left unsheathed, mayhap we would not have been discovered just then. Yet I think we would have fled west on the Brega Path when Bane's flame cried '*Rûpt!*' And we would have run into the band of Yrm coming up that way. Of course we could have run east on the Path and into the arms of the other Spawn back that way. Perry, Bane is a wondrous Elven-blade, yet it does not tell us where the danger lies, only that it is near or far or not at all. Let me say this: as we came to the Grate Room you remarked that there were no side passages off the Brega Path for the next mile; and the last mile we travelled to that place also had no corridors or crevices off to the side. True?"

"Yes, there are only those passages right at the Grate Room," replied Perry, "four eastward, one westward."

"And of those ways," continued Kian, "two had Yrm forces in them: one behind us on the path, and one ahead. Heed me: we would have seen Bane's glimmer and run along the Path into one *Rûptish* band or the other, with no place to hide; and we would have been trapped between the two gangs, overwhelmed by their very numbers in those broad halls." Lord Kian fell silent, and though Perry had to agree with the Man's reasoning, still he felt somehow guilty that the Seven had been discovered.

"Lord Kian is right," said Shannon to Perry, softly. "He has the wisdom to see that what has befallen would have done so one way or another no matter the circumstance, for we were already trapped yet did not know it. Some who call themselves leaders would have leapt at the chance to fix the blame on you, Perry, deserved or not; to them, finding fault is more important than finding solutions to their dilemmas. With them it is more important to punish in the name of justice than it is to right a wrong.

"But I stray far afield. Lord Kian knows that our task is to somehow rescue our quest from the jaws of adversity, and it is not our concern to blame one small Waerling for all the *Spaunen* that teem in these caverns—" Suddenly, with a screeching howl a large, spear-bearing Hlōk leapt onto the dead-Rūck barricade, only to be gutted by Delk's axe. Three more Rūck were slain by Delk and Borin. Again the attack was shorn off short, the Rūcks fleeing back up the notch.

Two more hours passed without attack, except now and again a black shaft or two would hiss into the chamber to fall with a clatter at the far wall. The guard on the cleft had been rotated, and in turn each of the Seven had walked the chamber—staying out of line of the black arrows, looking for a hidden door or passage—but none had been found, for this was indeed the Lost Prison, the Gargon's Lair: that terrible creature had been sealed in this chamber from the overthrow of Gyphon, at the end of the Ban War, to the year 780 of the Fourth Era: nearly three thousand years in all. The Dwarves had inadvertently set it free while mining silveron, led this way by Modru's evil art; it could be seen that the Dwarves had delved up to the wall of the chamber, but from all appearances, the Gargon had blasted through the weakened wall—whether by spell or by sheer strength, the Squad could not say.

The old tales told that the Gargon had slain many Dwarves, including a Dwarf King and his son: Third Glain fell in 4E780, and with him Orn was killed. After they and others were slaughtered in a bloody day of great butchery, the Dwarves fled Kraggen-cor. Yet Dwarves were not the only ones driven from this region: great numbers of Elves of the bordering Realm of Darda Galion fled from the Dread, as well as steaders of Riamon. The Gargon ruled Black Drimmendeeve for more than one thousand years, til slain by Tuck, Galen, Gildor, and Brega in a fiery doom. It took all of their efforts to vanquish this terrible foe, and even then it was but by chance circumstance that they slew the Dread, for it was a mighty creature.

Yet, as mighty as it had been, still it had not been able to break out of this prison until a wall had been weakened by delvers. The Seven were dismayed by this knowledge, for it meant that this chamber was a dungeon of extraordinary strength: it had defied the power of a mighty Gargon for nearly three millennia. Hence, how could the comrades even hope to break free in a matter of mere hours in order to aid Durek—especially in the teeth of a force of Spawn?

"What is the hour, Shannon?" asked Perry, for he was bone weary.

"It is midmorn of the twenty-fourth of November," answered the Elf.

Lord Kian's face took on a grim look at Silverleaf's words, for the time was perilously short, and they were yet trapped. Lord Kian knew, however, that for whatever plan—if any— they devised for winning free, rested warriors were needed. They also needed water, for theirs was nearly gone. He did not know what mischief the Yrm were devising, but it was certain that they would attack sooner or later. "The Rukha seem to have fallen quiet," said Kian, "planning some deviltry. They can afford to wait for reinforcements, for we are trapped. We must use this time to recover our own spent strength: While we are under siege, we will take turns resting. Two will hold the way while the others rest, perhaps even sleep. Keep nearby to aid in the event of attack. Stay out of arrow flight from the cleft. Think on ways that we may escape—though Adon knows how that may be.''

Perry lay down off to one side. He was exhausted: the flight had taken much of his strength, for the way had been hard and he was of small stature. He rested his head against his pack, and his thoughts were awhirl. He felt something tugging and nagging at the back of his mind, but he could not bring it to the fore. He believed that something was being overlooked, yet he knew not what. He gazed at the smooth carven walls, ceiling, and floor of the chamber. The silveron vein came through the guarded broken wall and ran on across the floor to vanish into the shadows. The argent line had many offshoots, running short distances, tapering off into thinner and thinner veins, to finally disappear. One such seam zigged across the ceiling, to end in a whorl. Another seam ran to the large stone block in the center of the chamber and up the side, to come to an end among the writhing runes set thereupon by the Gargon. Yet another silver line shot up a side wall, to crash back to the floor. Perry lay there letting his gaze follow the precious seams, and even though the Rūcken enemy was but a few paces away, he gradually drifted into slumber as his eyes roamed along glittering pathways streaking across the prison.

Perry slept for five hours without moving, exhausted, exempted from guard duty by the others; but then he began to dream: He was back on the Argon, riding the raft. But the river wasn't water; instead it was flowing silveron. The argent stream rushed into a roaring gap, and the raft was borne into a tunnel. Perry looked about and saw that he was riding with the other companions, yet there was a hooded Dwarf sitting on the far end of the float whom Perry did not recognize, for he could not see the Dwarf's face.

The starsilver river rushed through dark caverns, carrying the raft along, and Rūcks sprang up to give chase. Onward the raft whirled, to come to many Dwarves delving stone and scooping up treasured water into sacks, which they bore away. The float sped toward a stone wall, but just before the craft crashed into it, the wall burst outward and a dark Gargon jumped forth with four warriors in pursuit. The raft whirled into the chamber and sped on the silveron vein out the other side, but all the companions were tumbled off by the far stone wall, even though the float somehow went on through. The wall became transparent, and Perry could see that the raft was caught in an eddy of silveron, and the mysterious Dwarf was still aboard in spite of the invisible wall. Perry looked at the Dwarf and called, "Help us. Help us get through. You got out; how can we get out too?"

The Dwarf turned and threw back his hood. It was Barak! The dead Gatemaster! Slain by the Rūcks far away on the shores of the Argon River! *"All delved chambers have ways in,"* Barak intoned in a sepulchral voice, *"and ways out, if you can find the secret of the door and have the key. Without the key even a Wizard or an evil Vûlk cannot pass through some doors."* The raft burst into flames, and Barak lay down on the platform and uttered one more word: *"Glâr!"*

The burning raft whirled off on the swift-running silveron vein, and Perry woke up calling out, "Barak! Barak! Come back!"

When Perry opened his eyes, Shannon Silverleaf was bending over the Warrow shaking him by the shoulder. "Wake up, Friend Perry," urged the Elf, "your slumber disturbs you."

"Oh, Shannon, I had the strangest dream," declared the Warrow, rubbing his eyes and squinting at the far wall to see if it was truly transparent; but he saw only solid stone. "It was all mixed up with rivers of silveron, the Rūcks, this chamber, the Dread, and a conversation I had with Barak long ago in our last camp by the Great River Argon, where he was slain."

"Though Elves do not sleep as Men, Drimma, and Waerlinga do," stated Shannon, "still I believe I can understand the way of some dreams. Though many are strange and appear to make little sense, now and again darktide visions do seem to have significance; mayhap yours is one of those."

"Maybe it is," agreed Perry. "I've got to talk to Delk. He's a Gatemaster, as was Barak." The Warrow rose and went to the brown-bearded Dwarf who was standing guard at the notch with Ursor. "Delk," began Perry, "Barak and I often chatted at night. Once he told me that all delved chambers had doors, some secret; and for those what is needed is to divine each secret and to have the key it calls for. Delk, this Gargon's Lair is a delved chamber. Surely there must be a way out other than through a hole in a broken wall. Barak must be right."

"Were this chamber Châk-delved, I would agree," grunted Delk, "but it is not. The work is more like that of . . . of . . ." Delk fell silent in thought, then continued. "Old beyond measure, I deem, like the work of an ancient Folk called the Lianion-Elves—though but traces of their craft remain that I have seen."

"Lianion-Elves?" exclaimed Shannon. "The Lianion-Elves are my Folk, the Lian!" Now it was Silverleaf's turn to fall silent and study the chamber. "You are correct, Drimm Delk: this chamber *does* resemble the work of my ancestors, though it is different in some ways. I knew that my Folk had known of the Lost Prison, but that we delved it would be news to me. And if delved by the Lian, I doubt that originally it was meant to house such a guest as a Gargon—though as to its initial intent, I cannot say."

"Well, if Barak was right," said Perry, "there is a secret way out strong enough to defy even an evil Vûlk. And if we can find it, maybe we can divine the way to open it. You are a Gatemaster, Delk; surely you can locate a hidden door. And you, Shannon, your Folk perhaps made this place; maybe you can find the secret way. We've got to try."

"Ah, but Friend Perry," protested Delk, "we all have searched every square inch—walls and floor alike—and we have found nought." Delk looked from the cleft to the far wall and finally at the slain Rūcks; then he growled thoughtfully, "Nay, not all; we have not searched it all. We have not searched where the Grg arrows can reach. But the dead-Ükh barricade is now high enough that if we stay low we can safely examine the stone block in the center of the chamber."

Delk awakened Borin to take his place at the cleft, and then Gatemaster, Elf, and Warrow crawled to the central platform and began the search.

Perry watched as the other two carefully inspected the stone, but his mind kept spinning back to his dream of Barak:

the Dwarf had said, *"Glâr!"* yet Perry knew as a Ravenbook Scholar that *glâr* was the Slûk word for "fire." Though the raft in the dream had burst into flames, why would he dream that Barak had said a Slûk word? How did fire bear on their problem? Maybe it meant nothing. Perry watched as the search continued.

Delk had begun to examine the silveron seam running up the side of the block, and suddenly he gave a start. "This vein is not native to the stone," he muttered after long study, "it is *crafted!*—made to look like a natural branching of the starsilver offshoot. And see! Here the silveron is shaped strangely, like two runes—though I cannot fathom their message."

Shannon crawled around to join Delk, staying well below the Rūck arrow line, and peered at the silver thread. "These are vaguely like ancient Lian runes, made to look like odd whorls of silveron in the stone. This rune, I would guess it to say 'west,' and the other rune says 'point'—or mayhap 'pick' is more accurate, I'm not sure. West-point or west-pick, that is the best I can guess these odd runes to mean."

"Hola!" exclaimed Delk, "Here is a thin slot in the stone at the end of the crafted vein, as if the silveron had run its course but the crack ran on a bit. Mayhap—"

"The Wrg are up to something," rumbled Ursor at the notch, interrupting Delk. "They may be preparing another rush. They are chittering like rats, and again I can hear them calling, *'glâr!'* "

"Glâr!" exclaimed Perry, startled. "That's what Barak . . . Ah yes, I see: I heard it in my sleep. Ursor, *glâr* is a Slûk word for fire." The three crawled away from the stone block and out of arrow flight, and stood beside Ursor. "What can they be up to?" asked Perry, listening to the Slûk jabber.

"I have my suspicions," growled Ursor. "We've been trapped here many hours. Time enough for them to devise some terrible plot and secure the means to carry it out."

"Look!" cried Delk, pointing to the floor at the cleft. In through the entrance a dark liquid flowed. They could hear a wooden barrel being broken, and a surge of fluid gushed in through the notch. "It is lamp oil," growled Delk, testing it with his finger and smelling it. Then his eyes widened— "They seek to flood the chamber with oil and set it afire!"

Shannon fitted an arrow to his bow and quickly stepped across the entrance, loosing the bolt as he went. A scream came from the dark notch as the longbow-driven shaft found a victim. Delk awakened Anval and Lord Kian. The young Man joined Shannon, and they sped missiles into the cleft, and the Spawn answered with bolts of their own. In spite of the arrows, oil continued to gush forth from the notch to overspread the chamber floor.

Perry watched in desperation, for he knew that the maggot-folk were nearly ready to transform this prison into a burning tomb. *We have to get out!* thought the Warrow frantically, on the edge of panic. But then with a conscious force of will he wrenched his terrified mind toward the paths of reason. *Now settle down. Don't bolt. And above all, use your scholar's brains to think!* The buccan believed that there was a hidden door, and he felt that the secret and its solution was within his grasp if he could only get the time to think it through. What had Barak said that night long ago on the banks of the River? Something about Lian Crafters. *"These doors are usually opened by Elven-made things,"* Barak had said, *"carven jewels, glamoured keys, ensorcelled rings,"* and something else, but what? What did the runes on the stone block mean, "west-point"? Perry glanced up at the Elf.

"Lord Kian," urged Silverleaf, "before they put the torch to this oil, let us rush them. At least we will take some of that evil spawn with us." Ursor grunted his agreement, Delk thumbed the blade of his axe, and Anval and Borin nodded. Shannon drew his long-knife, shaped much the same as Bane. "This edge of the Lian, forged in Lost Duellin—the Land of the West—will taste *Rûpt* blood for perhaps the last time; yet this pick, though it has not the power bound into the blade as that of the Waerling's pick, will—"

"I've got it!" shouted Perry. "I know the way out!" He flashed Bane from its scabbard, and its edges blazed with flaming blue light streaming from the rune-carven jewel. Perry held the sword high and laughed. "Here, as Barak would have said, is a spellbound blade. The key! Made by the Elves in the Land of the West. In your words, Shannon Silverleaf—and in those of the silveron runes on yon block—it is a west-pick. No wonder the Gargon couldn't get out: he hadn't a key. If I am right, then this blade—or any like

it—will do with a simple thrust what the Gargon in all his awesome power could not do in three thousand years.''

Crouching low, the small Warrow stepped through the inflowing oil to the stone block and plunged the blade into the slot at the end of the silver line. The Elven-knife went in to the hilt. There was a low rumble of massive stone grating upon stone, and a great slab ponderously swung away from the far wall; a black opening yawned before them where solid stone had been.

Shouts of astonishment burst forth from the Squad, yet Gatemaster Delk had the wit to call out above their cries, ''Withdraw the sword and do not plunge it in again, else the portal will close once more!''

Heeding Delk's words, Perry immediately withdrew the dazzling blade, and the door remained open; but the Warrow's thoughts were upon another Gatemaster, now dead: the one who had shown him the way. ''Barak, you were right,'' whispered the Warrow quietly. ''Thank you.

A Rūcken horn blared from the notch and a stentorian voice snarled, ''*Glâr!*'' They were bringing a torch to fire the oil.

''Quickly!'' shouted Kian, catching up his pack. ''We must fly!'' Each of the companions took up his own bundle and headed for the open door: Kian in the lead, Delk last. The oil made the stone floor as slippery as ice, and the footing was difficult; haste was needed yet could not be afforded. ''Hurry!'' Kian urged as he reached the door and stood by the open portal.

Just then there was a great *Whoosh!* as the oil was fired and flames ran into the chamber, lighting it a lurid red. The dark shadows were driven from the far recesses of the room, and through the blaze the *Spaunen* could see for the first time the opened, secret door. They snarled and howled in rage—their victims were escaping!—and their own Spawn-set fire would cut off pursuit!

As the companions tumbled across the doorsill, inches ahead of the flames, a burst of black arrows whined across the room, most to splinter against the stone wall; but one shaft took Delk through the neck, and he fell dead at the threshold. Lord Kian reached for the fallen Dwarf, but a hot blast of fire drove the Man backwards through the door as the last of the oil ignited.

The portal had opened into an undelved cavern leading away from the chamber. The companions were waiting just around a corner when Kian stumbled into their midst, singed and gasping. "Delk is dead. *Rûpt* arrow." Anval and Borin cast their hoods over their heads, and Perry bit his lower lip and tears sprang into his sapphire-jewelled eyes.

The raging flames behind them pitched writhing shadows on the walls of the cavern, and the grotto was illuminated a dull red. Towering stark stones stared silently at the group huddled below, and the sound of weeping was lost in the roar of the blaze. Massive blocks and ramped ledges stood across the cave, barring the way for as far as the firelight shone, and the rock yielded not to the grief.

Lord Kian looked at the group standing numbly before him. "He is wreathed in flame," said Kian above the sound of the fire, "and his funeral chamber contains the weapons of the foes he slew. Thus he goes in honor on his final journey. Delk will be missed; he will be remembered. But he would urge us to mourn not, and to go on—for Durek needs us, and we are late."

For long moments no one spoke, and the only sound heard was the brawl of the fire. Then finally:

"You speak true, Lord Kian," concurred Anval, casting back his hood with effort. "There will come a time when we will mourn the loss of Delk Steelshank, but now we must go on to the Dusken Door—though how we will repair it without his aid, I cannot say. Our Gatemaster has fallen, and there is little hope for our mission without his gifted hand."

"But we must try," interjected Perry, choking back his grief, "else all this has been in vain. We must get back to the Brega Path and on to the western portal—though whether there is yet time to do so, I know not."

"It is sunset of the twenty-fourth of November," announced Shannon. "There remains but one and thirty hours until Durek is to attempt the opening of the Door."

"Now that Delk has fallen, I will lead," stated Borin, casting his own hood from his head, "though I cannot take his place. And I shall try to hew to his plan, turning always back toward the Brega Path when fortune allows me the choice."

"Then let us go away from this bitter place now," urged Perry. Lord Kian nodded, and Borin set forth, climbing up the ramps and across the looming stones to an exit on high. And they entered a rough-floored cavern that led them generally south and west.

The way was slow and difficult, for they had to clamber up and down steep slopes and over great obstacles. Giant Ursor often lifted Perry up to ledges just out of the Warrow's reach, or lowered him down drop-offs just a bit too far for the buccan to jump. Without the big Man's help, the journey would have been beyond Perry's abilities. Even the Dwarves were hard pressed to negotiate this passage. Only nimble Shannon seemed at ease on the rugged way. There were no offshoots from the cavern, and so a smoother way was not a matter of choice. It took them three hours to traverse just four miles of this arduous cave; and their thirst had grown beyond measure, for their water was gone.

But then they were brought up short by both a welcome and at the same time a disheartening sight: the cavern deadended at an underground river. The water rushed out of the stone on the right side of the cave, and plunged under the wall on the left side. The far bank was a narrow ledge of rock, shelving out from a sheer stone wall that ran to the ceiling with no outlet. Though he was desperately thirsty, and water was within reach, Perry flung down his pack and broke into tears of frustration. "If this doesn't beat all," he vented bitterly. "Trapped again. Stone and water before us, and Rūcks and fire behind us."

And then, from far off, faintly echoing down the cavern, came a discordant horn blare. "I fear the fire is no longer burning," declared Lord Kian, "and the *Spaunen* are once more in pursuit."

CHAPTER 4

WIZARD WORD

Two Dwarves, a Warrow, and a Man threaded their way along the Great Loom of Aggarath as they walked toward the pile of stone covering Dusk-Door. Everywhere they stepped, it seemed, they came to another fallen Dwarf warrior, slain by the monstrous Krakenward during the fearful retreat along the causeway. Durek and Bomar had cast their hoods over their heads, as is the manner of Dwarven grief; tears silently coursed down Cotton's cheeks as the Warrow passed the broken bodies; and Rand's countenance was bleak. But they did not stop to mourn, for as Durek had said, "There will come a time to lament, but now we must think of the living. Our companions in the halls of Kraggen-cor depend upon us; we must not fail them."

Where the lake once stood, a black crater now scarred the land. Of the Dwarves drawn underwater by the malevolent creature, there was no sign. Along the sundered causeway the four strode, and over the ancient bridge. Far below in the muck-laden bed of the drained lake they could see the ancient stonework of the old Gatemoat at last revealed to the light of day after long, dark ages. With the Troll-dam destroyed, water once again flowed through an unseen fissure under the Loomwall and into the moat, filling it to spill over a formed lip in the massive bulwark, shaping the beginning of a stream. After centuries of silence, the Duskrill once more fell asplash to meander across the upper vale—now a black crater—to come to the linn of the Sentinel Falls and cascade down into the stream bed below to flow onward through the ravine of Ragad Vale.

Onward strode Cotton, Durek, Bomar, and Rand. Now

they could see, here and there, the pave of the ancient courtyard before the Dusken Door, a courtyard no longer drowned, yet one burdened with mire and silt. There, too, they could see the ancient remnants of great trees that had once grown before the western portal.

The four finally came to the bank of rubble over the Door; it was immense: the evil creature not only had put back all the stone removed by the Dwarves; it had heaped even more rock on the pile.

Cotton looked at the great mound in dismay, for the buccan did not see how even a Dwarf army could move this mass of stone in a week—much less in the scant hours remaining before the appointed rendezvous. Rand retrieved Brytta's spear, and picked up his own sword from where he had dropped it and had caught up Durek's axe during the Krakenward's attack. Grey Bomar stood and surveyed the ramped heap. "King Durek," rumbled the Masterdelver, "I know not whether we can move all this stone twixt now and mid of night tomorrow." Bomar glanced at the forenoon sky. "Already I judge it to be drawing upon midmorn, and whether there are enough hours for this labor is questionable. Yet we must try. Berez and I will set the shifts and oversee the work: one of us will guide the delving by day, the other will lead the toil at night, for we must work nonstop by lantern light throughout the eventide, too, if we are to succeed by tomorrow night."

Durek nodded, and the foursome turned and walked back along the causeway and around the north end, to come to the broken dam and the Sentinel Falls.

Still the Dwarf companies were in turn casting stone blocks down on the now-lifeless carcass of the Monster. The mound had grown large in the basin below the precipice, and the Duskrill plunged over the linn to cataract down onto the jagged heap; and only here and there could the mottled green hide of the hideous creature be discerned. Cotton looked on and shuddered in revulsion, for even though only slight glimpses of the Krakenward were visible, that which could be seen was repulsive to behold.

Durek summoned Berez and called his Captains together; and the Dwarves gathered in a great circle, along with Cotton the Warrow and two Men: Prince Rand and Reachmarshal Brytta. As soon as the Council was seated, the Dwarf King spoke: "The broken stones over the Door are piled yet higher. The task of uncovering the portal by midnight tomorrow may prove impossible, but Bomar has a plan for working day and darktide, too. But ere he speaks, I would say this:

"First, there are many fallen kindred on the sundered causeway. We cannot stop to mourn the slain, although they deserve the honor. Even though we shall not mourn, let those who sorrow work with hooded heads, and use stone from over the Door to build cairns against the Great Loom for the dead to rest within. After we have defeated the Squam, we shall decide whether to let the cairns stand for all time, or instead to delve stone tombs or set funeral pyres for all those the Madûk slew.

"Second, there are those among the Host wounded by the Monster of the Dark Mere. The injured will not issue into the caverns to fight the Grg, but will stay behind. Those among them who can, will help the healers with the more severely afflicted and prepare them for a short waggon trip south; all wounded will go with the Vanadurin when they drive the horses to better pasturage.

"Third, as Bomar will explain, we will toil in shifts. But only those removing the rubble will be working; all others must rest until it is their turn at the labor. The one exception to this rule of rest will be you, the Captains: Friend Cotton will meet with you on the morrow to describe the major features of the Brega Path, so that we will be better prepared for the War. The Chief Captains will gather here midmorning tomorrow, and all other Captains as their work shift permits that same afternoon.

"Finally, I have faith that the Host shall succeed in this task of removing the stone, for they are staunch and have the will to overcome even this. And remember, at this very moment seven of our comrades and kindred are within, and they depend upon us. *We must not fail!*" Durek then gave the Council over to Bomar, who began outlining the shifts and the way of working.

Cotton tried to pay heed, but his mind simply could not concentrate upon Bomar's words. Had the Dwarf been speaking of growing a garden, or of shaping wood, or of treating an animal or a bird, then the buccan's attention would have been riveted to every syllable Bomar uttered. But the

Masterdelver was speaking of stone and levers, of slings and prybars, of work shifts and duties; and even though these words were vital to the mission and vital to the rescue of Mister Perry and the others, Cotton's thoughts purely would not stay focused upon Bomar's work plan.

Instead, the Warrow again fretted about Mister Perry, wondering where the Squad was, and whether they had met with mischief: how had they fared? And his thoughts scurried along these endless paths to nowhere, for how long he did not know.

But suddenly, he became aware that he was listening intently, not to Bomar, but to the valley, for it seemed as if, above the shush of Sentinel Falls, he had heard a faint cry; yet it was so dim, so far away—just on the edge of perception— that he wasn't at all certain whether he had actually heard it, or had merely imagined it.

The Warrow swept his emeraldine eyes around the circle; no Dwarf there appeared to have noted anything other than Bomar's words; yet both Rand and Brytta seemed to be listening intently for a distant call—especially Brytta, who had risen to his knees and turned his face toward the west.

There! It came again! To Cotton the call had the sound of a far-off horncry. Brytta cocked his head and held up his broken hand. "Quiet!" he barked. A hush fell upon the Council, and only the cascade of the falling water failed to heed Brytta's sharp command.

Once more! Again! It *was* a horncall! Now all heard it, and it grew stronger:

A-raw, a-rahn! A-raw, a-rahn! A-raw, a-rahn! Over and again it belled, growing louder, and Marshal Brytta leapt to his feet. "A foe! Alert!" he cried, his good left hand gripping his spear as he sprang to the rock in circle center, his sharp gaze piercing the length of the valley to the west.

"A horseman comes!" cried down a Dwarf lookout from atop the Sentinel Stand.

A-raw, a-rahn! came the call again; and at last bursting into sight along the valley floor came a rider flying at full gallop; clots of flood-dampened earth were flung behind from plunging hooves as the horse thundered down the vale and toward the Host along the Old Rell Spur. "It's Arl!" cried Brytta. "From Redguard Mountain! From Quadran Gap!"

Couching his spear, Brytta blew a signal upon his own black-oxen horn—*Hahn! Hahn! (Here! Here!)*—and he sprang toward the stairs beside the linn and plunged down them to meet the flying scout.

No sooner, it seemed, had Brytta reached the bottom of the steps than Arl pounded up, hauling his lathered mount short as he leapt to the ground. Quickly the two Men spoke in Valur—the warrior tongue of Valon—with Arl gesticulating fiercely, his hands and spear describing numbers, directions, and actions. In but a moment Marshal Brytta brought him up to the Council circle as all eyes followed them, and Cotton discovered his heart was racing. Brytta spoke: "It's Wrg! Some know we are here! *They go to warn Gnar!*"

Angry shouts burst forth from many in the circle, while others spat oaths and gripped their axes. Durek held up his hand, and when silence returned he motioned for Brytta to continue. "It seems as though the secret High Gate is known to the Spawn after all, and we are revealed. But here, let Arl tell it."

The tall young rider of Valon stood before them. As with all the Harlingar, he was clothed in leathern breeks and soft brown boots, while a fleece vest covered his mail-clad torso. Arl's steel helm sported a flowing black horse-tail crest, and his flaxen locks fell to his shoulder. He bore a spear in his left hand, while a long-knife was at his belt, and a bow and arrows could be seen at his horse's saddle, as well as a scabbarded saber. At his side depended a black-oxen horn, taken from the wild kine of the south—the mark of a Son of Harl.

It could be seen that the youth was weary; yet his manner belied the fatigue, for he stood warrior straight. With a quick sweep of his eyes, Arl's intense gaze took in the Council circle, and in a firm voice he spoke, his scout's report stripped starkly bare of all but the essential facts: "For those here who know it not, three nights past, Eddra, Wylf, and I were left atop Redguard Mountain to watch for a Wrg army should they come to attack from Quadran Col.

"Last night a torch-lit Rutchen band of thirty or so scuttled down from the Gap and turned south toward this valley.

"Leaving Wylf behind to watch for a larger force, Eddra and I rode from Redguard and trailed the Spawn at a distance.

Our plan was to divert them were they nigh to discovering the
Host; or, should we fail to deflect them, our plan was to warn
the Legion if the Wrg espied you here in this place.

"We followed them south for some leagues, when the
band we trailed met up with a like number coming north from
the direction of this vale.

"They joined forces and turned back for Quadran Gap. *Yet
heed!* As they loped past where we were hidden, we overheard them cursing: '. . . *we tell Gnar of the lake-draining
army of foul-beards at the buried door!'* "

"*Kruk!*" burst out Durek, slamming fist into palm, his
face dark with rage. "They know who we are, where we are,
our exact numbers, and our very goal!"

Again angry shouts swept forth from the Council circle,
and many pounded the flats of their axes to the ground while
venting oaths. Durek struggled to master his own passion,
and held up his hands for silence; and Dwarves swallowed
their rage and clenched their jaws. And when quiet returned
the Dwarf King motioned for Arl to continue.

"Eddra is tracking them yet, or did so til dawn," the
young rider spoke on, "leaving sign along the Grg path,
marking their dash for the hidden High Gate. I came as
quickly as I could to warn of the danger."

Arl turned to Brytta. "Sire," he spoke urgently now to his
commander, "there are perhaps seventy of them, and they are
swift. Yet I think they have not now reached the pass, for
dawn was nigh and first light of day will find them holed up
until sunset, when once again they will take up the race for
the Black Hole. They must be intercepted ere they can carry
word to Gnar, else we are foredone; and the riders of the
Valanreach are the only ones fleet enough to overhaul their
track." The youth, pale and harried from his all-night venture, looked into the drawn, tired faces of Brytta and the
Council, weary, too, from their night-long struggle with the
Krakenward.

Durek, rubbing his eyes with the heels of his hands, rasped,
"Marshal Brytta, Warrior Arl is right. Only the Vanadurin
can thwart this threat." As the Dwarf King looked up at the
Reach commander, others in the Council grunted and nodded
their agreement, for it was clear that only the horse-borne
Harlingar would be swift enough to overtake the fleeing

Squam. No one there knew just how far the two bands of maggot-folk had gotten before dawn broke, the oncoming dayrise forcing the Spawn to take cover in the splits and cracks of the western side of the range to await the onset of night and the final dash for the High Gate. Indeed, perhaps some had already reached that goal and even now were on their way to Gnar with news of the Dwarves at Dusk-Door.

Brytta's voice was grim: "Arl, get a fresh mount; you will lead us back to Eddra. If they have not yet done so, these Wrg must not escape to alert Gnar. Go now; and bring Nightwind to me." And as Arl sprang down the steps, the Reachmarshal glanced at the morning sky. "Prince Rand, by the straightest horse route, how far lies the road to Quadran Gap?"

"Nine leagues, perhaps ten, through the foothills by horse-back will set you upon the way to the pass," answered Rand after some thought. Both Brytta and Durek grunted in agreement, for the estimate confirmed their own. Rand continued: "The route through the margins will be rock-strewn and slow, rugged, broken, though I can see no swifter way to cut off the Yrm." Rand then turned to the Dwarf King. "Even so, King Durek, when the Vanadurin reach the road, how far upwards should they ride? Where lies the secret High Gate?"

Durek shook his head. "Lore only tells us that it is some-where within the pass. Yet it cannot be more than a league or three upslope, for we now know that it is this side of the high snow, the deep snow, else the Grg could not have used it. How they found it and discovered the way of its working, we may never learn, though they have had more than a thousand years to know of it."

"Oh, no sir," spoke up Cotton. "Beggin' your pardon, King Durek, but I think they've not known about it all that time. Why, if they knew of that High Gate just as recent as Tuck's time—two hundred thirty or so years past—well then, Sir, you can stake your last copper on the fact that they'd've used the High Gate to get at him and the other three when those four tried to cross over Stormhelm during the Winter War." Cotton looked around and saw nods of agreement. "So, as I'd say, since they didn't grab at Tuck in the pass, well, they must have got that secret door open since then."

Brytta glanced down into the vale and saw Arl riding a

fresh mount and leading Nightwind to the Sentinel Falls.
"Regardless as to when it was discovered by the Wrg, they
know of it now. No more time can be spent in speculation. It
is time for deeds, not talk." And Brytta raised his black-oxen
horn to his lips to signal the Harlingar.

"Wait, Sir!" cried Cotton. "What about the wounded?
What about those hurt in the fight with the Monster? Who
will take them south? And, for that matter, what about the
horses? We can't just leave them here in this dead place; how
will they live?"

"Cotton, my gentle friend, unforeseen events are running
roughshod o'er us, trampling our careful stratagems," declared Brytta. "Hence, for those things you name—and perhaps more—other plans must needs be made; for, wounded or
not, horses or not, still the Spawn must be stopped ere they
reach the High Gate; and none else can do that but the
Vanadurin. We must ride now!"

Astride a fresh mount and leading the Reachmarshal's
steed, Arl had come to the foot of the linn; and Nightwind
reared and his forelegs pawed the air, sharp hooves flashing.
Brytta glanced down, and then spoke to all in Council: "Fare
you well, Lords. May each of you succeed in your mission,
and we in ours."

And Brytta again raised the black-oxen horn to his lips,
and this time an imperative call split the air. Nightwind belled
a challenge, and other notes rang forth as Brytta's call was
answered in kind by each of the Harlingar; and horn after
horn resounded, which set the echoes to ringing, and the
Ragad Vale pealed with the fierce calls of the untamed horns
of Valon.

'Mid the Vanadurin horncries to battle, Brytta sprang down
the steps and vaulted to Nightwind's back. And with yet
another blast upon his horn, the Reachmarshal spurred his
dark steed to the west toward the mouth of the valley, and at
his side rode Arl on a grey. High upon Arl's upright spear
flew the War-banner of the House of Valon: a white horse
rampant upon a field of green, an ancient sigil ever borne into
battle by the Harlingar. And as Brytta and Arl went swiftly
past each of the other riders, they, too, spurred in behind.
Soon all the Vanadurin were in the column, riding at a fast
pace, in pairs, a forest of spears bristling at the morning sky:

thirty-seven grim warriors upon whom the hopes of the Dwarf Army rested.

And as the Valanreach column rode forth, Cotton turned to Prince Rand. "Sir, what about Marshal Brytta's broken hand?" asked the Warrow, fretting. "How can he fight? How can he defend himself?"

Rand did not take his eyes from the distant riders, and his answer was a long time coming: "Fear not, Cotton, for he shall manage," said the Prince finally; yet Cotton was not comforted by the words.

Slowly the day crept forward, and Cotton's weary mind continued to churn with worry: over Perry and the Squad; over Brytta and the Vanadurin; over the vast amount of rubble covering the Door; and over the mission in general. Realizing at last the state he was in, he decided to try to break this darkling mood with a trip to see Brownie and Downy, and to visit with the cook-crew of the last waggon.

Tiredly the buccan trudged along the Old Spur back to where the rear of the train was encamped upon the vale sides. All along the way there was torn landscape where the loosed water had whelmed the ravine. Most of the black rot from the lake bottom had been washed away by the Duskrill flowing once more along the ravine, yet some of the decay still clung here and there to the rocks and crevices of the valley floor. And where the rot was, an unclean odor emanated; but there was a cool breeze blowing along the vale and toward the mountain and up, and the reek of centuries of accumulated foulness, though prevalent, did not overpower those at the wains.

After visiting the horses, Cotton ate a meal with Bomar's cook-crew. They seemed pleased to see the small, gold-clad Warrow; yet at the same time, *something* about the buccan's presence unsettled them. Uneasily, they sat in a circle; and what conversation there was turned again and again toward Brytta's mission, and toward the upcoming invasion of Kraggen-cor. And in the fashion of Dwarves, the talk went from Dwarf to Dwarf around the circle:

"Just how did the foul Squam discover the High Gate into Quadran Pass?" growled Nare.

"If a thieving Grg found it, then it has to be easily

done—no doubt from the inside," answered Caddor. "It is, after all, a secret door, Châkmade. Yet, in this, I think it is concealed only on the outside."

"Let us hope the Vanadurin can intercept them before they regain the High Gate," said Belor, to a general murmur of agreement.

"Why were the Foul Folk on this side of the Mountains anyway?" snapped Naral. "There are no homesteads nearby, nor villages, no one to ravage or plunder."

"For aught we know, they were trailing us," responded Oris. "We marched by the pass. In open view."

Crau leaned forward, poking the fire. "Aye, Oris, may-hap. Yet there were two bands."

"One band trailing us and another band trailing them? Spies watching spies?" queried Funda, scratching his head.

"Who knows?" growled Littor, exasperated. "Ravers, scouts, trackers, spies: the only thing that matters is they have seen us and must be stopped!"

"Wull," chimed in Cotton, "if anyone can stop 'em, it's Marshal Brytta and his horse riders!"

Shifting edgily at Cotton's words about horse riders, most of the Dwarves glanced at the silver horn the Warrow bore and then quickly away, and a strained silence fell upon the group. Finally, after a time, with visible effort, Nare again took up the conversation, and soon all were engaged:

"It is an ancient dream, the retaking of Kraggen-cor," observed Nare. "We of Durek's Folk have dreamed this dream for many a long age."

"Aye," responded Caddor. "An ancient dream of an elder race. It is a dream yearned for by many: bethink! we here do not fight just for ourselves; we also fight for our kith who remained behind in Mineholt—and in the Quartzen Caves, too."

"Not to mention those down in the Red Hills," added Belor, pouring himself a cup of tea.

"For that matter," spoke up Naral, "some of Durek's Folk dwell in the far western Sky Mountains and in the rewon halls of the Rigga Mountains to the north."

"But it is not only Durek's Folk we fight for," said Oris thoughtfully, "or just the Châkka. The foul Squam raid the

Lands of Valon and Riamon, where they maim and slaughter the innocent and plunder that which others' labors won.''

"I have heard the Elves of Blackwood and the Baeron think on action against the raiders," declared Crau as he threw a log on the cook fire.

"I know the Men of Pellar stand ready to aid us if we call," added Funda.

"It means that our Captain has the right of it," stated Littor. "We must strike and strike hard in the coming conflict. Dwarves, Men, Elves: all will gain from our victory."

"Hey!" exclaimed Cotton, "What about us Warrows? I mean, we'll benefit too. You left us out, Littor."

"Ho, my Friend Cotton," laughed Littor, standing up and bowing low to the buccan, "Waerans, too. I did not intend to exclude you, though it is not likely that Grg would bother the Boskydells—or the Waerans of Weiunwood near Stonehill, for that matter."

"Wull, that's where you might be wrong, Littor," asserted Cotton. "I mean, we fought the Spawn in the Bosky during the Winter War . . . and over in Weiunwood the maggot-folk tried more than once to invade—but the Rūckslayer drove 'em out, he did."

"Rūckslayer?" asked Caddor.

"That's what he was called," answered Cotton. "His real name was Arbagon Fenner. He led the Warrow force in the Battle of Weiunwood and drove the Rūcks and such out; that was back in the time of the Winter War too. The Rūckslayer must have been quite a buccan: why, they say he once even rode a horse into battle—and I don't mean a pony, I mean a real horse."

At this second mention of horse riding, all the Dwarves again uneasily glanced at and then hastily looked away from the silent horn that Cotton now carried in plain view—a horn no longer stowed out of sight in the Warrow's pack. An irredeemable pall fell upon the conversation, and Cotton soon started back toward the head of the column.

The Dwarves at Dusk-Door toiled without pause, and slowly the great rock pile diminished. The stone itself was used to build cairns for the fallen against the Great Loom. All Dwarves worked hooded out of respect for their dead kindred, but they took not the time for formal mourning, though grief-stricken they were. Several cairns also were made near the broken dam for those killed by the Krakenward during the drilling. Gaynor's remains were recovered and put to rest, as well as were the slain Drillers and Hammerers and the members of the fireteam broken by the clutch and slap of great tentacles. The Monster itself had been crushed by stone, and now it, too, was completely covered by rock, all Dwarf companies and Brytta's scouts having tumbled blocks down upon it.

Late in the afternoon, Farlon, a Valonian scout, rode in from the south. Not finding Brytta, he located Prince Rand to report that good pasturage with hearty grass and sparkling water lay in a wide vale but eleven miles downchain. After giving his report to the Prince, Farlon swept his eyes about the flood-whelmed valley and noted, "Much seems to have happened here since yesternoon, when last I saw this vale—as if a great stroke has hammered this land. The stream that was dry now flows again. The falls that were not, now tumble free. The dam that was whole is now shattered. A foulness lingers on the air. And gone are my comrades, and Marshal Brytta. Where are they? Where are the Vanadurin? And what has befallen this vale?"

Rand now realized that Farlon had ridden south at noon the day before to look for fair pastures for the horses. Hence, the scout knew nought of the events concerning the battle with the Monster, nor of the discovery of the Host by the spying bands of maggot-folk. And so the Prince told the horseman of the struggle with the Warder of the Dark Mere, while Farlon stared with eyes wide with wonder at the broken dam and the black crater, at the Duskrill and the Sentinel Falls, at the Great Loom of Aggarath and the pile of rubble over the Door, at the toiling Dwarves, and at the cascade-shrouded mound of stone covering the creature's carcass.

Then Rand spoke of the prying *Spaunen* and explained Brytta's mission, and Farlon railed at the Fates for separating him from his brethren on this thrust to intercept the Rück spies. Even then Farlon would have ridden to join the Vanadurin, and he strode resolutely to his horse. But ere he could mount, "Hold!" commanded Rand. "Your fellow horsemen are by now too far toward the pass for you to overtake ere nightfall, when the Yrm begin to stir. And a lone

rider running at speed in the dark or by moonlight perchance
would spoil any ambush set for the Foul Folk.''

Farlon began to protest, but his words were cut short by
Rand: "Horse rider, think! Would you gamble our quest
'gainst your desire to join your comrades in battle?'' At
Farlon's sullen silence, Rand spoke on: "In sooth, horseman,
we have more need of you here than there, for someone must
lead the wounded south to the haven you have found."

"Garn!" growled Farlon, "I'm a warrior, not a nursemaiden."

Cotton, who had been listening to the exchange, flushed
with anger. "Warrior? Nursemaiden?" he cried, stepping in
front of the scout. "Those words have no meaning in this!
Ally! Helper! Friend! That's what's needed now! Come with
me, *warrior*, and look!" And the small enraged Warrow
grasped the Man by the wrist and stormed off toward the
white waggons standing nearby, hauling the astonished rider
in tow.

Long minutes fled, til nearly an hour had passed. Yet
finally the two returned to Rand's side. And Farlon was most
subdued, for he had seen and spoken with many Dwarves
lamed and broken by the evil Monster's might in the long
battle with that hideous creature. "Sire," said the rider to
Rand, "I am much shamed by my unthinking words. I do
humbly place my service at your command, to succor the
needs of the *Dwarvenfolc* wounded in that dire struggle."

And Farlon turned to Cotton. "Little friend, you spoke
truth: neither warrior nor nursemaiden are words to be bandied here; rather ally, helper, or friend best describes the
need." And Cotton shuffled his feet and peered at the ground,
all too embarrassed by his own temperamental outburst.

Rand clapped the horseman on the shoulder, and the awkward moment was dispelled. "Good! Now we must think
upon how best to move the injured south; in this we must
seek the advice of a healer. As to when to move them: *if* the
Door opens at the mid of night on the twenty-fifth, and *if* the
Host enters Kraggen-cor, then you *must* move them no later
than the morn of the twenty-sixth, perhaps e'en sooner, to get
them out of harm's way should Spawn flee the battle and
come forth through this vale."

"Aye," answered Farlon, "there is that to think on. And

there are the horses, too. My original mission was to find
them good pasturage, which I have done. Yet how will I get
them south? Drovers are needed, but all my brethren are
gone, and the wounded cannot move the herd. Yet the steeds
cannot be left here.''

"You can do nought but loose them and hope that most
will follow behind your waggons bearing the hurt Dwarves,''
stated Rand. "They are horses of Riamon, more tame than
the fiery steeds of your Land, more likely to follow. Even so,
if they do not come with you, I think they will stay together
in a great herd and wander to other pastures upon the western
wold, to be found again once the issue of Drimmen-deeve is
over and done with.''

"Mayhap we should leave some of the horses behind, here
near the Door; perchance there will be a need,'' suggested
Farlon. "Come, let us see how that might be done. And, too,
let us find a healer and speak upon the move south.''

And the scout and the Prince strode away, leaving Cotton
behind. And the Warrow watched across the black crater as
the work at Dusk-Door went on. The Sun set and darkness
fell, yet the toil at the distant Loom continued by lamplight.
Shifts changed and fresh workers replaced weary ones. Dwarves
not working slept, as Cotton finally did, succumbing at last to
his fatigue.

The next morning, Cotton awakened to find that more than
half the stone had been removed from the Door, and he was
overjoyed until he tallied up the hours to find that more than
half the work time also was gone. He breakfasted with Rand,
who said, "It is going to be close. Whether we reach the
portal by mid of night depends upon whether any more great
stones are found like the one last eventide that took more than
an hour to move.'' No sooner had he said that than word
came that another massive block barred the way.

After breakfast, Cotton went to the remnants of the dam
above the falls and sat and once again watched the work.
Time passed, yet by midmorn the pile did not seem to have
diminished. The Warrow let his sight stray up along the
reaches of the massif and down into the black crater. And
then his jewel-like eyes swept to the Sentinel Stand. He could
see someone—Farlon it was—carrying a bundle of wood up

the steps to the top of the spire. Now why would the rider be carrying a fagot up there? But ere Cotton could puzzle it through, Durek brought his Chief Captains to the buccan, and Cotton began to describe the main features that the Army would see along the Brega Path, starting at the Dusk-Door.

Using copies of Perry's map, Cotton began by telling of the stairs leading up behind the western doors, and he went on to speak of the halls and chambers and passageways they would encounter within Kraggen-cor. The Captains were especially interested in places where there would be bottle-necks, or where maggot-folk could lie in ambush. Cotton had to draw upon all of his knowledge of the Brega Scroll to answer their enquiries, particularly those of Felor the Driller, who asked many penetrating questions, dwelling almost exclusively upon the first several miles of the Brega Path. Cotton was later to discover that Felor's companies were to be in the forefront of the invasion—the spearhead of the Dwarf Army.

Though he couldn't answer all their queries, Cotton had done well, and the Chief Captains thanked him for the review, and at noon they withdrew. But shortly thereafter, Cotton went over the same information with another group of Captains. Three more times, meetings were held at which the Warrow spoke of the Brega Path in terms of bottlenecks, ambuscades, deployments, and other tactical features. It was sundown when he finished, and at last all the Captains had heard his words.

During the time Cotton was speaking, the work at Dusk-Door continued. At times it went swiftly, at other times slowly, yet progress was being made. More than three quarters of the stone was now out of the way, yet only seven hours remained until midnight. Lanterns were again unshielded, and the toil went on.

Cotton ate his evening meal, then sat once more atop the broken dam and watched the labor at the far wall. The stars began to shine in the vault above, and still the effort went forth. Time passed, and Rand joined the Warrow. "In just three hours night will be at its deepest," remarked the Man, peering at the starfield.

They continued to watch the work in silence, each immersed in his own thoughts. Farlon came and joined them, but said nothing as he, too, regarded the sky and judged the depth of the night. Shortly, however, there came a cheer from the Great Loom, and Cotton sprang to his feet. "They're done!" he shouted. "They must be! See, the light shows only a few rocks remain, and they are being rolled into the black crater even now."

The three watched, and soon the lanterns began bobbing northward as the workers returned to the encampment. Word finally came: the task was indeed finished—the massive job done with. Durek, smiling, came carrying a lantern to the top of the falls. "Well, Friend Cotton," he rumbled, "we have succeeded, and with yet two hours to spare."

Durek summoned a herald to him and spoke a word or two. The herald stepped to the edge of the falls precipice and raised a golden horn to his lips, and blew a blast that echoed throughout the vale, causing all who heard it to leap to their feet with hands flying to axe hafts. And even though Cotton was standing next to King Durek, still the Warrow found himself reaching for the hilt of the Atalar Blade, so compelling was the hight to arms of the War Horn.

At this sound, Farlon raised his own black-oxen horn to his lips, and an imperative call split the air. Again Cotton felt his heart thud and his blood surge, and his gaze leapt in wonder from Durek's golden War Horn to Farlon's black-oxen horn. And he glanced to the silver Horn of the Reach hanging by the green and white baldric over his own shoulder, recalling its heartlifting voice. The peals of these three clarions seemed, somehow, irresistibly compelling, though their calls were different: the golden horn was resonant and commanding; the black, flat and challenging; the silver, sharp and calling.

Cotton, too, felt the urge to sound the trumpet he carried—the silver Horn of the Reach—and his hand grasped the bugle; yet he did not set the wind to it, for he knew the dread this token held for the Dwarves; and so he let it fall back to his side unvoiced.

Yet other sounds pealed forth as Durek's and Farlon's calls were answered by the shouts of Dwarf warriors and by the clack of axe upon buckler, a sonance which soon became a great rhythmic pounding of steel upon bronze.

And Cotton's heart pounded too, and his blood surged and his spirit flamed as the Ragad Vale rang with the great hammering and with the roar of the fierce War calls of the Châkka. And above this din pealed the wild cry of a horn of Valon, but above all belled the great golden command of Durek's mighty War Horn.

And the Dwarves of the Army came to the golden call, for it was the summons of their King. Their blood was up and their hearts aflame, and as they came they shouted and flourished their weapons to the sky, and their Dwarvish passions blazed. And when the clamoring Host had gathered on the sides of the vale near the Sentinel Falls, a great proud cry burst forth from the Legion entire as above them Durek stepped to the edge of the linn and stood.

The light of the lanterns filled the valley before the Dwarf King, and he was wreathed in the blue-green phosphorescence. The Moon was full and shone down on him, and the circlet of stars on his black mail-shirt glittered silver in the moonlight. And at his side the water tumbling o'er the linn shimmered brightly. His black and silver locks fell from his helm, and his forked beard shone with luster. He grasped his silveron-edged axe in his right hand, and the blade sparkled. And he looked somehow greater than his stature, for he was King.

Durek raised his arms, and when quiet fell, he spoke; and though he did not seem to raise his gravelly voice, still all the Host heard him: "We stand ready to issue into our rightful homeland and drive the foul usurpers out. This ancient foe we have met in battle many times, and never yet have we suffered defeat at their hands. But heed me: My meaning is not that the Grg is a soft, easy opponent. To the contrary, the Squam are evil and cunning, and in every battle the struggle has been mighty and the outcome uncertain. Yet we defeated the Foul Folk in the Wars of Vengeance; we defeated them again in the Battle of the Vorvor; and we again defeated Squam in the Great War, as well as in the Winter War. And now, once more we go to fight the Grg, and this time the victory may be yet harder to grasp, for this time they shall be in their strength, for the battle will take place underground, where the Sun threatens them not. But we, too, shall be strengthened, for we shall be in our rightful homeland. And when this War is done with, Kraggen-cor shall again be ours!"

There was a great roar of voices, and a pounding of axe haft upon stone, and the black and golden horns blew wildly.

After a time, Durek once more held up his arms for quiet, and slowly the swell of voices and horncalls and clatter of axes subsided, til only the susurration of the tumbling glitter of the Sentinel Falls remained. And above the shush Durek spoke: "We have conquered much that has stood in our way to come to this moment: we outfought the blizzard in the Crestan Pass; we overcame the deep snow on the Mountainside; we quick-marched long to defeat time and distance; we slew the vile Monster of the Dark Mere; and we moved a great mass of stone to uncover the Dusken Door. There is but one thing more that stands in our way, and that is the Grg Swarm. But as we have done before, so shall we do again: we shall meet them in battle and crush them! Victory shall be ours!"

Again there was a mighty shouting and a wild pealing of the black and golden horns, and the strike of axe haft on stone became a great rhythmic beat, and four thousand voices chanted, *Khana-Durek! Khana-Durek! Khana-Durek! [Breakdeath-Durek!]* over and over and over.

At last Durek held up his hands for quiet, but it was a long time coming. "I go now to the Dusken Door to speak the words of power at that portal. If the Squad of Kraggen-cor has won through the caverns to the goal, then at the mid of this night we shall set foot into our ancient homeland. Yet hearken: it may not be the Squad we meet at the Door but, rather, the Squam army, for we know not the success or failure of Marshal Brytta's mission, and the Grg spies may have slipped past the Vanadurin and borne to Gnar word of our Army here at the Dusken Door. Regardless, if it is the Grg Swarm we meet, then we will begin the War just that much sooner and regain our ancient homeland all the quicker. Heed: We all know our battle assignments. Form into your Companies, for the hour is nearly arrived. And may Elwydd smile upon each of us, and Adon strengthen our arms."

Then Durek flashed his axe up to the moonlit sky and cried the ancient battle challenge of the Dwarves: "*Châkka shok! Châkka cor! [Dwarven axes! Dwarven might!]*"

And thrice a mighty shout went up from all the Host: *Châkka shok! Châkka cor!* and Cotton felt his heart leap and his blood surge. The Warrow stabbed his sword to the sky and he, too, shouted with all the Legion the battle cry of the Dwarves. And he turned to see that Rand, also, had his Riamon blade upraised in solemn pledge; and Farlon stood with the butt of his spear grounded to the earth of the Valley Ragad as a steadfast vow that he would lead the wounded to the south, out of harm's way.

Then Durek spun on his heel and started for the Door with Cotton and Rand at his side; and the Dwarf Legion surged along the Old Rell Spur and up the cliff to follow after, while Farlon of the Valanreach stood firm.

As the warriors strode around the crater and by the cairns along the Great Loom, desperate thoughts whirled through Cotton's mind: *Oh, please let Mister Perry be at the Door. He's just got to be there. It won't be right if he ain't.* But then he thought, *Whoa now, Cotton Buckleburr, why are you thinkin' he might not be there? You know he'll make it. Nothing can stop him, not even a black mine full of maggot-folk. It'll sure be good to see him again—if he's there. If he ain't there, well, then, I'll just lead the Dwarves down the Brega Path til we find him and the others, even if Marshal Brytta didn't stop those spies and we have to go through a whole Spawn Horde. But I won't have to do that, 'cause Mister Perry'll be there and the maggot-folk won't be . . . I hope. Then he'll lead and I'll follow. But if I do have to lead then it's: two hundred steps up the broad stair; one and twenty and seven hundred level paces in the main passage 'round right, left, right, and right turns passing three arches* . . . And as Cotton strode with the others toward the Door, through his mind marched the beginning steps of the Brega Path.

At last they halted at the place of the Dusk-Door. Blank stone loomed where the portal should appear. It was not quite midnight, and so they stood and waited. Behind them the Host moved into position: Felor's companies were first, standing ready with axes, and some sported small bucklers on their left arms. Cotton could see rank after rank of Dwarves stretching back around the black crater toward the Sentinel Falls. Lanterns glowed softly, carried by the warriors. Cotton's eyes followed the lights all the way to the last group of lanterns: Bomar's company: the rear guard.

Atop the Sentinel Stand stood Farlon and a head-bandaged Dwarven observer, peering at the stars overhead and at the bright Moon riding high. At last the two looked to one another and nodded; and the Dwarf took up his lantern and threw the shutter wide, and a beam sprang toward the Door, toward those under the great hemidome who could not see the whole of the spangled heavens wheeling through the ebon sky. And as the lantern flashed its signal, Rand drew his sword, and Durek gripped his axe. Hastily, Cotton, too, drew his blade. It was midnight, the appointed hour—time to attempt the opening. They did not know whether the doors would swing wide; and if the portal opened, would the Host be met by friend or foe?

King Durek stepped to the towering Loom and set his axe down, leaning it against the massif, and placed his hands upon the surface of the blank stone, muttering strange words under his breath. *And springing forth from where his hands pressed, there spread outward upon the stone a silvery weft that shone brightly in the lantern glow and by the moonlight and starlight. And as the tracery grew, it took form. And suddenly there was the Door!* At last they could see its outline shining on the smooth stone, and they could see within the glittering web three runes set thereupon, wrought of theen, the Wizard metal: a glowing circle in the center of the Door; and under the circle and off to the right, the Wizard Grevan's rune *G*, and to the left, Gatemaster Valki's glyph *V*.

Durek caught up his weapon by the helve and stepped back from the high portal; all that remained was for him to say the Wizard-word for "move," and the Door, if able, would open. The Dwarf turned to Cotton, Rand, and Felor. "Stand ready," he warned, "for we know not whom we meet."

Cotton gripped his sword and felt the great pressure of the moment rising inside him. The tension was nearly unbearable, and he felt as if he needed to shout, but instead he thought, *Let Mister Perry be at the Door and not no Rŭck.*

Durek turned back to the Door and gripped his axe; he placed his free hand within the glittering rune circle; then his voice rang out strongly as he spoke the Wizard word of opening: *"Gaard!"*

CHAPTER 5

SPEARS OF VALON

Forty hours before Durek spoke the words of opening at the Dusk-Door, the horse column of the Harlingar quickly moved out of the Ragad Valley. The warriors rode two abreast with spears bristling to the sky; favors fluttered from the hafts, while in the lead the War-banner of Valon snapped and cracked in the breeze. The dark helms of the Vanadurin threw back no glints, yet gauds of horsehair and wings and horns flared from the steel. Swiftly they passed, yet not at full gallop, for they had far to go and must needs save their mounts. And the earth trembled at their passage.

Brytta rode in the fore with Arl at his side, and all cantered at the steady ground-devouring pace of a Valanreach long-ride. And no rider spoke as their grim eyes swept the bleak high wold for sign of movement but saw none. The column rode thus as the Sun clambered up through the winter sky, and miles fell away beneath the hooves. Slowly the land changed as they went, the rolling western wold yielding to rugged hills, which in turn gave way to a rough, broken region of shattered rock and deep defiles, of high stone walls and jagged slopes, and of flint-hard paths twisting through a splintered land, as if the world's crust had been thrust asunder by the towering mountains bursting forth from the fettering rock below.

Brytta's force rode with relentless determination to succeed in this desperate mission to intercept the two bands of spying Wrg ere they could reach the hidden High Gate in Quadran Pass, for the Spawn were carrying to Gnar word of the Dwarf Army at the western Door. And but a bare four hours of daylight remained; and then the Sun would set and the Foul

Folk would again take up their dash for the Gate. And the
riders had yet some leagues to go to reach their goal: the road
to the Gap.

The land now consisted of huge upjuttings of red granite,
striated in places with hued bands of layered stone. It would
have taken great skill for the Harlingar to track the Rutcha
through this tangle of rock, yet early on Arl had unerringly
led the column to find Eddra's wake: Eddra, who had trailed
the Spawn throughout the previous night, leaving clear
Valanreach signs indicating the Wrg path for the pursuers to
follow. And the Vanadurin had now followed that track for
hours.

'Mid the red crags and rudden bluffs wended the riders,
strung out in their long column of twos, their gait slowed to a
mere picking walk through the tumble of shattered stone. As
Nightwind stepped through the broken rock, Brytta, seeking
some tactical advantage over the foe, reflected back upon the
tale Arl had told him during other slow passages such as this,
a tale not stripped bare as would be a scout's terse report but,
rather, one told in full:

"Three days agone, after the Legion marched away from
the fork in the road toward that . . . that dead vale back
there"—Arl gestured toward the Ragad Valley—"Eddra, Wylf,
and I took the other fork and rode like the wind to the small
watch-mountain, Redguard, where we set vigil o'er the pass.
We huddled atop that cold stone peak for what seemed an
endless time, wood for the balefire ready but unlit, awaiting
the coming of a Wrg army. And we burned no campfire at
night, for that would signal our presence to enemy eyes.

"And cold we were, so cold. . . . A bitter, rimed grip was
upon the land; and the very stone cracked under heel—frost-
riven, broken by that dread clime's grasp. Even Wylf's luck
at finding comfort failed, and we lurked there among the icy
rock in the long, bitter nights; and the cruel wind cut like
sharp knives as we huddled shivering, urging on the morn so
that we could then light a small campblaze for its feeble
warmth. At times we even japed that should a Rutchen army
come, we then could kindle the balefire and warm by its
flames; yet it did not happen. For two nights nothing happened.

"But, on the third night—last night—thirty or so Rutcha

bearing torches came marching down from Quadran Col just after sunset.''

"Hold!" interrupted Brytta. "Whence came they? How far up were they? Did you see them come from the High Gate?"

"I have thought long upon that," answered Arl, his brow furrowing, "and this is the way of it: the first we saw of their torches, they were nearly at the snow line, high up on the roadway o'er the Gap."

Brytta grunted, then motioned for the young rider to continue his tale, and so Arl did: "Though we had hoped for some action to fire our blood, when the Spawn came all thoughts of discomfort, all longing for warmth fled in our dismay, for we knew that here could spell the doom of the quest. There were only thirty or so of them, but still it could mean discovery of the Host. Yet down the flanks of Stormhelm they tramped, and turned south. And while they marched, we considered our course.

"Because there were so few, we did not light the balefire, for that signal was meant to warn the Legion of the coming of a full Wrg army, not just a mere squad. Too, a beacon would only serve to warn the Spawn that something was stirring on this side of the mountains. Yet it seemed likely that their spying eyes had seen our Army bear south along the Old Rell Way, and this force had come to see what was afoot.

"They marched for two hours, or a bit more, going perhaps six or eight miles, down from the snow line and passing below us on the east flank of Redguard. Yet suddenly they stopped, seeming to mill about in fear or confusion, and we wondered at the cause. Then we, too, saw what had affrighted the Foul Folk, and we ourselves were taken aback, for it was indeed a bodeful sight: that great cusp of a stone wall at the head of the Valley of the Door . . ." Arl turned and swept his hand back toward the hemidome of the Great Loom, which, through the granite crags behind, could be seen towering up the side of Grimspire, "that wall was flaring and blooming red and orange and yellow in the night, like the very forge of Hèl, and great dark shadows were guttering and twisting and writhing up the mountain flank and into the blackness, as if some vast fire was ablaze in Ragad Vale."

"Indeed, 'twas a great conflagration," verified Brytta, turning

Nightwind through the jumble of rock, "set ablaze atop the dam last night to thwart the evil Warder as the Dwarves strove to break the stone and loose the lake. But that is a tale to be told later, after yours is finished. Speak on."

But at that moment the land opened somewhat, calling for a faster pace. Arl shifted the banner spear from the left stirrup to the right, couching the haft butt in the cup there, and spurred his horse to a swift canter. They rode thus for a time before coming again to shattered land where the column had to slow. And when the pace dropped back, Arl continued as if there had been no break in his narrative: "We were filled with foreboding, whelmed by the unknown yet dire portent of the flaring upon the Loomwall. It seemed as if some great battle perchance raged in the Valley of the Door while we three on Redguard stood mayhap a less necessary duty. We argued whether or not to ride to the vale to help; yet we knew not the cause of the flaming, thus could not easily decide upon our course: at hand directly below us was the given threat of a small, perhaps unimportant, force of Wrg; while far off was the sign of a great raging effort of some unknown action, which for aught we knew could be entirely peaceful, though we three thought elsewise."

"*Arn!*" snorted Brytta. " 'Twas anything but peaceful. Yet I interrupt. Go on."

"In the end," continued Arl, "we chose to hew to our original duty—to watch the Gap for a Rutchen army—but also to watch the track of this Wrg band below us. In any event, in spite of the fact that we would rather be at our comrades' sides in any conflict, we knew that surely the Host could face any foe and fare as well without us as with us, though it goes against the grain to admit so. On the other hand, we alone knew of this squad of ravers. We knew, too, that should they espy the Host at the Dusk-Door, then Gnar would be alerted, to the ill of our quest."

"You chose aright," commented Brytta, "though difficult it is to forbear rushing to the aid of arms-mates."

"After a time," Arl went on, "the Spawn once again started south, toward the valley, and we came to the decision that one of us should ride to warn the Host, mayhap to set a trap or to divert the Foul Folk if it seemed they were near to discovering the Army. Yet, to set a trap, we needed to know their goal; and to divert them, if that became necessary, we needed to be on their track. The ravers had just passed beyond sight within the foothills, and we were not certain as to their course.

"In haste, we drew lots. Wylf lost, pulling the short twig, and was left atop that cold Redguard Mountain while Eddra and I rode down to trail the Spawn. I had drawn the long stick and would be the messenger to warn the Host should the need arise.

"Ahorse, we followed their path along a rocky trace, and in the full moonlight we set a goodly pace. Soon we came to where we could again see their torches, and we lagged far behind, trailing their slow march southward. After the mid of night, as if a vast fire had been drowned, the Great Loomwall suddenly went dark, and again the Wrg milled about in confusion or fright, as if they were undecided as to what course to follow. And both Eddra and I were sore beset with doubt, for we knew not the meaning either, but we guessed yet again that something dire was happening south in the Ragad Valley. But we knew our duty was to follow the Spawn, as we had planned.

"Once more the Wrg started toward the Ragad Vale, and again we trailed them. Some time passed, and we covered two leagues or so. They drew nigh to the Valley of the Door, and Eddra and I knew we had to decide soon on how we would act: to ride among them, shouting, and then away to draw them off; or to wait to see their goal, and then warn the Host. But ere we could act, a *second* torch-bearing gang of thirty *more* came through the night—but *they* came *from* the direction of the *valley*. The two bands clotted together and shouted and snarled and cursed one another, and the two leaders argued; but then with a lashing about of thongs, the Drōken leaders turned the Rutcha back toward Quadran Pass.

"Moving quickly now, no longer uncertain, loping at Rutch-pace, they began running toward the Quadran Gap, coming straight at Eddra and me. We quickly stepped our mounts off the path and into the surrounding dark scrub and rock, and we dismounted, holding our steeds' muzzles to prevent a challenge. The returning Wrg loped past without seeing us, and among their words both Eddra and I heard one of them snarl something about '. . . *we tell Gnar of the dam-breaking lake-draining army of foul-beards at the buried door!*' Though we knew not what all overheard meant, we did know that the Host had been discovered by these Spawn now on their way to the High Gate to warn Gnar.

"As soon as they were beyond hearing, Eddra told me to ride to warn the Legion while he stayed behind to trail the Wrg and leave Valanreach signs along their track for pursuers to follow. And we parted, Eddra following Rutcha and Drōkha north while I hastened south.

"Swiftly I rode, and the Moon was bright; yet I could not fly apace until the coming of first light, and then at last Firemane could see to run in full. And as I rode, I knew that only the Vanadurin would be fleet enough to intercept the two bands of Wrg ere they reached the pass—if they have not yet attained that goal. But I think the dayrise will have found them short of the Gap, and they will be holed up awaiting nightfall—at least I hope their Wrg-lope was not fast enough to carry them to Stormhelm before the coming of the Sun.

"And you know the rest of the tale, Sire." Arl fell silent, and onward they rode, following Eddra's well-placed markers.

Thus had Arl told his full tale; and now, miles later, Brytta reflected upon the scout's words for some shred, some scant fact, that would give the Vanadurin added advantage over the foe—but beyond knowing their number and their goal, the Reachmarshal found nought he could use.

Once more the column of Valanreach riders came upon an open flat, and again the pace quickened as swiftly they coursed north, and the high stone of the flanking mountain ramparts flung back the thunder of their passage, and the plateau drummed beneath the driving hooves.

Ahead they could see a towering scarp rear up from the land and stand athwart their path, and a great dark crack jagged upward into its flank. And toward this yawning split, Eddra's signs pointed. Black it looked, dark though the Sun still rode the sky. And the closer they came, the more dreadful it seemed. And into this fissure, Eddra's track plunged.

The column rode into the forbidding cleft, now single file, for the walls were close upon them. Though it was daytime still, a shadowy muffled murk clutched at them, and the rays

of the Sun fell dim and feeble into the cold depths. Splits and
cracks radiated away into the flanks, their ends beyond seeing,
lost in darkness. Horses shied and started at the black gap-
ings, sensing the disquiet of the riders they bore as they
passed these holes. Ancient Vanadurin legends told of the
haunted Realm of the Underworld, where dwelled the living
dead; and ever in these hearthtales, heroes came to woe and
grief and unending agony. And always these paladins had
entered into the halls of the dead through caves and rifts and
clefts in the land, ignoring the warnings of a loved one to stay
clear of these fissures. Hence, for those accustomed to open
skies and grassy plains, these dark legends gave rise to
inchoate yet palpable feelings of dread whenever a dark pit
yawned before them. And the Vanadurin column now rode
through the dim light at the bottom of a black abyss while
splits and cracks and holes without number leapt at them from
the looming stone walls; and the pits cast back shattered
echoes, reverberating hollowly like laughter from Hèl.

These dim legends scuttled on spider claws through Brytta's
mind as he felt his hackles rise, but he dismissed them, for
warriors believe they have long since cast aside the hearthtales
of youth. Still, the thought of being underground was dire,
and the prospect of fighting a War below earth—as the
Dwarves were wont to do—caused Brytta to marvel at the
Dwarves' staunch courage, and unformed feelings of apprehension rose within his own heart. But uneasy or not, the
column rode ahead, as Brytta fleetingly thought of Hèl. And
his sight darted from hole to hole. And it seemed as if he
could feel the presence of hundreds of malevolent Rutchen
eyes glaring out at the passing horsemen—if not the Spawn
they were pursuing, then perhaps others; for despite Durek's
assurances to the contrary, the Valanreach Marshal was more
than convinced that the walls of this region were riddled with
a thousand secret bolt holes to the great Black Hole of
Drimmen-deeve—a thousand places for sudden assault or
surreptitious spying or swift escape. Yet even if there were
not here secret shafts boring away to the Black Maze, still
Brytta felt watched. Were the eyes of the undead staring out
from the blackness? Hèl's spawn?

Shaking his head to dispel these fey thoughts, Brytta squinted
up the looming walls to the jagged rift of sky far above,

knowing that if foul Wrg or aught else lurked in the splits of
this dreadful crack, the wan light of day dimly reaching these
depths was not enough to keep the creatures pressed back into
the dark shadows at the deep roots of the riven fissures.

The walls of the cleft twisted tortuously, and the long path
before the line of horsemen began to rise. Slowly they rode
up out of the stifling narrow crack, to come at last to another
open plateau. And as they came out upon the high plain, out
into the cold crisp air of day, the sense of cloying suffocation
left Brytta and he breathed freely again. And the wisps of
fables and lurking Wrg fled Brytta's mind, though he still
marveled at the courage of the *Dwarvenfolc*.

"Sire!" Arl exclaimed and pointed. Far ahead they could
see a dun horse standing near several huge boulders where yet
another bluff lunged upward, and again a great split fissured
away into blackness.

"It's Eddra's mount," growled Brytta, and his heels clapped
into Nightwind's flanks and the great black horse sprang
swiftly forward. "Sound no horns," Brytta ordered as the
column matched his stride.

As they rode toward the towering cliff, Eddra stepped out
from the shadow of a boulder and hand-signalled that all was
well. The Marshal felt a surge of relief that his scout was
alive, for Brytta, seeing what appeared to be a riderless,
abandoned horse, had fleetingly feared the worst. Yet Eddra
was hale, in fact was less weary than his brethren, for he had
dozed under the Sun while awaiting the Harlingar, whereas
none of them had rested for nearly two days: Arl had ridden
throughout the preceding night, while Brytta and the others
had struggled without letup in the battle with the Krakenward.

"*Hál!*" cried Eddra, pleasure upon his features, as the
riders wheeled 'round him in a semicircle and brought their
steeds to a halt, half to the left of Brytta, half to the right.

Brytta dismounted and signed to the others to do the same,
for they had been long in the saddle. "*Hál*, rider! Clear was
your track and long have our eyes sought you. How fares
your mission? Where be the Spawn?"

"The Wrg spies lie up in yon crack," answered Eddra,
gesturing at the dark split in the face of the bluff, "waiting
for the westering orb to fall." Many glanced at the late-
afternoon Sun, and but two hours or less remained before it

would set. "Far did they run through this broken land, and weary was I with the chase. Yet there they lurk in the deep black shadows, soon to fly out the crack's far side.

"Still we may head them, for to the west but a ways lies a path around this dark cranny, where we may pass beyond them without their knowledge. North, too, is water for the horses. A short ride, then, will bring us to a deep stony defile through which they must pass, for it is upon the road to the Quadran Gap and the secret High Gate, a defile with steep walls where we may entrap them and they cannot escape our spears."

"Hai!" cried Brytta, and his dour features broke into a wide smile, and he clapped Eddra upon the shoulder; for his warrior had scouted the lay of the land and had found a snare for the foe, a place where at last the Harlingar could stand athwart the fleeing Spawn's path. "Let us spend no more time in idle chatter," he grinned. "I would as lief be on our way. Lead, fair Eddra, and we shall follow."

Once again the warriors mounted, and this time their hearts sang, for now they had the knowledge that they were not on a shadow-mission—a mission of little or no hope—for each had secretly feared that they would be too late, and now they knew they were not.

Following Eddra, swiftly they rode to a narrow path pitching shallowly up the face of the bluff. Along this slant the horses went, steeds and riders seemingly oblivious to the steep fall on their left. And at the top they came out upon the last plateau. In the distance before them they could see the road leading up to the Gap of Stormhelm. To the west lay Redguard Mountain, and they knew that even now Wylf, at its crest, watched them ride forth into the open and toward the col. They pressed ahead and at last came to the side of the road, and here and there an ancient pave-stone could be seen, though most were buried and a few were thrust aside by weed and hidden in the tangle. And at roadside, a spring thinly crusted with ice bubbled down from the snows in the pass; and they paused long enough to water the steeds and to refresh their canteens.

Slowly the Sun sank, and just as it lipped the earth, they came to the defile spoken of by Eddra. The sides were steep and the canyon long; Quadran Road wended upward through its flanks, to pass beyond sight at a far turn, rising toward the Gap. Up to the turn they rode, there to lay their trap for the Wrg.

Brytta gathered his riders about him, and in the dimming dusk he set forth his plan. And when he was done, each knew his assignment and was pleased, for Brytta was a mighty Captain, and his strategy suited their nature. He spoke in Valur, the enduring Battle-tongue of the Valanreach, which hearkened back even unto the ancient days when their forebearers had ridden free on the high northern steppes, a time long before any had come south to the grassy plains of Valon. And as darkness fell, Brytta repeated an elder benediction of the Vanadurin:

> "Arise, Harlingar, to Arms!
> Fortune's three faces now turn our way:
> One smiling, one grim, one secret;
> May the never-seen face remain always hidden.
>
> Hál, Warriors of the Spear and Saber!
> Hál, Warriors of the Knife and Arrow!
> Hál, Warriors of the Horn and Horse!
> Ride forth, Harlingar, ride forth!"

And in the gathering darkness, the fierce Valanreach warriors, their hearts pounding and spirits surging, mounted and rode to take up their battle positions to await the coming of the Spawn.

Brytta, far up the defile, sat his horse and stared down the dark road rising up to meet him. Riders four abreast formed a long column behind their Marshal. And as they held, the horses were calm, occasionally shifting their weight; and saddle leather creaked and the thicket of upright spears stirred to and fro.

The night deepened and the stars shone forth. To the east beyond the range, the bright Moon climbed up the star-studded sky, and at last the silver rays spilled through the gap between Grimspire and mighty Stormhelm, bathing the defile with pale, glancing light. And sharp-edged blackness clung to boulders and crags and streamed darkly away. To the west, Redguard's peak jutted up out of the shadows of the range and into the moonlight, and past Redguard lay the western wold stretching beyond sight to the River Caire. The air was cold and crystalline, and the night was still, and the breath of horses and warriors alike rose in white plumes.

And the spears of Valon waited.

Ppfaa! Nightwind suddenly snorted and tossed his head, and Brytta listened sharply. At first he heard nothing; then dimly came a sound, faint: a scrabbling, like a chitinous scuttling. Stronger it grew, resolving at last into the distant slap of iron-shod Rutch boot.

"*Stel! [Steel!]*" hissed Brytta, reining to the side, and the lances in the first row dropped level, held steady by firm grips, and clear eyes watched the far turn. Louder came the sound of running, and now all could hear the clack of harsh voices, cursing and snarling, whining, panting, grating, the speech foul. Louder it came, and louder still, nearly upon them. Suddenly, a ragged loping column of torch-bearing Rutcha burst into view, scrambling around the turn below, and they jostled and jolted and elbowed and railed at one another as they swarmed up the road.

"*Tovit! [Ready!]*" Brytta hissed a second command in the Valonian Battle-tongue, and the horse-column seemed to bunch itself, as a tautly drawn bow ere the arrow is loosed. Yet tense and quivering, still they held their places; and onward came the Spawn, as yet unaware of the danger ahead.

And when it seemed that the Wrg must at last see the Harlingar, a flat horncry sounded from below, from behind the Foul Folk, as the Vanadurin posted there took station upon the road when the last of the Rutchen column passed by.

And the trap sprang shut!

"*V'ttacku! [Attack!]*"] barked Brytta, and swift as an arrow loosed at last, the first four riders charged forth, spears leveled, thundering death.

"*Stel!*" called Brytta, and the lances of the second row

dropped level. *"Tovit!"* His voice was sharp and clear, and he paused but a moment; then: *"V'ttacku!"* And another line charged forth, havoc upon four horses, ten running strides behind the first.

"Stel!" the command came again, and again, and again, and rows paced forward, and lances lowered, and file after file of swift-running doom was launched down the road, down from the high ground.

At first the Spawn did not realize their plight, and when the Valonian horncall sounded from behind them they quickened their pace, fleeing unknown pursuit. And it was not until the last moment that those in the fore saw by moonlight and torch flare the first strike swooping down upon them, and then it was too late as wave after wave of lethal spears, hard driven by full-running horses, shocked into and through and over the Rutchen column. And screams rent the air as victims fell underfoot to be trampled, and lances impaled others, some spears to shatter in the impact. Sabers were drawn and slashed to and fro, felling foes, and Valanreach battle cries burst forth:

> *Hál Vanareich! [Hail Valon!]*
> *B'reit Harlingar! [Ready, Sons of Harl!]*
> *Kop'yo V'ttacku Rutcha! [Now whelm the goblins!]*

A few Rutcha tried to flee, but the walls of the defile were too steep to clamber, and the dreaded horsefolk were both before and behind them. Yet most of the foul breed, though taken by surprise, fought with feral savagery, for they were cornered: Torches were thrown in the faces of horses, and steeds shied and reared. Iron bars were swung with cunning force to crack across the forelegs of several charging coursers, and they fell screaming among the enemy, and the riders were set upon by the Wrg. Yet other horses, riderless, trained for War by the Vanadurin, lashed out with sharp hooves, felling Rutcha with their crushing blows. And warriors rose up out of piles of Spawn and cast the foe aside, and many Harlingar sang as they slew, a terrible burning light in their eyes.

Into the fray came Brytta, hewing left-handed with his saber, slashing Death borne upon Nightwind's back. And it was a mighty slaughter, and Brytta's arm grew weary with the reaping of Rutcha. Yet the battle raged on, for the Foul Folk were savage. And lance pierced, and saber slashed, cudgel smashed, and hammer crushed. Scimitar clashed with long-knife, and flashing hooves struck o'er iron bar. Grunts and screams and oaths and cries filled the air, and so, too, did the harsh clang of steel upon steel. And the struggle swept to and fro. Yet slowly the Vanadurin prevailed, and the Wrg numbers dwindled.

All Rutchen torches had been flung aside, or at riders, or at their steeds, and now only the bright Moon illumed the battleground, though here and there a brand sputtered on the road. Surviving Spawn flicked in and out of dark shadows, striking quickly then leaping back into blackness.

And slowly the fight became a grim stalking, as the Vanadurin dismounted and took up torches and spread across the road and searched each cleft and shadow. And the Foul Folk were found, sometimes singly, sometimes clotted together in pockets. And no quarter was given.

Brytta sat upon Nightwind, looking down the defile; he watched as the Harlingar sought living Spawn in the blackness, and made certain that those lying upon the ground were dead and not feigning. It was long-knife work, and saber, too; and struggles were short and fierce. And as he looked, a stone rattled down from above.

On the wall! A Drōkh! No, two! Flitting through the shadows above Brytta were two Drōkha who had managed to scale up a cranny to a high path along the south wall of the defile, a path running to the top. And now they were fleeing along it, escaping the defile, fleeing for the High Gate.

With effort, Brytta strung his bow, cursing the pain and clumsiness of his broken right hand. Another rider was nearby; "Didion! To me!" cried Brytta. "Wrg! On the wall! Your bow!" And as Didion rode to him, Brytta set an arrow to string and tried to draw the weapon with his broken hand. A low agonized groan hissed between his clenched teeth, and with the bow but half drawn the arrow fell from the weapon and clattered to the ground. *"Rach!"* Brytta cursed, and changed hands, shifting the bow to his clumsy right, reaching for arrow with his left. The Drōkha now scrambled the last

few steps toward the top of the wall, an open plateau—and if
they reached it, they were free!

Again Brytta set arrow to string, this time drawing the bow
against the heel of his shattered right hand and gritting against
the grinding pain while beads of sweat burst forth upon his
brow. "Take the right, Didion, I'll take the left," he gasped,
and as the Drōkha momentarily reappeared from the shadows, two arrows hissed through the air, one well aimed, the
other less so. Now at the top and just entering the shadow
again, one of the enemy flung up his hands and a piercing
scream rent the air as he plunged backward down the defile
wall to land with a sodden thud in the roadbed. The other
Drōkh pitched forward into the blackness, and if he was
arrow-struck, they did not see.

"Didion, after him! He must not escape!" Brytta barked.
"Ged!" he called to another rider coming nigh. "Go with
Didion! Drōkh on the height!" And Ged leapt from his
horse and scrambled up a cleft behind Didion, finding the
steep climbing no easy task.

And the search for Rutchen survivors went on.

Night passed and the Moon set, and dawn crept upon the
land to find stricken Harlingar: exhausted, for they had spent
two nights without sleep; wearied by struggle, first with the
Krakenward, then with Wrg; drained, for some, weeping, had
had to slay their own steeds, legs broken in battle; afflicted,
for nearly half the warriors bore wounds, some serious, some
minor, now bandaged; filled with heartgrief, for five of the
Vanadurin would never again answer horncall. Thusly did the
dayrise find the riders of the Valanreach.

Earlier, a count showed that three and seventy Rutcha and
one Drōkh had fallen to the riders; and in the predawn the
carrion were dragged down out of the defile and flung into a
ravine, where the coming of the Sun would shrivel them to
dust, as Adon's Ban decreed. The Wrg weapons were gathered, and in dull rage the riders snapped the blades and
shattered the hafts and bent the iron bars beyond repair, and
these, too, were cast into the ravine.

In midmorn, Didion and Ged returned to the defile and
sought out Brytta. "Sire," said Didion, drawn and weary,

"long we hunted, and this we found." He held up an arrow, broken in twain, covered with dried black Wrg gore. Brytta examined it closely and grunted: it was his. "Yet," Didion went on, "no Drōkh did we find, not near nor far; and by dawn's light we searched even unto the snow line. At the first, a spotted trail we followed, and quickly found the arrow. Soon the trail diminished, at last to disappear on the edge of a deep crevasse with a black still pool at bottom. Ged, here, climbed down while I cast about, but neither he nor I found aught else."

"*Skut!*" spat Brytta, flinging the fractured arrow from him and looking bitterly at his broken hand. "The Drōkh may have been but fleshwounded, snapping the arrow in twain and pulling it through himself. As to the Wrg's fate thereafter, we know not whether he pitched off into the crevasse by accident, or while dying, or not at all. He may have escaped entirely; if so, then even now word goes forth to Gnar.

"Yet you have done all I could ask, and though no Drōkh was found, feel no blame; the hand that failed was mine." And Brytta dismissed the two and cast himself to the ground. And he sat with his back to the wall, and his brooding stare bore into the stone opposite him. His mood was black and bitter, and in his eyes lurked fault.

Yet after a long while of smoldering thought, he again stood and gathered his warriors to him: "Vanadurin," he spoke, "I deem we must remain on guard in this defile, for other bands of ravers may be about the land. Yet all must come through this slot to reach the secret High Gate. And though this is the night appointed when King Durek will attempt the Dusk-Door, still it may not open, for the Squad of Seven may be delayed.

And it is in my mind that other trials may come, and we stand at guard here at the Dwarf Army's back. Even now, word may be going forth to Gnar, and he may set a Rutchen army on the inside of the Door to await the Dwarves. And in that event, if the Squad be delayed, then likely they will not be able to penetrate Gnar's waiting Swarm to reach the Door hinges. And if the Squad cannot reach the inside of the Door, then who will let Durek's Legion within?

"Too, there may be other doors, other gates, through which Gnar may launch an attack upon the Host. Yet the secret Gate in yon Quadran Gap is the only one we are certain of. And if an army marches down this way, then we with quick slashing strikes must bait and harass and divert their energies aside for as long as our War-skill permits, to give the Squad and the Legion precious time to ope the Door.

"And so, here we must stay, both foreguarding and hindguarding the Dwarf Army. And a long wait it may be, for we know not when the Door may yield: tonight, tomorrow, in a seven-night, or never.

"Yet even though we wait, there is still much to do: Place our slain comrades 'neath stone cairns, until proper burial. Tend your steeds. Then rest, for you are weary. Go now, and know you stand a vital duty."

And the warriors saluted Brytta—*Hál!*—and turned to take up their tasks.

"Hogon," Brytta called, "set forth a ward of eight: four upslope, four down, two-hour watches."

And while Hogon selected the guard, Brytta turned to a flaxen-haired youth: Brath, Brytta's bloodkith. "Brath, sister's son, to me," he said wearily as he sat down upon a small boulder.

The younger Man, his left arm bound in splints and held in a sling, stepped to his kinsman's side. "Sire?"

"Your arm is shivered and your leg gashed," observed the Marshal, a fierce pride in his eyes, for Brath had accounted for many of the Rutchen slain. "Were we in other times or other places, I would send you to the hearth." Brytta held up both hands, forestalling the protests leaping to the young warrior's lips. "Instead, I would have you go to yon mountain"—he pointed to Redguard—"and relieve Wylf, for he is hale and we need his strong arm. In this, go with honor, for we must have one to tend the balefire, to signal the Host if need be. Take an extra overgarment, for Arl said it is cold; his cloak will do, for he needs it not and would give it gladly could he say."

And Brath went forth, and Gannon went with him, for both of wounded Gannon's hands were shattered, and he could no longer bear arms, though his vision was sharp and he could set watch.

And temporary cairns were made for the slain riders, to shelter them until they could be brought forth to the wide grasslands below and laid to rest 'neath turves. The Vanadurin withheld show of their grief for their fallen brethren—though it cut to the quick—for it is the custom of the Harlingar to mourn not until the final burial.

The Sun climbed high and passed overhead, and warriors rested. Two hours ere sunset, Wylf rode into the quiet encampment. He sat in the afternoon Sun, basking in its warmth as Brytta slept. Wylf spoke to one of the warders, and in the Valonian War-tongue the companion told the tale of the Krakenward, the Rutchen spies, and the battle in the defile; and Wylf listened grimly, and his eyes took on a steely glint.

In foredusk, the camp awakened, and a quick meal of waybread and dried venison was taken, and the horses were gathered from the sward downslope. And warriors girded themselves for what the eventide would bring.

Night fell, and again the devastating trap was set, ready to spring shut should Spawn come. This time the Vanadurin posted a bowman upon each wall of the defile, to stop Wrg from fleeing that way; yet Brytta thought that this was latching the stable after the stallion has fled, for it yet burned within him that perhaps a Drōkh had escaped to carry word to Gnar, to the great ill of the quest—a Drōkh that he, Brytta, should have slain; and the Marshal again glanced with bitterness at his broken hand.

The darktide deepened, and stars wheeled above. Again the Moon shone silvery, full and bright. And the warriors spoke quietly of the Dusk-Door and wondered if it would open, for this was the night.

Time crept by at a slow-moving gait, and each moment seemed frozen in stillness.

Yet of a sudden the twelfth hour was upon the land. Now was the time for King Durek to say the words of opening. Silent moments fled and mid of night passed, and Brytta yearned to know what befell at the Door, and his heart felt taut with foreboding. And again time plodded.

Suddenly the bowman upon the south steep shouted in wonderment: "Ai-oi!" he cried, his voice loud in the hush. "Sire!" he called to Brytta, "at the Great Loomwall in the Valley of the Door, a balefire flares!"

''What? Balefire? At the Dusk-Door?'' cried Brytta. ''A
recall beacon! Spawn! Or does it mean the Door opened? If
so, was the Host met by friend or foe? Or have the Wrg fallen
upon them from another gate? Fie! Whether or not we knew
the which of it, it is of no moment, for we must ride!''

And Brytta sprang to Nightwind's back and raised his horn
to his lips and blew a mighty blast that rent the air. And
Nightwind reared and pranced and curvetted with sidle-steps,
eager to answer the Valonian hight to arms. And Brytta called
to the Vanadurin: ''Mount up, Harlingar, and ride! Ride to
the Dusk-Door! Let any who fall behind come at their own
pace, for we are summoned! Forth, Harlingar, ride!''

And he clapped his heels into Nightwind's flanks, and
down the shadowed road they sprang, hooves thundering,
horn pealing, racing through the moonlit night. And so went
all the Vanadurin, bursting forth from Stormhelm Defile,
sparks flying from steel-shod hooves. And the fierce horns of
Valon blew wildly.

CHAPTER 6

TRAPPED AGAIN

A day earlier, with the Squad lost at a dead-end passage and with no Gatemaster, and but twenty-eight hours remaining ere the appointed time of the rendevous at the Dusk-Door, Perry drank his fill from the clear cold water of the underground river and refilled his leather water bottle. He was putting in the stopper when another faint hornblat echoed down the cave behind them. "Oh, why didn't we search for a way to close the secret door to the Gargon's Lair?" he asked. "Then the Rūcks wouldn't have been able to follow us."

"We were fortunate just to have found the way out," rumbled Borin, "and we had not the time to spare to look for the way of closing the portal; it is not our mission to discover the workings of all hidden gates in Kraggen-cor; our goal is to reach the Dusken Door and set it right."

"Well, we've got to get out of here," responded Perry. "The Spawn will be upon us shortly."

"I judge they are only about an hour or so behind us in that hard passage," said Shannon. "In the meanwhile, I urge that we look for another hidden door. The secret way at the Lost Prison opened onto this passage, and so there must be another door in and out of this cave."

"But that hidden door could be anywhere over the miles we just travelled!" cried Perry. "There's no reason to believe that it's here, near this dead end. Besides, we don't even know what we are looking for: it could be another slot for a west-pick, like Bane, or a stone that gets pressed, or a special word that must be said, a glamoured key, or a hundred other things. And our Gatemaster is dead."

91

"But we must try, Friend Perry," insisted the Elf softly, "we must try."

"Oh, Vanidar Silverleaf, you are right, of course," admitted the Warrow, abashed at his own behavior. "I am just bitterly disappointed at this setback."

"So are we all," said Lord Kian. Above the gurge of the river came another faint horn sound. "Ursor, can you swim? Good. Doff your clothes and cross the river with me, and we will search the far wall for slots, runes, hidden levers, and other such devices. Anval, Shannon, take the right-hand wall. Borin, Perry, search the left side. Let us see if we can locate a way out."

Long and hard they searched by lantern light. Anval and Shannon found only one strange-looking rock, which, when they twisted it, merely came loose from the wall. Borin and Perry ranged along the left side, and Bane was thrust into several crevices to no avail. Kian and Ursor disrobed, then cast a grappling hook to the opposite bank of the river; it caught between two rocks, and when they tugged, it remained well anchored; after tying the line to a boulder on the near shore, they pulled themselves across the swift current and over to the far bank. But after a careful search, the sheer end-wall proved to be a blank. All the while the Squad looked, the Rūcken horn sounded closer and closer. Finally the comrades also examined the rough floor of the cavern for sign of an exit from the cave; but that, too, proved fruitless. "We must have passed it," called Kian from the far bank, waving a hand toward the Gargon's Lair as he prepared to cross back over.

The Squad came back together on the bank of the river, Ursor coming last, casting loose the grapnel and grasping the boulder-tied rope to ride the swift current and swing to the near shore. The Rūcken horn echoed again, and Bane blazed fiery blue. "We'll make our last stand there," decided Lord Kian as the Baeran came out of the water and into the group; Kian pointed at a high ledge running athwart the cavern. "That stone wall will be our rampart, and we will give good account of ourselves before their very numbers overcome us."

"Sire," spoke up Ursor, "there is but one other thing I'd like to try first. If I fail, it may mean you will be without my strength in the final battle. But if I succeed, then we will yet escape the Spawn.''

"Escape?'' exploded Perry in astonishment. "How can we escape? There is no way out!''

"There may be one, little friend,'' answered Ursor. "The river. As I was crossing back over I was swept toward the left wall, and I wondered where the river goes on the other side of it, if indeed there *is* another side; it occurred to me that the river may run into another cavern.''

"It may,'' rumbled Anval, "but then again it may not, and you may drown finding out.''

"He also may succeed,'' countered Borin.

The Rūcken horn blatted again, and Kian looked back the way they had come. "The gamble is worth the risk,'' he said after a short moment. "Our mission is to reach Dusk-Door, not to engage Yrm. If Ursor does not try, we will die fighting *Spaunen*. If he tries and fails, again we will perish. But if he succeeds, then we will go on. Yet hurry, for not much time remains.''

Their longest line was swiftly fixed to Ursor's waist, and he took a Dwarf-lantern for light, for they are unaffected by water. "Let Wee Perry count one hundred heartbeats,'' Ursor instructed, "then pull me back.''

"But my heart is racing,'' protested Perry as the Rūcken horn sounded again. "One hundred frightened-Warrow heart-beats will take but a moment. Let Shannon count instead.''

Shannon nodded; and after four deep breaths, the giant Man ducked under, the lantern around his neck casting a rippling glow through the crystal-clear water as his powerful strokes and the current carried him under the wall. The others watched the glow recede and payed out the line. In spite of the fact that Shannon was counting, Perry also kept track of his own racing heart. The Warrow's count was nearing two hundred and Perry was feeling frantic when Shannon called, "Time!'' and they began hauling in the rope.

At last the glow of light appeared and became brighter as they pulled strongly, and then Ursor emerged from beneath the wall and surfaced, blowing and gasping. "Nothing,'' he panted after a bit, "not even an air pocket.''

Perry's hopes were dashed, but then Ursor spoke: "I'll try the opposite side.''

The echo of a Rūcken horn sounded down the cavern.

"They come," gritted Kian.

The giant moved to the upstream wall and again entered the water. Once more the Baeran breathed deeply, and on the fourth breath he dived under and swam now against the strong current and slowly passed out of sight beneath the wall. Again Perry's racing heart passed the count of two hundred, and once more the blat of Rūcken horn clamored along rock walls. The raucous blare was much closer, and Borin ran to the rampart and looked down the length of the dark tunnel. "Their torchlight is faint but growing swiftly," he called back. "They will overtop this ledge in less than a quarter hour."

Lord Kian, who was tending Ursor's line, announced, "He's taking no more rope. He's stopped."

A moment later, Shannon called, "Time!" and Anval and Kian hauled on the line.

"It will not budge!" shouted the Dwarf. "He must be caught on something!"

Shannon and Perry sprang to the line and pulled also, but still it would not haul in. "We've got to do something!" cried Perry. "He'll drown!" But the rope stubbornly refused to be drawn in and only grew iron-rod taut under the strain.

Then Shannon cried, "Look! A light!"

And a faint glimmer appeared in the water and swiftly grew to a bright glow, and then Ursor came under the wall and burst to the surface. "It's there. Another cavern," he gasped. "I tied the line to a boulder. We can use it to hale ourselves against the swift current."

"Quickly!" cried Kian, beginning to don his clothes in haste and motioning Ursor to do likewise. "Shannon, you go first. Perry, you second. Then Anval and Borin. Pull yourselves hard hand over hand along the line. Leave your packs, but carry your weapons, and wear your armor. Don't let go of the rope. Here, Shannon, carry this lamp at your waist. Go now, swiftly. The Spawn draw near." As if to spur them on, a discordant bugle blatted loudly.

Shannon hurriedly tied the lantern to his waist and entered the flow. He took a deep breath and disappeared under the wall. Perry was frightened, but he knew he had to move quickly or all would die. His thoughts had returned to the terror-fraught time he tumbled helplessly under the floodwaters at Arden. Oh! he did not want to go into the rush; but in spite of his fear, he plucked up his courage and entered the underground river. The water was icy, and he gasped in the coldness. He grasped the rope and took four deep breaths as he had seen Ursor do, and on the fourth one he plunged beneath the surface, his eyes tightly shut. The last thing he heard as he went under was a loud horncall.

Hand over hand the Warrow desperately hauled himself; and he gripped to the limit of his strength, for he knew that if he let go of the line he would be swept to his doom under the opposite wall. The current was swift and buffeted him. Bane slapped against his legs, and his armor for the first time felt heavy. Hand over hand he pulled, and he needed air. *Oh, don't let me breathe water again,* he thought in dread, and hauled with all his might. Just as he was certain his lungs would burst, his head broke through the surface, and he explosively gulped sweet breaths of air and opened his eyes for the first time since starting.

By the light of Shannon's lantern the buccan could see the Elf reaching out to help him, and he took Silverleaf's hand and stumbled up to the shore in the cave. No sooner had he reached the bank than Anval and then Borin came. After a moment, giant Ursor surfaced, closely followed by Lord Kian. As soon as Kian reached the bank he called to the company to reel in the line, and tied to the end were knapsacks and lanterns.

"Well," declared Kian, "that'll give the *Spaunen* a riddle to read. Let us hope they believe we went through another secret door."

The companions stripped off their sodden clothes and searched through their packs for drier garments. Although the backpacks were not made to be submerged, still they were to a degree waterproof, and the clothing inside, though wet in places, was for the most part relatively dry. The bedrolls were not so fortunate, and, at Lord Kian's suggestion, were abandoned along with the drenched garments they had removed. Perry's warm Elven-cloak, however, seemed to shed water as effectively as a duck's back, and he rescued it from his roll. All ropes and tools were retained, but most of the food had been ruined by the underwater jaunt, and the waterlogged crue as well as the mian—a tasty, Elven waybread carried by Shannon and Ursor—were discarded. Perry's map and his copy of the Brega Scroll were preserved in their waterproof wrappings. The weapons, armor, and lanterns were no worse for the trip.

Borin wrung water from his black forked beard and then caught up a lamp and went exploring. An undelved cavern ran down out of the north, swung west over the river, and curved away to the south. As in the last cavern, the river itself issued from one wall, cut across the cavern, and dived back under the other wall. Borin crossed over the water on a ledge along the northwest wall, and soon his lantern light disappeared around the curve to the south; but shortly he returned. "The way looks open, but this cavern, too, is arduous, with many shelves and slabs and cracks on our path. I deem we are walking in channels never before trod by Châkka, paths as old as the Mountains themselves. Yet the southern way should lead us back toward the Brega Path, and we must begin."

Once more the Squad took up the trek, and as Borin had said, the way *was* arduous: ledges, splits, ramps, boulders, and ravines stood across their path. Twice they edged along a lengthy narrow path etched on the face of a sheer precipice. At one place they walked under a roaring cataract that leapt from a distant hole in a high wall to fall into a churning black pool far below the wet, slippery path they trod along a narrow stone ledge. But most of all they clambered: up, down, over, and across. Once Borin had to drive rock-nails and tie a rope so that the company could ascend a sheer precipice. Another time they thought that they would have to do just the opposite, sliding down a steep cliff on a rope tied at the top; but Anval lay on his stomach and dangled his lantern over the edge to espy a ledge aslant down the face of the bluff; and they followed this shelf to the cavern floor.

They had struggled for six hours and had gone only five miles when the cavern came to an end at a high wall with great boulders strewn at the base or canted against the end wall. "Oh, no!" cried Perry, distressed, "we've come all this hard way only to find another dead end!"

*   *   *

Dejectedly, the Squad slumped to the cavern floor, weary and bitter. Suddenly, Shannon called, "*Hsst!* I hear *Spaunen* boots."

The lanterns were shuttered, and Perry drew Bane; the blade was blazing, and quickly the Warrow resheathed it to hide its light. Now they all heard the Spawn, yet where could the foe be? This cavern had no side passages.

Quietly, facing the way they had come, the Squad knelt in readiness, all weapons save Bane in hand, but the comrades could see no enemy. At Perry's side was Anval, who turned his head this way and that, searching for the Squam in the darkness; after a moment he leaned toward the buccan and whispered, "Look to the end wall."

Perry turned and saw a dim glimmer of torchlight shining through the base of the wall, faintly backlighting one of the huge slabs leaning against a fold. Perry whispered to the Dwarf, "I'm going to take a look." And before Anval could object, Perry was gone, slipping noiselessly toward the great rock.

Behind the stone was a cleft, blocked completely except for a small opening at the base. The torchlight came glimmering through that crack. It was a way out! But the hole was barely large enough for the Warrow to crawl through. Cautiously, he poked his head and shoulders into the opening. The crevice curved away, and from around the bend came the far-off flicker of burning brands and the faint sound of maggot-folk. The buccan wriggled through and into the cleft, where he could stand. Beyond the turns, the slot widened and issued out into a huge, delved chamber. Remembering the words that Delk had said back at the pine grove outside Dawn-Gate, Perry shielded his tilted, jewel-like eyes with his hand and, standing behind a rock outjutting, he peered through the cracks between his fingers and cautiously looked around the corner and toward the firelight in the chamber.

In the center of the floor, sprawled all about, was a Hlök-led band of Rūcks, nearly one hundred strong. By the light of their torches, Perry looked at the features of the chamber: It was nearly circular. From one end he could hear the sound of running water, and he saw a natural stone arch crossing a wide stream, His heart leapt for joy, for once again he knew where he was: this was the Bottom Chamber, a watering spot on the Brega Path. Dusk-Door was yet fifteen miles away, Rūcks and a huge slab barred the route, and there were only twenty hours remaining til Durek was to try the words of opening, but Perry again felt hope, for he was no longer lost.

As Perry watched, he saw one of the Rūcks slink secretively away from the others and come straight toward the cleft and the Warrow. Perry drew back. *What could the Rūck be coming this way for? Did my eyes catch the light in spite of looking through the cracks of my fingers?* Then Perry saw that his right sleeve was unbuttoned—perhaps had never been buttoned from the time he had changed out of the wet shirt back at the underground river. And the cuff had fallen away from his wrist as he'd held his hand over his eyes, and the firelight had reflected on his silveron armor; the Rūck was coming to claim for himself what he believed to be a long-lost gem gleaming in the dark. Perry scurried back along the cleft and popped through the opening and into the other cavern.

"What did you see?" whispered Anval from the darkness beside the great slab.

"There's a Rūck coming this way," hissed Perry, "and a lot more are sprawled in the chamber on the other side of this barrier."

Ursor's great hand drew the Warrow into the darkness along the wall. "Fear not," breathed the Baeran, "I'll handle the Rutch."

Perry could hear the Rūck scuffling down the cleft, cursing and muttering. It reached the end and stopped. Then the Warrow heard the Rūck drop to its hands and knees; the faint glow of torchfire reflected from the stone was blotted out as, grunting and swearing, the Rūck started squeezing through the opening. The cave was too black to see what happened next, but Perry heard a choked-off intake of breath and the thrashing of limbs and a scuffling sound that was quickly repressed. Then there came a *snap!* and all was quiet. "It's done," Ursor hissed, and Perry was glad that he had not seen what had just occurred.

In the darkness the Warrow gathered the Squad together. "The Brega Path is just beyond the end wall," he said quietly. "We are at the Bottom Chamber, fifteen miles from

Dusk-Door. There is a Rücken company barring the way; but even if the Rücks weren't there, the way into the Chamber is blocked with that great slab of stone, and unless we get rid of it, I am the only one here small enough to get through the hole.''

"Perhaps we can topple the stone," conjectured Anval. "But the crash will bring all the Grg rushing."

"Then let us decoy them," said Shannon. "After all, that is one of my purposes for being here: to draw off the *Rûpt* if there is no other choice. Here is what I propose: We locate three places nearby to hide. Then we topple the stone. When it falls, Perry, Anval, and Borin get to the hiding places while Lord Kian, Ursor, and I hie back the way we came, lanterns brightly lit, drawing the *Spaunen* behind. As soon as the way is clear, you three will make for the Door while we three will escape underwater."

"But there are maggot-folk back that way, too," protested Perry. "You'll just be running from one Spawn force to another. Why don't we simply wait for this Rück company to move on?"

"The Wrg back at the underground river are likely gone by now," responded Ursor, "and we know not when this company will move. No, Shannon is right: we must draw them off."

"But Perry speaks true too," countered Borin. "If the Squam move soon, there is no need to take this risk."

"These are my thoughts," announced Anval: "Borin and I can do but a limited amount at the Door without the guidance of a Gatemaster. If the trouble is simple, we may be able to set it aright. If not, then we could work for weeks and still not succeed. Hence, I deem it will matter little if we get there with ten hours to work, or with but one. With that in mind, let us set the toppling ropes on the slab now and get everything in readiness. Then we wait. If the Grg have not moved in good time—say, four hours—then we go ahead with Silverleaf's plan; on the other hand, if they *do* move on, we can all proceed to the Dusken Door together."

"That plan, though well thought, may just lose us four hours," pointed out Shannon.

"Aye. But it may also save us from dividing our strength," retorted Borin.

The Squad fell silent while Lord Kian weighed the alterna-
tives. Finally he chose: "Set the lines, seek out the hiding
places; as soon as all is ready, we topple the stone; we shall
not wait. Our mission now is for Perry to deliver Anval and
Borin to the Door as quickly as possible; we must not delay
any longer, for the time may be needed for other tasks, as yet
unseen, between here and Dusk-Door."

Quietly the Squad set about to carry out Shannon's plan.
The hole was covered with Perry's cloak, and lanterns were
dimly unhooded. Ursor cast the dead Rūck into one of the
wide cracks in the floor as the rest of the Squad searched for
and located three places to take cover: one on a ledge high on
the west wall, the other two behind boulders along the east
wall. And Perry, Anval, and Borin made sure that they could
quickly get concealed in their selected hiding places: Borin on
the ledge, Anval and Perry behind the boulders. Then a trio
of toppling ropes were tied to the great slab up high, Borin
clambering to do it. That done, the lanterns were hooded, and
Perry made one more trip through the hole and down the
cleft, this time with his sleeve well buttoned. When he returned he reported that the maggot-folk showed no sign of
moving on.

"Then we must delay no longer," declared Lord Kian, and
he turned to Anval and Borin. "We have come far together,
and it saddens me that we are to be sundered. Yet the mission
is our first concern and makes this separation necessary. In
my heart I believe we will meet again."

Then Lord Kian knelt on one knee before Perry and placed
a hand on each of the buccan's shoulders. "Friend Waerling,
though we have known one another but a brief time, I value
your friendship. Take care and guide well." He embraced the
Warrow and then stood.

Shannon and Ursor in turn said a simple "Fare you well"
to the Dwarves and the Warrow. Perry was too overburdened
with emotion to say anything, and Anval and Borin managed
to say only, *"Shok Châkka amonu."*

Lord Kian stepped forward and took up one of the toppling
lines, and so did they all: Borin assumed a stance behind
Kian on that line; Ursor, and behind him Shannon, took up
the second line; and Anval with Perry grasped the third and
last line. At Kian's quiet command, they all hauled back; the

ropes grew taut as the Squad pulled, yet the stone yielded not. Again Kian gave the command, and all put forth maximum effort: grips tightened, arms knotted, backs straightened, and legs strained; still the rock remained stubborn and did not move. "Enough," panted Kian, and released his grip.

Dejectedly, Perry dropped his end of the rope and sat down with the others, rubbing his forearms. "Now what do we do?" asked the Warrow.

Borin glanced at the top of the slab. "When I fastened the lines," he recalled, "I saw a notch high up behind the rock. I deem a Châk could climb into it and use his legs to lever the stone. Anval, you are strongest. Climb to the cleft, brace between the rock and the wall, and give it enough more of a push with us pulling to o'erbalance it."

No sooner did Borin speak than Anval swarmed up the slab and into the notch. He then placed his feet on the rock and braced his back against the stone wall. The rest of the Squad took up the ropes: Borin, Kian, and Ursor on the three separate lines, Shannon behind Kian, and Perry behind Borin.

At Kian's soft command, again they pulled: Perry leaned into the rope with all his might, straining to his uttermost limits. Borin's great shoulders knotted, the muscles becoming iron hard as he hauled on the rope. Kian and Shannon threw all their weight and strength into their line, their arms rigid and their legs trembling with the effort. Giant Ursor had braced his feet against a fissure in the floor, and his body leaned almost level, his mighty thews drawing down hard on his rope.

But it was Anval who proved to be the key: He summoned all of his power into pushing against the slab; perspiration beaded his brow; ligaments and tendons and blood vessels stood out in bold relief on his arms, neck, and forehead; his teeth ground together; and his face distorted with effort. His fingers clawed into their hold on the stone of the notch, and his arm muscles knotted. His back and shoulders braced hard against the wall, and his thigh muscles trembled with the strain. He emitted a low moan as the stress became nearly unbearable, and then slowly, slowly his legs began to straighten as the massive slab inched away from the cleft.

Ursor's great legs, too, began to uncoil as the slab gradually stood upright, and the Baeran's mighty back straightened. Perry's foot slipped, and he fell to one knee, but he quickly recovered and threw his strength back into the struggle. Borin, Kian, and Shannon felt the rock pulling away from the wall and strained mightily to haul with all their strength for just a moment longer.

And then the rock passed over center to fall to the cavern floor with a thunderous *CRACK!*

And the black fissure into the Bottom Chamber stood open before the Squad, lighted by a lantern at this end and by far-off burning brands at the other.

Momentarily the Squad slumped back, drained of all energy. Then Kian struggled upright. "Quickly!" he gasped, "we must act now."

As Perry retrieved his cloak, Anval dropped down from the cleft, and he and the Warrow limped to the crannies behind the boulders while Borin wearily scaled up to the high ledge. Kian, Shannon, and Ursor, their strength returning, unhooded three lanterns and fled back down the cavern. A shout came from the chamber, and the slap of running Rücken boots could be heard. Perry scuttled behind his boulder. He could see through a crack between rocks. Torchlight shuttered down the notch, and a large Hlōk-led band of Rücks burst through the mouth of the cleft and into the cave. From far off Perry heard Shannon Silverleaf call, "Hai, Rucha!" and two arrows whined into the enemy, felling two Rücks. Then two more arrows hissed through the air to thud into another pair.

The Rücks quailed back, but the Hlōk snarled, *"Ptang glush! Sklurr!"* and cracked the thongs of a cat-of-tails. Most of the Rücks leapt forward in pursuit, but the Hlōk shouted more orders, and ten of the maggot-folk stayed behind while the leader sprang after the others, torches pursuing lanterns. Soon the sound of the chase was remote, and the notch-warding Rücks fell to squabbling among themselves.

Perry was dismayed. *This is awful,* he thought. *They've left behind a rear guard, to the ruin of our plan, Now we can't get through. Oh, why did this have to happen? Hey! that's a fair question. Why would a rear guard be left behind? Are they waiting for something? If so, what?*

As Perry pondered the questions, he glimpsed Anval behind the other boulder; and the Dwarf made shushing, stay-where-you-are hand signals at the Warrow. Perry nodded his understanding and leaned back against the stone wall behind, waiting.

An hour went by, then another, and another. Perry cautiously shifted about uncomfortably; it seemed, no matter where he moved, there was always a rock or a hump or a lump in the wrong place, and it ground into his back or thigh or seat. He wondered what Anval's plan was, and then he could see that the Rūcks were nodding off, one by one. *How did Anval know that they would sleep?* Perry wondered; then: *Perhaps it is the nature of the maggot-folk to shirk duty at every opportunity.*

In another hour all the Rūcks were asleep, including the one who was supposed to be standing guard.

Anval cautiously signalled Perry, *Go quietly*—and they slowly and soundlessly crept from behind their boulders as Borin silently descended from the ledge. Both Dwarves held their axes in readiness, and Perry unsheathed blazing Bane. On tiptoe they threaded their way among the sleeping Spawn. As they passed the guard, Borin's foot rolled a pebble that went clattering toward a crevice in the floor, sounding to Perry as loud as thunder itself. The three froze, and Perry held Bane ready to slay the slumbering watch, the sword point poised steadily over the Rūck's heart. Restlessly, the sleeping guard moaned and shifted his weight, while the pebble rattled to a stop down in the crack to leave silence behind, broken only by the snoring of the maggot-folk. None of the Rūcks awakened, and the Dwarves and the Warrow passed into the cleft.

As they emerged into the Bottom Chamber, Perry sheathed Bane's light and led the way toward the arch over the stream. Swiftly they crossed the floor, passing over the bridge and beyond the running water. But before they could reach the west corridor, they saw light coming down the passageway toward them.

Quickly the trio dived behind a low parapet of delved stone off to one side. A large company of Spawn loped into the Chamber. *This is why ten Rūcks were left behind: to meet this gang,* thought Perry, and he watched them lope to the center of the Chamber and halt. "We got out just in time," the Warrow breathed to Borin. "They've got the way we came stopped up like a cork in a bottle."

As the three looked on, several of the notch-warding Rūcks trotted out of the crevice and spoke with the newly arrived Hlōk leader, but Perry and the Dwarves were too far away to hear what was being said. To the dismay of the three, however, the Hlōk snarled orders, and Rūcks jumped up and ran to guard each of the entrances and exits of the Bottom Chamber, including the west portal. Then runners were dispatched: one east, one west, and one south. "He sends messages to other Hrōken leaders," hissed Anval. "No doubt, Gnar also will be informed as to the 'intruders' in this part of the caverns. *Kruk!* This will make it even more difficult for us to reach the Dusken Door."

"How do we get past the guard at the west corridor without raising the alarm?" whispered Perry. Borin touched his finger to his lips for quiet, and silently crawled off into the dimness.

Perry and Anval watched the guard slouching against the wall beneath a torch lodged in an ancient lantern bracket on the delved wall, a bracket put there in elden times by the Dwarves. Minutes fled by and nothing happened. As the two watched, time seemed to stretch out endlessly, and the Warrow could see no sign of Borin. Still they waited. Suddenly it seemed as if one of the shadows behind the guard detached itself from the wall and soundlessly engulfed the Rūck. Perry heard a quiet thump, and then Anval was pulling on the Warrow's arm and hissing, "Now!"

Swiftly they flitted along the wall and into the corridor; Borin carried the dead Rūck over one shoulder, and hid the body at the first wall crevice. The three then fled down the passageway. Behind them, all was still; their escape had not been noted.

The next four miles was a nightmare of hide and run. Repeatedly, the companions dived into crevices, notches, and side passages, to remain hidden as Hlōks and Rūcks came loping eastward. Many small squads and large companies passed by. Perry guessed—rightly—that the news of a few "intruders" had spread, and the Spawn were flocking to the sport of hunt and slaughter.

At last the threesome approached a room called the Oval Chamber in the Brega Scroll. Once more the trio found the way blocked by maggotfolk, but Anval motioned, *Follow me,* and taking an enormous gamble they began crawling from shadow to shadow along the north wall.

At times they lay without moving for long minutes as one or more Rūcks in the chamber came near. At other times they crawled swiftly from rock to pillar to crevice, only to find that again they had to remain motionless in the darkness with Spawn barring the way. Finally they came to the passage leading on toward Dusk-Door, and after a long wait they managed to slip out of the chamber and into the corridor.

Though they met no maggot-folk, the three found the next few miles arduous, for there were cracks in the floor that yawned unexpectedly. Yet, one crevice that they came to was foreknown to Perry, and dreaded by him: it was the Drawing Dark, so named because of the awful *sucking* sound that could be heard in its lost depths, thought by the Deevewalkers to be a slurking whirl of water in an underground river at the bottom of the crack; but to Perry this explanation was of no comfort, for it sounded as if *something* below were *alive* and questing for victims.

Although Perry had been expecting this rent—for it had been mentioned both in *The Raven Book* and in the Brega Scroll—still he found it difficult to summon up the courage to leap it, for it was fully eight feet across, and he could not banish the specter of being sucked down into the deep crack, drawn down into an unseen maw ravening in the black depths. But at last he took three running steps and sprang with all his might and cleared it by a good three feet.

The trio pressed on for the Long Hall, and as they neared it, Bane's fire grew. Soon Perry sheathed the sword, for its flame was bright. Yet when they came to the chamber, they could see neither torchlight nor *Spaunen*. "Let us cross the floor quickly, before the Rūcks arrive and block our way again," urged Perry, and they started across the Hall.

As they reached midchamber they heard shouts and snarls, and looked around to see a company of maggot-folk issue out of a corridor behind them. The trio had been detected!

"Fly!" cried Perry, and the three ran toward the west corridor; but as they approached they could see light reflected around a bend moving swiftly *toward* them from the passage ahead. Perry darted a look over his shoulder: the other exits

were already cut off by the howling Spawn closing behind. *Trapped!*

At a glance, Anval took in the situation. "The force before us is as yet unaware of us, and there may be only a few. Let us charge through if we can. If not, then we will slay many before we fall."

Borin brandished his axe. *"Châkka shok! Châkka cor!"* he cried. Anval, too, gripped his double-bitted weapon and vented the ancient battle cry. Perry whipped out flaming Bane, determined to sell his life dearly.

Forward they charged, running toward the oncoming force. Behind them the yawling Rūcks pursued, weapons and armor clattering, boots slapping against stone. Ahead and toward them came the others, suddenly rounding a corner and bursting into view. And Perry's racing heart leapt to his throat, and he gave a great shout, for at the forefront of the oncoming force ran a small form in golden armor with a bright sword. *It was Cotton! And Durek! And Rand! And four thousand others! The Dwarf Army was within the Halls of Kraggen-cor!*

CHAPTER 7

INTO THE BLACK HOLE

Three hours earlier, the Host had stood before the Dusk-Door, and Durek had said the words of power, and by moonlight and starshine and Dwarf lantern the theen tracery and runes and sigils had appeared.

Durek caught up his weapon by the helve and stepped back from the high portal; all that remained was for him to say the Wizard-word for "move," and the Door, if able, would open. The Dwarf turned to Cotton, Rand, and Felor. "Stand ready," he warned, "for we know not whom we meet."

Cotton gripped his sword and felt the great pressure of the moment rising inside him and he felt as if he needed to shout, but instead he thought, Let Mister Perry be at the Door and not no Rŭck.

Durek turned back to the Door and gripped his axe; he placed his free hand within the glittering rune-circle; then his voice rang out strongly as he spoke the Wizard-word of opening: "Gaard!"

The glowing web of Wizard-metal flashed brightly, and then—*as if being drawn back into Durek's hand*—all the lines, sigils, and glyphs began to retract, fading in sparkles as they withdrew, until once again the dark granite was blank and stern. And Durek stepped back and away. And slowly the stone seemed to split in twain as two great doors appeared and soundlessly swung outward, arcing slowly, the black slot between them growing wider and wider, becoming a great ebon gape as the doors wheeled in silence, til at last they came to rest against the Great Loom.

A dark opening yawned before the vanguard of the Legion, and they could see the beginnings of the West Hall receding into blackness; to the right a steep stairwell mounted up into the ebon shadows. And those in the fore of the Host—weapons gripped, thews tensed, hearts thudding, hackles up—stared with chary eyes at the empty darkness looming mutely before them.

And they were astonished and baffled, for no one was there, neither friend nor foe, only silent dark stone!

And of all those in the vanguard, only one did not seem rooted in place: "Mister Perry!" shouted Cotton, and before any could stop him, he sprang through the doorway and bolted up the stairs, holding his lantern high and calling as he ran: "Mister Perry! Mister Perry!" he cried, but his voice was answered only by mocking echoes: *Mister . . . ister . . . Perry . . . erry . . . ery . . . ister . . . erry . . . ery . . . y . . .*

"Cotton! Wait!" shouted Rand, breaking the grip of his bedazement. " 'Ware *Spaunen!*" And he and Durek and Felor and the forefront of the Host leapt forward after the Warrow. And they could see the light of Cotton's lantern dashing up the steps far above them to disappear from sight over the top.

"Fool!" Prince Rand cursed the Waerling's rashness, and sprang up the steps two at a time, his long shanks outdistancing the Dwarves behind. The steps were many, and soon he was breathing deeply, for the climb was strenuous; but in a trice he o'ertopped the last one. Ahead and around a bend he found Cotton at the first side passage, his lantern held high, peering through the arch and into the dark. Several swift strides brought the Prince to the Warrow's side. "Cotton," he gritted through clenched teeth, angered by the Waerling's thoughtless actions.

"He . . . he's not here, Prince Rand," stammered the Warrow, turning in anguish to the Man. "Mister Perry's not here."

"Cotton, you are our only guide. The Yrm . . ." but ere Rand could say on, he saw that the Waerling was weeping quietly.

"I know, Sir. I know," sobbed Cotton, miserably. "I've acted the fool, rushing in like I did, and all. But Mister Perry wasn't there, and I couldn't stand it. I just had to see, had to see for myself. But he's not here at all. He's not here; the Squad's not here; the Rūcks are not here; nobody's here. But the Door opened. It *opened!*"

There was a clatter of weaponry and a slap of boots and a jingle of armor as Durek and Felor and the vanguard of the Host topped the stairs and started forward, their sharp eyes sweeping the shadows.

"As you say, Cotton, the Door opened," replied Rand, "yet no one met us. Mayhap the Squad was here, for the Door worked."

"Wull, if they were here, where are they now?" Cotton demanded.

"I know not," replied Rand, his voice grim. "Perhaps Spawn . . ." His words trailed off.

"Spawn!" cried Cotton, bitterly, turning as Durek strode up.

King Durek stood before the Warrow, an angry glim in his eyes. "Cotton," he gritted, "the fate of this quest lies in your hands, for where you lead, we must follow. Without you, we are lost. Henceforth, stay at hand where our axes may protect you; never again dash off into the dark alone." The Dwarf King's voice held the bite of command that brooked no disobedience, and the Waeran nodded meekly. "As to these empty halls," continued Durek, his flinty eyes sweeping the passage, "we can only press forward and hope to find the Squad of Kraggen-cor safe, and not Grg-endangered, or worse."

"Grg-endangered? Worse?" blurted out Cotton. Then his viridian eyes became fell and resolute. "Let's go," he said sternly. "We've got to find Mister Perry and the others."

And at a nod from Durek, the Warrow went forth, with Rand at one side, Durek and Felor at the other, and four thousand axes behind. And along the Brega Path they strode.

A mile went by, and another, and yet one more, and still they saw no sign of life, friendly or otherwise. Only dark splits and black fissures and delved tunnels did they see, boring off into the ebon depths. Through this shadowy maze Cotton unerringly led. And the axes of the Dwarves stood ready, but no foe appeared. Another mile, and another, and still more; and time trod on silent feet at their side. An hour had passed, no, two, then a third; and swiftly they marched into the depths of Drimmen-deeve.

Suddenly: *"Hist!"* warned Felor, and held up his hand, and the command quickly passed back-chain and the Army ground to a silent halt.

In the quiet they could hear the far-off yammering of many voices—yelling and howling—yet they could make out no words. Ahead in the curving tunnel they could see a glimmer of distant light dimly reflected around the bend.

"They know not that we are here," hissed Durek. "Weapons ready! Forward!"

And the Host moved swiftly, running now to catch the foe unaware and suddenly fall upon them. Forward they dashed, toward the Long Hall just ahead. And as they ran they could hear more shouts—battle cries, it seemed—their meaning lost in reverberating echoes. Ahead the light grew brighter as the oncoming force neared. And suddenly bursting into view came three forms running.

CHAPTER 8

THE SILVER CALL

At first Cotton thought that these three figures plunging head-long at him and the Army were Rūcks, for the faces of Perry, Anval, and Borin were covered with blackener, and Perry's starsilver armor was hidden beneath his shirt; and so this charging trio did not at all look like the friends and companions that Cotton had last seen by the Argon River. But as the three ran toward the vanguard, Cotton saw the flaming sword borne by the one and the Dwarf axes of the other two and the Dwarf-lanterns the trio carried, and by these tokens alone he knew that they were not Rūcks. And suddenly there came a voice he recognized, a voice calling his name: "Cotton! Cotton!"

"It's Mister Perry!" cried Cotton, and he leapt forward, running to meet his master.

"Mister Perry! Mister Perry!" he shouted and wept at one and the same time, for when the portals of Dusk-Door had silently swung outward and none of the Squad of Kraggen-cor had been waiting inside, Cotton had feared the worst. But he had led the Army along the Brega Path in spite of his fears. And here were Mister Perry and two Dwarves seven miles from the Door, alive after all.

As the two Warrows ran together and embraced one another, Anval shouted, "King Durek, Squam pursue us! A hundred fly at our heels!"

"Felor!" barked Durek, "Axes! Forward!" And the spear-head of the Host sprang around the curve and into the Long Hall.

The onrushing maggot-folk wailed in dismay as hundreds of Dwarves issued into the chamber. Some Spawn stood and

111

fought and died, some turned and ran and were overhauled from behind and felled, others escaped. The skirmish was over quickly, and the Dwarves were overwhelmingly victorious in this opening engagement of the War of Kraggen-cor.

After the battle and before resuming the northeastward march, Durek called the trio to him; and Cotton for the first time saw that these two blackened Dwarves were actually Anval and Borin. Prince Rand and Felor joined the circle of the small council kneeling on the stone floor of Long Hall. "Tell me not your entire tale," Durek bade the three, "but for now speak of the Grg along the route before us; tell me of any problems with the Brega Path for which we must change our battle strategy; tell me where Prince Kian, Barak, Delk, and Tobin are; and finally, speak on any other thing of importance to our campaign that you think pertinent but about which I know not enough to ask."

Anval spoke first: "As to the Grg, our suspicions were correct: there are great numbers of the vile enemy in Kraggen-cor, for often we had to hide or flee from large bands within the passageways and chambers. We saw many of the foul foe on our journey, at least ten or twelve companies—a total of more than a thousand Squam—and that just on the path we trod. I have no count of the true number of thieving Grg in Kraggen-cor, but I gauge it to be many times more than we saw."

"The Brega Path we trod," added Borin, "posed no special unforeseen problems, but we did not see it all; we left the Path twice. Perry, give me your map." Ere Perry could act, Felor quickly pulled a copy from his own jerkin and gave it to Borin, who spread the map before Durek.

"Here at Braggi's Stand, the way at the Fifth Rise is blocked. We went around it by going west at the Third Rise to the first north passage, from there to the Sixth Rise, and thence east and south to the Great Chamber, coming back to the Path at this point." Borin traced the route they had taken, a sturdy finger moving through part of the blank area on the map. "We left the Path a second time here, at the Grate Room; we were discovered by Squam and fled thusly"—again Borin traced their route—"passing down a tortuous path to emerge in the Bottom Chamber. And so, we know not the Brega Path between the Grate Room and the Bottom Chamber; but the Path is nearly certain to be better than the hard way we ran." Borin fell silent.

King Durek turned to Perry. "And the others, where are the others? Where is Barak?"

"Dead," answered Perry, his eyes brimming, "slain by Spawn on the banks of the Argon." Durek, Anval, Borin, and Felor cast their hoods over their heads.

"Tobin, and Delk, where are they?" demanded Durek from his cowl.

"Tobin is with the Elves in Darda Erynian, wounded in the same battle at the Great Argon River," replied Perry. "Delk was slain by Rūck arrow as we fled the Gargon's Lair here in Kraggen-cor." Perry pointed at the approximate location of the Lair on the map.

"*Gargon?*" blurted Durek, his voice filled with surprise and dread.

"The Ghath slain by Brega and the others in the time of the Winter War," responded Anval. "We found its ancient prison when we fled. There, too, is a vein of starsilver."

"And my brother," asked Prince Rand, his face bleak, "where is Kian?"

"We don't know," said Perry, anguish in his voice. "He and the Elf Vanidar Shannon Silverleaf, and Ursor the Baeran— new companions who joined us at the Argon—those three decoyed a company of Rūcks so that we three could reach Dusk-Door. They fled back from the Bottom Chamber toward the Lair, drawing the maggot-folk behind them. But I fear for their safety, for later we saw many Spawn moving—we think to join the hunt. The three may escape by the underwater path we found, but I fear they may be trapped between Rūcken forces. And the terrible truth is, their decoy strategy went for nought, for we didn't even reach Dusk-Door."

"You didn't?!" burst out Cotton. "Well then, who fixed 'em? I mean, they opened just as slick as a whistle."

"It seems," replied Durek, "that no one repaired them. Hence, the Warder did not damage them when he wrenched and hammered at the doors centuries agone. Valki builded them well, for they withstood the awesome might of even that dreadful Monster."

"You speak as if you saw it," spoke up Perry, "the Krakenward, I mean. Did you see it? Was it there?"

"We slew it," growled Durek, "but it nearly proved our undoing, for it killed many of us and buried the Door under yet more rock ere we succeeded." The Dwarf King fell silent for a moment. "Where best to array the Host?" he then asked Anval.

"The Mustering Chamber, the War Hall of Kraggen-cor," replied Anval; and Borin nodded his agreement. "It is vast, and will be a good location to meet the Squam Swarm—or to sortie from."

"But that's all the way back to the Great Deep!" cried Perry, weary and exasperated. "Nearly to Dawn-Gate!"

"Naytheless," insisted Borin, "it is the best battleground for our Legion, for though it was delved long ago as an assembly chamber to array the Host against invaders coming over the Great Dēop, it will serve equally well to array the Army against the Grg within the caverns. We must go there quickly to gain the advantage of a superior formation."

"But what about Lord Kian, and Shannon, and Ursor?" demanded Perry, fearing the answer. "What are we going to do about them?"

"Nothing," replied Prince Rand, his voice trembling in helpless agony. "We can do nothing, for we must race to the battleground to arrive first and array in the strongest formation, which will force the Spawn to take a weaker one, if they come. We cannot jeopardize the entire Host for the sake of three; nor can we send a small force to search for them, for as you say, the Yrm flock in great numbers to hunt the trio, and a small force of Dwarves would be o'erwhelmed in that mission. No, we must make haste to the Mustering Chamber, and hope against all hope that the three somehow elude the enemy until we are victorious." Prince Rand turned his face away, and his hands were trembling.

At Prince Rand's words a great leaden weight seemed to crush down upon Perry's heart, and he despaired. "You are saying we must abandon them. Surely there is some other choice."

"Choice?" barked Durek, his face shadowed by his hood in the lantern light, his voice tinged with grim irony. "Nay, we have no choice. And we will get no further choices til the issue of Kraggen-cor is settled. As with the very act of living, there are but few true times of choosing, for most of life's so-named *choices* are instead but reflections of circumstance. And now is not a time of choosing; nay, our last time of choosing was at my Captain's Council at Landover Road Ford. Since then, Destiny alone has impelled each of us along that selected path. Yet, Friend Perry, we all knew our course would lead us into harm's way, and that some of us would cast lots with Death and lose, for that is one of War's chiefest fortunes. Nay, Waeran, we cannot send aid to that trio of comrades now, for their lot, too, is cast, and their future is as immutable as ours.''

''But to abandon them all but assures their doom, if it is not yet upon them,'' Perry said bitterly. ''By doing nothing we might as well have sentenced them to death. And there's been too much needless death already: first Barak and then Delk, and now Kian, Shannon, and Ursor.'' The buccan's eyes filled with tears of frustration, and he hammered his fist against his leg. ''And all for nothing! All for a door that wasn't even broken! All for a needless mission!''

''Yes!'' Rand gritted angrily through clenched teeth at Perry, for the Warrow had not yet admitted to the reality of their strait plight. And the Prince sprang to his feet and paced to and fro in agitation. ''Yes!'' he spat, ''all for a *needless mission!* But one that had to be assayed at all costs, for we knew it not that the Dusk-Door had survived the wrenching of that dire creature. The Door was not broken, but we were ignorant of that knowledge. It is ever so in warfare that *needless missions* are undertaken in ignorance.

''Ignorance! Pah! That, too, is one of the conditions of War. And good Men and Dwarves and others die because of it. This time our ignorance may have cost me my brother; but worse yet, it may have cost my people a *King!* So prate not to me about *needless missions*, Waerling, for it is time you realized to the uttermost what being a warrior means, and the necessity of the cruel decisions of War, for you seem to think that we do not grasp the fullness of our course.

''But we *do* know! *Yes*, it is abandonment! *Yes*, it spells doom! *Yes*, we *know!* But it is *you* who does not seem to grasp what it means to do otherwise! This Army *must* be held together to meet the strength of the Yrm, and must *not* be fragmented into splinter parties searching for a mere three; for in that foolish action lies the seeds of the destruction of our quest—and the needs of the quest gainsay all else, no matter who is abandoned.''

Like crystal shards, the jagged truth of Rand's angry words tore at Perry's heart, and the Warrow paled with their import.

''Hold on there, now!'' Cotton protested sharply, starting to rise to defend his master, upset not by the meaning of Rand's words but rather at the angry manner in which Rand had spat them at Perry, ''there's no cause to—'' but Cotton's words were cut short by a curt gesture from Borin. And Cotton reluctantly fell silent, unsaid words battering at his grimly clamped lips as he tensely settled back, ready to speak up for Perry if need be.

But then the Prince halted his caged pacing and for the first time looked and saw how utterly stunned Perry was. And Rand's own heart softened, and his voice lost its edge of wrath as he turned and reached out to the buccan. ''Ah, needless missions, times of no choice. There is no choice, Perry, no choice; and in that I grieve with you, for it is *my brother* we abandon to War's lot. I would that it were otherwise, yet we can do nought but hope, for instead we must set forth at once to array the Host against the foul Spawn.''

Anval had listened to the Prince speak sharply to Perry, but in spite of the harshness, the Dwarf was in accord with Rand's meaning; yet at the same time Anval also had seen the anguish in the Waeran's eyes. The Dwarf leaned forward and gently placed a gnarled hand upon Perry's forearm and spoke: ''Aye, Friend Perry, you, I—the Squad—we all went on a necessary yet needless mission; and now you despair, for our staunch companions are missing, facing dangers unknown, fates dire; and you have said that their sacrifice has gone for nought, for it claws at you that we did not even reach the unbroken Dusken Door, the sought-for goal, our mission's end. Yet, take heed: *missions fail!* Only in the faery-scapes of children's hearthtales do all goodly quests succeed. But in this world many a desperate undertaking has fallen full victim to dark evil, or has been thwarted: turned back or shunted aside or delayed, not reaching the planned end, costing the coursing lifeblood of steadfast comrades. Such thwart fell upon our mission. Yet heed me again: all warriors who encounter such calamities and who live on must learn to accept these truths and go forth in spite of unforeseen setbacks.

"Once I said unto you that you must become a warrior; and you have. But times as these test a warrior's very mettle, and he must be as stern as hammered iron. We live, and so might our lost comrades; but in any case, we must now go forth and war upon the thieving Grg, for that is our prime reason for being here ready for battle." Anval fell silent and turned and looked expectantly at his King.

With effort, Durek cast his hood back and reluctantly agreed: "Though I am loath to abandon our comrades to the Grg's hunt, Prince Rand is correct, and so too is Anval: we must hasten to the War Hall at the Great Dēop to meet the Squam Swarm. Gnar soon will know that we are within the corridors, and he will muster to meet us. We must needs be arrayed in our strength, for the numbers of his force may be great indeed. But hearken to me, Friend Perry: after our victory, I will send search parties for any of the three who still may live. Yet now the Host must hie forth to the War Hall and array in our strongest formation."

And Perry's heart at last admitted to the grim truth, and he nodded bleakly as Durek issued the commands; and once again the Army began to move deeper into Kraggen-cor, striding to the northeast at a forced-march pace.

Borin led the way back toward the Bottom Chamber. Once more, when they came to the Drawing Dark—the eight-foot-wide crack in the tunnel floor—Perry overcame his fear and made the running leap over the fissure, this time with less hesitation; but Cotton delayed long, while others passed over, mustering his courage for the hurdle above the sucking depths, the leap a long one for a Warrow. At last the buccan stepped into the line of warriors and took his turn, and cleared the wide crack easily; Perry had waited for him, and together they ran to catch up with the head of the column.

At the Oval Chamber, as signalled by Bane's jewel-flame, a force of Rūcks was arrayed to meet the Dwarves: some of the enemy who earlier had escaped had told of the Dwarves' coming, and the Spawn did not yet know that it was an entire army they faced, believing instead that they were meeting, at most, a company-sized troop. And so, once again the Dwarves issued against the maggot-folk in overwhelming force, and the skirmish was short and decisive.

Durek had ordered Cotton and Perry to remain out of the

fray, saying that although Anval and Borin knew most of the
Path now, he wanted to hold the Waerans in reserve, at least
until the Great Dēop was reached—then he would have an
entire legion of guides. And so Cotton and Perry remained
back in the corridor until the engagement was over.

The march toward the Mustering Chamber continued, and
as they tramped, Cotton, who was happy simply to be reunited with Perry, chatted about the Army's trek from Landover
Road Ford to Dusk-Door. In spite of his low spirits, Perry
soon found himself becoming more and more interested in
Cotton's venture; and Perry was slowly drawn out of his
black mood by the tale he was told. Cotton spoke of: the
shrieking, clawing wind at the Crestan Pass; Waroo the Blizzard and the blind guides and lost Dwarves; being snowbound
and the great dig-out; the forced march down the Old Rell
Way, and the mud mires; the arrival at Dusk-Door; the battle
with the Krakenward and the breaking of the dam and slaying
of the Monster of the Dark Mere; the discovery of the Host
by the Rūcken spies and Brytta's troop riding from the
valley to intercept them; and the removal of the mountain of
rubble and the opening of the Door at midnight.

Perry was fascinated by the story. "Why, Cotton," he
declared when the other finished, "you have lived an epic
adventure, one as exciting as even some of the old tales."

"Wull, I don't know about that, Mister Perry." Cotton
shrugged doubtfully. "It seems to me that most of it was just
a bother, if you catch my meaning."

"Oh, it's an adventure, alright," assured Perry, "and
when we're through with all this, I'll want to set it down in a
journal for others to see." He began asking questions, seeking more detail about Cotton's venture, and Perry's bleak
mood ebbed as he and the other Warrow marched north and
east with the Host.

And both Warrows soon fell to speculating as to the outcome of Brytta's mission. Each worried that the Harlingar
had met up with a Swarm; yet Cotton surmised, "Oh, I
believe the Valonners did their job, Sir, 'cause Gnar's army
wasn't waiting at the Dusk-Door when it opened. In fact,
nobody was. Not even you. But I knew you'd be alright. And
since the maggot-folk weren't there, well, that means Gnar

hadn't got the word, so as the Valonners must have succeeded in stopping the Rūcken spies."

"I'm not sure of that, Cotton," mused Perry, "not sure at
all. I mean, I'm not sure that some Spawn didn't get through
to Gnar. After all, if they did get through, there would have
been only a bit more than a day for Gnar to muster his forces.
And perhaps he has—has mustered them, that is. Perhaps
there's a great ambush awaiting us ahead and we're walking
into an enormous trap."

Cotton's heart gave a lurch at these ominous words. "Wull,
if that's true, Sir, then that means that Marshal Brytta may
have met up with more than he bargained for; and that would
be news I'd rather not know about." Yet, in spite of his
remarks, Cotton fretted over the fate of the riders of the
Valanreach, and would have given much to know their state
of health and their whereabouts.

At that very moment, it was early morning in the Ragad
Valley, and Brytta, at the fore of the Harlingar, had just
ridden in to find the vale empty of all but his kinsman Farlon
and the Dwarven wounded, preparing to embark on the journey south to the grassy valley.

Farlon was overjoyed to see the Vanadurin arrive, for he
had longed to know their lot; and now he could see that most
were safe, though his searching eyes failed to find some of
his comrades in the column. Too, he felt relief, for now he
would have escort in moving the wounded. And now, also,
the herd could be driven south, and not left to wander the
wold. The horses had been loosed, yet in their tameness had
not gone from the valley.

At Brytta's query, Farlon explained that it was he who had
fired the recall beacon atop the great spire of the Sentinel
Stand after the Door had opened and the Host had entered.
Brytta then ordered that yet another signal fire
be laid high upon the towering spike to call the riders back
should Wrg come fleeing out of the Dusk-Door; the top of the
spire was the best place for the beacon, for, as reported by
Farlon, a fire upon the tall spire should clearly be visible
from the southern pasture. Three scouts, Trell, Egon, and
Wylf, were named to this balefire duty. Taking turns, one of
the trio always would be atop the stand to set the beacon

ablaze if the Rutcha came. As Brytta said when he gave over
the guard duty to the three, "I'm certain you would rather
ward against a danger that never comes, than to wait with the
rest of us in a pasture watching horses crop grass."

Then Brytta and the Harlingar rounded up the horses and
waggons bearing the wounded and began the drive south,
following Farlon's lead. And Farlon was pleased, for not only
was he reunited with his fellow Vanadurin, he also was
fulfilling the pledge he had made to Prince Rand and to that
fiery little Waldan, Cotton: a pledge to guide the wounded
Dwarves to safe haven.

But neither Perry nor Cotton knew of those events then
occurring in the Ragad Valley, and so they fretted over the
unknown fate of the Harlingar; yet in spite of this uncertainty,
Perry had nearly regained his former pluck. Even so, when
they came to the Bottom Chamber, where last he had seen the
missing trio of companions, Perry's high spirits crashed.

The Chamber was empty of Spawn; the word of a Dwarf
army had passed ahead of the Host, and the Rūcks and
Hlōks had fled before them. As the Legion marched across
the arch over the stream and into the huge round room, Perry
looked toward the notch in the north wall; no light came
through it from the cavern beyond. "There, Prince Rand,"
said the Warrow, pointing, "there's where Lord Kian, Shannon Silverleaf, and Ursor the Baeran misled the Rūcks."

Rand looked on bleakly as they tramped by. Suddenly the
Prince ran to the cleft and down its length, and peered into
the black cave beyond, and whistled a shrill call that echoed
and shocked along the cavern to be lost in its dark distance.
Twice more he whistled, and each time at echo's death he was
answered only by ebon silence. When he returned to the column, his face bore a stricken look, and he spoke not. Perry,
too, fell into mute despair. And the Army marched on.

Here Cotton took over the guide chores from Borin; the
Host now began moving into the corridors between the Bottom Chamber and the Grate Room, a part of the Brega Path
not yet trod by Borin, for the Squad had fled through the
Gargon's Lair instead.

Bane's blade-jewel spoke only of distant danger, and the
long column soon reached the Side Hall, where the floor of

the corridor began its long, gentle upward slope out of the lower Neaths and toward the upper Rises. During this part of the trek, Cotton chatted gaily, trying mightily to draw Perry out of his black mood, but to no avail.

As they marched away from the Side Hall, Bane began to glimmer more strongly, and word was passed that Squam were coming nigh. They tramped for two more miles and Bane's light slowly faded; but then a great hubbub washed over the Legion from the rear of the column. "Hey," questioned Cotton, "what's all this commotion about?" But no one there could answer him.

Finally, word was passed up-column to Durek that a large force of Rūcks had boiled out of the Side Hall and had atacked the rear guard of the Host. A savage battle had ensued, and the Spawn were once again routed, but this time some Dwarves had fallen in the fight.

"So it begins at last," rasped Durek. "The foul Grg will harass and ambush us from coverts until Gnar musters his forces for battle. Pass the word that the War has begun. Henceforth, the slain shall lie where they are felled, and we shall remain unhooded until the last battle is done."

The march began again, and now Cotton fell into a black mood too, for he knew not the lot of Bomar, Captain of the Rear Guard, nor the fate of his friends of the cook-waggon crew. But though the Warrow fretted, he continued to guide well, and the Legion made good time in their trek toward the Grate Room. Again Bane's rune-jewel began to glow brighter as they marched east; and the nearer they came to the Room, the more luminous became the blue flame. They trod swiftly, and the vanguard of Felor's forces gripped their axes in readiness as they quickstepped up the passageway. And then from ahead they heard a great shouting of maggot-folk and a clatter of weapons.

Felor's companies sprang forward, and they raced toward the last turn before the Grate Room. As they rounded the curve, up a long straight corridor they could see torchlight, and there were Spawn clamoring and milling about the door of the Room, battering it with hammers and a ram. Momentarily, the Rūcken band did not see the Dwarves; and Felor's Companies made many running strides toward the enemy before the Host was detected; and then it was too late, for the Rūcks had not enough time to array themselves to meet the rush.

There was a clash of axes on scimitars, and the Spawn were borne backwards by the charge. Again the battle was swift and savage: the Dwarves hewed the Squam, and black Rūcken gore splashed the stone as the maggot-folk were felled.

And in the midst of the fray, Perry saw the Grate Room door fly open, and out sprang two tall, face-blackened figures ready to join the fight. It was Lord Kian! And Shannon Silverleaf! They were alive!

From a distance, Prince Rand, too, saw his besmudged brother and gave a shrill whistle, and he and Kian looked upon one another, and they were glad. Then Rand raised his sword and inclined his head toward the retreating Spawn, and they both plunged after the Dwarves to join the battle against the foe.

Perry shouted in his glee. His friends were safe! But, wait . . . where was Ursor? As the battle receded before him, Perry made his way to the Grate Room and stepped in. The Warrow saw that two of the iron stone-wedges, tools carried for work on the gate, had been used to jam the door of the Room against the maggot-folk. Perry could see the corroded grille had been wrenched away from the square shaft, and the dark hole gaped at him; cautiously looking into it, he could see nought but the massive, rust-stained chain dropping down sheer, strait walls into the blackness below. Shuddering, Perry turned away and found Kian's and Shannon's backpacks. But of the Baeran, the room was empty of all sign. Fearing the worst, Perry scooped up the wedges and packs and stepped back into the corridor, to find Cotton searching for him.

The engagement had ended, the Rūcks had been slain or had fled, and the head of the column was forming up again when Rand, Kian, and Shannon finally came to where Perry and Cotton were waiting. Kian embraced both of the Warrows, and Shannon greeted Perry with a grin and a hug. "You came barely in time, Friend Perry," said the Elf. "We were just preparing to start down the dark square shaft to who-knows-where when you led the Drimma to our rescue."

"Oh, but it wasn't me," protested Perry, "my good friend here, Cotton Buckleburr, was leading." Perry then intro-

duced a self-conscious Cotton to Shannon; at first Cotton felt
somehow clumsy and awkward in the presence of the lithe
Elf, but Shannon's lighthearted manner soon put the Waerling
at his ease. "Lord Kian," asked Perry, his apprehension
growing, "Ursor, where is Ursor?"

A troubled look came over the Man's face. "We do not
know where he is," answered Kian. "We led the *Spaunen* on
a desperate chase back to the underground river. When we
got there, we debated whether to go on up the north passage
or to swim under the wall and go through the Gargon's Lair
and on to await the Host at the five corridors by the Grate
Room. Ursor asked us to stand ready while he swam to see if
the Yrm were gone from the cave leading to the Lair. He tied
a rope to a boulder and let the swift current carry him under
the wall. When he returned, he said all was black in the other
cavern—those Rukha were no longer there. He had lashed the
line securely on the far side, and he asked us to go ahead of
him in the water. By this time the pursuing Yrm were nearly
upon us. Shannon and I plunged in and pulled under to the
opposite tunnel. Almost as soon as we got there, the rope
went slack, and we hauled it in, and tied to the end were our
backpacks. But Ursor never came. We tried to go back, but
neither Shannon nor I was a powerful enough swimmer to
battle back through the rush without the aid of the line, and
we could not get to the other side to find him and aid him.
We know not his fate, though I fear it was grim." Lord Kian
stopped speaking, a pained look in his eyes.

"We took a long rest," said Shannon after a moment,
taking up the rest of their tale, "and then we made our way
back through the Lost Prison, up the silveron delving, and
finally through the tunnels to the Grate Room. Again we
rested, this time in the upward middle corridor of the four
eastern ways. But it was not our lot to idle our time away
until the Drimm army arrived, for *Rûpt* forces came at nearly
one and the same time along all passageways, including the
west one. We were revealed and fled into the Grate Room,
where we drove wedges under the door to jam it shut. We
indeed were about to try to escape down the shaft when we
heard the ancient *Châkka shok! Châkka cor!* battle cry of the
Drimma and were saved that perilous descent."

Shannon fell silent, but before Perry or Cotton could ask

any questions, Durek, Anval, and Borin returned, and once more the march resumed, Borin again in the lead, for the Legion now marched in passageways he had trodden before.

The Host halted for a rest in the great Round Chamber. Patrols were maintained along the corridors, and Bane was posted in the center of the gallery as a ward for all to see. Perry fell instantly into slumber, for he was exhausted, having had no sleep since he had rested in the Gargon's Lair. Cotton, on the other hand, before settling down made certain that his friend Bomar was unhurt, for the Warrow had been deeply concerned ever since the Legion had marched past the Side Hall and the Spawn had attacked the rear guard. Bomar laughed and told Cotton it would take more than a Grg or two to do him and the cook-waggon crew in, and not to worry. Relieved, Cotton returned to where Perry slept and lay down nearby. Cotton, too, quickly went to sleep, and his and Perry's slumber was undisturbed.

But all too soon it was time to move on; and so, after but six hours of respite, the Army again headed east along the Brega Path, Borin still in the lead.

As they marched, Cotton seemed withdrawn, as if bemused by some deep thought. Finally, when Perry sounded him out, Cotton grasped the Horn of Valon and held it for Perry to see and said, "Well, Sir, I mean, look here: ever since we've come into Kraggen-cor, the Horn of the Reach has . . . changed. It seems more polished, or, well, as if it were somehow shinier. I don't know what it is exactly that's different, but it seems to be, as it were, more . . . more *alive!*"

Perry looked closely at the bugle, and he, too, sensed that it had changed. The metal appeared to have more depth, the racing figures seemed to have taken on greater dimension, the carven runes higher luster. Yet Perry could not say whether this silvery *life* was due to an actual change in the horn or, rather, a change in the way he himself viewed it. "Perhaps, Cotton, it only *seems* to glisten more because this cavern is dull and dark and provides great contrast to the shining silver; or perhaps it glimmers more because it now is illumed only by the light of Dwarf lanterns."

As if in response to Perry's words, the bugle glinted and

flashed in the blue-green phosphorescent glow; yet, deep within, it seemed to burn with a light of its own.

"That may be, Sir," replied Cotton, looking with perplexed wonderment at the glittering metal, "but I think it's got more *life* because it's back to its home again, back to its birthing place, back to where it's meant to be."

About the horn, Cotton said no more, and the buccen strode onward in silence, each deep in his own thoughts, as the Army pressed on through Kraggen-cor.

The Host covered the remaining twenty miles in six hours, and they were attacked twice: The first time was a minor assault: arrows hissed at them out of the side passages of Broad Hall; Felor's companies rushed the corridors, and the maggot-folk scuttled away in the darkness, and the attack was over. The second time was a major engagement: a force of nearly four hundred maggot-folk had lain waiting in ambuscade in the Great Chamber; but Bane had alerted the Legion that Spawn were near, and the Army avoided the concealed assault and fell upon the enemy in fury, driving them out of the chamber. In both engagements, Dwarves died, though the number was small.

The Legion then made its way along the two-mile detour around the wreckage of the Hall of the Gravenarch and then marched the final mile to come down at last to their chosen battleground: the vast Mustering Chamber, the War Hall of the First Neath.

Dwarf lanterns were affixed to each of the ancient cressets, and the Hall was brightly lighted. Patrols were again posted in the corridors, and the Host was arrayed to meet Gnar's Swarm. But the *Spaunen* did not come. Dwarves were sent over the rope bridge to Quadmere to fetch its cool clear water, and the Army rested. Again Perry and Cotton slept.

Upon awakening, both Warrows were well rested but famished. Unfortunately, the only food at hand was the crue Cotton had brought in his pack. And so they ate the tasteless waybread and drank water for their meal. Rested, with his stomach full, and in the spacious, bright Hall, Perry's spirits began to recover at last. He had washed his face clean of the face blackener, and had removed the shirt hiding his armor;

now he was a resplendent silver warrior. And though he was troubled by Ursor's unknown fate, still he started joining in conversation with Cotton.

Before he realized it, Perry began telling the other buccan all about the journey down the river, across the wold, and through the caverns. The words came tumbling out, his voice hesitating only when he painfully spoke of Barak's death and funeral, and of Delk felled by Rūck arrow in the Lair fire. When Perry fell silent at the end, his tale told, Cotton leaned back in wonderment, his jewel-like green eyes wide. "Why, Mister Perry," declared Cotton, "*you're* the one that's had a real adventure, not me. That's the story you've been wanting to write: not *my* adventure, but *yours.*"

Perry shook his head in disagreement, for as it is with many a neophyte adventurer, his own story seems insignificant alongside others'. Cotton, seeing the self-doubt in Perry's eyes, then added, "Wull, maybe you just ought to write 'em both up, and we'll have a contest and vote on 'em, and then we'll see which one is the more adventuresome."

Perry laughed outright at the absurdity of the suggestion, and Cotton joined him, and it was the first time mirth had visited either in a long, long while. Before they could say more, a Council of Captains was called, and the two Warrows were summoned to attend.

As soon as all had gathered, Durek spoke: "Cruel Gnar seems too timid to bring his forces to face ours; and so we must draw him out. We must lure him into battle here in the great Mustering Chamber." Durek gestured at the mighty War Hall. This enormous gallery was more than two thousand Dwarf-strides long, and half that wide, its ceiling a hundred feet high. A fourfold row of huge delved pillars marched down its length, carven to resemble great Dragons coiling up fluted columns, each graven monster glaring in a different direction, some with stone flame or spew splashing against the roof. Along the walls were lesser sculptings of bears, eagles, owls, Wolves, and other creatures of rock perched on interior cornices, looking down from the high shadows cast by the hundreds upon hundreds of Dwarf-lanterns that brightly illuminated the Hall.

"This chamber shall become the center of our forays into the passages to destroy the Squam," Durek rasped, then paused; but what he was going to say next shall forever remain a mystery, for it was at that moment that Gnar announced that the Foul Folk were indeed coming to fight: A great rolling *Doom!* of a huge drum thundered into the cavern; so vast and loud was the beat that Perry's small frame shook in its echo.

Boom! Doom! came the beats again, and the very stone itself seemed to rattle and sound with their call.

Boom! Doom! Doom! The mighty vibrations caused rock dust to sift out of cracks and drift to the floor.

"To your Squadrons! Array the Host!" shouted Durek. "Gnar comes at last!" And the Captains sprang to their feet and sped to their Companies.

Boom! Doom! Perry's heart leapt in terror at the great booming sounds, and the blood drained from his face. *Hold on, bucco,* he thought, *settle down. You know what that is: it's a great marching drum of a Rücken Horde*—The Raven Book *speaks of them.* Perry looked at Cotton, and the other buccan's features were drawn, his lips pressed into a thin white line.

Perry reached out and squeezed his comrade's hand, and Cotton cast Perry a fleeting smile from his stricken face.

Boom! Boom! beat the great pulse, as if the mountain itself were being struck by a mighty hammer to ring in response. And then clamant, discordant hornblats sounded, and there came echoing horns from each of the passageways leading into the vast chamber, followed by a shattering volley of harsh clashing of scimitar and tulwar upon dhal and sipar.

Boom! Doom!

As foreplanned, the Dwarf Legion formed up in the center of the great floor, all warriors facing outward with axes and bucklers at the ready. On three sides of the Host stood the stone of the chamber walls, with many dark holes showing where passageways bored off into the black reaches of Drimmen-deeve. It was these portals that the elements of the Army watched, for through these ways would come Gnar's forces. On the fourth side was the Great Deep, and only a few of the Host looked thereupon, for it guarded the Army's back better than another Legion could. Across the floor from sidewall to sidewall and through the Host ran several wide fissures—great cracks in the stone; here and

there, huge slabs spanned the fissures, footbridges placed
there ages agone by the Dwarven Folk.

Doom! Boom!

Both Perry and Cotton were too short to see over the
warriors' heads, and so they mounted up on the base of one
of the pillars and watched; Perry drew Bane, and Cotton the
Atalar Blade, and Bane's flame was nearly bright enough to
hurt the eyes, while the golden runes on the sword of Atala
glinted in the phosphorescent glow of the Dwarf-lanterns.

DOOM! DOOM! whelmed the vast pulse, and then fell
silent. There was one more bray of horns, as one raucous
blare was answered from all corridors by other blats. From
afar the Host could hear the sound of running Rūcken boots
slapping against the stone. Louder and louder the footsteps
sounded, until they became a veritable thunder of feet.

And then Rūcks began to issue into the Hall out of every
corridor, every orifice, like black ants vomited from a thousand holes. And among the Rūcks scuttled armored Hlōk
leaders. Still the maggot-folk poured through the portals and
into the chamber. And they deployed themselves along the
walls and around the Host.

The Dwarves stood their ground in silence, though many
faces were grim to see the awful flood of Squam. And then at
last the Spawn were arrayed, and they shouted and clamored
in a thunderous din, brandishing their weapons and threaten-
ing the Dwarves by making menacing swipes and swirls and
starts. But though they raised a great outcry, they attacked
not, for they were awaiting the coming of Gnar.

And then he came; the supreme Man-sized Hlōk came.
Into the far end of the chamber he strode, and through the
massed ranks of Rūcks. When he reached the forefront of
his Horde, he stopped and stood on widespread legs with his
fists on his hips: cruel and proud, swart and yellow-eyed,
armored in black scale mail and a high-peaked helm, and
armed with a great long scimitar. And the shouting voices of
his Swarm proclaimed him to the Dwarven Army. Gnar stood
'midst the clamorous roar; then he raised up a clenched fist,
and the ranks of his Horde abruptly fell silent, as if their very
breath had been choked off. And Gnar laughed in the sudden
stillness, for there were ten thousand Rūcks to but four
thousand Dwarves.

"What slime comes into my kingdom?" Gnar bellowed in a great snarly voice across the distance that separated the two armies. "Who is the stupid fool leading this paltry group of foul-beards? Why have you of little wit blundered into my caverns?" And a great derisive shout went up from the Rūcken Swarm, as if Gnar had somehow scored a victory with insults alone. Yet the Dwarves stood grim and silent, facing the gibing enemy, not responding, waiting for this *noise* to subside. At last Gnar again raised his fist, and once more the Horde's voice chopped shut.

Still the Dwarf Legion stood fast; and when the cavernous echoing died, Durek spoke: He did not seem to raise his voice, yet he was plainly heard by all in the Hall: "I, the Seventh Durek, and mine Host have come to take back that which is rightfully ours. And we have come to avenge old wrongs and hurts. And more, we have come to stop your rape of the land around. But above all, we have come because you are Squam and we are Châkka." And the Dwarf King fell silent, but with a deafening clap of axe on buckler and with a single great voice, the entire Army shouted once only: *CHÂKKA SHOK!*

At this thunderous call the Rūcken Horde cringed, but seeing the Dwarves stand fast, blustered up again. Gnar glared at his craven Swarm and then turned to the Legion and laughed derisively. "Do you rabble *truly* expect to evict us? Look about you, imbeciles! You are doomed, for we are nearly thrice your numbers. Even so, we could conquer you weaklings with less, in fact, perhaps with but two of us." And Gnar turned and shouted, "Goth! Mog!"

And as the Horde howled in evil glee, from the dark shadows of the end-cavern ponderously came two great, hulking creatures: nearly fourteen feet tall, swart, greenish, scaled, red-eyed, each monster clutching a massive iron pole in one thick hand, each brutish face filled with a vile, malignant leer. They were Cave Ogrus. They lumbered through the massed Rūcken ranks to stand aflank of Gnar. And Gnar threw back his head and laughed cruelly.

The Dwarf Army blenched, for even though there were a full ten thousand Rūcks surrounding them, til this moment the Dwarves had not truly felt fear. But now their eyes were drawn irresistibly to the great Cave Trolls, and the massive

strength of rock-hard flesh seemed to spell doom, for they
were an awful enemy. At last Perry knew why Ogru-Trolls
were so feared: they were direful behemoths of crushing
power, and they looked unstoppable. Perry tried to remember
the places of Ogru vulnerability, but his wit fled in his fright,
and he could only recall that a sword thrust under the eyelid
and into the brain would kill one.

Holding up his fist to stop the jeering of his Swarm, Gnar
sneered from between the massive Trolls, "I will give you
but one chance to surrender, fools. All I ask in tribute are
your inferior weapons and pitiable supplies, and eternal bond-
age as my groveling slaves." Raucous laughter swelled up
from the Horde, and they jittered in revelment. But their
shrill gaiety was cut short by another dinning clash of axe on
buckler, again followed by a single thunderous shout bursting
forth from the entire Legion: *CHÂKKA COR!*

And quickly upon the ensuing silence, Durek roared in
wrath, "We did not come to parley with a foul usurper! We
are here to fight to the death!" And the Dwarf King signalled
his herald, who raised the great War Horn to his lips and
blew a blast that sprang from pillar to post to wall and roof.
The Hall seemed to tremble and shudder with its sound, and
all the Host took heart. An answering blare came from the
Spaunen horns, and the two mighty armies came rushing
together with hoarse shouts and a great resounding crash of
weapons.

Perry and Cotton sprang down from the base of the pillar
and rushed to the fray. Faced by the Rūcken Horde, the
Dwarves had formed a wall of flashing axes, and the maggot-
folk could not break through the phalanx. Likewise, neither
Warrow could reach the Rūcks; the two ran up and down
the lines, but to no avail. The axes hewed and slashed and cut
the foe with dreadful effect. Dwarves also were felled, but
the ranks somehow closed, and still the Spawn failed to
penetrate.

Gnar had withheld the great Ogru-Trolls, for they were the
last in Drimmen-deeve, and the secret of his power; and the
prowess of Dwarf Troll-squads was legendary. Hence, only
shouting Rūcks and snarling Hlōks clashed with the Dwarves
in this first charge.

Blood and gore splashed the stone of the hall, and screams

rent the air, and corpses littered the floor. The Dwarves' compact deployment defied the enemy attack, and at last the Horde withdrew. Dwarf wounded were drawn into the center, and fresher warriors stepped to the fore.

Twice more the Spawn charged, only to suffer dismaying losses, for twice more the Dwarves' formation held, and the Horde was beaten back; the Rūcks could not break through to bring their greater numbers to bear. Many of the Châkka, however, were felled, and the Dwarves yielded back a bit to consolidate their perimeter.

Gnar knew that he would have to use the great Trolls, even though he could not replace them, even though were they to fall, his rule in Drimmen-deeve might fall with them, for other Hlōks could then challenge him without fear. Yet without the Ogrus, the Hlōk-led Rūcks could not break the Dwarf array, and unless the array were broken, Gnar would suffer defeat at the hands of the Châkka.

Hence, once again Gnar ordered a charge, but this time he loosed the Cave Trolls. These mighty engines of destruction waded into the forefront of the Dwarves, their great iron War-bars swinging to and fro to crush all before them. The Dwarves gave back, and there stood a gap in the wall of axes. Hordes of Rūcks streamed into the center, and the Dwarves' mighty phalanx disintegrated: the formation was broken and the Dwarf defence was sundered into Companies, squads, pairs, and single Dwarves fighting against desperate odds.

In the center, fifty or more Dwarves surrounded each Ogru, hewing and hacking at their vitals and great legs; but Gnar ordered Rūcks to attack the Troll-squads, and whether the Dwarves would have succeeded in felling the giants will never be known, for the Rūcks assaulted the squads and turned the Dwarves' energies aside.

Perry and Cotton found themselves facing the foe at last, and the relentless hours of Kian's sword-instructions now showed their worth, for the Warrows' blades wove swift nets of death upon the enemy.

Perry lunged under a hammer, and blazing Bane drank black Rūck blood; the foe fell, but another took his place, and Elven-blade clashed against Rūcken-scimitar. A parry, riposte, and thrust ended that duel, but another Rūck lashed a bar at the Warrow, And amid snarling Rūcks and cursing

Dwarves and the clash and clangor of War, Perry dodged and whirled and darted, and hacked and stabbed and cut, felling Rūck after Rūck in the swirling battle.

Cotton, too, was pressed by a great number of the maggot-folk: they seemed to come at him from all points. Twisting among ally and foe alike, Cotton hewed and clove and pierced with his Atalar sword; and Rūcks fell about the Warrow like grain before the scythe.

And as circumstances would have it, the two Warrows found themselves battling back to back near the lip of the Great Deep, hindguarding one another while dealing death to the foe at hand.

Soon the assailants fell back, for these small warriors were much more skilled than they, and the two in glittering silver and shining golden armor seemed bright and invincible.

But then a great Hlōk jumped forward to challenge Cotton. Even as the Hlōk engaged Cotton's sword, a Rūck tried to take the buccan from the rear; but Perry and Bane cut down the foe, the Rūck's death scream to be lost among the shouts filling the War Hall. And with Perry guarding his back, Cotton fought the enemy before him. *Clang!* went sword on scimitar, and the clash and skirl of steel upon steel rang out. Cotton was pressed hard, for the Hlōk was skilled, but at last the Warrow turned a thrust aside and slashed his blade through the throat of the Hlōk. Blood flew wide, and the enemy fell.

Ai! wailed the Rūcks and drew back; but one set an arrow to his bow and drew it full to the cruel barb and let the black shaft fly at point-blank range. But Perry had seen the danger, and with a warning shout he leapt forward to knock Cotton aside. And the arrow slammed into Perry, its force so great that it penetrated even the silveron mail, bursting through a chink high on the chest where an amber gem was inset among the links. And the Warrow slammed backwards against the base of one of the great Dragon Pillars, and crumpled to the stone, the buccan pierced through. Cotton sprang forward with a cry of rage, and his blade mortally clove the Rūck from helm to breast. The remaining Rūcks fled from the small enraged warrior in the golden mail. And Cotton's wrath turned to dismay as he fell to his knees beside Perry's still form.

"Mister Perry! Mister Perry!" wailed Cotton, hugging the fallen Warrow to his breast. And then Perry moaned, and Cotton saw that he wasn't dead. "Oh, Mister Perry, you're alive! Oh, don't die, Mister Perry. I couldn't bear it if you died."

With chaos and confusion and slaughter all around, and with a savage and desperate battle raging back and forth above them, Cotton knelt at the edge of the Great Deep and held on to Perry and wept and rocked back and forth in torment.

Perry opened his eyes, his vision swimming in a sea of pain, and looked to see Cotton's face dimly before him. "Oh, Cotton, Cotton, what have I done?" whispered Perry. "I have dragged you off into a quest where neither one of us belongs. And you may be slain. Oh, Cotton, when I reached for this adventure, I did not stop to consider anyone's feelings but my own. The only thing that mattered was my own lust for excitement. I did not stop to think how you felt, or Holly . . . poor Holly . . . Did you see how she cried, Cotton? I didn't know. I didn't think. That's it! I didn't think. Me, the bright scholar, the glorious Fairhill Scholar, and I can't think my way past a foolish dream of bold achievement.

"It was all foredoomed anyway. My whole witless venture was unnecessary. No single part of it was necessary. Look at our mission: We tried to sneak through Drimmen-deeve, and the Dusk-Door wasn't even broken. Barak died for nought. Tobin suffered needlessly. Delk died for nought. And Ursor. And what for? . . . What for? . . . What for?"

Cotton looked into Perry's sapphirine eyes. "Oh, no, Mister Perry," he protested, "you've got it all wrong. That's not the way of it at all. They *needed* us. Without us the raids of the maggot-folk would go on. Without us the Dwarves might not have gone to Dusk-Door and would have died in the Great Deep." Cotton gestured at the nearby gulf. "Without us the Dwarves wouldn't have stood a chance."

A grimace of pain crossed Perry's features, and he gasped through clenched teeth. "Leastwise now, leastwise now . . ." A shuddering sigh racked the wounded buccan, and unconsciousness mercifully washed over him.

"Mister Perry!" cried Cotton, fearing the worst, but before he could press his ear to Perry's breast, one of the huge Cave

Trolls, seeing two small, helpless targets hidden in the shadow of a Dragon Pillar, lumbered toward the Warrows.

Cotton saw the Ogru coming, and gently eased Perry to the floor. Catching up his sword, Cotton sprang between the Troll and the wounded buccan. And as he ran into the path of the dire creature, the story from *The Raven Book* of Patrel and the Ogru on the bridge flashed into Cotton's mind, and he shouted, *"Hai!* Troll! You great clumsy oaf! Look at me! I am the golden warrior!" And the buccan held his arms wide and danced to one side, drawing the Troll's full attention. The huge Ogru stared stupidly at the small creature in the shining gilded mail; then he raised his great iron bar and struck.

Crack! The bar smashed to the stone, but the nimble Warrow was not there. Cotton sprang to the side and forward, and hewed with his Atalar sword, hacking just above the great Ogru's knee, for that was the highest the small Warrow could reach with his blade. But the edge clanged into the Troll's armor-like hide and glanced down.

Crack! The great iron bar missed again, and once more Cotton's blade failed to cut the stone skin. As the Warrow dodged away, he knew that sooner or later the Troll would make contact, and the fight would end then and there. Cotton knew he needed help; and in that moment he glimpsed from the corner of his eye Bane's blue flame burning on the stone where the sword had skidded when Perry had been felled.

Crack! The Ogru missed again, and Cotton darted to the side and scooped up the blazing Elven-blade. Yet the monster shouted in vile gloat, for it now had Cotton trapped: to get at Bane, the Warrow had dashed beyond the Troll to the precipitous edge of the Great Deep; and the only way to freedom led back past the great foe. To cut off escape, the Ogru spread its arms wide and took a ponderous stride forward.

Cotton, his eyes locked upon the massive War-bar, stepped back, and his foot came down upon the edge of the great split. He teetered and gasped in fear, his arms windmilling. And the vast dark gulf gaped blackly, and waited. Yet with a twisting motion, the Warrow managed to fall forward. And as he had been trained, Cotton rolled as he landed, to come back to his feet in a balanced stance with sword in hand to again face the foe. The great Cave Troll snarled in anger, yet its

eyes took on a look of evil cunning, for it still had the wee
Warrow trapped; and the monster swooshed the bar in a feint
followed by a swift overhand stroke.

Crack! The iron pole just missed the dodging Warrow, so
close it ticked a golden scale.

Again Cotton leapt to one side and then lunged forward;
and the blazing rune-jewelled Troll's Bane flashed up as
Cotton plunged it into the Ogru's kneecap: the stone-like skin
that easily turned aside axes and swords yielded like soft
butter to the flaming Elven-blade; the point sank through the
cap and into the knee joint, plunging nearly to the sinews at
the back of the leg. Cotton jerked Bane out and twisted aside;
black blood dropped from the bitter blade to the stone floor,
and where it fell a reeking smoke coiled up from the hard
rock.

The great Troll roared in agony and clutched at its pierced
knee, and stumbled with a sliding crash to the stone at the lip
of the great black abyss, to slip over the edge, grasping
frantically but in vain at the smooth floor. And with a bellow
of terror and its eyes wide in fear, and still gripping the
massive War-bar, the huge Ogru fell howling beyond the rim
and down into the bottomless black depths.

Cotton stared for a moment at the place where the Troll
had gone over the edge; then the Warrow scooped up the
Atalar Blade and ran back to Perry, who was conscious
again. Once more Cotton cradled the wounded buccan.

As Cotton watched the hideous battle, Perry gazed up into
the shadows on the ceiling. The War was going badly for the
Dwarves: the Spawn now controlled the center of the chamber and the Dwarves were at the perimeter. The great numbers of the Rücken forces and the strength of their position
weighed the battle heavily in their favor; though much more
skillful, the Dwarves were in weak array, and by the hundreds they had fallen to Gnar's Swarm. As Cotton looked on
in dismay, Perry whispered, "That's where Borin climbed."

"Wha . . . what, Mister Perry?" asked Cotton.

"That's where Borin climbed over the ceiling. When we
crossed the gulf, I mean," rambled Perry, lying on his back,
looking upward above the chasm. "Over there. Above the
bridge."

"You said he didn't make it all the way. The ceiling was

all cracked, *zig . . . zig* something," wept Cotton, crying for the Dwarf dead as he tried to comfort his wounded master.

"*Ziggurt.* The roof is *ziggurt.* As far as the eye can see. Borin told us." Perry's blurred gaze roamed down the Hall along the roof above the pillars.

Though he was weeping, Cotton felt strangely at peace— sitting here, holding his friend, chatting about inconsequential things—as the mighty clash and clangor of weapons and War swirled back in the main chamber just a stone's throw away.

"Rocks, stone, that's all the eye can see," muttered Perry. "No green growing things, no soft comfortable things, just hard rock and stone. I had enough of rocks when the slide nearly got us back in the Crestan Pass, oh so long ago. Those were the days. Just you and me, and Anval, Borin, and Kian."

"True," answered Cotton, "those were the days. They taught us a lot, Lord Kian and the Dwarves." And Cotton again looked at the black shaft standing out from Perry's shoulder. "I just wish they'd taught me about healing instead of about swords, and rock slides, and snow avalanches, and—"

A startled look had come over Perry's face, and a fierce energy suffused his pained lineament, and he urgently interrupted Cotton: "That's it! Cotton, that's it!" he gasped through his pain. "You've solved the riddle! We've got to get to Durek! We can win the War yet! Get me to Durek. Get me to Durek." And he clutched desperately at Cotton's arm, and struggled to rise. "Get me to Durek."

Cotton helped Perry to stand, and the wounded buccan fought to keep from swooning. His good arm was over Cotton's shoulders, and he absently clutched Bane in his other hand, having grasped it when Cotton had laid it aside. Slowly they started along the south wall; Cotton didn't know why, but his master urgently needed to get to Durek.

As they crept forward, Cotton's emeraldine eyes cast about for the Dwarf King. Perry's eyes, too, sought Durek as the Warrows limped slowly along the perimeter, the black shaft standing full neath Perry's left collarbone. Cotton saw Dwarves striving desperately with two, three, or four Rūcks at once. He also glimpsed Kian and Rand in a small force battling the remaining Ogru:

Only a handful hewed at the Troll where fifty were needed, yet at bay they held the creature. Of those facing the Ogru, it was Prince Rand who had harassed and baited the fell beast into a foaming rage; for after the two Trolls had burst through the Dwarves' defense, Rand had seen that these great monsters if unchecked would assure a Yrm victory. And he had run before one of them, shouting and waving his arms, leaping away from the crashing iron bar, drawing the Ogru out of the general mêlée in the creature's rage to smash this puny Man-thing that it couldn't quite seem to hit. Again and again Rand had leapt aside, and again and again the great iron pole had smashed to empty stone where Rand had stood but an instant before. But the Prince was growing weary, for he had baited the beast long, and the great bar was becoming more difficult to dodge.

Then Lord Kian saw his brother and the Ogru, and he ran to aid Prince Rand. Kian fell upon the Troll from the rear and lashed his sword in a mighty arc, but the blade crashed into the stone hide and glanced away notched. Three Dwarves joined the fray, but their axes proved no better. "His heel!" cried Prince Rand. "Go for his heel when I draw him forth!" And Rand stood motionless at a long reach for the Troll.

The monster lunged forward, swinging his bar in a wide sweep; and as he extended his body, the creature's ankle bent sharply and one of the scaled plates of his greenish hide lifted away from his heel. Lord Kian stepped up, and using two hands he swung his sword of Riamon with all the strength he could muster. The blade sped true, and the keen edge flashed under the scale and into the flesh to sever the heel tendon and chop to the bone and lodge in the joint. Kian's sword was wrenched from his grasp to shatter in twain upon impact as, with a great bellow, the Ogru crashed forward onto the stone, to roll and clutch at his ankle; the great beast was now out of the battle and would aid the Rūcks no more, for it could not stand.

"Rand, we did it!" Kian shouted, elated, and looked up and saw to his horror that his brother had stood fast so that the Troll could be felled, and Rand had been smashed to the wall by the cruel iron bar.

And as he saw his brother's crumpled form, and the howling Ogru rolling in agony upon the stone, a madness of fury possessed Lord Kian. Weaponless, he seized hold of the Troll's great War-bar which had been flung from the monster's clutch, *and even though the mass of the bar was beyond the strength of two Men to heft, in his wrath Lord Kian raised up the huge pole and violently smote it down upon the thrashing Troll.* The Ogru saw the strike coming and warded with his forearm, but the force of the blow was so great that the rock-hard limb was broken as if it were a twig, and the War-bar drove on to smash into the Troll's thick neck, crushing its throat; and the great creature's eyes bulged out as it tried to breathe but could not, and its limbs flailed about in desperation. And though the monster was mortally struck and falling swiftly unto Death, Lord Kian tried to raise up the War-pole for yet another blow, but could not, for with that one strike the towering fury had been spent and the bar was now far beyond his power to wield.

Catching up a fallen axe from the lax hand of a slain Dwarf, Lord Kian turned from this heel-chopped, throat-crushed monster, and made his way toward Prince Rand's fallen form.

Slowly the Warrows went forth, and they both saw Anval: he was battling Gnar! There was a great clanging as axe and scimitar clashed together. Anval drove the great Hlōk back, but then the tide turned as more Rūcks joined Gnar to attack the Dwarf. "Get back! Get back!" cried Perry, feebly, but his whisper was lost in the shouts and screams of others and in the din of steel upon steel. Suddenly a Rūck behind Anval hurled a War-hammer, and it struck the Dwarf on the back of his helm! And Anval staggered! And Gnar's great scimitar flashed up and back down, and clove into the Dwarf, blood flying wide, and Gnar threw back his head in wild laughter as Anval fell dead.

Cotton and Perry both gasped in horror, and their minds fell numb with shock. Then they heard a raging scream above all others, and they saw Borin rush at Gnar roaring, "For Anval! For Anval! Death! Death!" And he fell to with a rage unmatched by any. The Rūcks shielding Gnar were cut down by Borin's bloody axe like wheat before a reaper, and then the Dwarf and Hlōk rushed together in savage combat.

Cotton tore his eyes away from Borin and Gnar, and at last he saw Durek. The Dwarf King and Shannon Silverleaf stood back to back, battling Rūcks, besieged near one of the entrances into the War Hall. Cotton drew Perry as close to the fracas as he dared, and sat the wounded buccan to the floor, his back to the wall. "Don't move!" Cotton cried, and then he drew his blade of the Lost Land and attacked the Rūcks from behind.

Cotton felled three before the enemy realized that another foe had joined the fray. Two more dropped, but then the Warrow's foot skidded in gore, and the buccan fell. A scimitar came slashing down and Cotton started to roll to one side, but he was not quick enough to avoid the cut. Another blade seemed to flash out of nowhere to clash with the descending curved edge: it was Shannon's long Elf-knife, and it turned the scimitar aside to crash with a sheet of sparks into the stone floor. Then Shannon cut upward, and the Rūck fell dead. Cotton sprang to his feet to see the remaining Rūcks flee screaming from this deadly trio.

"King Durek!" cried Cotton, "Mister Perry calls you to him. He is wounded and says you must come. Here, this way." And he led the Dwarf King to Perry's side. Perry had swooned again, but he opened his eyes when Durek knelt at his side and called his name.

As Shannon and Cotton stood guard, Perry spoke: *"Narok,"* whispered Perry, and Durek leaned closer to hear. *"Narok!"* Perry said more strongly. "The roof is *ziggurt*. The slide in the mountains—Anval told us about rock slides and how they are started. But Anval is dead." Perry began to weep. "Borin fights on for him. But the sounds . . . you must make the right sounds."

Durek looked upon the weeping, incoherent Waeran. The Dwarf had no idea what it was that Perry was trying to tell him. With an arrow standing forth from high on his chest, the small warrior sat against the wall: wounded, crying, looking up with pain in his eyes, bloody Bane blazing, held in the hand of his hurt arm. "Friend Cotton," asked Durek, "do you fathom what Friend Perry is trying to tell me?"

Cotton shook his head in anguish. "No, Sir, I don't, but whatever it is, he's got a good reason."

Durek turned back to Perry, but the Warrow was staring through his tears at the mighty battle between Cruel Gnar and raging Borin. "Friend Perry," rumbled Durek, "you are sorely wounded and I grieve for you, but I must return to the fight." And he started to rise to his feet.

But Perry desperately clutched him by the wrist. "*No!* No! It's time that Dwarves come on horses, King Durek," pled Perry. "You must sound the Horn of Narok. Sound assembly! *Now!* Before all is lost! It is our only hope!"

The Dwarf looked doubtfully away at Cotton, and then again at Perry, who was struggling to reach the trumpet on Cotton's shoulder. Cotton quickly removed the bright horn and handed it to Perry who, in turn, held it out with trembling hand toward King Durek. "Believe me . . . oh, please believe me," begged the Warrow.

In an agony of indecision, Durek looked at the fearful token and then away to the savage mêlée in the Hall and back to Perry again. And the Dwarf dreaded touching the glittering silver. "We are at our uttermost extremity. More than half of my warriors have fallen, and it seems certain that the Grg will have the victory. This trump we Châkka have feared all of our days, yet you say it is our only hope—but I do not know why. Yet I deem I must believe you, though I do not understand. You may be right, Friend Perry: perhaps the wind of *Narok* is our last hope. Perhaps the Châkka must at last ride the horses." The Dwarf King looked away from the dreadful clarion and into Perry's wide, tilted, gemlike eyes. Tears glittered in the sapphire-blue gaze, and desperate urgency welled up from the jewelled depths. "Aye, I believe you, Friend Perry. Quickly now, before I change my mind, before I lose my courage, give me the trumpet; I will sound it ere all is lost."

And Durek, full of apprehension, accepted the brilliant horn from Perry's trembling fingers. And *lo!* at Durek's touch the metal shimmered with light, and sparkling glints shattered outward; and the Dwarf King set the dazzling horn to his lips and began to blow:

The silver call electrified the air. Its clarion notes rang up to the roof and sprang from the walls and sounded throughout the great War Hall. Everywhere, Dwarves' hearts were lifted; and the Rūcks and Hlōks quailed back in fear. Again and again the call resounded as Durek blew the signal to assemble; and the sound leapt into the Great Deep, falling to its depths and running out into the vast rift in the walls; and then it seemed to spring back from the nether parts of that great split, magnified by the sheer stone faces of the mighty fissure. Durek blew the shining horn again and again, and the whole of the War Hall appeared to tremble in response to the silver notes.

Imperceptibly at first, but swiftly growing, the floor began to resonate as a crescendo of sound mounted up from the depths of the Great Deep and the echoes piled one upon the other; and still the Dwarf King winded the sparkling trumpet. Stronger and stronger came the vibrations, racking through the floor in continuous waves. And then the entire Chamber began to quiver, and rock dust drifted down from the cracks above. And still the echoes and vibrations grew as Durek sounded the bright horn and the stone shook. The Rūcks huddled together, screaming in fear in the center of the thrumming floor, the place of strength they had won. All battle and fighting had ceased in the shivering Hall. *Nay!* Not all! For mighty Borin yet raged against Cruel Gnar to avenge fallen Anval.

Durek blew, and still the echoes grew. Now all of the War Hall wrenched: the floor rattled, the walls groaned, the pillars lurched, and the roof pitched. *And there came from the stone a sound like that of an endless herd of horses wildly thundering by in racing stampede.* Cotton became aware that Perry was chanting, and Cotton listened in wonder:

> *"Trump shall blow,*
> *Ground will pound*
> *As Dwarves on Horses*
> *Riding 'round."*

It was the Staves of Narok! Perry chanted the Staves of Narok as Borin's axe and Gnar's scimitar clashed together again and again, and sparks flew up from their collisions. The two fought on as the Hall groaned and rumbled and shook, as if an earthquake strove within the mountain.

And Cotton looked at Durek. Now the horn seemed to be blazing, flaming with a bright internal fire; and the figures, riders and horses, *were they moving?* Galloping through runes 'round horn-bell? Or was it just a judder-caused illusion? Cotton squeezed his eyes tightly shut and rubbed them with his fists and then looked again, but he could not tell, for the quake jolting through the Hall blurred his vision.

Still the Dwarf King blew, and except for Borin, all the surviving Dwarves, their numbers now less than a thousand, flocked to Durek's signal and arrayed themselves along the southern wall. The Rūcks wailed with dread, for they knew not what was coming to pass. And Perry chanted on:

> *"Stone shall rumble,*
> *Mountain tremble,*
> *In the battle*
> *Dwarves assemble.*
>
> *Answer to*
> *The Silver Call."*

And still Durek continued to sound the flaring trumpet, and the silver notes grew, and the mountain shook. Pebbles fell from the *ziggurt* ceiling, and rocks, and slabs. And great clots of Rūcks and Hlōks jerked this way and that as the stone smashed into their ranks.

Borin pressed Gnar back to one of the huge shuddering pillars. A great slab of rock crashed down from above to land beside the battling pair, but they gave it no heed. Now they grappled, and Borin's great shoulders bunched, and he forced the Hlōk back against the quaking stone support. Gnar screamed hoarsely in terror, and Borin's axe flashed as stone fell all around. Up went the double-bitted blade, and then down it fell with a meaty smack, *and Gnar's head was shorn from his thrashing body.* Borin laughed wildly as rocks and slabs, summoned by the Silver Call, crashed from the ceiling to the floor and giant pillars toppled with thunderous wrack; and the Dwarf held up the grisly trophy by the hair, shouting, "For Anval!" And he flung it bouncing and skidding across the wide stone floor as the entire roof of *ziggurt* rock at last ripped completely away from the cavernous vault above, and the great, invincible, rushing mass fell with a cataclysmic roar to smash across all of the broad center of the vast War Hall.

> *"Death shall deem*
> *The vault to fall."*

And as the rock thundered down, the surviving remnants of the Dwarf Army reeled back aghast against the southern wall, their eyes locked in awe upon the crashing mass, their hands clapped over their ears. Durek desperately held the Horn of Narok in his white-knuckled grip, and he winded it a few notes more, but its silver echoes were lost in the deafening roar of thundering stone.

Tons upon unnumbered tons shattered down, crashing into the Hall, a great, bellowing, endless, rolling roar. Rock smashed upon rock, hammering, shattering, pulverizing, destroying. It seemed as if the vast collapse would never stop . . .

But suddenly it was over: the thundering rockfall ended. Slowly the rolling echoes of cracking stone and cleaving rock died away. Billowing stone dust whirled and settled, and the survivors gazed stunned across the wreckage. Volume upon volume of stone had crashed down into the chamber. Only along the walls had the roof been sound, and the Dwarves who had assembled there had, for the most part, escaped the carnage, although here and there a few huge rocks had bounded and crashed to crush some unfortunate Dwarves. But in the center of the chamber, all living things had perished: All the myriad Rūcks and Hlōks. And Borin.

The battle was finished, the War over. Four fifths of the Dwarves had been slain in battle; ten thousand *Spaunen* had died, two thirds at the hand of the Host, the rest by falling stone. Perry looked out across the wreckage:

> *"Many perish,*
> *Death the Master,*
> *Dwarves shall mourn*
> *Forever after."*

Durek had taken the silent bugle from his lips. Stunned, he looked across the shattered sea of stone. He turned to Cotton and gave him the Horn of the Reach, now softly glowing with but the gentle sheen of fine silver and no longer flaring with glitterbright fire. Cotton took it with numb fingers and unconsciously hung it over his shoulder.

At last Cotton had seen the connection between Perry's

pain-driven, rambling speech and the crashing down of the ceiling. Cotton, too, now remembered Anval's warning in the Crestan Pass of just how the right sound would cause rock to jink and come roaring in avalanche. And he remembered Anval's exact words: *"We Châkka believe that each thing in this world will shake or rattle or fall or even shatter apart if just the right note is sounded on the right instrument."* And the Horn of the Reach—the Horn of Narok, the Death-War—crafted ages ago by an unknown hand, had been created for just this event: created against the day when Dwarves, driven to their uttermost limits, would have to bring the vast *ziggurt* roof of the immense War Hall down upon some great horde of enemies. The Staves of Narok were not made to warn Dwarves against riding on horseback. No, for that line in the ode spoke only of the drumming sound the rock would make in the event the horn was winded. And to Cotton it was now plain that the vault referred to in the rede was the wide ceiling of this huge stone chamber; til now, Cotton had suspected that the vault of the poem was the sky above and that somehow the Staves were related to the Dwarves' belief that falling stars foretold of Death's coming. But Mister Perry had figured it all out, and just barely in time, too.

Cotton was wrenched from his stunned thoughts and back to the here and now by an anguished cry from Perry, who was staring toward the center of the chamber. "Oh, Borin, Anval, we loved you and now you are gone." And the wounded buccan began weeping as, slowly, the healers started moving among the Host, tending the injured. And Shannon came to Perry and examined the arrow standing forth from the juncture between the Waerling's chest and shoulder.

As the Elf prepared to extract the barb, with Cotton hovering nearby, ready to aid, King Durek began to make his way along the wall, at the edge of the wrack, seeing but too benumbed to fathom the total destruction wrought in the War of Kraggen-cor: The great War Hall was destroyed. Tons unnumbered of fallen *ziggurt* ramped upward toward the center of the chamber; like a vast cairn, it covered the crushed bodies of all the Úkhs and Hrōks, all the Châkka slain in battle, the Troll felled by Rand and Kian, and Gnar's slayer, Borin Ironfist. Here and there a broken Dragon Pillar jutted upward through the great heap, a jagged reminder of the ancient rows of columns, now collapsed and part of the rubble. Durek also made his way past many of the eight hundred or so surviving Châkka quietly and methodically binding up each other's wounds. All were stunned by the cataclysmic ruin, and had not yet realized the staggering cost of their victory.

King Durek saw the devastation, but he, too, did not comprehend, until at last he came upon Lord Kian. Nearby lay the axe Kian had carried back into battle: one bit broken, the other blade chipped and jagged, the helve cracked, the iron and oak now awash with black Grg-blood; Lord Kian had wielded it beyond its endurance, for his vengeance had been mighty. Kian also was drenched, some of it Squam gore, some of it his own blood, for he, too, was wounded—by spear thrust and scimitar cut—although not mortally; but Prince Rand was dead, slain by Troll War-bar. And Lord Kian huddled on the stone floor, hugging his brother's lifeless body to his breast, and he wept and rocked in distress.

Durek gazed on in sorrow, and Lord Kian looked up through his tears at the Dwarf. "When we were but lads," wept Kian, "we were in the market, and Rand took up a turtle-shell comb in his hand. And he laughed happily over the raft we had made and ridden to Rhondor and sold for two silver pennies. And Rand bought that comb for Mother, and we went home and gave it to her, and Rand glowed in the pleasure of her delight. We began planning a new raft: two children rejoicing in the flush of youth, as close in life as two brothers who loved one another could ever be. But now he is dead and nevermore will we laugh together, for the lad who plied rafts with me to Rhondor has now sailed without me on his final journey." And Lord Kian rocked and keened in his grief.

It was in this poignant moment of kin-death lamentation that at last the cost of the victory came clear to Durek. And the overwhelming despair of the War-loss uncontrollably welled up in the Dwarf King; and he quickly pulled his hood over his head, and his face fell into shadow, for no one should see the heartgrief of Dwarves—for to look upon Dwarf bale is to gaze upon sorrow beyond measure. And the Dwarf King sank to his knees and choked upon his own woe. His glistening tears fell to splash upon the stone, and great sobs racked his frame as he and Lord Kian and uncounted others grieved in deep despair along the wall behind the jumble and scree of fallen *ziggurt*. But the slain of the Death-War heeded them not.

CHAPTER 9

THE JOURNEY BACK

Two weeks passed, and Perry's wound steadily healed. The black shaft had driven through muscle, all vital parts having been missed, and the barb had not been poisoned. Both Warrows' spirits, however, were greatly injured, for four out of every five of the Host had fallen, and nearly all of their comrades had perished. Cotton was often seen searching, looking for some sign of Bomar and the cook-waggon crew; but he found them not, for they had been slain in combat and were buried under tons of stone in the ruined War Hall; and he wept for them and for Rand and for all the others lost. And Perry, too, spent long days in anguish, remembering Delk and gruff Barak, and huge Ursor, and the Ironfist brothers, Anval and Borin. And the Warrows thought upon all the times that were, and they grieved for all the times that might have been but now would never be. Of their close companions, only Durek, Shannon, and Kian remained, and a desolate mood haunted them as well as each of those of the Host who had survived: King Durek looked upon his won Kingdom, but felt only grief. Lord Kian stood for long moments and stared without seeing into the dark corners of Kraggencor. Often someone—anyone—would be seen with his face buried in his hands. All were stunned by the overwhelming losses of their victory. And their heartgrief filled them.

On the seventh day after the battle, word came from the Dusk-Door of Brytta's safety and that of the Vanadurin; yet this good news caused no celebration, only quiet relief. Even the arrival on the tenth day of a force of Dylvana Elves from Darda Galion stirred little excitement. How the Elves had become aware of the victory, none knew—or would say—

although Cotton did overhear an Elf Captain speaking to Silverleaf, asserting, "We came at your summons, Alor Vanidar." But the buccan did not see how Shannon could have sent a message, and thus dismissed it from his mind.

At last Perry came to King Durek and said, "I can stand this sorrow no longer. My physical wound is well enough to travel"—and the Warrow flexed his fingers and turned his hand over and again, and then stiffly he eased his arm from the sling and set the cloth aside—"but my very being is sorely injured. I must go to a place of quiet and solitude, a place far removed from the reflections of War and evil memories, a place where pleasures are simple and time goes slowly. King Durek, I am returning home to the Bosky, for The Root calls me with an irresistible voice, and I must answer, and rest, and be drawn forth from this bleak place where my heart and spirit have been driven."

And Durek saw that the Warrow was indeed injured far beyond what the eye could see. "Come with me," Durek rasped, and they strode forth from the Great Chamber, where the remnants of the Host were now quartered. Out through the north entrance they went, and up within the mountain. High they climbed, and higher still, mounting up stair upon stair delved within the stone of Stormhelm, passing through Rise after Rise; many times they rested, yet still they ascended, and the stair was ancient, but lightly trod. Once more they rested and then pressed on, and finally they entered a carven hall. But the Dwarf held his lantern high and led the Warrow into a dark, twisting crack with shoots branching off in many directions.

At last they came to a small but massy bronze door, and the rune-laden surface flung brazen glints back unto the eye. The Dwarf King took hold of the handle—a great ring of brass—and muttered strange words under his breath; and then he turned his wrist, twisting the ring post, and pushed the door outward.

Bright light streamed in through the open portal, and blue sky could be seen beyond. The Dwarf King crossed over the bronze doorsill and bade Perry to follow. And blinking his watering eyes in the brilliance, his hand shading his sight, the Warrow stepped through into the light.

And Perry found he was upon a windswept ledge on a

towering vertical face of stone on the outer flanks of
Rávenor—of Stormhelm. High up he was, yet still the mountain reared above him, rising toward the snow-laden crest. A
low parapet was before him, and there King Durek stood,
leaning forward upon both hands and looking down into the
land. But Perry shrank back from such a view, for the drop
was sheer and awesome. Yet Durek turned and held out his
hand, and in spite of his fright, Perry stepped forward and
took it; and strength seemed to flow from Dwarf to Warrow,
and never again was Perry to fear heights.

It was a rare day upon Rávenor, for no storm hammered its
peak. The cold thin air was crystalline, and the endless sky
was calm, and a few serene clouds drifted past. To the north
and south the great backbone of the Grimwall marched off
into the distance. The other three peaks of the Quadran—
Aggarath and Uchan, south and southeast, and Ghatan, east—
shouldered up nearby. The clear-eyed Warrow could see far
and away: to Darda Galion and beyond; to the Great Argon
River; even unto the eaves of Darda Erynian. Perry's vision
swept outward, over the southwest borders of Riamon and
into the North Reach of Valon, where perhaps horses thundered across the plains. And it seemed to Perry as if the very
rim of Mithgar itself might be seen from here.

And Durek directed the Warrow's eyes down onto the
Pitch, and like tiny specks, a work crew of Dwarven Folk
could be seen fetching water from the Quadmere. And Durek
and Perry looked deeper down into the Quadran, and there in
a great fold of stone on Ghatan's flank stood the Vorvor, a
whirling churning gurge deeply entwined in Dwarven legend:
There a secret river burst forth from the underearth to rage
around a great stone basin and plunge down into the dark
again; and a great gaping whirlpool raved endlessly and
sucked at the sky and funneled deep into the black depths
below. Dwarves tell that when the world was young and First
Durek trod its margins, he came unto this place. And vile
Úkhs, shouting in glee, captured him and from a high stone
ledge they flung him into the spin, and the sucking maw drew
him down. According to the legend, none else had e'er
survived that fate; yet First Durek did, though how, it is not
said. To the very edge of the Realm of Death, and perhaps
beyond, he was taken, yet Life at last found him on a rocky

shore within a vast, undelved, undermountain realm; and
First Durek strode where none else had gone before—treading
through that Kingdom which was to become Kraggen-cor.
How he came again unto the light of day, it is not told; yet it
said that Daūn Gate stands upon the very spot where he
walked out through the mountainside; but how he crossed the
Great Dēop remains an enigma, though some believe that
he was aided by the Utruni—the Stone Giants. And the
enmity with Squam began here too, more deadly than the
ravening whirl of the roaring Vorvor.

Yet none of this legend did Perry and Durek speak upon at
length, for the violence of the Vorvor was remote down
within the Quadran; and the distant whirling waters seemed to
twist around in silence, for only a winking glitter of the
far-off wheeling funnel reached up into the lofty aerie.

Durek glanced at the sky, gauging where stood the Sun.
"Here, Friend Perry," the Dwarf King counseled, "sit here."
And he led the Warrow to an unworked quartzen outcrop, in
part naturally shaped much the same as the bench of a
massive throne. "Look east to the peak of Ghatan, just there
where the high cleft and grey crag meet. And wait, for the
time is nearly upon us."

And so they waited in silence, Perry's gaze locked upon
the place Durek had directed. Slowly the Sun came unto the
zenith, and lo! a circlet of light bejewelled with five stars
sprang forth from deep within the crags. Perry looked in
wonder at the Dwarf King and saw that the studded circlet
and stars on Seventh Durek's armor were arrayed in the same
number and fashion as those reflected from the spire of
Ghatan.

"You see before you the Châkkacyth Ryng—the Dwarvenkith Ring," declared the Dwarf, "spangled with a star for
each Line of the Châkka Kindred. Ever has the Ryng lived in
our legends. Ever has it signified the unity of our Folk. And I
came to Kraggen-cor to claim the Ryng for myself and my
kith. But alas! I did not know the terrible cost that such a sigil
would bear.

"I now feel that I will be the last King of Durek's Folk,
and that after me we shall be no more. Oh, we shall not die,
nor leave Mitheor; but instead, I deem we must come together with others of our Race to merge our blood with theirs,

and the pure line of Durek will vanish. For if we do not meet and merge with others of our kind, Durek's Folk will fall into weakness and futility; our losses were staggering, and alone, we who were the mightiest cannot recover.

"Already Châkkadom is spread thinly, and our numbers gradually dwindle, for we are slow to bear young. I think that this War has sounded the death knell of the separate Châkka Kindred, and to survive, the Five Kith must become but one. Accordingly, I have sent out the word of our . . . victory— not only to Mineholt North, where my trothmate Rith and the families of my warriors even now prepare to join us, but also to the other Châk Kindred both near and distant, asking any who would come to do so.

"I brought you here, Friend Perry, to show you that Ryng, to show you that symbol of our dream: five stars upon a perfect circle. But I also wished to show you the cost of that dream—for as it can be with each great dream, sometimes the cost to the dreamer is staggering.

"All dreams fetch with a silver call, and to some the belling of that treasured voice is irresistible. And in many quests, the silver turns to dross, while in others, it remains precious; but in the harsh crucibles of some quests, the silver is transformed into ruthless metal. Such was the case with both of our dreams, Waeran, yours and mine: we answered to the lure of a silver call, but found instead cruel iron at quest's end. Yet what is done is done, and we cannot call it back, we cannot flee into yesterday.

"That does not mean that it is wrong to dream, nor does it mean that one should not reach for a dream. But it does mean that all dreams exact a price: sometimes trivial, sometimes more than can be borne.

"Some dreams are small: a garden patch, a rosebush, the crafting of a simple thing. Some dreams are grand: a great journey, a dangerous feat, the winning of a Kingdom. And the greater the dream, the greater the reward—yet the greater can be the cost. One cannot reach for a dream and remain unchanged, and that change is part of the cost of the dream. But when events go awry and disaster strikes, each of us who dreams must not let his spirit be crushed by the outcome.

"A person can be safe and never reach for his dream, never risk failure, never expose his spirit to the dangers inherent, but then he will never reap the rewards of a dream realized, and he might never truly live.

"Friend Perry, you reached for your dream, you grasped it, and held on to the very end. You found that the cost was high—higher than any of us had anticipated. And now you would go and rest and be at peace, and I believe you should. But do not hide away and brood, and fester, and become small in spirit; instead, rest, and reflect, and grow."

Durek then fell silent. And as the Sun passed beyond the zenith, Perry and the Dwarven King sat upon the Mountain Throne, and together they watched the Ring fade from sight— and as the glitter dimmed, the grasping bitterness gently fell away from the Warrow's heart, though the deep sadness remained. After a while, they stood and walked in silence back into Kraggen-cor, closing the bronze door behind.

The next morning, Cotton and Perry prepared to leave. They would head back through Kraggen-cor to Dusk-Door, and Silverleaf would go with them: Shannon was to be their guide through Lianion to the place called Luren. And as the Warrows prepared, so did Lord Kian; in the company of the Elves of Darda Erynian he would go east to the Rissanin River and then northeasterly to Dael, returning to Riamon and his Kingdom.

At last all was ready. Perry and Cotton, Shannon and Kian, all stood with Durek in the Great Chamber of the Sixth Rise. None knew what to say, for it was a sad moment. The Man looked to the center of the hall, to a white stone tomb—a tomb upon which lay an unadorned blackhandled sword of Riamon—a tomb wherein Prince Rand had been laid to rest in honor. And tears sprang into Kian's eyes. Durek followed the young Lord's gaze and said, "Your brother died in glory and is the only Man ever to be so honored by the Châkka."

Tears coursed down the cheeks of the Warrows, and Kian turned to them and pledged, "I shall come to the Boskydells after a time, and we'll have a pipe and speak of better things. Look for me in the spring, summer, or fall, not the next but perhaps the ones after; but do not look for me in the winter, for it will be bleak and stir up too many painful memories. I will come when the grief has faded to but an old sadness." He embraced the Waerlinga and clasped the forearm of Shannon and Durek, and without another word, turned and walked swiftly away through the lantern light, striding toward the Dawn-Gate, where awaited his escort of Elves.

"Fare you well," called Cotton after him, but Perry could say nought.

Then Perry and Cotton in turn took the hand of Durek and said goodbye. And Durek gave Cotton a small bag of silver pennies to see to their expenses on the way home, and a small silver cask, locked with a key, that they were not to open until they had returned to The Root—and what was inside was for the both of them. He returned to Perry the silveron armor; and the quarrel hole had been repaired by Durek himself, the arrow-shattered amber gem now replaced by a red jewel, and all the gems were now reinforced behind by starsilver links. And Durek bade him to put the armor on. Perry donned the mail but vowed, "I have had enough of fighting and War, and though I wear this armor, I will fight no more.

The Warrows and Shannon turned and began trudging west across the floor, along the Brega Path. Durek watched them go, and before they entered the west corridor he called out after them, "Perhaps I, too, will come to your Land of the Bosky."

And only silence followed.

The trio spent that night in the Grate Room, and the next morning they went on. When they came to the Bottom Chamber, Perry did not look at the cleft in the wall where Ursor had gone, but instead he hurried past with his eyes downcast to the stone floor. They came to the eight-foot-wide fissure and found that the Dwarves had constructed a wooden bridge over it to carry the supplies across, and the Warrows were relieved that they didn't have to leap above the dreadful depths of the Drawing Dark. Onward they went until they came to the stairs leading down to Dusk-Door, and at the bottom they found the gates standing wide and two Dwarves guarding the portal.

"This is where the Dark Mere was," said Cotton, pointing at the black crater, "and all that rock down there is what used to cover the Door." Perry looked at the tons of debris strewn

over the ancient courtyard, and wondered how the Dwarven
Army had ever managed to move all that mass.

In silence they passed the cairns along the Great Loom,
and only the sound of the free-flowing Duskrill intruded upon
their thoughts. As they came to the vale, Cotton called Perry's attention to the Sentinel Falls, now a silver cascade,
falling asplash upon a great mound of rock. "There stood the
dam that was broken, and down under that heap of stone is
the dead Monster." Perry looked on and shuddered.

That night they talked with members of the Dwarf Company at Dusk-Door and with two Valonian riders, messengers. They were told that most of the waggons now stood
empty, the supplies having been taken into Kraggen-cor.
Messages had been borne by rider south to Valon and Pellar
and the Red Hills, and Dwarven kindred would be coming
north to bring more supplies and to gather the wain horses
from the Vanadurin and to take the surplus waggons and
teams south. And some Dwarves would be coming north to
remain in Drimmen-deeve.

Durek had sent word to the Company of the Dusken Door
that Cotton, Perry, and Shannon would be coming, and a
waggon with a team had been prepared with the provisions
needed for the trip to Luren and to the Boskydells beyond.

The trio ate a short meal and then retired for the night.

The next morning, waving goodbye to the Dusk-Door Company, the trio in the wain started west down the Spur, Cotton
at the reins. They emerged along the foothills and turned
south, following the Old Rell Way toward the River Hâth.
The Old Way wended toward Gûnar, and slowly the waggon
rolled along its overgrown, abandoned bed. Shannon spoke of
the days when there was trade between the Realms of Drimmen-deeve and Lianion—called Rell by Men—and the city of
Old Luren, now destroyed. The roadbed they followed would
lead to the new settlement on the site of those ancient ruins.

In late morning they crested a ridge and looked down into a
wide grassy valley, where they saw a great herd of a thousand
horses grazing beside a glittering stream in the winter pasture.
Soon they came to the camp of the Harlingar, and there they
were hailed by raven-helmed Brytta. And the riders were
pleased to look once more upon the *Waldfolc*, and they

treated the Elf with the utmost respect. And the three travellers took a meal with the Vanadurin; and Brytta ate with his left hand while he loosed an occasional oath at the awkwardness caused by his tender bandaged right. And in his oathsaying, he was joined by his bloodkith, Brath, whose left arm was broken, and by Gannon with the shattered fingers, who was fed by both of them, much to his disgust and their amusement.

They spoke on the War, and talked of the final battle, and then Cotton asked the Valanreach Marshal to tell his tale.

Brytta told them of the desperate ride to Quadran Pass in pursuit of the foul Rutchen spies, and the ambush and battle with the ravagers. Brytta's voice dropped low when he spoke of the Drōkh who may have escaped, for the Marshal yet held himself at fault in this, even though it was now clear that whether or not the Drōkh had reached the High Gate to warn Gnar, it had had no bearing on the outcome. Brytta then spoke of the long dash back to the Ragad Valley, summoned by Farlon's recall beacon, only to find the vale empty of the Dwarf Army, the Host having entered the Black Hole. And he told of bringing the wounded and the herd south, and of setting the guard atop the Sentinel Stand to signal should the Wrg flee the Dwarves' axes out through the Dusk-Door: "But the Spawn never came . . ." His tale done, his voice dwindled to silence.

"Just so!" groused Wylf in the lull, his countenance chapfallen. "The Wrg never came . . . not while I was near. For during the battle of Stormhelm Defile, I was stuck atop Redguard Mount. And they came not the next night when I sat ambush on the road to Quadran Col. Nor did they flee out of the Door while I warded atop the Sentinel Stand. They never came to me, or to Farlon. We alone of all the brethren did not get to share in the great vermin-slaughter. Yet I suppose we served as well by watching for the enemy—though he never stood before us—and by tending the wounded and the herd. Even so, it seems that fortune could have thrown at least one or two Wrg our way."

"It was not ill fortune that kept the Spawn from you," declared Perry. "Rather, it was to your good, for War is bitter luck indeed." And the small Warrow fell silent and said no more, and Brytta looked at him with surprised eyes.

The Sun was bright and the air still, and in the grassy vale a gentle warmth o'erspread the land. All was quiet. But then the startling sound of sharp fife and tapping timbrel floated through the calm, and Perry saw nearby a loose circle of Brytta's Men sitting upon the earth. And from this circle came the pipe and tap. One by one the Men joined in the music, their hands clapping time to the air. Soon all there were sounding the beat, and some gave over their long-knives to comrades, who added the iron tocsin of blade on blade to the rhythm. Quickly the tune became more barbaric, wild fife and drum and steel on steel and strong hands clapping. And as Perry watched, a young warrior sprang to circle center and whirled 'round the fire, his feet stamping the earth, joining the savage beat. He spun and gyred and leapt high, and fierce shouts burst forth from his companions as the wild dancer whirled and tumbled and cartwheeled over the flames.

Perry's heart was tugged two ways, and he turned to Brytta: "How can they be so festive?" he asked, and his silent thoughts went on to add, *when so many have perished*.

Brytta's gaze strayed far away to a coppice of silver birch at the distant high eastern reach of the grassy vale. A great curving stone upjut on the mountain flanks cupped the grove, sheltering the clean-limbed trees from harsh mountain winds. Beyond Brytta's sight, but nevertheless seen by him, there, too, were five fresh mounds in the sward; five barrow mounds where five warriors slept the eternal sleep 'neath green turves: Arl, Dalen, Haddor, Luthen, and Raech, forever standing guard o'er the sheltered glen. And this dale became known in later years as the Valley of the Five Riders. It was said that weary, riderless horses often made their way to this place, to rest and heal and become strong again, to eat of the green grass and drink of the crystalline water springing forth from the stone bluff and flowing out and down through the peaceful land. And it was also said that at times in the dim twilight shadows or misty early dawn, the faint sound of distant oxen horns hovered on the edge of hearing.

Brytta's eyes rested momentarily upon the far wooded dell, and his sight misted over, and then he answered Perry: "It is not a gay dance, not a happy tune my scouts tap to. No, not festive; they are not festive. Yet in time they will be. For life continues, and grief fades."

Of a sudden, the wild piping and stamping dance, the
tattoo beat and steely claqué, and fierce clapping and savage
shouts, all stopped; silence fell heavily down upon the still
vale, and not an echo or whisper of the frenzied music
remained. And Perry looked and saw that deep dolor pressed
a heavy hand down upon them all.

At that moment, Hogon rode up leading two horses, and
Cotton shouted in glee, "Brownie! Downy!" And he leapt up
and ran to greet them as Hogon and Brytta smiled widely.

"We thought you would come hence," explained Hogon,
"so we have kept them nearby."

"Oh, thank you, Hogon; thank you, Brytta," bubbled
Cotton, and his face was aglow. "They are a sight for sore
eyes." Then he turned to the horses, and they nuzzled and
nudged the Warrow. "Why, you rascals, you've grown fat
and frisky in these parts! Wull, we're just going to have to
work some o' that stoutness off of you."

And so, when Perry, Cotton, and Shannon said goodbye to
the Men of Valon, it was Brownie and Downy in harness
pulling the waggon toward the south. And as they at last
crested the austral rim of the valley, the trio paused and
looked far back into the vale, and waved to the distant
Harlingar. And floating up to them on the breeze came the
lornly cry of Brytta's black-oxen horn: *Taaa-tan, tan-taaa,
tan-taaa! [Til we meet again, fare you well, fare you well!]*
And with that faint call echoing in their hearts, Cotton flicked
the reins and they passed from the sight of the Vanadurin.

The waggon rolled southward for two days, and just before
sunset of the second day, they reached the River Hâth. The
ford was shallow, and they made the crossing with ease. The
abandoned Old Way turned westward, and they followed its
course. They drove by day and camped at night, and because it was winter they found the days short and blustery and
the nights long and cold. They dressed as warmly as they
could, donning the quilted down-suits given to them by the
Dwarves; at night they camped in sheltered ravines and built
warm fires. Still, by night and day alike, the icy chill drove a
dull ache deeply into Perry's tender shoulder; and each morning when he awakened, his arm was stiff and could be moved
but gingerly.

*   *   *

On the evening of the sixth day from the Dusk-Door, they arrived at the Ford of New Luren. Here, the abandoned way they followed joined the Ralo Road, and when that track passed north of New Luren, it became known as the North Route by some and as the South Route by others, yet most called it the Post Road. Just above Luren, the rivers Hâth and Caire joined, and the ever-changing swirl of the waters of their meeting was named the Rivermix. From that point on down to the sea, the river was called Isleborne by all except the Elves, who named it the Fainen. At Luren crossed the trade routes between Rell, Gûnar, Harth, and Trellinath, for here was the only ford in the region. And on the west bank of the ford was the site of Luren.

Old Luren had been a city of free trade serving river traffic and road commerce from all the regions around. It had suffered mightily during the ancient Dark Plague—more than half its populace had died—but slowly it had recovered, and though it did not reach its former heights of commerce, still it was a city of importance. But then a great fire raged throughout the city, and Luren was devastated and abandoned.

It was not until about fifty years ago that New Luren sprang up on the site, mainly serving travellers going up and down the Post Road and the Ralo Road. New Luren was but a small village surrounded by the great Riverwood Forest, yet it had an inn—the Red Boar—where the food was plentiful, the beer drinkable, and the rooms snug and cozy. Cotton drove the waggon across the ford and into the village.

When the three travellers stepped across the threshold and into the Red Boar, all conversation among the locals came to a halt as they craned their necks to get a look at these strangers. At first the Lurenites thought a fair youth and two boys had entered the inn; but then Perry and Cotton doffed their warm jackets, and there before the patrons stood two small warriors in silver and golden armor—and the fair youth in green was suddenly recognized to be one of the legendary Elf Lords. And a murmur washed throughout the common room:

Lor! Look at that. One of the Eld Ones. A Lian! If these are people out of legend, then the two small ones must be Waerlinga, the Wee Folk.

The proprietor, Mister Hoxley Housman, stepped forth.

"Well now, sirs, welcome to the Red Boar," he boomed, drawing them toward the cheery fireplace, and unlooked-for tears sprang up in Cotton's eyes, for it was the first "proper place" he'd been in since that night, oh so long ago, at the White Unicorn in Stonehill.

The next morning was one of sadness, especially for Perry, for Shannon Silverleaf was turning back to Drimmen-deeve and then going beyond to Darda Galion. Three ponies had been purchased from innkeeper Housman, one for each of the Warrows to ride and one to carry their goods. Shannon would return the horses and waggon to the Dwarves.

Cotton stood outside saying goodbye to Brownie and Downy, while inside the Red Boar, Shannon looked at Perry and smiled. "Friend Perry, I, too, think I'll visit you in the Bosky—in summer, when the leaves are green and the flowers bloom and your gardens begin putting forth their fruit. Not this coming summer, but the next one instead, for I deem it will be that long ere all will be ready for that encounter. But fear not, I shall come, and I think others will too."

Together the Elf and the Warrow stepped out of the Red Boar to join Cotton; and the pair of buccen said their goodbyes to Shannon, and the Elf climbed up on the waggon and flicked the reins, and drove back in the direction of Luren Ford as the Warrows watched. Finally Perry and Cotton turned and clambered aboard their ponies and began the journey north and west, up the post Road toward the Boskydells, their pack pony trailing behind.

On the fourth day along the route, the Warrows came to a fork in the road: the Post Road turned northwards, heading for Stonehill; the left-hand road, the Tineway, swung westerly, making for Tine Ford on the Spindle River, and the Boskydells beyond. Along this way the buccen turned, and in the afternoon of the next day they came to the great Spindlethorn Barrier. Into the towering bramble they rode, following the way through the vast tangle. It was late afternoon when they crossed over Tine Ford and again entered the long thorny tunnel on the far side. Another hour or so they rode, and it was dusk when they finally emerged from the

Barrier and came into the region known as Downdell. At last they were back in the Boskydells.

On the west side of the Spindlethorn they stopped the ponies and dismounted and stood looking out upon the land. Cotton peered through the twilight to the north and west, and filled his lungs with air. "It sure does feel good to be back in the Bosky," he observed, "back from them *Foreign Parts*. Why, here even the air has the right smell to it, though it's winter and the fields are waiting for the spring tilling, if you take my meaning. But though we're back in the Dells, we've still got a good bit left to go before we're back to The Root—about fifty leagues or so. Right, Mister Perry?" And Cotton turned to Perry, awaiting his answer.

But Perry was gazing back toward the thorny growth, along the dark road that they had come, looking in the direction of faraway Kraggen-cor, and his eyes brimmed with tears. "Wha . .. what, Cotton? Oh yes, another fifty leagues and we'll be home." And he quickly brushed his eyes with his sleeve and began fumbling with his pony's cinch strap.

The way from the Spindle River toward Eastwood and beyond to Woody Hollow, though long, was not arduous. And the Warrows rode during the day and camped at night, as they had throughout their journeys. On the fourth morning after entering the Boskydells they awakened to a light snow- fall. They had camped south of Brackenboro on the eastern side of a trace of a road in the eaves of the Eastwood standing near. After breakfast they prepared to cut cross-country, strik- ing directly for Byroad Lane through Budgens to Woody Hollow.

As they rode, the snow thickened, but there was little wind and the flakes fell gently. And for the first time in a long, long while, Cotton burst into song, and soon he was joined by Perry:

> *The snowflakes fall unto the ground,*
> *In crystal dresses turning 'round,*
> *Each one so white,*
> *Their touch so light,*
> *And falling down upon the mound.*

Yo ho! Yo ho! On sleighs we go,
To slip and slide on a wild ride.
Yo ho! Yo ho! Around the bend,
I wish this ride would never end.

The snow lies all across the land
And packs and shapes unto the hand,
Rolls into balls,
Shapes into walls,
Makes better forts than those of sand.

Yo ho! Yo ho! Let's throw the snow,
From bright fort walls sling white snowballs.
Yo ho! Yo ho! Here comes a hat,
Let fly the snow, knock it kersplat!

Let fly the snow, knock it:
Kersplat!

And both Warrows found themselves laughing in glee.

They rode all through the daylight hours and came to Byroad Lane at dark. By then the snow was nearly a foot deep, and their ponies chuffed with the effort. Still the flakes swirled down thickly, but there was only a slight breeze, and neither Warrow was uncomfortable.

The ponies plodded through Budgens and past the Blue Bull. Yellow light shone out through the inn windows and across the white snow. Singing came from within; and as the two rode by, someone stepped through the door, and the song burst forth loudly, only to be muffled again when the door swung shut.

The Warrows rode on, and finally crossed the bridge over the Dingle-rill and passed beyond the mill. Their ponies plodded up into Hollow End, and they came at last to the curved hedge along the snow-covered stone walkway to The Root.

They had dismounted and were tethering the ponies to the hedge fence when the oaken door burst open, and out flew Holly. She hugged them both and kissed Perry. And Perry held her tightly and tears coursed down his cheeks, but he said nothing. And she held him close for a moment, and then drew them both inside. And there they found waiting a rich meal of roast goose and *three* places set at the table, for as Holly explained through her tears of happiness, "It's Year's End Eve, and I've been expecting you all day."

CHAPTER 10

THE HEROES

A year and a half had passed since Mister Perry and Cotton had come home, and the Bosky was bubbling with excitement. For on this day—Year's Long Day—there was to be a Ceremony. Oh, not just an *ordinary* Ceremony—with Mayor Whitlatch giving a speech and cutting a ribbon—but a real *King's* Ceremony. In fact, it was even better than that, for it was to be a *High King's Ceremony:* High King Darion *himself* had come with a great retinue to the Boskydells. But it wasn't only the High King that had come: it seemed as if every King in Mithgar was in the Dells . . .well, maybe not *every* King, but all the *important* ones had come; and the gossips and the tittle-tattles were having a field day:

There is that King from North Riamon, Kian, the one as what fought the Rūcks and such; there's that King Eanor from Valon and his Man Brytta, the ones as what came with all those horse riders; and lawks! there's even a Dwarf King, Durek, the one as what gave Mister Perry and Cotton that box of jools! Yes, and he's got that Dwarf with him the one as limps, Tobin something-or-other, and all his Company of Dwarf warriors what came in riding ponies, wouldn't you know, except for them two Dwarf striplings, them as what came riding on horses, just grinning and lording it as if they were doing something really special. But more, there's that Company of Elves with the Elf Lord, Vanidar Shannon Silverleaf, and if he ain't the King of the Elves, I'll eat my hat! And who knows what other Folks might come, what with more Outsiders *arriving all the time. Why, another whole bunch of them big Kingsguards rode in from Dael just this morning. Oh, it's a big day in the Bosky, alright, one that'll be remembered when it's long past.*

Yes, the Boskydells were all aflutter, because the *important* thing about the Ceremony was that all those Kings had come to honor two Warrows: Peregrin Fairhill and Cotton Buckleburr.

It's like the folks down to Budgens always say, ''Whenever them Kings get into trouble they allus find they got to call on a Warrow or two to settle them troubles, whatever they might be.''

But the folks of the Boskydells thought that the very *best* thing about the Ceremony was that right afterward there was going to be a big free meal down at the Hollow Commons, and everybody—I mean *everybody*—was invited.

And inside The Root, Holly fluttered about her husband of one year, getting him ready for the Ceremony. ''I'm so proud of you, Perry, and Cotton, too,'' she chatted as she straightened his cloak collar and brushed back a stray curl, thinking how splendid her buccaran looked in his starsilver armor. ''Imagine, you're to be named a Hero of the Realm.''

''Oh, piffle,'' protested Perry, uncomfortably, ''I'm not a hero. Anyone who's read my journal knows that I'm just an ordinary Warrow and not some great warrior.'' On the table by his bedside was his journal; it was open, and on the first page, in Perry's fine script, was written:

The Silver Call

A Tale of Quest and War as Seen by Two Warrows

The Journal of Peregrin Fairhill

''Well, I've read your journal,'' said Holly, ''and a lot of others have too: the Ravenbook Scholars, to name a few. And we all think that your story, and Cotton's, well, it's a tale of a noble quest.''

''Ah, but my dammia, that's just it,'' sighed Perry. ''My tale wasn't meant to be noble; it was meant to tell of the horror of War. I wanted to tell of War as it *really* is. In so many tales, none of the heroes ever get killed or even hurt.''

Perry paused, raising his hand to touch the blood-red jewel that marked the armor where the Rūck-arrow had pierced through. "Oh, some hearthtale heroes now and then have been slightly wounded, nothing more. But in most tales, only the villains die. And the heroes never suffer the pangs of fear or doubt, and the villains can't seem to do anything right. Well, that isn't what War is really like. In *real* War, many, many heroes are slaughtered, and feel fear, and make blunders. And the villains are victorious . . . oh, so often.

"And as to it being noble: this War, well, it was just fleeing and fighting and killing down in a great, dark hole in the earth. We slew living beings, Holly, without warning when we could—Rūcks and Hlōks to be sure, and an Ogru or two, but living things all the same."

"But it was necessary," insisted Holly. "Cotton says it was necessary; Kian says it was necessary; Shannon says it was necessary; Durek says so, and so does High King Darion, and all the Dwarves, Elves, and Big Men that have come to honor you."

"Necessary, yes; still it was abhorrent," said Perry. "And so many comrades, who didn't deserve to die, fell in battle. So who am I to be singled out with Cotton to be a hero? I'm just an insignificant character in the role of the world."

"Why, Mister Peregrin Fairhill, don't you go saying such a thing!" protested Holly, golden fire flashing deep in her great amber eyes. "If it weren't for you and Cotton, the maggot-folk would have won. They'd still be raiding and killing in the Lands around; and more: Shannon Silverleaf told me that if the Spawn had won, they would have started spreading out in the Grimwall Mountains again, and that would have spelled trouble for everyone. Why, they might even have tried to invade the Bosky after a time. But thanks to you and Cotton, that won't happen. You *are* Heroes of the Realm: Cotton's sword saved Durek from the Monster of the Mere, and Cotton was a Brega-Path guide, and he killed the Troll, and he carried the Horn of Narok; without Cotton doing those things, the quest would have failed. And you, Perry, you carried Bane that warned of maggot-folk, and you were a Brega-Path guide, and you found the key to the Gargon's Lair, and you solved the riddle of Narok; without you the Spawn would have won.

"Oh, you're heroes alright, but you just don't see that you are. Instead you say you are just some 'insignificant' character in the world. Well, don't you see that it is just the ones that you seem to think 'insignificant' that are truly important? It's on folks like you and Cotton that major events turn. Without you 'insignificant' ones, the world would fall before the cruel and evil.

"Now don't you go downplaying yourself just because you're a Warrow and not a King or a Big Man or a high Elf, or even a clever Dwarf. You're a Warrow, the best there is, and a Hero of the Realm, and that's why all the Kings are here to honor you and Cotton: King Eanor's Land of Valon is no longer being plundered; King Kian's subjects in Riamon no longer live in fear of Rūcks and Hlōks; and Shannon Silverleaf, Elf Lord of Darda Erynian, his Land of Galion is free of spoilers; the Halls of Kraggen-cor are once more filled with Dwarves, and King Durek reigns; and High King Darion, well, all is at peace in his Kingdoms again. And without you it would not have happened, and they've all come to pay you the highest homage because of it."

Not quite convinced, yet unwilling to argue further with his dammia, Perry stood still while Holly fastened the silver brooch at his collar. Again he fingered the blood-red jewel inset among the links of his armor; and deep within his shoulder there pulsed a dull ache, and he knew that within two days the weather would change. But he said nought and instead wished that these *formalities* would just get over and done with.

Holly, flicking one last invisible speck from Perry's cloak, stepped back and appraised her buccaran with a critical eye. "Well," she said at last, pride shining in her face, "it looks like you're ready. Now there's a Big Man waiting in the study with Cotton to escort you both before the assembled Kings. You'd better hurry on now before you're late."

Perry sighed and stepped out of the bedroom, and went down the hall and around the corner toward the study. As he approached that chamber, he saw an object on the table outside the study door. And his heart leapt, for it was a great black mace!

"Ursor!" he shouted, and ran into the room just as the great bear of a Baeran was getting to his feet. "Ursor!" cried

Perry, and he wept and laughed, and the Big Man smiled, and Cotton grinned from ear to ear.

"Well, little one," huge Ursor rumbled, "we meet again." And he caught up the wee Warrow and embraced him with a *whoof!* and then sat him down on the edge of a table like a small child, the buccan's feet dangling and swinging.

"Ursor, we thought you were dead!" exclaimed Perry, an incredulous look on his face. "What happened? How did you escape? Tell me before I burst with perplexity!"

"It's a long tale, and we can't be late before the Kings," smiled the Baeran, fingering a deep scar that ran down his left cheek from the corner of his eye to his jaw. "I'll tell it in full after the Ceremony. Let me just say that I decided to mislead the Spawn up the north passage from the underground river, to make certain that they didn't follow my Liege Lord, Kian, now King of North Riamon. My running battle with that company of Wrg in the undelved halls of the Black Hole lasted long, and I did nearly die, but it was of starvation and not by Rutchen hand. I was lost, but at last found my way to the Dwarves—or they to me, for Durek had sent them searching right after the great battle. And they finally found me, and I was saved, three days after you had gone.

"But we will speak of the full story later, for I want to hear your tale from your own lips too," declared Ursor, Commander of the Kingsguard of Riamon. "But now the Kingdom awaits its Heroes."

And so they stood and stepped into the hall, where Ursor took up his great black mace and hung it from his belt; and they strode to the oaken door of The Root. Ursor opened the portal, and the sunshine outside was bright.

Through the doorway Perry could see, to his wonder, the Kings of Pellar, Valon, Riamon, and Kraggen-cor, and an Elf Lord of Darda Erynian: each down upon one knee, paying high homage to him and Cotton. Beyond the Kings, all the knights and warriors and attendants—Men, Dwarves, and Elves—of all the retinues also knelt on one knee. And beyond them it seemed as if every Warrow of the Boskydells stood quietly in End Field, waiting.

Perry looked up at Ursor, and over at Cotton, and last of

all to Holly, and she beamed and inclined her head toward the open door. And Perry and Cotton, smiling, stepped forth into the sunshine, resplendent in their sparkling silver and glittering golden armor; and from the waiting multitude a mighty roar flew up to the sky.

The End

" . . . stature alone does not measure the greatness of a heart."

Lord Kian
October 7, 5E231

APPENDICES

A WORD ABOUT WARROWS

Common among the many races of Man throughout the world are the persistent legends of Little People: Wee Folk, pixies, leprechauns, sidhe, pwcas, gremlins, cluricaunes, peris, and so forth. There is little doubt that many of these tales come from Man's true memories of the Eld Days . . .memories of Dwarves, Elves, and others, harking back to the ancient times before The Separation. Yet, some of these legends *must* spring from Man's memory of a small Folk called Warrows.

Supporting this thesis, a few fragmentary records are unearthed once in a great age, records that give us glimpses of the truth behind the legends. But to the unending loss of Mankind, some of these records have been destroyed, while others languish unrecognized—even if stumbled across—for they require tedious examination by a scholar versed in strange tongues—tongues such as Pellarion—ere a glimmering of their true significance is seen.

One such record that has survived—and was stumbled across by an appropriately versed scholar—is *The Raven Book;* another is *The Fairhill Journal.* From these two chronicles, as well as from a meager few other sources, a factual picture of the Wee Folk can be pieced together, and deductions then can be made concerning Warrows:

They are a small Folk, the adults ranging in height from three to four feet. Some scholars argue that there seems to be little doubt that their root stock is Man, since Warrows are human in all respects—i.e., no wings, horns, tails, etc.—and they come in all the assorted shapes and colors that the Big Folk, the Men, do, only on a smaller scale. However, to the contrary, other scholars argue that the shape of Warrow ears—pointed—the tilt of their bright, strange eyes, and their longer life span indicates that some Elven blood is mingled in their veins. Yet their eyes do set them apart from Elvenkind: canted they are, and in that the two Folk are alike; but

Warrow eyes are bright and liquescent, and the iris is large and strangely colored: amber like gold, the deep blue of sapphire, or pale emerald green.

In any case, Warrows are deft and quick in their smallness, and their mode of living makes them wood-crafty and nature-wise. And they are wary, tending to slip aside when an *Outsider* comes near, until the stranger's intentions can be ascertained. Yet they do not always yield to intruders: should one of the Big Folk come unannounced upon a group of Warrows—such as a large family gathering of Othens splashing noisily in the waters of the fen—the *Outsider* would note that suddenly all the Warrows were silently watching him, the dammen (females) and oldsters quietly drifting to the rear with the younglings clinging to them or peering around from behind, and the buccen (males) in the fore facing the stranger in the abrupt quiet. But it is not often that Warrows are taken by surprise, and so they are seldom seen in the forests and fens and wilds unless they choose to be; yet in their hamlets and dwellings they are little different from "commonplace" Folk, for they treat with *Outsiders* in a friendly manner, unless given reason to do otherwise.

Because of their wary nature, Warrows usually tend to dress in clothing that blends into the background: greys, greens, browns. And the shoes, boots, and slippers they wear are soft and quiet upon the land. Yet, during Fair Time, or at other Celebrations, they dress in bright splashes of gay, gaudy colors: scarlets, oranges, yellows, blues, purples; and they love to blow horns and strike drum, gong, and cymbal, and in general be raucous.

Some of the gayest times, the most raucous, are those which celebrate the passing from one Warrow age to another, not only the "ordinary" birthday parties, but in particular those when an "age-name" changes: Children, both male and female, up to the age of ten are called "younglings." From age ten to twenty, the males are called "striplings," and the females, "maidens." From age twenty to thirty, males and females are called respectively "young buccen" and "young dammen." It is at age thirty that Warrows reach majority— come of age, as it were—and until sixty are then called "buccen," or "dammen," which are also the general names for male or female Warrows. (The terms "buccen" and "dammen" are plurals; by changing the "e" to an "a", "buccan" and "damman" refer to just one male or female Warrow.) After sixty, Warrows become "eld buccen" and "eld dammen," and beyond the age eighty-five are called respectively "granthers" and "grandams." And at each of these "special" birthday parties, drums tattoo, horns blare, cymbals clash, and bells ring; gaudy colors adorn the celebrants; and annually, on Year's Long Day, during Fair Time, bright fireworks light up the sky for all who have had a birthday or birthday anniversary in the past year—which, of course, includes everyone—but especially for those who have passed from one age-name to the next.

Once past their youth, Warrows tend to roundness, for ordinarily they eat four meals a day, and on feast days, five. As the elders tell it: "Warrows are small, and small things take a heap of food to keep 'em going. Look at your birds and mice, and look especially at your shrews: they're all busy gulping down food most of the time that they're awake. So us Wee Folk need at least four meals a day just to keep a body alive!"

Warrow home and village life is one of pastoral calm. The Wee Folk often come together to pass the day: the dammen klatch at sewings or cannings; the buccen and dammen gather at the field plantings and harvests, or at the raising or digging of a dwelling, or at picnics and reunions—noisy affairs, for Warrows typically have large families.

Within the home, at "normal" mealtimes all members of a household—be they master, mistress, brood, or servantry—flock 'round the table in one large gathering to share the food and drink, and to speak upon the events of the day. But at "guest" meals, customarily only the holtmaster, his family, and the guests come to the master's table to share the repast; rarely are other members of the holt included at that board, and then only when specifically invited by the head of the house. At meal's end, especially when "official business" is to be discussed, the younger offspring politely excuse themselves, leaving the elders alone with the visitors to deal with their "weighty matters."

Concerning the "hub" of village life, every hamlet has at least one inn, usually with good beer—some inns have the reputation of having better beer than the average—and here gather the buccen, especially the granthers, some daily, others weekly, and still others less frequently; and they mull over old news, and listen to new happenings, and speculate upon the High King's doings down in Pellar, and talk about the state that things have come to.

There are four strains of northern Warrows: Siven, Othen, Quiren, and Paren, dwelling respectively in burrows, fen stilt-houses, tree flets, and stone field-houses. (Perhaps the enduring legends concerning intelligent badgers, otters, squirrels, and hares, as well as other animals, come from the lodging habits of the Wee Folk.) And Warrows live, or have lived, in practically every country in the world, though at any given time some Lands host many Warrows while other Lands host few or none. The Wee Folk seem to have a history of migration, yet in those days of the *Wanderjahre* many other Folk also drifted across the face of the world.

In the time of the writing of both *The Raven Book* and *The Fairhill Journal*, most northern Warrows resided in one of two places: the Weiunwood, a shaggy forest in the Wilderland north of Harth and south of Rian; or in the Boskydells, a Land of fens, forests, and fields west of the Spindle River and north of the Wenden.

The Boskydells, by and far the largest of these two Warrowlands, is protected from *Outsiders* by a formidable barrier of thorns—Spindlethorns—growing in the river valleys around the Land. This maze of living stilettoes forms an effective shield surrounding the Boskydells, turning aside all but the most determined. There are a few roads within long thorn tunnels passing through the barrier, and during times of crisis, within these tunnels Warrow archers stand guard behind movable barricades made of the Spindlethorn, to keep ruffians and other unsavory characters outside while permitting ingress to those with legitimate business. In generally peaceful times, however, these ways are left unguarded, and any who want to enter may do so.

In that warm October of 5E231, when this tale begins, it was a time of peace.

An Abbreviated Family Tree
of Peregrin Fairhill

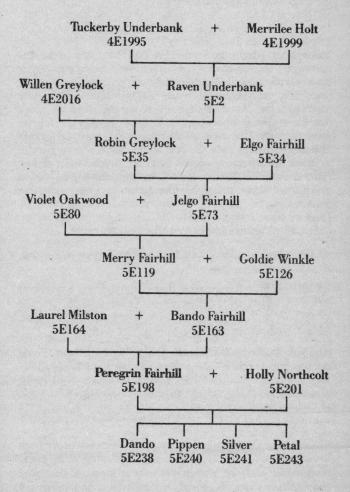

Tuckerby Underbank   +   Merrilee Holt
4E1995   4E1999

Willen Greylock   +   Raven Underbank
4E2016   5E2

Robin Greylock   +   Elgo Fairhill
5E35   5E34

Violet Oakwood   +   Jelgo Fairhill
5E80   5E73

Merry Fairhill   +   Goldie Winkle
5E119   5E126

Laurel Milston   +   Bando Fairhill
5E164   5E163

Peregrin Fairhill   +   Holly Northcolt
5E198   5E201

| Dando | Pippen | Silver | Petal |
| 5E238 | 5E240 | 5E241 | 5E243 |

CALENDAR OF THE SILVER CALL

Some Events of the Second Era

In the final days of the Second Era, the Great War of the Ban is fought. On the High Plane, Adon prevails over the Great Evil, Gyphon; on the Middle Plane, by an unexpected stroke the Grand Alliance is victorious and vile Modru is defeated upon Mithgar. Adon sets His Ban upon the creatures of the Untargarda, who aided Gyphon in the War: they are forever banished from the light of Mithgar's Sun, and henceforth those who would defy the Ban suffer the Withering Death. Gyphon, swearing vengeance, is exiled beyond the Spheres. Thus does the Second Era end and the Third Era begin . . . and so matters stand for some four thousand years, until the Fourth Era.

Some Events of the Fourth Era

4E1995: Tuckerby Underbank born in Woody Hollow, Eastdell, the Boskydells.

4E2013: Comet Dragon Star flashes through the heavens of Mithgar, nearly striking the world. Great flaming, gouting chunks score the night skies, some pieces hurtling to earth. Many see this hairy star as a harbinger of doom.

4E2018: Tuckerby Underbank, Danner Bramblethorn, Patrel Rushlock, and other Thornwalkers set out from Woody Hollow to join the Eastdell Fourth Company to walk Wolf Patrol and stand Beyonder Guard. This mission ultimately will become the quest that will culminate in Modru's downfall. In this year the Winter War begins.

4E2019: The Deevewalkers pass through Drimmen-deeve from Dusk-Door to Dawn-Gate; the Dwarf Brega is one of the Four. Also in this year, the Winter War ends as Modru is destroyed and Gyphon's Gate is closed. Rūcks, Hlōks, and Ogrus are slain or flee, and over the next few years many Spawn come to Drimmen-deeve to join the Horde there.

Some Events of the Fifth Era

October 15, 5E2: Raven Underbank is born in Woody Hollow, Eastdell, the Boskydells.

Circa 5E7: Tuckerby Underbank is commissioned by the High King to gather and record the history of the Winter War, a work that is to take his lifetime and will be called *Sir Tuckerby Underbank's Unfinished Diary and His Accounting of the Winter War.* In the work, Tuck will be assisted by many scholars and scribes, but mainly by his daughter Raven. In later years, Tuck will refer to the work as *The Raven Book.*

5E26: Brega the Dwarf, DelfLord of the Red Hills, at the urging of Tuckerby Underbank, records the Brega Scroll, detailing the path taken by the Deevewalkers through Kraggen-cor.

5E31: Raven Underbank marries Willen Greylock. They move to the Cliffs, Westdell, the Boskydells, where Willen founds the Ravenbook Scholars.

Circa 5E40: Tuckerby's Warren, The Root, becomes a museum housing artifacts of the Winter War.

Circa 5E47: Rumors abound of many Elves passing to Adonar upon the High Plane, leaving Mithgar behind.

December 31, 5E73: Eleventh Yule: Year's End Day: Tuckerby Underbank, Bearer of the Red Quarrel, 'Stone Slayer, Hero of the Realm, dies at the age of 97.

5E193: Brega, Bekki's son, DelfLord of the Red Hills, dies at the age of 242. Thus passes away the last of the mortal Heroes of the Winter War.

5E198: Peregrin (Perry) Fairhill born at the Cliffs.

5E205: Cotton Buckleburr born in Brackenboro, the Boskydells.

5E222: Perry makes his copy of *The Raven Book.*

5E228: Perry comes of age and moves to Woody Hollow as the new Scholar of The Root. Holly becomes homekeeper of The Root. Cotton is hired as general handywarrow of The

Root, where he becomes Perry's friend and companion. Perry discovers the Brega Scroll.

5E229: Gnar the Cruel arises as supreme leader of all Rūcks, Hlōks, and Ogrus in Drimmen-deeve; Raids in Riamon and Valon begin.

5E230: Seventh Durek, Dwarf King in Mineholt North, asks Lord Kian to guide Anval and Borin Ironfist, Dwarf warriors and Mastercrafters, to High King Darion in Pellar to advise him of the Dwarves' plans to reoccupy Drimmen-deeve. At court, the two Dwarves learn of the Spawn in Drimmen-deeve and pledge to cleanse the caverns of that evil. King Darion informs the Dwarves that the tale of the Deevewalkers, told in *The Raven Book*, in the Boskydells, may reveal detail of Drimmen-deeve's halls and passageways, detail useful in any War conducted in the caverns.

The Quest of Kraggen-cor
5E231

October 9: Lord Kian, Anval, and Borin arrive in Woody Hollow and come to The Root. Perry's copy of *The Raven Book* is examined, and the tale of the Deevewalkers is told. Perry shows the visitors the Brega Scroll, which has the detail the Dwarves seek. Perry has memorized the complicated Brega Scroll and volunteers to guide the Dwarves along the Brega Path.

October 10: Cotton decides to go with Perry on the quest.

October 11–12: Perry, Cotton, Anval, Borin, and Lord Kian leave The Root and Woody Hollow by waggon, heading for the rendezvous with Durek's Army at Landover Road Ford, beyond the Grimwall Mountains. Cotton sounds the Horn of the Reach in Budgens; the Dwarves examine the horn and regard it as a token of fear, muttering the word *Narok*. Travelling by the east-west Crossland Road, they stay at the Happy Otter Inn in Greenfields the first night out. Travel the next day carries them out of the Boskydells, and they camp in the eaves of Edgewood.

October 13–23: Travel eastward continues, and sword training begins. Nights are spent: encamped on the southern slopes slopes of the Battle Downs, at the White Unicorn Inn in Stonehill, and in encampments north of the Bogland Bottoms, at Beacontor, within the Wilderness Hills, along the margins of the Drearwood, and then at Arden Ford. The ford is flooded and they cannot cross.

October 24–26: Arden Ford floodwaters slowly recede. (Full Moon, October 26)

October 27–28: Arden Ford is crossed. Perry and Cotton are swept downriver by the floodwaters, but they are rescued. That night the comrades camp in the foothills of the Grimwall Mountains, and the next night up in the high country.

October 29: The travellers cross through the Crestan Pass, over the Grimwall Mountains. The waggon is destroyed by a rockslide.

October 30–31: The companions continue on foot toward the Landover Road Ford. In the foothills they meet Passwarden Baru and his sons. Marching onward, the travellers follow the Landover Road beyond the foothills and across the plains to come at last to the river-border forest along the Argon River, arriving at the ford to await Durek and the Dwarf Army.

November 1: Durek and the Army arrive at Landover Road Ford at midnight.

November 2: The Dwarf Army crosses the river. They are accompanied by forty riders of Valon who act as scouts, led by Brytta, Marshal of the North Reach. Also, Lord Kian's brother, Rand, is with Durek. The Warrows discover that Lord Kian is heir to the Throne of North Riamon. The Council of Durek is held. It is decided that the Army will march over the mountains and south to Dusk-Door and try to enter; it is also decided that a small squad will not cross the mountains, but instead will go south down the Argon River and then west across the wold and attempt to sneak through Dawn-Gate and penetrate the length of the Spawn-infested caverns and, from the inside, repair the hinges of Dusk-Door, if they are broken. Cotton is to go with Rand, Durek, Brytta, and the Army as their Brega-Path guide; Perry is to go with the squad, consisting of Lord Kian and the Dwarves Anval,

Borin, Barak, Delk, and Tobin. That night, Durek tells Perry and Cotton the Legend of Narok, a riddle of the silver horn foretelling a doom of sorrow to befall the Dwarves.

November 3: The Army and Cotton leave the ford and march toward the Crestan Pass, heading over the Grimwall Mountains toward Dusk-Door, on the west side of the range.

The Squad and Perry stay at the ford, and Kian outlines how to build a raft.

November 4: The Army arrives at the Passwarden's cottage in the foothills.

The Squad cuts logs for the raft.

November 5: The Army marches to the edge of the timberline below the Crestan Pass. Late at night, Rolf, Baru's son, arrives and warns that the cold wind blowing down means that a blizzard is on the way.

The Squad fashions the log bed of the raft.

November 6: The Army crosses the Crestan Pass in a blizzard and struggles to a sheltering pine forest on the far side of the mountains.

The Squad completes the raft, and a cold rain begins that evening.

November 7: The blizzard continues, trapping the Army in the shelter of the pines.

The Squad embarks downriver and arrives at Great Isle by nightfall; the cold rain continues.

November 8: The blizzard ends, but the Army is snowbound; the digout begins.

The rain ends and the river brings the Squad to the far northern reaches of the Dalgor March.

November 9: The dig-out ends at sundown, and the Army moves down out of the snow.

The Squad floats past the mouth of the Dalgor River and comes to the far southern reaches of the Dalgor March.

November 10: The Army begins a forced march to Dusk-Door; they are three days behind schedule because of the blizzard.

The Squad rides the raft through the Race, and at nightfall

they come to the final campsite on the river; Drimmen-deeve and Dawn-Gate lie five days' march overland to the west.

November 11–14: The Army forced march continues; rain on the thirteenth causes waggons to mire and the march is slowed.

The Squad makes final plans while waiting to set out for Dawn-Gate.

November 15: The Army forced march continues.

A Rücken raiding party falls upon the Squad: Barak is slain; Tobin is wounded; the Squad is saved by the Elf Shannon Silverleaf, Ursor the Baeran, and a company of Elf warriors.

November 16: The Army forced march continues.

Barak's funeral is held. Tobin is borne toward Darda Erynian by the Elf Company. Shannon and Ursor join the Squad.

November 17–21: The Army's forced march ends on the eighteenth as they draw nearly even with their schedule, and they continue at a normal pace toward Dusk-Door, passing beyond the old road that leads up toward Quadran Pass on the twentieth. Brytta learns of a legendary but lost High Gate in the Pass and posts a guard to watch for Spawn should they come from that way.

The Squad marches over the wold toward Dawn-Gate. On the twentieth they arrive at the foothills that border the valley leading onto the Pitch. The Squad arrives at Drimmen-deeve on the twenty-first.

November 22: The Army arrives at Dusk-Door, one day late.

The Squad enters Drimmen-deeve through Dawn-Gate and slays the guards and a large number of *Spaunen*. The Squad crosses the Great Deep and finds a way around the collapsed Hall of the Gravenarch.

November 23: The Army begins removal of the rubble blocking the way into Dusk-Door. At sunset the Krakenward attacks. The battle between the Army and the Monster rages all night.

The Squad sneaks to the Grate Room, about halfway to

Dusk-Door, where they are discovered by *Spaunen* and flee to the Gargon's Lair and are trapped.

November 24: The Krakenward is finally slain by the Army at dawn. A short while later, one of the Valonian scouts left at Quadran Pass arrives bearing news that the Dwarf Army has been discovered by Rūcken spies now fleeing for the High Gate in Quadran Gap. Brytta's riders depart on a desperate mission to intercept the Spawn. At Dusk-Door, rubble removal begins again; cairns are built for the many Dwarf dead.

That night, Brytta's force springs a trap on the Rūcken spies, slaying all, they think, but one Hlōk, who may have escaped to warn Gnar.

The Squad free themselves from the Gargon's Lair, but Delk, the last Gatemaster, is slain. Later, the Squad finds the underwater path to again elude the Spawn.

November 25: The stone rubble covering Dusk-Door is finally removed; the Dwarf Army enters Kraggen-cor at midnight. (Full Moon)

Just after midnight, a Valanreach recall beacon in Ragad Valley is lit, and Brytta's force, not knowing the reason for the balefire, begins a race from Stormhelm Defile to the vale.

The Squad topples the stone blocking the way into the Bottom Chamber. Kian, Shannon, and Ursor mislead the *Rûpt* while Perry, Anval, and Borin press on toward Dusk-Door through Spawn-infested passages. Kian and Shannon are separated from Ursor.

November 26: The Army rescues Perry, Anval, and Borin from a company of Spawn. The Host marches toward the Second Hall. Kian and Shannon are rescued at the Grate Room.

Brytta's force arrives back at the Valley of the Door to find the Dwarves have entered Kraggen-cor. The Vanadurin withdraw to a grassy vale to tend the wounded and to put the Dwarves' great herd of horses to pasture.

November 27: The Army arrives at the War Hall.

November 28: The final battle is fought between the Spawn and the Dwarves in Kraggen-cor; Perry is wounded. Many comrades are slain. The Horn of Narok is sounded and the *Spaunen* Horde is destroyed.

November 29 to December 13: Perry sufficiently recovers from his wound so that on the thirteenth he decides to return to The Root.

December 14–15: Perry, Cotton, and Shannon travel the Brega Path to Dusk-Door and leave Drimmen-deeve.

December 16–21: Perry, Cotton, and Shannon travel from Drimmen-deeve to New Luren. On the sixteenth they pass through the valley where the Vanadurin tend the herd, and they bid farewell to Brytta and his Men. On the twenty-first the three come to New Luren, where they stay overnight in the Red Boar Inn.

On the seventeenth, a Dwarf search party finds Ursor alive but starving in the caverns.

December 22: Shannon turns back from New Luren, heading for Drimmen-deeve and beyond to Darda Erynian. Perry and Cotton, riding ponies, leave New Luren for the Boskydells.

December 23–29: Perry and Cotton follow the Post Road to the Tineway, crossing Tine Ford and entering the Boskydells on the twenty-sixth. (Full Moon, December 25)

December 30: Year's End Eve. Snow. Perry and Cotton arrive in the evening at The Root. End of Quest.

Three Later Events

5E232: Perry writes *The Silver Call*, a journal of the quest. **June 5:** Perry marries Holly Northcolt.

5E233: June 21: Year's Long Day: Perry and Cotton are named Heroes of the Realm by High King Darion. The Ceremony is attended by High King Darion of Pellar, King Kian of Riamon, King Eanor of Valon, King Durek of Kraggencor, Elf Lord Vanidar Shannon Silverleaf of Darda Erynian, Ursor the Baeran, Brytta of the Valanreach, Tobin Forgefire, and many Elves, Dwarves, and Men of the Realm, and by a great number of Boskydell Warrows.

SONGS, INSCRIPTIONS, AND REDES

[Listed by: type; title; first line; volume and chapter(s) of appearance]

Warrow saying: Brave as Budgens (Vol. I, Chap. 6)

Warrow song: "Song of the Night Watch": The flames, they flicker, the shadows dance (Vol. I, Chap. 6)

Free Folk saying: Vulg's black bite slays at night (Vol. I, Chap. 7)

Inscription on the Tomb of Othran: Blade shall brave vile Warder (Vol. I, Chap. 7)

Stonehill song: "The Battle of Weiunwood": From northern wastes came Dimmendark (Vol. I, Chap. 7)

Warrow song: "The Road Winds On": The Road winds on before us—(Vol. I, Chap. 8)

Dwarf rhyme: "Time's Road": The Past, the Present, the Future (Vol. I, Chap. 8)

Warrow saying: Yesterday's Seeds are Tomorrow's Trees (Vol. I, Chap. 8)

Warrow saying: Word from the Beyond (Vol. I, Chap. 10)

Dwarf pledge: *Shok Châkka amonu!* (Vol. I, Chaps. 13, 14; Vol. II, Chap. 6)

Dwarven inscription on the Horn of Narok: Answer to/The Silver Call (Vol. I, Chap. 13)

Dwarven (?) staves: *The Rime of Narok:* Trump shall blow (Vol. I, Chap. 13; Vol. II, Chap. 8)

Elven dirge: From mountain snows of its birth (Vol. I, Chap. 17)

Dwarf War cry: *Châkka shok! Châkka cor!* (Vol. I, Chap. 3; Vol. II, Chaps. 4, 6, 7)

184

Vanadurin benediction: Arise, Harlingar, to Arms! (Vol. II, Chap. 5)

Valonian Battle cries: Hál Vanareich! (Vol. II, Chap. 5)

Warrow song: "Yo Ho! Yo Ho! Here Comes the Snow!": The snowflakes fall unto the ground (Vol. II, Chap. 9)

TRANSLATIONS OF WORDS
AND PHRASES

Throughout *The Fairhill Journal* appear many words and phrases in languages other than the Common Tongue, Pellarion. For scholars interested in such things, these words and phrases are collected in this appendix. A number of tongues are involved:

Châkur	=	Dwarven tongue
OHR	=	Old High tongue of Riamon
OP	=	Old tongue of Pellar
Slûk	=	Spawn tongue
Sylva	=	Elven tongue
Twyll	=	ancient Warrow tongue
Valur	=	ancient War-tongue of Valon

The following table is a cross-check list of the most common terms found in various tongues in *The Raven Book* and *The Fairhill Journal*.

	——Men——			
Warrow (Twyll)	Valon (Valur)	Pellar (Pellarion)	Elf (Sylva)	Dwarf (Châkur)
Rūck	Rutch	Rukh	Ruch	Ùkh
Rūcks	Rutcha	Rukha	Rucha	Ùkhs
Rūcken	Rutchen	Rukken	Ruchen	Ùkken
Hlōk	Drōkh	Lōkh	Lok	Hrōk
Hlōks	Drōkha	Lōkha	Loka	Hrōks
Hlōken	Drōken	Lōkken	Loken	Hrōken
Ghūl	Guul	Ghol	Ghūlk	Khōl
Ghûls	Guula	Ghola	Ghūlka	Khōls
Ghūlen	Guulen	Gholen	Ghûlken	Khōlen

Warrow (Twyll)	Men: Valon (Valur)	Men: Pellar (Pellarion)	Elf (Sylva)	Dwarf (Châkur)
Dread	Dread	Dread	Dread/*Draedan*	Dread
Gargon	Gargon	Gargon	Gargon	Ghath
Gargons	Gargons	Gargons	Gargoni	Ghaths
Ogru	Ogru	Troll	Troll	Troll
Kraken	Kraken	Kraken	Hèlarms	Madûk
maggot-folk	Wrg	Yrm	*Rûpt*	Grg
Spawn	Spawn	Spawn; *Spaunen*	*Spaunen*	Squam
Dwarf	Dwarf	Dwarf	Drimm	Châk
Dwarves	Dwarves	Dwarves	Drimma	Châkka
Dwarven	Dwarven	Dwarven	Drimmen	Châkka
Elf	Deva	Elf	Lian;* Dylvan	Elf
Elves	Deva'a	Elves	Lian; Dylvana	Elves
Elven	Deven	Elven	Lianen; Dylvanen	Elven
Giant	Giant	Utrun	Utrun	Utrun
Giants	Giants	Utruni	Utruni	Utruni
Warrow	Waldan	Waerling	Waerling	Waeran
Warrows	Waldana	Waerlinga	Waerlinga	Waerans
Wee Folk	*Waldfolc*	Wee Folk	—	—

*The Elves consist of two strains: (1) the Lian, the First Elves, and (2) the Dylvana, the Wood Elves.

In the following text, words and phrases are listed under the tongue of origin. Where possible, direct translations () are provided; in other cases, the translation is inferred from the context {} of *The Fairhill Chronicle* or *The Raven Book*. Also listed is the more common name [], where applicable.

Châkur
(Dwarven Tongue)

Aggarath {stone-loom} [Grimspire]
Baralan {sloping land} [the Pitch]
Châk (Dwarf)
Châk-alon {Dwarf pure-spirit}
Châkkacyth Ryng (Dwarvenkith Ring)
Châka dök! (Dwarves halt!)
Châkka shok! Châkka cor! (Dwarven axes! Dwarven might!)
Châk-Sol (Dwarf-Friend)
Ctor (shouter) [Bellon Falls]
Daūn {sunrise} [Dawn]
DelfLord {Lord of the delvings}
Dēop {deep}
Dusken {sundown}
Faugh! {untranslated exclamation of contempt or disgust}
Gaard! {a Wizard-word perhaps meaning Move!; Act!}
Ghatan {ringmount = Mountain of the (Châkkacyth) Ring} [Loftcrag]
Ghath (horror) [Gargon]
Hauk! (Advance!)
Hola! {Untranslated exclamation used to express surprise or to call attention}
Kala! (Good!)
Khana (Breakdeath)
Khana Durek! (Breakdeath Durek!)
Kraggen-cor {Mountain-might} [Drimmen-deeve]
Kruk! {untranslated expletive of frustration or rage}
Madûk {evil monster} [Hèlarms, Kraken, Krakenward, Monster]
Mitheor {mid-earth} [Mithgar]
Mountain {living stone} [living stone, mountain]
Narok (Death-War)
Rávenor {storm hammer} [Stormhelm; the Hammer]
Shok Châkka amonu! (The axes of the Dwarves are with you!)
trothmate {true-pledged mate}

Uchan {anvil} [Greytower]
Vorvor {wheel} [Durek's Wheel]
ziggurt {shatter-rock}

OHR
(Old High Tongue of Riamon)

myrk {murk}
swordthane {sword warrior}

OP
(Old Tongue of Pellar) ·

Larkenwald {lark wood} [Darda Galion; Eldwood]
Rach! {untranslated expletive expressing frustration}
Untargarda {Under Worlds}
Weiunwood {wee-one-forest}

Slûk
(Spawn Tongue)

Glâr! (fire)
Gnar skrike! {Gnar commands!}
Ngash batang lûktah glog graktal doosh spturrskrank azg!
{untranslated invective}
Ptang glush! {After them!}
Sklurr! {Now!}
Tuuth Uthor {dread striker; fear lash}
Waugh! {untranslated exclamation expressing startled fright}

Sylva
(Elven Tongue)

Aevor {wind-dark = Darkwind Mountain} [Grimspire]
Alor (Lord)
Chagor {jag-top} [Loftcrag]
Coron (king/ruler) [Stormhelm]
Dara {Lady}
Darda Erynian {leaf-tree hall-of-green = Greenhall Forest}
[Greenhall Forest; the Great Greenhall; Blackwood (of old)]

Darda Galion {leaf-tree land-of-larks = Forest of the Silver-larks} [Larkenwald; Eldwood]
Draedan (Dread One) [Gargon]
Drimm (Dwarf)
Drimmen-deeve (Dwarven-delvings) [Kraggen-corr]
Dylvana {wood-Elves}
Falanith {valley rising} [the Pitch]
Gralon {grey stone} [Greytower]
gramarye {spell-casting} [sorcery]
Hèlarms {hell arms} [Kraken, Krakenward, Madûk, Monster]
Lian {First Elves}
Lianion {first land}
mian {waybread}
Mithgar {mid-earth}
Ogruthi {Trollfolk}
Vanidar (vani = silver; dar = leaf) [Silverleaf]
Vanil (silvery)
Vani-lērihha (Silverlarks)

Twyll
(ancient Warrow Tongue)

Cor! {untranslated exclamation used to express wonderment}
Hoy! {untranslated exclamation used to express surprise or to call attention}
Lawks! {Lord!; Mercy!; Lord of mercy!; Lord have mercy!}
Lor! {Lord!}
Lumme! {Love me!}
Wanderjahre (wandering days)

Valur
(ancient Battle-tongue of Valon)

A-raw, a-rahn! (A foe, alert!) [Valonian horncall]
Ai-oi! {untranslated exclamation to express astonishment or to call attention}
Arn! {untranslated interjection used to express ironic reversal}
B'reit, Harlingar! (Ready, Sons of Harl!)
Dracongield {Dragon-gold}
Dwarvenfolc {Dwarvenfolk}

Garn! {untranslated expletive used to express disappointment or frustration}

Hahn! (Here!) [Valonian horncall]

Hai roi! {untranslated exclamation, an enthusiastic call of greeting}

Hál! (Hail!)

Hál Vanareich! (Hail Valon!) {Hail our nation!}

Harlingar (Sons of Harl) [Men of Valon]

Hèl {Hell}

Hola! {untranslated exclamation used to express surprise or a greeting}

Kop'yo V'ttacku Rutcha! (Now whelm the goblins!)

Rach! {untranslated exclamation used to express frustration}

Skut! {untranslated exclamation used to express rage or frustration}

Stel! (Steel!)

Ta-roo! Ta-roo! Tan-tan, ta-roo! (All is clear! All is clear! Horsemen and allies, the way is clear!) [Valonian horncall]

Taaa-tan, tan-taaa, tan-taaa! (Til we meet again, fare you well, fare you well!) [Valonian horncall]

Tan-ta-ra {Answer me} [Valonian horncall]

Tovit! (Ready!)

Valanreach {Valon-reich}

Vanadurin {bond-lasting = our lasting bond}

V'ttacku! (Attack!)

Waldfolc {wood-folk = folk of the woods} [Warrows]

A NOTE ON
THE LOST PRISON

As to the Gargon's Lair: It remains uncertain to this day whether or not the chamber was delved specifically to be a prison for the Gargon. It seems more likely that the room was delved as a treasure store, and the Gargon, fleeing Adon's Ban, became trapped when the door closed behind it, and the creature had not the means or the power to escape. But then we are left with the mystery of whom the room belonged to, and why they did not inadvertently release the Dread when visiting the chamber.

Concerning this second point—why they did not accidentally free the creature—perhaps the unknown delvers knew the Gargon was trapped inside the room; in fact, they might have sprung the trap knowing the evil Vûlk would be captured in the chamber.

As to who delved the room, that, too, is a mystery; the work was both like and yet unlike that of the Lian (see Volume II, Chapter 3); but we know from Dwarven lore that the Châkka believe that the Eld Durek was the first to stride Kraggen-cor when he survived the Vorvor (see Volume II, Chapter 9); and then he brought his folk to make it into a mighty Kingdom, and that was ere the Ban War; which leads to the following dilemma: Would the Dwarves permit the Lian to delve a Vûlk prison or a treasure store within the Dwarven Realm? On the other hand, had the Dwarves known of the chamber, would they later have forgotten and delved the starsilver shaft toward the prison? Perhaps they knew of the chamber but not that the Gargon could burst through stone walls and layers of mineral-veined rock.

The runes "west-pick" were vaguely similar to those of the Lian. The chamber was like yet unlike Lian work. Dwarves learned much craft from the Lian, according to Delk (see Volume II, Chapter 3). Yet whether the chamber was Dwarven-delved, Elven-delved, or Other-delved, many questions remain unanswered.

Elven lore spoke of the Lost Prison, and maintained that great evil was entrapped beneath the Grimwall; yet how they knew of it is not told. It was further believed by the Elves that Modru, preparing for the coming of the Dragon Star, somehow used his evil art to cause the Dwarves to drive a silveron shaft toward the Gargon's Lair, according to Silverleaf (see Volume II, Chapter 3). And thus it was Modru who caused the Gargon to be freed.

If not Dwarf-delved, or Lian-delved, then who made the chamber? Ravenbook Scholars continue to debate the issue. Most believe the room was delved as a treasure store by a group of Dwarves with Lian help. The Scholars further believe that all those who knew of it, and of the silveron lode, were later slain in the Great War of the Ban, and thus the secret of the chamber died with them, though rumors of the chamber's existence persisted. It is also the general belief that the Gargon accidentally trapped itself within the chamber as it was fleeing from Adon's Covenant, but that somehow this became known to the Lian Guardians, who then told of the vile creature trapped in the legendary Lost Prison.

Recall the words of Barak (see Volume I, Chapter 17): "Some doors lead to secret treasure rooms, or secret weapons rooms, or secret hideaways . . . Yet such rooms must be entered with caution, for once inside the door may close and vanish, trapping the unwary in a sealed vault—it is a defence against looters and other evil beings . . . without the key, even a Wizard or evil Vûlk cannot pass through some hidden doors." Ravenbook Scholars believe that Barak essentially described how the Gargon came to be entrapped in that chamber, but none profess to know how the chamber itself came into being.

GLOSSARY

In this glossary:	
Châkur =	Dwarven tongue
OHR =	Old High tongue of Riamon
OP =	Old tongue of Pellar
Slûk =	Spawn tongue
Sylva =	Elven tongue
Twyll =	ancient Warrow tongue
Valur =	ancient War-tongue of Valon

(the) Account: Tuckerby Underbank's accounting of the Winter War as told to the scriveners of *The Raven Book*. Also the accounts of others recorded in the same book.

Adon: the high deity of Mithgar. Also known as High Adon, the High One, The One.

Adonar: the world on the High Plane, where Adon dwells. Also known as the High World.

Adon's Covenant. See (the) Ban.

Aevor (Sylva: wind-dark): Elven name for Grimspire (q.v.) meaning Darkwind Mountain.

age-names: names used by Warrows to indicate their general ages. These names change as Warrows grow older (see Appendix: A Word About Warrows).

Aggarath (Châkur: stone-loom). See Grimspire.

Ai-oi: an exclamation of surprise or to call attention.

ale-night: Cotton's term for a drinking bout.

(the) Alliance: the forces of Men, Elves, Dwarves, and Warrows opposed to Modru's forces in the Winter War. Also the name by which the Weiunwood Alliance was at times known.

(the) Allies: Folk of the Alliance. Also a general term given to any alliance of Free Folk.

Alor (Sylva: Lord): an Elven word meaning Lord.

Alor Vanidar (Sylva: Lord Silverleaf). See Vanidar.

amonu (Châkur: are with you): Dwarven term meaning "are with you."

Anval Ironfist: a Dwarf of Durek's Folk. Brother of Borin Ironfist. Masterwarrior. Mastercrafter. Member of the Squad of Kraggen-cor. Hero of the War of Kraggen-cor. Slain by Gnar in the Battle of Kraggen-cor.

Arbagon Fenner: a buccan Warrow of the Weiunwood. Leader of the Wee Folk in Weiunwood during the Winter War.

Arden. See Arden Valley.

Arden Falls: a cataract between high canyon walls at the narrow mouth of Arden Valley. The mist from this waterfall hides the valley from the view of outsiders.

Arden Ford: a ford along the Crossland Road where it crosses the Tumble River near Arden Valley.

Arden Gorge. See Arden Valley.

Arden Vale. See Arden Valley.

Arden Valley: a forested valley of crags in the north of Rell. Home of Talarin's band of Lian Guardians. Perhaps deserted in the time of the War of Kraggen-cor. Site of the Hidden Stand. The Hidden Refuge. Two hidden entrances lead into the Vale: the one in the north is a tunnel-like cavern through Arden Bluff; the one in the south is a road beneath and behind Arden Falls. Also known as Arden, Arden Gorge, Arden Refuge, Arden Vale, the Hidden Stand, the Hidden Vale, the Refuge.

(the) Argon River: a major river in Mithgar, running along the eastern flank of the Grimwall Mountains and emptying into the Avagon Sea. Also known as the Great Argon River and as the Great River Argon.

Arin: an Elfess. Companion of Egil One Eye in the Quest of the Green Stone of Xian.

Arl: A Man of Valon. One of the riders in Brytta's force. Slain at the Battle of Stormhelm Defile. One of the Five Riders (q.v.).

(the) Army: generally taken to mean any Army of the Free Folk.

Arn (Valur: untranslated interjection): an oathword of Valon used to express ironic reversal.

(the) Arrow Bearer. See Tuckerby Underbank.

Atala: a continent that cataclysmically drowned beneath the sea. Also known as the Lost Land.

(the) Atalar Blade: a long-knife of the Lost Land, found in the tomb of Othran the Seer by Tuck. Borne by Galen, who used the blade against the Krakenward to save Gildor. Borne by Patrel during the Battle of Challerain Keep. Placed on display at Tuckerby's Warren after the Winter War. Borne to the War of Kraggen-cor by Cotton, where it was used again to wound the Krakenward to help save Durek.

Aurion: a Man of Pellar. High King of Mithgar. Slain at the Battle of Challerain Keep during the Winter War. Known as Aurion Redeye because of a scarlet eye-patch worn over an eye blinded in combat against the Rovers of Kistan when he was a young Man. Also known as King Redeye and as Redeye.

(the) Avagon Sea: a sea bordering upon the southern flanks of Garia, Pellar, Jugo, Hoven, Tugal, and Vancha; on the eastern flanks of Alban, Hurn, and Sarain; and on the northern flanks of Chabba, Karoo, and Hyree. The great island of Kistan is in the western Avagon Sea.

Aven: a Realm of Mithgar. Bounded on the north by the Grimwall and on the south by North Riamon.

Aylesworth Brewster: a Man of Stonehill. Husband of Molly. Owner of the White Unicorn Inn.

Baeron (singular: Baeran): Men of great strength living in the northern vales of the River Argon and in the forest of Darda Erynian. This branch of Mankind fought with the Alliance against Modru's Hordes during the Winter War. Also known as the woodsmen of the Argon vales.

Baeron Holds: dwelling places of the Baeron.

balefire: a signal fire used to summon help or to communicate disaster.

(the) Ban: Adon's banishment of all the creatures of the Untargarda from the light of Mithgar's Sun as punishment for aiding Gyphon during the Great War. Daylight strikes dead any who defy the Ban: their bodies shrivel into dry husks and blow away like dust; this is called the Withering Death. Some creatures of Mithgar, such as some Dragons, also suffer the Ban—but in the case of Dragons, although they die, they do not suffer the Withering Death. Also known as Adon's Covenant, the Covenant, the Eternal Ban, High Adon's Ban, High Adon's Covenant.

Bane: an Elven-blade forged in the House of Aurinor in the Land of Duellin for use in the Great War. Bane, a long-knife, is one of several Lian sharp-edged weapons equipped with a blade-jewel that shines with a werelight when Evil is near; the light of Bane is blue. Bane was borne by Gildor and Tuck during the Winter War. Tuck used the blade to wound the Gargon. Bane was placed on display in Tuckerby's Warren after the Winter War. Bane was borne on the Quest of Kraggen-cor by Peregrin Fairhill and aided the Squad of Kraggen-cor on their mission. Used by Cotton to cause the death of one of the Cave Trolls during the Battle of Kraggen-cor. Also known as Troll's Bane.

(the) Ban War. See (the) Great War.

Barak Hammerhand: a Dwarf of Durek's Folk. Gatemaster. A member of the Squad of Kraggen-cor. Slain by Rūcks on the banks of the Argon during the Battle of the Last River Camp.

Baralan (Châkur: sloping land). See (the) Pitch.

(the) Barrier. See (the) Spindlethorn Barrier.

(the) barrow of Othran the Seer. See Othran's Tomb.

Baru: a Baeran Man. Warden of the Crestan Pass in 5E231.

(the) Battle Downs: a Wilderland range of hills to the west of the Weiunwood. Here was fought a mighty series of battles during the Great War.

(the) Battle of Budgens: a Winter-War battle at the village of Budgens, where Warrows trapped Ghûlen reavers in an ambush. The first battle of the Struggles (q.v.).

(the) Battle of Kaggen-cor: the last great battle of the War of Kraggen-cor. Fought between Gnar's Horde and Durek's Legion in the vast War Hall. Many perished. The Dwarves were barely victorious as the Doom of Narok befell.

(the) Battle of the Last River Camp: the skirmish between the Squad of Kraggen-cor and a Hlōk-led band of Rūcks, fought on the west bank of the Argon River. Here Barak was slain and Tobin severely wounded. The Squad was rescued by Ursor the Baeran, Shannon Silverleaf, and Shannon's Company of Elves.

(the) Battle of the Vorvor: a battle between Dwarves and Spawn. Fought in the Ravine of the Vorvor.

198 GLOSSARY

(the) Battle of Weiunwood: generally refers to the first battle fought between elements of Modru's Horde and an alliance made up of Warrows (from Weiunwood), Men (from Stonehill), and Elves (from Arden). The three-day battle was fought during the opening days of the Winter War. The alliance set many ambuscades and defeated the Horde.

(the) Battle-tongue of the Valanreach. See Valur.

Beacontor: the southernmost of the Signal Mountains. The Crossland Road passes near its flanks.

Bekki: Brega's sire.

Bellon Falls: a great cataract where the Argon River plunges over the Great Escarpment to fall into the Cauldron. Also known as Ctor (Châkur).

Belor: a Dwarf of Durek's Folk. One of Bomar's cooking crew. Slain in the Battle of Kraggen-cor.

Berez: a Dwarf of Durek's Folk. Masterdelver. One of the guides in Crestan Pass during the blizzard.

(the) Beyond: a term used by Boskydell Warrows to indicate any place outside the Thornwall.

Beyonder Guard: warders posted along the entrances into the Boskydells to guard against unsavory *Outsiders*. Also known as the 'Guard, the Thornwalker Guard.

Bigfen: a great marshland in Centerdell.

Big Folks: a Warrow term meaning Mankind.

Big Men: a Warrow term meaning Mankind.

Bill: a Man of Stonehill. Aylesworth's helper in the time of the War of Kraggen-cor.

(the) black crater: the black lake bed left behind when the Troll-dam was broken and the Dark Mere drained.

(the) Black Deeves. See Drimmen-deeve.

Black Drimmen-deeve. See Drimmen-deeve.

blackener. See Dwarf blackener.

(the) Black Hole: a name given to Drimmen-deeve by Men.

Black Kalgalath: the Fire-drake that captured Elgo's hoard. Kalgalath was so mighty that only the Kammerling could slay him.

(the) Black Maze: a name given to Drimmen-deeve by Men.

(the) Black Mere. See (the) Dark Mere.

Black Mountain: a great dark mountain in the Land of Xian. Home of Wizards.

black oxen: wild black kine living in the Lands of Hoven,

Jugo, Tugal, Valon, and Vancha. Source of the black-oxen horns. Also known as the wild kine of the south.

black-oxen horns: War horns used for signalling and borne by the Men of Valon. These horns, coming from the black oxen (q.v.), are much prized by the Vanadurin.

Blackstone: the Dwarvenholt in the Rigga Mountains invaded by Sleeth the Orm. Also known as the Châkka Halls of the Rigga Mountains.

Blackwood: the eld name for Darda Erynian (q.v.).

blade-gem. See blade-jewel.

blade-jewel: a special gem set in the blade of an Elven weapon that emits light when Evil is near—specifically when creatures of the Untargarda are in proximity, although some Mithgarian beings (such as the Krakenward) also cause the jewel to glow. The brighter the light, the nearer the Evil. Also known as a blade-gem.

(the) Blue Bull: a Boskydell inn in Budgens.

Bockleman Brewster: a Man of Stonehill. Owner of the White Unicorn Inn during the Winter War. Hero and leader of the Men of the Weiunwood Alliance. Also known as Squire Brewster.

Bogland Bottoms: a large boggy region south of the Crossland Road and thirty or so miles east of Stonehill.

Bomar: a Dwarf of Durek's Folk. Bossed a cooking crew on the way to Kraggen-cor. Masterdelver. Captain of the Rear Guard. Slain in the Battle of Kraggen-cor. Also known as Grey Bomar.

(the)'*Book*. See *(The) Raven Book*.

(the) Boreal Sea: a frigid sea north of the Dalara Plains, Rian, Gron, and other Lands, and bordering on the Northern Wastes.

Borin Ironfist: a Dwarf of Durek's Folk. Brother of Anval Ironfist. Masterwarrior. Mastercrafter. Member of the Squad of Kraggen-cor. Hero of the War of Kraggen-cor. Gnar's slayer. Killed as the Doom of Narok befell.

Boshlub: a Hlōk of Gnar's Horde.

(the) Bosky. See (the) Boskydells.

(the) Boskydells: a Warrow homeland surrounded by the Spindlethorn Barrier. Bounded to the north by Rian, to the east by Harth, to the south by Trellinath, and to the west by

Wellen. Also known as the Bosky, the Dells, the Land of the Waldana (Valur), the Land of the Wee Folk, the Seven Dells.

(the) Bottom Chamber: one of the chambers in Kraggen-cor along the Brega Path.

bower shelter: a tiny form of shelter made from evergreen boughs; their way of making is known to mountain dwellers.

Brackenboro: a Boskydell village south of the Crossland Road and inside the western edge of Eastdell. Here was fought the Battle of Brackenboro during the Winter War. Also known as the 'Boro.

ᚠᚱᚢᚫᚫᛁ: Châkka runes meaning Braggi. (See Braggi's Rune.)

Braggi: a Dwarf warrior. Leader of a doomed mission into Kraggen-cor to slay the Ghath.

Braggi's doomed raid: Braggi's doomed mission.

Braggi's Raid: Braggi's doomed mission.

Braggi's Rune: Braggi's name written in large letters of Squam blood on the wall of the Hall of the Gravenarch.

Braggi's Stand: the place in Kraggen-cor—the Hall of the Gravenarch—where Braggi and his Raiders fought their last battle against the Squam. The Dwarves were overcome by the Ghath and slain.

Brak: DelfLord of Kachar during Elgo's time.

Brath: a Man of Valon. One of the riders in Brytta's force. Brytta's sister's son.

Brave as Budgens: a Warrow saying indicating great courage, harking back to the time of the Winter War when a force of Warrow archers overcame a company of Ghülen reavers in the Battle of Budgens.

Breakdeath Durek: a name given to Durek (q.v.) by the Dwarven Folk, who believed that Durek now and again broke the bonds of Death to be reborn among his Folk. Also known as Deathbreaker Durek, Khana (Châkur) Durek.

(the) breath of Waroo: a cold, transmountain wind indicating the onset of a blizzard. (See Waroo.)

Brega: a Dwarf of the Red Caves. Bekki's son. Hero of the Winter War. One of the Deevewalkers. Leader of the squad to lower the drawbridge and open the gate of the Iron Tower on the Darkest Day. Scriber of the Brega Scroll. DelfLord of the Red Caves after Borta. Also called Axe-thrower and Warrior Brega.

Brega, Bekki's son. See Brega.

(the) Brega Path: the route through Kraggen-cor taken by the Deevewalkers during the Winter War. Because of the Brega Scroll, this route became known as the Brega Path. Also known as the Path.

(the) Brega Scroll: Brega's record of the route taken by the Deevewalkers through Kraggen-cor. The scroll was found by Peregrin Fairhill years after its making. Also known as Brega's record and as the Scroll.

Brega's record. See (the) Brega Scroll.

B'reit (Valur: ready): a Valonian word meaning ready.

(the) bridge: the Warrow name for the bridge along the Crossland Road over the Spindle River.

(the) Bright Veil: a haze of stars in an east-west band across the skies of Mithgar. (Thought to be the Milky Way.)

(the) Broad Hall: one of the chambers in Kraggen-cor along the Brega Path.

(the) Broad Shelf: the name given to the wide stone floor on the east side of the Great Deep of Kraggen-cor. Also known as the Great Shelf and as the Shelf.

Brownie: a workhorse used by Cotton and others during the Quest of Kraggen-cor.

Brytta: a Man of Valon. Warder of the North Reach. Valanreach Marshal. Captain of the forty horse-borne Vanadurin scouts who accompanied Seventh Durek on the march to Kraggen-cor. Fought in the Battle of Stormhelm Defile.

buccan (plural: buccen): the general name given to a male Warrow. Also the specific age-name given to male Warrows between thirty and sixty years old.

buccaran: a Warrow term of endearment used by dammen Warrows when speaking to or about their husbands or sweethearts.

bucco: a Warrow term meaning son.

Budgens: a Boskydell hamlet. Site of the first battle of the Struggles during the Winter War.

(the) buried door: the name used by Hlōks to mean Dusk-Door.

burrow: an underground Warrow dwelling.

Buttermilk Springs: a Boskydell spring near Thimble, cold enough to keep melons and buttermilk cool in the summer. Owned by Jayar Northcolt.

Byroad Lane: the road running south from Budgens to the Crossland Road.

Caddor: a Dwarf of Durek's Folk. One of Bomar's cooking crew. Slain in the Battle of Kraggen-cor.

Caer Lindor: an Elvenholt on an island in the River Rissanin between Darda Erynian and the Greatwood. Destroyed in the Great War.

Caer Pendwyr: southern strongholt, winter home and Court of the High King. Situated on Pendwyr Isle, Pellar, between Hile Bay and the Avagon Sea.

(the) Caire River: a river with northern origins in the west side of the Rigga Mountains and running south to the Rivermix at Luren.

Captain: a rank or position of authority among the Free Folk. Typically, Captains commanded up to one hundred warriors.

Captain Patrel. See Patrel Rushlock.

(the) Cauldron: a great churn of water where Vanil Falls and Bellon Falls plunge down the face of the Great Escarpment to thunder into the River Argon.

Cave Ogru. See Ogrus.

Cave Troll. See Ogrus.

(the) Cellener River: a river flowing into the Quadrill in Darda Galion in southwestern Riamon.

(a) Ceremony: a public gathering of Warrows at which both formal and informal speeches are made.

Chagor (Sylva: jag-top). See Loftcrag.

Châk (plural: Châkka) (Châkur: Dwarf): Dwarven word meaning Dwarf.

Châk-alon (Châkur: Dwarf pure-spirit): the Dwarven name for the Quadmere (q.v.).

Châkka (Châkur: Dwarves; of the Dwarves): Dwarven word meaning "Dwarves" and "of the Dwarves."

Châkkacyth Ryng (Châkur: Dwarvenkith Ring): a sigil shining forth from Ghatan Mountain, seen from the Mountain Throne on Rávenor. The Ryng, a circlet of light studded with five stars, one for each of the five Châkka kindred, only appears as the Sun passes through the zenith. Also known as the Dwarvenkith Ring, the Ring, and the Ryng.

Châkkadom (Châkur: Dwarfdom): the totality of Dwarven Folk.

Châkka doors (Châkur: Dwarven doors): doors, usually concealed, made by Dwarves. Also known as Dwarf doors.

Châkka Halls of the Rigga Mountains. See Blackstone.

Châkkaholt (Châkur: Dwarvenholt). See Dwarvenholt.

Châkka Kindred: the five branches of the Dwarven Folk. Also known as the Kindred.

Châk-Sol (Châkur: Dwarf-Friend): an honorary rank of Dwarf Kith given to a rare few non-Dwarves throughout the history of Mitheor. Perry and Cotton each were named Châk-Sol—Dwarf-Friend—by Anval and Borin. Also known as Dwarf-Friend, Friend.

Châk Speech. See Châkur.

Châkur (Châkur: our tongue): the secret language of the Dwarves. Also known as Châk Speech, the Dwarf speech, Dwarf tongue, the hidden language, and the hidden tongue. (For various Châkur words and phrases, see Appendix: Translations of Words and Phrases.)

Challerain Keep: northern stronghold, summer home and Court of the High King. Situated in Rian. Also known as the Keep.

(the) Chamber: a term applicable to many rooms in Kraggencor: e.g., the Bottom Chamber, the Oval Chamber.

Chief Captain: a rank above Captain in Dwarf armies.

(the) Chieftain: the leader of the Baeron (q.v.).

(the) Cliffs: a western Boskydell Warrowholt. A honeycomb of Warrow dwellings in a limestone cliff along the Wenden River in Westdell.

Cold-drakes. See Dragons.

(the) Cold Iron Tower. See (the) Iron Tower.

Common: a term meaning "of the Common Tongue" (q.v.).

(the) common room: a large public room at an inn where both guests and locals gather to eat, drink, and talk.

(the) Commons: a town square generally without buildings other than a pavilion or two for entertainment or speechmaking purposes.

(the) common stables: a public barn or corral for keeping horses and ponies.

(the) Common Tongue: q.v., Pellarion.

(the) Company of the Dusken Door: a Dwarven Company set to ward the Dusken Door. Also known as the Dusk-Door Company.

(a) copper. See copper penny.

copper coin. See copper penny.

copper penny: one of three types of coins used for commerce in Mithgar (silver and gold being the other two types). Also known as a copper, a copper coin, and a copper piece.

cor (Châkur: might): a Dwarven term meaning might (power). Also, a Warrow exclamation used to express wonderment.

Coron (Sylva: King/Ruler): Elven name for Coron Mountain (King of the Mountains) (see Stormhelm). Also the Elven name for their own Elven King (see Eiron).

(the) corpse-foe. See Ghûls.

cot. See cote.

cote: a small dwelling (cottage); usually a small, stone fieldhouse or a tiny house in the woods. Also known as a cot.

Cotton Buckleburr: a buccan Warrow of the Boskydells. Handywarrow at Sir Tuckerby's Warren. Member of the Quest of Kraggen-cor. Bearer of the Horn of Narok. Member of Durek's Army. Brega-Path guide. Wielder of the Atalar Blade. Drimmen-deeve Rūck-fighter. Hero of the Realm. Also known as Friend Cotton, Master Cotton, Mister Cotton, Pathfinder.

(the) Council of Durek: a council held at Landover Road Ford to plan the strategy of the invasion and War of Kraggen-cor.

(the) Council of Captains: a gathering of Dwarf Captains to advise a Dwarf King.

(the) Covenant. See (the) Ban.

(a) Crafter: one who takes up a crafting skill. Among Dwarves, there are Gatecrafters, Tunnelcrafters, Minecrafters, Doorcrafters, etc.

Crau: a Dwarf of Durek's Folk. One of Bomar's cooking crew. Slain in the Battle of Kraggen-cor.

Crestan Pass: a pass above Arden Valley, crossing the Grimwall Mountains, connecting the Crossland Road with the Landover Road.

(the) Crossland Road: a major east-west road of Mithgar, west of the Grimwall Mountains.

Crotbone: a Hlōk of Gnar's Horde.

crue: a tasteless but nutritious waybread.

Cruel Gnar. See Gnar.

Ctor (Châkur: shouter): Dwarven name for Bellon Falls (q.v.).

Dael: the capital city of North Riamon. Also know as Dael Township.

Daelsman: a Man from the vicinity of Dael.

Dael Township. See Dael.

Daelwood: a forest in Riamon within the ring of the Rimmen Mountains.

Dalen: a Man of Valon. One of the riders in Brytta's force. Slain in the Battle of Stormhelm Defile. One of the Five Riders (q.v.).

(the) Dalgor March(es): a region of Riamon west of the Argon River and east of the Grimwall, through which the Dalgor River flows.

(the) Dalgor River: a river flowing eastward from the Grimwall into the Argon River.

damman (plural: dammen): the general name given to a female Warrow. Also the specific age-name given to female Warrows between thirty and sixty years old.

dammia: a Warrow term of endearment used by buccen Warrows when speaking to or about their wives or sweethearts.

dammsel: a Warrow term meaning daughter.

Danner Bramblethorn: a buccan Warrow of the Boskydells. Hero of the Winter War. Leader of the Struggles. One of Tuck's companions. Thornwalker. A member of Brega's squad. Slain at the Kinstealer's holt. Also known as Captain Danner, Sir Danner, and the King of the Rillrock.

Dara (Sylva: Lady): an Elven title for an Elfess consort.

Darda (Sylva: leaf-tree): Elven word meaning forest.

Darda Erynian (Sylva: leaf-tree hall-of-green): Elven name meaning Greenhall Forest. A great forest east of the Argon River in Riamon. Also known as Blackwood of old, and as the Great Greenhall.

Darda Galion (Sylva: leaf-tree land-of-larks): Elven name meaning Forest of the Silverlarks. A great forest of Eld Trees in southwestern Riamon, west of the River Argon. Last true home of the Lian in Mithgar. Also known as Eldwood and as Larkenwald.

Darion: the High King of Mithgar during the time of the Quest of Kraggen-cor.

(the) Dark Mere: a black lakelet under the Loom at the

Dusk-Door. Abode of the Krakenward. Also known as the
Black Mere.

(the) Dark Plague: a ravaging plague that swept Mithgar in
days of yore and slew as much as one third of the total
population. Commonly believed to be a sending of Gyphon or
Modru.

darktide: night.

(the) Daūn Gate (Châkur: Sunrise Gate). See Dawn-Gate.

(the) Dawn-Gate: the great eastern entrance into Kraggen-
cor. Situated on the southeastern flank of Stormhelm Mountain. Opening onto the Pitch less than a mile from the
Quadmere. Also known as Daūn (Châkur) Gate, the Gate, and
Quad Gate.

(the) Dawn Sword: a special sword said to have the power
to slay the High Vūlk, Himself. This weapon disappeared in
the region of Dalgor March.

dayrise: sunrise.

daytide: daytime.

Deathbreaker Durek: an appellation of Durek. The Dwarves
believe that, after death, spirits are reborn to walk the earth
again, some more often than others. They believe that the
spirit of First Durek is one that breaks the bonds of Death
often; hence the name Deathbreaker Durek. (See Durek, First
Durek.)

(the) Death-War. See Narok.

(the) Deep. See (the) Great Deep.

(the) Deeves. See Drimmen-deeve.

(the) Deevewalkers: the name given to the four companions
who strode through Drimmen-deeve during the Winter War:
Brega (Dwarf), Galen (Man), Gildor (Elf), and Tuck (Warrow).
Slayers of the Gargon. Also known as the Dread Slayers, the
Four, the four heroes, the Four Who Strode Drimmen-deeve,
the Four Who Strode Kraggen-cor, the Four Who Strode the
Deeves, and the Walkers of the Deeves.

delf: a common Mithgarian term meaning a digging of some
sort, such as a quarry or a mine.

DelfLord: a title given to Dwarf Lords of outlying mineholts.
Second in power only to Dwarven Kings.

Delk Steelshank: a Dwarf of Durek's Folk. Gatemaster.
Member of the Squad of Kraggen-cor. Slain by Rūck arrow
in the Gargon's Lair.

(the) Dellin Downs: a low range of hills central to Harth.
(the) Dells. See (the) Boskydells.
Delon: an island in the Argon River, north of Landover Road Ford.
Delver: a Dwarf whose craft is delving, generally in or through stone.
(the) Dēop (Châkur: Dēop = Deep): a Dwarven name for the Great Deep.
dhal: a Rūcken shield similar to a sipar in construction but slightly smaller. See sipar.
(the) diary of Sir Tuckerby Underbank: Tuckerby Underbank's original diary of his adventures during the Winter War.
Didion: a Man of Valon. One of the riders in Brytta's force. With Ged, vainly pursued the Drōkh that escaped the Battle of Stormhelm Defile.
(the) Dimmendark: a spectral dark over the land, cast by Modru using the power of the Myrkenstone during the Winter War to negate Adon's Ban. Also known as the 'Dark, Modru's myrk, the murk of the Evil One.
(the) Dingle: a term generally taken to mean the Dingle-rill (q.v.), but also can indicate all of the hollow bottom through which the Dingle-rill flows in the vicinity of Woody Hollow.
(the) Dingle-rill: a Boskydell river flowing from Bigfen eastward to empty at last into the Spindle River. Also known as the Dingle.
dōk (Châkur: halt): a Dwarven word meaning halt.
(the) Doom of Narok. See (the) Staves of Narok.
(the) Doomed Raid of Braggi. See Braggi's Raid.
(the) Door. See (the) Dusk-Door.
(the) Doors of Dusk. See (the) Dusk-Door.
Dot Northcolt: a damman Warrow of the Boskydells. Wife of Jayar Northcolt. Holly's dam (mother).
Downdell: the southeasternmost of the Seven Dells of the Boskydells. Noted for its leaf.
Downdell leaf: apparently tobacco. Downdell leaf is reputed to be the best.
Downy: a workhorse used by Cotton and others during the Quest of Kraggen-cor.
Dracongield (Valur: Dragon-gold): a Valonian word meaning Dragon-gold.

Draedan (Sylva: Dread One). See (the) Gargon.

(the)Draedan's Lair [Sylva: (the) Dread One's Lair]. See (the) Lost Prison.

(the) Dragon Pillars: four rows of great pillars in the War Hall of Kraggen-cor. The pillars are carved to resemble Dragons twining up around the columns.

Dragons: one of the Folk of Mithgar. Comprising two strains: Fire-drakes and Cold-drakes. Dragons are mighty creatures capable of speech. Most have wings and the power of flight. Generally they live in remote caves and ravage the nearby land. They sleep for one thousand years and remain awake for two thousand. Often they seek treasure, which they hoard. Fire-drakes spew flame. Cold-drakes spew acid but no flame, for they once were Fire-drakes but sided with Gyphon in the Great War and their fire was taken from them by Adon as punishment. Cold-drakes suffer the Ban—yet though they are slain by the Sun, the Withering Death strikes them not (i.e., when Sun-slain, they do not wither to dust in its rays). No female Dragons are known, and it is said by the Dwarves that Dragons mate with Madûks (Krakens). Dragons named in *The Raven Book* and in *The Fairhill Journal* are Black Kalgalath, Ebonskaith, Skail, and Sleeth the Orm. Also known as Orms (Worms).

Dragon spew: generally refers to the acid spat forth by Cold-drakes, but also can mean the flame of a Fire-drake.

(the) Dragon Star: a comet that nearly collided with Mithgar. Sent by Gyphon, it bore the Myrkenstone to the world, to be used by Modru.

(the) Drawbridge at Dusk-Door: a span across the Dusk-Moat at Dusk-Door.

(the) Drawbridge at the Great Dēop: a span across the Great Deep near the Dawn-Gate.

(the) Drawing Dark: a deep, eight-foot-wide fissure in Kraggen-cor from which emanates a hideous sucking noise (possibly a whirlpool down within the crack). So named by Tuck because it seemed as if the crevice were trying to draw one down into the darkness. Also known as the eight-foot-wide crack, the eight-foot-wide crevice.

(the) Dread. See (the) Gargon.

(the) Dread of Drimmen-deeve. See (the) Gargon.

Drearwood: a forest in Rhone through which wends the

Crossland Road. In this wood in days of yore were said to
dwell dreadful creatures, creatures driven out by the Elves of
Arden during the Purging. Also known as the 'Wood.
Driller: a Dwarf whose craft is drilling, one of the skills of
stone delving.
Drimm (plural: Drimma) (Sylva: Dwarf): Elven name mean-
ing Dwarf.
Drimmen-deeve (Sylva: Dwarven-delvings; Dwarven-mines):
Elven name for Kraggen-cor (q.v.). Also known as the Black
Deeves, Black Drimmen-deeve, the Black Hole, the Black
Maze, and the Deeves.
(the) Drimmen-deeve Rūck-fighters: the name in Stonehill
by which Anval, Borin, Cotton, Kian, and Perry became
known after the Quest of Kraggen-cor.
Drōken: a term meaning "of the Drokha."
Drōkha (singular: Drōkh) (Valur: vile-filth). See Hlōks.
(the) drowned courtyard: the ancient courtyard before the
Dusk-Door, inundated when the Duskrill was dammed by
Trolls.
Duellin: one of the Lost Lands of Atala. Also known as Lost
Duellin and as the Land of the West
Durek: a recurring name within the line of Dwarven Kings of
Durek's Folk. Durek was thought to be reborn often through-
out the Eras and thus was given the name Breakdeath Durek,
Deathbreaker Durek, Durek the Deathbreaker, the High Leader.
Durek's Army. See (the) Dwarf Host.
Durek's Folk: one of the five strains of the Dwarven Folk.
Also known as Durek's Kin.
Durek's Kin. See Durek's Folk.
Durek's Legion. See (the) Dwarf Host.
Durek's Wheel. See (the) Vorvor.
Durek the Deathbreaker. See Durek.
(the) Dusk-Door: the western trade entrance into Kraggen-
cor. Situated under the cavernous hemidome at the base of
the Great Loom on the western flank of Grimspire Mountain.
Crafted by the Dwarf Valki and by the Wizard Grevan. After
arcane words are spoken, the Dusk-Door can be opened and
closed by Dwarves using the Wizard-word Gaard. And just
inside the West Hall, a chain also can be used to close (and
perhaps open) the portal. Also known as the Door, the Doors
of Dusk, the Dusken (Châkur) Door.

(the) Dusk-Door Company. See (the) Company of the Dusken Door.

(the) Dusken Door (Châkur: Sundown Door). See Dusk-Door.

duskingtide: the march of evening, from its onset until full night falls.

(the) Dusk-Moat: a moat surrounding the courtyard before the Dusk-Door. A Dwarven defence at the Dusken Door. During the time of the Troll-dam, the moat was submerged under the Dark Mere. Also known as the Gatemoat.

(the) Duskrill: a stream flowing from Grimspire through Ragad Valley. Used to create the Dusk-Moat. Blocked for centuries by the Troll-made dam.

Dwarf blackener: a salve used by Dwarves to darken their features when going into combat at night or underground. Also known as blackener, face blackener.

Dwarf doors. See Châkka doors.

Dwarf-Friend. See Châk-Sol.

(the) Dwarf Host: generally taken to mean the Army that accompanied Seventh Durek to Kraggen-cor. Also known as Durek's Army and Durek's Legion.

Dwarf-lantern. See Dwarven lantern.

Dwarf speech. See Châkur.

(the) Dwarf tongue. See Châkur.

Dwarf Troll-squad: a force of fifty or more Dwarves especially trained to do battle with Trolls.

Dwarven: a term meaning "of the Dwarves."

Dwarvenfolc (Valur: Dwarven Folk): a Valonian word meaning Dwarves.

Dwarvenholt: a Dwarven strongholt. Also known as Châkkaholt.

(the) Dwarvenkith Ring. See (the) Châkkacyth Ryng.

Dwarven lantern: a small hooded lantern wrought of brass and crystal, glowing with a soft blue-green light. No fire need be kindled, no fuel seems consumed. Also known as Dwarf-lantern.

Dwarves (singular: Dwarf): one of the Folk of Mithgar. Comprising five strains. The adults range in height from four to five feet. Broad-shouldered. Aggressive. Secretive. Clever. Mine dwellers. Crafters. Also known as Châk(ka) (Châkur), Drimma (Sylva), Dwarven Folk, *Dwarvenfolc* (Valur), forked beards, and the forked-bearded Folk.

Dwarvish: a term meaning "of the Dwarves."

Dylvana (Sylva: Wood Elves): one of the two strains of Elves upon Mithgar.

Eanor: a Man of Valon. King of the Vanadurin at the time of the Quest of Kraggen-cor.

Eastdell: one of the Seven Dells of the Boskydells.

Eastdell Fourth: a Thornwalker Company of Eastdell. Also known by Tuck and his comrades as the Thornwalker Fourth.

(the) East Hall: one of the chambers in Kraggen-cor, just inside the Dawn-Gate, along the Brega Path.

Eastpoint: a Boskydell village in Eastdell, south of the Crossland Road, near the Spindle River.

Eastpoint Hall: a large warren in Eastdell. Here lived Tuck's cousins, the Bendels. Here, too, was housed one of the libraries of the Boskydells.

Eastwood: a large forest in Eastdell, in the Boskydells. Also known as the 'Wood.

Eddra: a Man of Valon. One of the riders in Brytta's force.

Edgewood: a large forest in Harth, on the eastern border of the Boskydells.

(the) edifice of the Dusk-Door. See (the) great portico (of the Dusk-Door).

Egil One Eye: a Man of Mithgar. Companion of Arin in the Quest of the Green Stone of Xian.

Egon: a Man of Valon. One of the riders in Brytta's force.

(the) eight-foot-wide crack. See (the) Drawing Dark.

(the) eight-foot-wide crevice. See (the) Drawing Dark.

Eiron: a Lian Elf. Coron (Sylva) of the Elves in Mithgar during the Winter War. Consort of Faeon.

eld buccan (plural: eld buccen): the age-name given to a buccan Warrow between sixty and eighty-five years old.

eld damman (plural: eld dammen): the age-name given to a damman Warrow between sixty and eighty-five years old.

Eld Days/eld days: old days.

Eld Durek. See First Durek.

Elden/elden: a term used to mean ancient, old, olden.

Elden Days: olden days.

Eld Ones: beings of ancient legend; e.g., Lian Elves were also known as Eld Ones.

Eld Trees: great trees, hundreds of feet tall, said to have the special property of gathering and holding the twilight if Elves live nearby.

Eld wood: The precious wood of an Eld Tree. Used to make things of great worth; e.g., Perry had an Eld-wood carrying case for his copy of *The Raven Book*.

Eldwood. See Darda Galion.

Elf Lord: a title given to all Elves by common Folk.

Elgo: a Man of Valon. The hero who slew the Cold-drake Sleeth by tricking it into the sunlight, thus winning the Dragon's hoard. Also known as Sleeth's Doom.

Elven: a term meaning "of the Elves."

Elven cloak: a cloak of the Elves; of a color said to blend into a background of limb, leaf, or stone. Danner, Patrel, and Tuck were given Elven cloaks by Laurelin; Patrel's and Tuck's ended up on display in The Root. Cotton and Perry wore these cloaks in the Quest of Kraggen-cor.

Elvenholt: an Elven strongholt.

Elven rope: a soft, pliable, strong, lightweight rope made by the Elves.

Elves (Singular: Elf): one of the Folk of Adonar, some of whom dwell in Mithgar. Comprising two strains: the Lian and the Dylvana. The adults range in height from four and one-half to five and one-half feet. Slim. Agile. Swift. Sharp-sensed. Reserved. Forest dwellers. Artisans.

Elves of the West: Elves who dwelled in the Land of the West ere it sank beneath the sea.

Elvish: a term meaning "of the Elves."

Elwydd: daughter of Adon. Held in special reverence by the Dwarves.

Elyn: a Woman of Jord. Companion of the Dwarf Thork in the Quest of Black Mountain.

(the) End Field: a large open field in Hollow End, in Woody Hollow.

(the) Enemy in Gron. See Modru.

Era: a historical age of Mithgar. These ages are determined by world-shaking events, which bring each Era to a close and begin the following Era. At the time of the beginning of the Winter War it was the Fourth Era (4E), the year 2018: 4E2018. The Winter War ended in 4E2019. The Fifth Era (5E) began on the next Year's Start Day. The Quest of Kraggen-cor took place in 5E231.

eventide: generally taken to mean the march of dusk, from its onset until full night falls; however, it also can mean all of the time between sunset and sunrise.

(the) Evil One. See Modru.

(the) Evil One's Reavers: generally taken to mean Ghûls (q.v.).

face blackener. See Dwarf blackener.

Faeon: Elfess. Mistress of Darda Galion. Consort of Eiron. Daughter of Talarin and Rael. Sister of Gildor and Vanidor. After Vanidor's death, Faeon rode the Twilight Ride to Adonar to plead with the High One to intercede in the Winter War.

(the) Fainen River (Sylva: Fainen = Fair): Elven name (Fair River) for the Isleborn River (q.v.).

(The) Fairhill Journal: the chronicle written by Peregrin Fairhill to describe the Quest of Kraggen-cor. Also known as *The Silver Call.*

(the) Fairhills: the Fairhill lineage.

(the) Fairhill Scholar: a title given by the Ravenbook Scholars to an outstanding student among them of the Fairhill lineage.

Falanith (Sylva: valley rising): the Elven name for the Pitch (q.v.).

(the) Falls of Vanil. See Vanil Falls.

False Elgo: a name given Elgo by the Dwarves after their dispute over Sleeth's hoard.

Farlon: a Man of Valon. One of the riders in Brytta's force. The scout who first found the Valley of the Five Riders.

(the) farmer: a Man of the Wilderland near Stonehill. Unnamed guest of the White Unicorn Inn when the Drimmendeeve Rück-fighters were also guests.

(the) Fates: the spinners of the skeins of the world; the personification of the ancient belief of the Men of Valon that unseen forces weave the fortunes of all peoples.

(the) Father of Durek's Folk. See First Durek.

Faugh: a Free Folk exclamation of contempt or disgust.

Felor: a Dwarf of Durek's Folk. Masterdriller. Chief Captain of the Spearhead of the Dwarf Army in the War of Kraggen-cor. Felor and his drillers helped break the Troll-made dam to empty the Dark Mere during the battle with the Madûk.

Fennerly Cotter: a buccan Warrow of the Boskydells. Owner of the Happy Otter Inn in Greenfields at the time of the Quest of Kraggen-cor.

'Fieldites: citizens of Greenfields.

(the) 'Fields. See Greenfields.

firecoke: a special charcoal used by the Dwarves in their forges.

Fire-drakes. See Dragons.

Firemane: a horse of Valon. Arl's mount.

First Durek: a Dwarf King and founder of Durek's Folk in the First Era. Discoverer of Kraggen-cor. Also known as Eld Durek and as the Father of Durek's Folk. (See Breakdeath Durek, Durek.)

(the) First Watchtower: an ancient sentry tower, now ruins, on the crest of Beacontor.

(the) five Châkka kindred: the five strains of Dwarves. Also known as the Five Kith.

(the) Five Kith. See (the) five Châkka kindred.

(the) Five Riders: the five riders of Valon slain in the Battle of Stormhelm Defile: Arl, Dalen, Haddor, Luthen, Raech.

(the) flatboats (of the River Drummers): barges, trade boats, used by river merchants.

flet: a tree house or tree platform used as a dwelling, notably by the Quiren strain of Warrows.

Fleetfoot: Gildor's horse. Slain by the Hèlarms during the Winter War.

(the) Fletchers: the Fletcher lineage.

Folk: a branch of the Free Folk (q.v.) or of the Foul Folk (q.v.). Also known as a Race.

(the) Ford of New Luren: the ford across the Isleborne River at the hamlet of New Luren.

forebearers: a Pellarion word meaning forebears (ancestors).

Foreign Parts: a Warrow term meaning anywhere beyond the borders of the Boskydells.

(the) forge of Hèl: Hell's smithery. A term used to mean a harsh or hellish experience or place.

(the) forked-bearded Folk: a term generally taken to mean Dwarves. In Mithgar, only Dwarves sported forked beards.

forked beards: a term generally taken to mean Dwarves. [See (the) forked-bearded Folk.]

Fortune's three faces: the three aspects of chance. The Valonians believed that Fortune had three faces: one fair, signifying good luck; one scowling, signifying bad luck; and one unseen, signifying not only Death's visage, but also misfortunes too terrible to contemplate.

foul-beards: a term used by Hlōks in general, and Gnar in particular, to mean Dwarves.

Foul Elgo: a name given to Elgo by the Dwarves after their dispute over Sleeth's hoard.

(the) Foul Folk: any or all of the Folk allied with Modru or Gyphon, the most notable of which are Cold-drakes, Ghûls, Hèlsteeds, Hlōks, Ogrus, Rūcks, and some Men (e.g., in the past, the Rovers of Kistan, the Lakh of Hyree).

(the) Four. See (the) Deevewalkers.

(the) Four Who Strode Drimmen-deeve. See the Deevewalkers.

(the) Four Who Strode Kraggen-cor. See the Deevewalkers.

(the) Free Folk: any or all of the Folk allied with Adon, the most notable of which are Dwarves, Elves, Men, Utruni, Warrows, Wizards. Also known as the High Folk.

Friend: abbreviated form of Dwarf-Friend. (See Châk-Sol.)

Funda: a Dwarf of Durek's Folk. One of Bomar's cooking crew. Slain in the Battle of Kraggen-cor.

Gaard: a Wizard-word perhaps meaning move, or act. Used by Dwarves to both open and close the Dusk-Door.

Galen: a Man of Pellar. Eldest son of Aurion. A Lord and Prince who became High King during the Winter War. Deevewalker. Hero. Founder of the Realmsmen. Husband of Laurelin. Sire of Gareth. Also known as Shatter-sword. Died at age 71 during a storm at Caer Pendwyr.

(the) Gammer (Alderbuc): a buccan Warrow of the Boskydells. A granther Warrow and past Captain of the Thornwalkers at the time of the Winter War. Organizer of the Wolf Patrols at the onset of the cold winter heralding the Winter War.

Gannon: a Man of Valon. One of the riders in Brytta's force.

(the) Gap. See (the) Gap of Stormhelm, Gûnarring Gap, Quadran Gap.

(the) Gap of Stormhelm. See Quadran Pass.

Gareth: firstborn of Galen and Laurelin. Gareth became King in 5E46.

(the) Gargon (plural: Gargons, Gargoni): a Vûlk aiding Gyphon in the Great War. Trapped in the Lost Prison by Lian Guardians. Freed by Modru's art. Ruler of Drimmen-deeve for more than a thousand years. Slain by the Deevewalkers. Also known as the *Draedan* (Sylva), the Dread, the Dread of Drimmen-deeve, the Dread of the Black Hole, the Evil, the Fear to the North (of Darda Galion), the Ghath (Châkur), the Horror, the Mandrak (Twyll), Modru's Dread, and the Negus (Slûk) of Terror.

(the) Gargon's Lair. See (the) Lost Prison.

Garia: a Land of Mithgar bounded on the north by Aven, on the east by Alban, on the south by the Avagon Sea, and on the west by the Inner Sea and Riamon.

Garn (Valur: untranslated interjection): oathword of Valon, used to express disappointment or frustration.

(the) Gate. See Dawn-Gate, (the) High Gate.

Gate Level: the level at the Dawn-Gate to which all other levels in Kraggen-cor are referenced: Deeper chambers have "Neaths" as their level designations (i.e., First Neath, Second Neath, etc.), whereas higher chambers have "Rises" as their level designations (i.e., First Rise, Second Rise, etc.); those chambers in Kraggen-cor at the same level as the Dawn-Gate are said to be at "Gate Level."

Gatemaster: one who has mastered the Dwarven craft of gate making.

Gatemaster Valki. See Valki.

Gatemaster Valki's glyph: a rune *V* inscribed in theen upon the Dusken Door.

(the) Gatemoat. See (the) Dusk-Moat.

Gaynor: a Dwarf of Durek's Folk. Masterdelver. One of the guides through Crestan Pass during the blizzard. Slain by the Krakenward.

Ged: a Man of Valon. One of the riders in Brytta's force. With Didion, vainly pursued the Drôkh that escaped the Battle of Stormhelm Defile.

Gerontius Fairhill: a buccan Warrow of the Boskydells. Peregrin Fairhill's uncle. A Master of the Ravenbook Scholars.

Ghatan (Châkur: ringmount); the Dwarven name for Loftcrag (q.v.), meaning Mountain of the Ryng. So named because the Châkkacyth Ryng shone forth from the crags of Ghatan.

(the) Ghath (Châkur: horror): Dwarven name for the Gargon (q.v.).

Ghola (singular: Ghol): Pellarion for Ghûls (q.v.).

Ghûlen: a term meaning "of the Ghûls."

Ghûls (singular: Ghûl): minor Vûlks. Savage, Hèlsteed-borne reavers. Very difficult to slay. All perhaps perished in the Winter War. Also known as the corpse-foe, the corpse-folk, the corpse-people, Ghola (OP), Ghûlka (Sylva), Guula (Valur), Khōls (Châkur), Modru's Reavers, reaving-foe, reavers.

Giants: the Warrow and Valonian name for Utruni (q.v.).

(the) gilded armor. See (the) golden armor.

(the) gilded mail. See (the) golden armor.

Gildor (Sylva: gold-branch): an Elf. Lian warrior. Elf Lord. Son of Talarin and Rael. Twin brother of Vanidor, brother of Faeon. Hero. One of the Deevewalkers. Also known as Alor Gildor, Gildor Goldbranch, Goldbranch, Lord Gildor, Torch-flinger.

Glain. See Third Glain.

Glâr (Slûk: fire): a Spaunen word meaning fire.

Gnar: a Hlōk. Leader of the Spawn in Drimmen-deeve. Anval's slayer. Slain by Borin in the War of Kraggen-cor. Also known as Cruel Gnar, Gnar the Cruel, his Nibs, and O Mighty One.

Gnar's Horde: the Horde of maggot-folk living in Kraggen-cor during the time of the Quest of Kraggen-cor.

Gnar the Cruel. See Gnar.

(the) golden armor: armor originally made by the Dwarves of the Red Caves for young Galen. The mail was given to Patrel by Laurelin to wear at her birthday feast and was worn by him throughout the Winter War. The armor was ultimately placed on display at Tuckerby's Warren, where it was to be left in possession of the Warrows until recalled by the shade of Aurion. Worn by Cotton in the Quest of Kraggen-cor. Also known as the golden mail, the gilded mail, and the gilded armor.

golden coin. See gold penny.

(the) golden mail. See (the) golden armor.

(the) golden War Horn: a golden horn of Durek's Folk used to summon Dwarves to battle. Also known as the War Horn.

gold penny: one of three types of coins used for commerce in Mithgar (silver and copper being the other two types). Also known as a gold, a gold coin, and a gold piece.

Gorbash: a Hlōk of Gnar's Horde.

Goth: a Cave Ogru of Kraggen-cor. A Troll in Gnar's Horde.

Grael: a Baeran Woman. Ursor's wife. Slain by Spawn on a trip to Valon.

Gralon (Sylva: grey-stone). See Greytower.

gramarye: the art of sorcery.

(the) Grand Alliance: the alliance of Dwarves, Elves, Men, Utruni, Warrows, and Wizards who fought on the side of Adon in the Great War against Gyphon, Modru, and the Foul Folk.

grandam (plural: grandams): the age-name given to a damman Warrow eighty-five years old and beyond.

granther (plural: granthers): the age-name given to a buccan Warrow eighty-five years old and beyond.

(the) Grate Room: a small chamber in Kraggen-cor along the Brega Path. Also known as the Room.

Grau: a Baeran Man. Eldest son of Baru, the Passwarden of the Crestan Pass in 5E231.

(the) Gravenarch: a Dwarf-crafted arch in Kraggen-cor in the Hall of the Gravenarch. Destroyed by Brega during the Winter War.

(the) Great Arch of the Loom. See (the) hemidome.

(the) Great Argon River. See (the) Argon River.

(the) Great Barrier. See (the) Spindlethorn Barrier.

(the) Great Chamber (of the Sixth Rise): one of the chambers in Kraggen-cor along the Brega Path.

(the) Great Deep: an unplumbed abyss in Kraggen-cor near the Dawn-Gate. Also known as the Deep, the Dēop (Châkur), and the Great Dēop.

(the) Great Dēop: (Châkur: Dēop = Deep): Dwarven name for the Great Deep (q.v.).

(the) Great Enemy. See Gyphon.

(the) Great Escarpment: a great uplift in the land running east from the Grimwall Mountains and curving south along Greatwood. Bellon Falls marks the place where the Argon River plunges down the Escarpment, just as Vanil Falls marks where the River Nith cascades.

(the) great flank. See (the) Loom.

(the) Great Greenhall (Forest). See Darda Erynian.

(the) great hemidome. See (the) hemidome.

Great Isle: an island in the Argon River some fifty miles south of the Landover Road Ford. Site of an ancient fort whose guardians were corrupted by Gyphon; the fort was subsequently destroyed by the Baeron.

(the) Great Loom (of Aggarath). See (the) Loom.

(the) Great Loomwall. See (the) Loom.

(the) Great Maelstrom: a giant whirlpool in the Boreal Sea between Gron and the Seabane Islands, where it is said that Krakens dwell. Also called the Maelstrom.

(the) great portico (of the Dusk-Door): an edifice of marble columns supporting a marble roof against the Loom at the Dusk-Door. Destroyed by the Krakenward during the Winter War. Also known as the edifice of the Dusk-Door.

(the) Great Purging. See (the) Purging.

(the) Great Retreat: the retreat of all Free Folk from the forces of Modru during the early stages of the Winter War.

(the) Great River Argon. See (the) Argon River.

(the) Great Shelf. See (the) Broad Shelf.

(the) Great Swamp. See (the) Gwasp.

(the) Great Treehouse: a huge treehouse in the Boskydells containing a library.

(the) Great War: the part of the War between Gyphon and Adon that was fought in Mithgar. Also known as the Ban War, the Great War of the Ban, and the War of the Banning.

(the) Great War of the Ban. See (the) Great War.

(the) Greatwood: a vast forest in South Riamon stretching from the River Rissanin to the Glave Hills.

(the) green-and-white of Valon: the colors of the flag of Valon. [See (the) War-banner of Valon.]

Greenfields: a Boskydell hamlet on the Crossland Road east of Woody Hollow. Also known as the 'Fields.

Greenhall Forest. See Darda Erynian.

(the) Green Stone (of Xian): a jade egg. Said to hold the spirit of the Dragon-King.

Grevan: a Wizard of Mithgar who helped Valki construct the Dusk-Door. Also known as Grevan the Wizard, the Wizard Grevan.

Grevan the Wizard. See Grevan.

Grey Bomar. See Bomar.

(the) Greylocks: the Greylock lineage.

Greytower: the southeasternmost of the four mountains of the Quadran beneath which Kraggen-cor is delved. Greytower was so named because of the grey stone of its composition. Also known as Gralon (Sylva), and Uchan (Châkur).

Grg (Châkur: worms of rot): the Dwarven name for the maggot-folk.

Grimspire: the southwesternmost of the four mountains of the Quadran beneath which Kraggen-cor is delved. Grimspire is a mountain of black stone, and along its west face is the Great Loom in which the Dusk-Door is delved, opening into the mountain. Also known as Aevor (Sylva), and Aggarath (Châkur).

(the) Grimwall. See Grimwall Mountains.

(the) Grimwall Mountains: a great chain of mountains in Mithgar generally running in a northeasterly-southwesterly direction. Also known as the Grimwall.

Gron: Modru's evil Realm. Barren and bleak, it is a great wedge of land between the Gronfang Mountains to the east, the Rigga Mountains to the west, and the Boreal Sea to the north. Also known as the angle of Gron, the Northern Wastes (of Gron), and the Wastes of Gron.

(the) Gronfang Mountains: a north-south chain of mountains running from the Boreal Sea to the Grimwall. Also known as the Gronfangs.

(the) Gronfangs. See (the) Gronfang Mountains.

Guardian(s). See (the) Lian Guardian(s).

Gûnar: an abandoned Realm in Mithgar bounded on the north by the Grimwall and on the east, south, and west by the arc of the Gûnarring.

Gûnarring Gap: a pass through the Gûnarring (Mountains) joining Gûnar to Valon. Also known as the Gap.

Gûnar Slot: a great wide slot through the Grimwall connecting Gûnar to Rell.

Gushdug: a Hlôk of Gnar's Horde. Probably the leader of the company of Rûcks slain by the Squad of Kraggen-cor, Ursor, and Shannon Silverleaf's Elven Company in the Battle of the Last River Camp. If so, Gushdug was killed by arrow from Silverleaf's bow.

Gushmot: a Hlôk of Gnar's Horde.

(the) Gwasp: a vast swamp in Gron. Also known as the Great Swamp.

Gyphon: The High Vûlk, whose struggle with Adon for control of the Spheres spilled over into Mithgar as the Great

War. Gyphon lost and was banished beyond the Spheres. Gyphon again attempted to gain control during the Winter War but was thwarted by Tuckerby Underbank. Also known as the Great Deceiver, the Great Enemy, the Great Evil, The Greatest Evil, the High Vûlk, the Master.

Haddor: a Man of Valon. One of the riders in Brytta's force. Slain in the Battle of Stormhelm Defile. One of the Five Riders (q.v.).

Hai: a Free Folk exclamation of delight, surprise, or fierce exultation.

Hai roi: an enthusiastic call of greeting, probably Valur in origin but common to all tongues of the Free Folk.

Hál: a Free Folk greeting: hail.

(the) Hall: a term applicable to many of the chambers in Kraggen-cor: e.g., the Great Hall, the Hall of the Gravenarch, the War Hall. Also, a term by which Woody Hollow Hall (q.v.) is known.

(the) Hall of the Gravenarch: a long, low, narrow chamber in Kraggen-cor with a rune-engraved arch supporting the roof. Site of Braggi's demise and Braggi's Rune. The Deevewalkers strode through the Hall of the Gravenarch. Brega broke the Gravenarch to thwart the Gargon by blocking the way. Thus, this part of the Brega Path could not be traversed, but a way around the blockage (the two-mile detour) was found by the Squad of Kraggen-cor.

(the) halls of the dead: the underworld (Hèl) of Valonian myth.

(the) Hammer: the Common-Tongue name given to Rávenor by the Dwarves because of the sudden storms that whelm its slopes. (See Stormhelm.)

Hammerer: a Dwarf whose craft is hammering, one of the skills of stone delving.

hammer-signalling: a Dwarven method of signalling one another by tapping out coded messages—hammer striking stone.

(the) Happy Otter Inn: a Boskydell inn in Greenfields. Also known as the 'Otter.

Harl. See Strong Harl.

Harlingar (Valur: Harl's line of blood): the lineal descendents of Strong Harl. Also the name given to horse-borne warriors of Valon.

Harl the Strong. See Strong Harl.

Harth: a Realm in Mithgar, south of the Wilderland, west of Rell, east of the Boskydells, north of Trellinath.

Hâth Ford: the ford across the Hâth River north of Gûnar Slot.

(the) Hâth River: a river flowing west from the Grimwall Mountains to the Rivermix north of Luren.

hauk (Châkur: advance): a Dwarven term meaning advance.

healer: a physician. A term also used to mean a battlefield helper who binds wounds and dispenses medicines and unguents.

hearthtale: a fairy story or adventure tale told for amusement or for illustrative purposes. So named because these tales were usually told in the evening around campfires, or around the fireplaces of dwellings.

hearthtale hero: a hero of a hearthtale. A term sometimes used to ascribe atypical powers, characteristics, or fortunes to a person. A person whose abilities or fate does not conform to reality.

Hèl: Hell. Also known to the Vanadurin as the halls of the dead, the Realm of the Underworld, and the Underworld.

Hèlarms (Sylva: Hell-arms): Elven name for a Kraken (q.v.).

Hèl's spawn. See (the) undead.

Hèlsteeds (singular: Hèlsteed): horse-like creatures with cloven hooves, long scaled tails, yellow eyes with slitted pupils, and a foetid stench. Slower than horses but with greater endurance. Ridden by Ghûls. Also known as 'Steeds.

(the) hemidome: a great cavernous arch of mountain within which the Dusken Door is situated. Also known as the Great Arch of the Loom and the great hemidome.

(a) Hero of the Realm: an honor bestowed by the High King upon extraordinary heroes.

(the) hidden language. See Châkur.

(the) hidden linchpins: linchpins set in strategic passages in Dwarven caverns which, when pulled, cause the collapse of the passage. A Dwarven defence.

(the) Hidden Refuge. See Arden Valley.

(the) Hidden Stand. See Arden Valley.

(the) hidden tongue. See Châkur.

(the) Hidden Vale. See Arden Valley.

High Adon. See Adon.

High Adon's Ban. See (the) Ban.

High Adon's Covenant. See (the) Ban.

(the) High Gate: a secret door from Kraggen-cor into Quadran Pass. Situated on the western side of the col. Also known as the Gate.

(the) High King: the Liege Lord of all of Northern Mithgar, to whom all other Kings swear fealty. He holds Court at Caer Pendwyr in Pellar, and in Challerain Keep in Rian. Also known as the High Ruler.

(a) High King's Ceremony: a Ceremony ordained by the High King.

(the) High Leader. See Durek.

(the) High One. See Adon.

High Plane: one of the three Planes of creation, holding the High Worlds.

hight: command; order; call; called; name; named.

(the) High Vûlk. See Gyphon.

his Nibs. See Gnar.

(the) History: generally taken to mean the written body of work of the Ravenbook Scholars.

Hlôks (singular: Hlôk): evil, Man-sized, Rûck-like beings. Though fewer in number, Hlôks were masters of the Rûcks. Also known as Drôkha (Valur), Hrôks (Châkur), Loka (Sylva), Lôkha (OP).

Hlôken: a term meaning "of the Hlôks."

(the) hoard of Sleeth: the treasure trove of Sleeth the Orm. Originally stolen by the Dragon from the Dwarves of Blackstone, centuries later the trove was won from Sleeth by Elgo. This treasure became a bone of contention between the Dwarves and the Men of the Steppes of Jord, leading to War and to the Quest of the Black Mountain.

Hogon: a Man of Valon. One of the riders in Brytta's force. A lead scout.

Hola: an untranslated exclamation, common to all tongues of the Free Folk, used to express surprise or to call attention.

(the) Hollow. See Woody Hollow.

(the) Hollow Commons: an open wooded parkland in Woody Hollow where the citizens gather for special events or to have picnics and games. Also known as the Commons.

Hollow End: the northwest end of Woody Hollow. Also named Hollow End because of the many burrow dwellings there.

Hollow Hall. See Woody Hollow Hall.

Holly Northcolt: a damman Warrow of the Boskydells. Wife of Peregrin Fairhill. Dam of Dando, Pippen, Silver, and Petal.

(a) Horde: usually taken to mean ten thousand or more maggot-folk ravaging across the land. In the time of the Fairhill Chronicle, however, Gnar's Horde was one that had been trapped in Drimmen-deeve at the end of the Winter War and remained there until destroyed in the War of Kraggen-cor.

(the) Horn of Narok: a Dwarven horn crafted by an unknown hand. A great token of fear to the Dwarves. Lost to Sleeth the Orm when he took Blackstone as his lair. Won by Elgo. Given to Patrel, as a token of his office, by Vidron. Used to rally Warrow forces in the Struggles during the Winter War. Kept on display at The Root until the Quest of Kraggen-cor. Returned to Kraggen-cor, by Cotton Buckleburr, where it called forth the Doom of Narok. Also called the Horn of the Reach and the Horn of Valon.

(the) Horn of the Reach. See (the) Horn of Valon.

(the) Horn of Valon: a Dwarven horn found in the hoard of Sleeth the Orm by Elgo, Sleeth's Doom. The horn was passed down through the generations until it became Vidron's property. For reasons unexplained—perhaps in a sweeping gesture of generosity but more likely because the horn sought to fulfill its destiny—Vidron gave the horn to Patrel as a token of the Warrow Captain's office. It was used by Patrel to rally forces during the Winter War, although a greater destiny for the horn lay in future events. Also called the Horn of Narok, the Horn of the Reach, and the silver horn of Valon.

(the) Horror. See (the) Gargon.

(the) horsefolk: a term used by Cotton to mean the Vanadurin.

(the) Host: an army (or armies) of a leader of the Free Folk. Also known as a Legion.

(the) House of Aurinor: a branch of weapons-making Lian Elves in the Realm of Duellin, one of the Lost Lands of Atala.

(the) House of Valon: the ruling House of the Kingdom of Valon.

Hoxley Housman: a Man of New Luren. Owner of the Red Boar Inn during the time of the Quest of Kraggen-cor.

Hoy: an untranslated exclamation, common to all tongues of the Free Folk, used to express surprise or to call attention.

Hrōks (singular: Hrōk) (Châkur: vile-vermin). See Hlōks.

Hrōken: a term meaning "of the Hrōks."

Hunter's Moon: the first full Moon after the Harvest Moon.

Hurn: a Realm of Mithgar situated at the easteern reach of the Avagon Sea.

Hyree: a southern Realm in Mithgar allied with Gron during the Winter War. Bounded on the north by the Avagon Sea, on the east by Karoo, on the south by wasteland, and on the west by the Weston Ocean.

Igon: a Man of Pellar. Youngest son of Aurion. A Lord and Prince of the Realm. Brother of Galen. Hero of the Winter War. A member of Brega's squad.

Inarion: an Elf. Lian warrior. Elf Lord of Arden Vale. Leader of the Elves in Weiunwood during the Winter War. Fought in the Battle of Kregyn.

(the) Inner Sea: a brackish-water inland sea joined to the ocean through an extraordinarily long, narrow strait. Bounded on the east by Garia and on the west by Riamon.

(the) Iron Tower: Modru's fortress in the Wastes of Gron. Also known as the Cold Iron Tower, the dark citadel, the Kinstealer's holt.

(the) Ironwater River: a river originating in the Rimmen Mountains and flowing southeasterly to the Inner Sea.

(the) Isleborne River: a river running south and west from Luren to the Weston Ocean. So named because of the many islands in the river. Also known as the Fainen (Sylva) River.

(a) jam: a mountain-climbing/stone-climbing device that is lodged in crevices and used with a snap-ring and a rope or climbing harness, giving purchase to climbers. Shaped like irregular cubes, jams are known as "nuts" by modern-day climbers. Used in Mithgar primarily by Dwarves.

Jayar Northcolt: a buccan Warrow of the Boskydells. Husband of Dot. Sire of Holly. Ex-postmaster. Squire. Owner of Buttermilk Springs, near Thimble. Also known as Squire Northcolt.

Jeering Elgo: a name given Elgo by the Dwarves after their dispute over Sleeth's hoard.

Jugo: a Realm of Mithgar bounded on the north by Gûnar; on the east by Valon, the Red Hills, and Pellar; on the south by the Avagon Sea; and on the west by Hoven and the Brin Downs.

Kachar: a Dwarvenholt in the Grimwall Mountains above Aven. Here it was that Elgo came to face Brak in the dispute over Sleeth's hoard.

Kala (Châkur: good): a Dwarven exclamation meaning good.

(the) Kammerling: a silveron hammer said to have been forged by Adon Himself. Used to smite Black Kalgalath, a Fire-drake.

Khana (Châkur: breakdeath): a Dwarven term meaning breakdeath; refers to the Dwarven belief in reincarnation, that the bonds of Death are broken as each spirit is reborn to walk the earth once again. ·

Khana Durek (Châkur: Breakdeath Durek): a Dwarven title for Durek; i.e., Khana Durek = Breakdeath Durek. (See Breakdeath Durek.)

Khōls (singular: Khōl) (Châkur: reaving-foe): Dwarven term for Ghūls (q.v.).

Kian: a Man of Riamon. Prince of Riamon during the Quest of Kraggencor. Realmsman. Guide to Anval and Borin, and to the Squad of Kraggen-cor. The Leader of the Squad of Kraggen-cor. Hero. King of Riamon after the War of Kraggen-cor. Also known as Lord Kian and later as King Kian.

(the) Kindred: generally taken to mean Châkka Kindred (q.v.).

King Kian. See Kian.

King's business: the specific purpose with which a King charges his emissaries.

(a) King's Ceremony: a Ceremony ordained by a King.

Kingsguards: the personal guards of a King.

Kingsmen: agents and soldiers of a King.

King's Messengers: couriers or heralds of a King.

King's-soldiers: warriors of the army of a King.

Kinstealer: a name given to Modru when his forces took Laurelin captive.

Kistan: an island Realm in the Avagon Sea north of Karoo

and south of Vancha. Ancient enemy of Pellar. Home of sea
rovers (pirates). Allied with Gron during the Winter War.

Kop'yo (Valur: now): a Valonian term meaning "now" or
"go now."

Kraggen-cor (Châkur: Mountain-strength, Mountain-might):
the Dwarven Realm mined under the Quadran. Mightiest of
all Dwarvenholts. Lost to the Dwarves for more than a thou-
sand years while ruled by the Ghath. One of the rare places in
Mithgar where silveron is found. Also known as the Black
Deeves, Black Drimmen-deeve, the Black Hole, the Black
Maze, the Black Puzzle, the Deeves, Drimmen-deeve, the
Mines.

Kraken (plural: Krakens): an evil creature of the sea. Huge.
Tentacled. Some Krakens are said to live in the Great Mael-
strom. Krakens are perhaps the female mates of Dragons.
Also known as Hèlarms.

(the) Krakenward: a Kraken, living in the Dark Mere,
guarding the Dusk-Door. Controlled by Modru and borne to
the lakelet by Skail the Cold-drake in preparation for the
coming of the Dragon Star. Slain by the Dwarves during the
Quest of Kraggen-cor. Also known as the Hèlarms (Sylva),
the lurker, the Madûk (Châkur), the Monster, the Monster of
the Dark Mere, the Monster of the Mere, the Warder, the
Warder from the deep black slime.

Kruk (Châkur: untranslated interjection): Dwarf oathword of
rage.

(the) Lady of the Root: title given to Holly by Perry.

(the) Lair. See (the) Lost Prison.

Land of Galion: Holly's name for Darda Galion.

(the) Land of the Waldana. See (the) Boskydells.

(the) Land of the Wee Folk. See (the) Boskydells.

(the) Land of the West: taken to mean Duellin (q.v.). A
Land in Atala where Elves once dwelled.

Landover Road: a great east-west road of Mithgar, running
eastward from the Crestan Pass in the Grimwall.

Landover Road Ford: the ford across the Argon River along
the Landover Road.

Larkenwald. See Darda Galion.

(the) Last River Camp: the place where the Squad of Kraggen-
cor last camped along the Argon River. It was there, on the

west bank, that they fought with Spawn in the Battle of the
Last River Camp.

Laurelin: a Woman of Riamon. Princess. Betrothed to Galen
in the time of the Winter War. Modru's captive during the
Winter War. Wife of Galen after the Winter War. Mother of
Gareth.

Lawks: a Free Folk interjection of surprise or awe meaning
"Lord," "Mercy," "Lord of mercy," or "Lord have mercy."

leaf: apparently tobacco. Smoked in pipes usually made of
clay.

(a) Legion. See (the) Host.

Levels: taken to mean the tiers or floors within Dwarvenholts.

Lian (Sylva: first): one of the two strains of Elves, the other
being the Dylvana. Also known as Eld Ones, the First Elves.

(the) Lian Guardian(s): Elf warder(s) of Mithgar, guarding
against evil. Also known as Guardian(s).

Lianion (Sylva: first land): Elven name given to Rell, where
the Lian once dwelled.

Lianion-Elves: the name given to the Lian when they dwelled
in Lianion.

(the) Line of Durek: the lineage of Durek and of Durek's
Folk.

Line of the Châkka Kindred: any one of the five strains
of Dwarves.

little uns. See Warrows.

Littor: a Dwarf of Durek's Folk. One of Bomar's cooking
crew. Slain in the Battle of Kraggen-cor.

Loftcrag: the northeasternmost of the four mountains of the
Quadran, beneath which Kraggen-cor is delved. A mountain
whose stone is tinged blue. Also known as Chagor (Sylva)
and Ghatan (Châkur).

Loka (singular: Lok) (Sylva: vile-ones). See Hlōks.

Loken: a term meaning "of the Loka."

Lōkha (singular: Lōkh) (OP: ones-of-filth). See Hlōks.

Lōkken: a term meaning "of the Lōkha."

(the) Lone Eld Tree: a single Eld Tree growing among the
pines in Arden Valley near Arden Falls. This tree was the
only known one of its kind in Mithgar other than those in
Darda Galion.

(the) Long Hall: one of the chambers in Kraggen-cor along
the Brega Path.

(the) Loom: a massif; the western sheer stone flank of Grimspire Mountain, containing the cavernous hemidome at Dusk-Door. Also known as the great flank, the Great Loom, the Great Loomwall, the Loom of Grimspire, the Loomwall.

(the) Loom of Grimspire. See (the) Loom.

(the) Loomwall. See (the) Loom.

(the) Looser of the Red Quarrel. See Tuckerby Underbank.

Lord Kian. See Kian.

Lost Duellin. See Duellin

(the) Lost Land. See Atala.

(the) Lost Prison: the place in Kraggen-cor where the Gargon was trapped for three thousand years. Also known as the *Draedan's* (Sylva) Lair, the Gargon's Lair, the Lair.

(the) Lower Plane: one of the three Planes of creation, holding the Low Worlds.

Lumme: a Free Folk interjection of surprise meaning "Love me."

Luren: a great city of trade situated on the west bank of the Isleborne River in the Riverwood Forest. Suffered through the Dark Plague; destroyed by fire and abandoned. Centuries later, the hamlet of New Luren was founded among the ruins of Old Luren, for at that place is the only river ford in the region.

Luren Ford: the ford across the Isleborne River at Luren.

Lurenites: citizens of Old Luren and of New Luren.

(the) lurker (in the Dark Mere). See the Krakenward.

Luthen: a Man of Valon. One of the riders in Brytta's force. Slain in the Battle of Stormhelm Defile. One of the Five Riders (q.v.).

Madûk (Châkur: evil monster): the Dwarven name for the Krakenward.

(the) Maelstrom. See (the) Great Maelstrom.

maggot-folk: a Warrow name for Spawn.

maiden (plural: maidens): the age-name given to a damman Warrow between ten and twenty years old.

Market Square: a town square in Woody Hollow with stores and an open market.

Marshal of the North Reach: the rank of the Valonian governor of the North Reach of Valon. Brytta was the Marshal of the North Reach in the time of the Quest of Kraggen-cor.

Marshal (of the Valanreach): any of the Reachmarshals (q.v.).

Mastercrafter: a Dwarven master of a craft.

Masterdelver: a Dwarf who has mastered the skill of delving the stone of a Dwarvenholt.

Master of the Ravenbook Scholars: a scholar-moderator elected by the Ravenbook Scholars (q.v.) to chair meetings, direct studies, and in general to guide the activities of that historical society. In the time of the Quest of Kraggen-cor, Gerontius Fairhill was the Master.

Master of The Root: the Ravenbook Scholar chosen to be the curator of The Root.

Master Perry. See Peregrin Fairhill.

(the) Memorial. See (the) Monument at Budgens.

Men: Mankind as we know it. One of the Free Folk of Mithgar. Allied to but separate from Dwarves, Elves, Warrows.

mian: a tasty Elven waybread.

(the) Middle Plane: one of the three Planes of creation, holding the Middle Worlds.

(the) mill: taken to mean the mill on the banks of the Dingle-rill in Woody Hollow.

Mineholt: a term meaning a Dwarvenholt.

Mineholt North: a principal Dwarvenholt in the Rimmen Mountains in Riamon. Also called the Undermountain Realm of Mineholt North.

Minemaster: a Dwarf who has mastered the skill of mining.

(the) Mines. See Kraggen-cor.

Mister Borin: an appellation given to Borin by Fennerly Cotter.

Mister Cotton: an appellation given to Cotton by Fennerly Cotter.

Mister Perry: an appellation given to Perry by a number of Warrows of the Boskydells.

Mitheor (Châkur: mid-earth): the Dwarven name for Mithgar (q.v.).

Mithgar: a term generally meaning the world. Also can refer to the Realms under the rule of the High King. Also known as the midworld, and as Mitheor (Châkur).

Modru: an evil Wizard. Servant of Gyphon. Master of the Myrkenstone. Slain by Tuck in the Winter War. Also known as the Enemy, the Enemy in Gron, the Evil in Gron, the Evil

One, the Evil up North, the Foe, the Kinstealer, the Master of the Cold, Modru Kinstealer.

Modru Kinstealer. See Modru.

Modru's Dread. See (the) Gargon.

Modru's Horde: all of the forces of maggot-folk commanded by Modru.

Modru's Mines: Spawn caverns thought to be in the Grimwall Mountains in the vicinity of Crestan Pass.

Modru's minions: all of the forces commanded by Modru.

Modru's Reavers. See Ghûls.

Mog: a Cave Ogru of Kraggen-cor. A Troll in Gnar's Horde.

Molly Brewster: a Woman of Stonehill. Wife of Aylesworth.

Monarch: generally taken to mean the High King, but also can mean any King.

(the) Monster. See (the) Krakenward.

(the) Monster of the Dark Mere. See (the) Krakenward.

(the) Monster of the Mere. See (the) Krakenward.

Mont Coron. See Stormhelm.

(the) Monument. See (the) Monument at Budgens.

(the) Monument at Budgens: a Boskydell monument in the hamlet of Budgens commemorating the first battle of the Struggles. Also known as the Memorial and as the Monument.

Monument Knoll: the hill in Budgens on which is situated the Monument.

Mountain (Châkur: MOΠΛ = living stone): a Dwarven word represented in the translation of *The Raven Book* and of *The Fairhill Journal* by the word Mountain. The symbol M indicates a special word for "mountain" signifying Châkka reverence for the living stone of Mitheor (Mithgar).

(the) Mountain Throne: a natural quartzen outcrop shaped like the bench of a great throne high upon the side of Stormhelm. From it can be seen the Châkkacyth Ryng.

Mount Redguard. See Redguard (Mount/Mountain).

(the) Mustering Chamber (of the First Neath). See (the) War Hall.

(the) Mustering Hall. See (the) War Hall.

myrk (Sylva, OHR: myrk = murk): murk.

(the) Myrkenstone: the piece of the Dragon Star that fell to Mithgar; used by Modru to create the Dimmendark. Destroyed by Tuck. Also known as the 'Stone.

(the) Myrkenstone Slayer. See Tuckerby Underbank.

*   *   *

Naral: a Dwarf of Durek's Folk. One of Bomar's cooking crew. Slain in the Battle of Kraggen-cor.

Nare: a Dwarf of Durek's Folk. One of Bomar's cooking crew. Slain in the Battle of Kraggen-cor.

Narok (Châkur: Death-War): a Dwarven term meaning Death-War. The Staves of Narok (q.v.) foretold of a Death-War (an apocalyptic struggle) in which the Dwarves would reap great sorrow.

Neaths: the name given to the levels in Kraggen-cor deeper than the entrance at Dawn-Gate. (See Gate Level.)

Neddra: the name of one of the Untargarda, whence came the Spawn.

Ned Proudhand: a buccan Warrow of the Boskydells. The wheelwright that was paid a gold coin for repairing the waggon used by Anval, Borin, and Lord Kian on their trip to the Boskydells.

New Luren: the settlement built upon the site of Old Luren. (See Luren.)

Nightwind: a horse of Valon. Brytta's great black stallion, trained for War.

ninnyhammer: dolt.

(the) Nith River (Sylva: nith = rising): a river in Darda Galion flowing east to plunge down the Great Escarpment at Vanil Falls into the Cauldron to join the Argon River.

(the) Northern Wastes. See Gron.

(the) North Reach (of Valon): the northern quadrant of Valon.

North Riamon. See Riamon.

(the) North Route. See (the) Post Road.

Ogrus (singular: Ogru) (Twyll, Valur: Trolls): evil creatures. Giant Rūcks. Twelve to fourteen feet tall. Dull-witted. Stone-like hides. Enormous strength. Also known as Cave Trolls, Cave Ogrus, Ogru-Trolls, Trolls.

Ogruthi (Sylva: Trollfolk): Elven name for the Ogru Folk.

Ogru-Trolls. See Ogrus.

Old Luren: a city of old, destroyed by fire. (See Luren.)

Old Man Tumble: Cotton's name for the Tumble River.

(the) Old Rell Spur: the ancient road joining the Old Rell

Way to the Dusk-Door. Also known as the Old Way Spur and as the Spur.

(the) Old Rell Way: an abandoned trade road running south from the Crestan Pass down the west side of the Grimwall Mountains to Luren. Also known as the Old Way and as the Way.

(the) Old Way. See (the) Old Rell Way.

(the) Old Way Spur. See (the) Old Rell Spur.

O Mighty One. See Gnar.

(the) One-Eyed Crow: a Boskydell inn in Woody Hollow. Also known as the 'Crow.

Oris: a Dwarf of Durek's Folk. One of Bomar's cooking crew. Slain in the Battle of Kraggen-cor.

Orm. See Dragon.

Orn: a Dwarf of Durek's Folk. Glain's son. Slain by the Gargon shortly after it burst free of the Lost Prison.

Othen Warrows: one of the four northern strains of Warrows. Othen Warrows traditionally live in fen stilt-houses in marshlands.

Othran the Seer: a Man from Atala, the Lost Land.

Othran's Tomb: a rune-marked stone tomb at the foot of Mont Challerain. Here lie the remains of Othran the Seer. Tuck found the Red Quarrel and the Atalar Blade in Othran's Tomb. Also known as the barrow of Othran the Seer.

(the) 'Otter. See (the) Happy Otter Inn.

Outside: a Boskydell Warrow term meaning the Lands beyond the borders of the Boskydells.

Outsiders: a Boskydell Warrow term meaning people living beyond the borders of the Boskydells.

(the) Oval Chamber: one of the chambers in Kraggen-cor along the Brega Path.

(the) Over Stair: the portage-way up the Great Escarpment at Bellon Falls.

Paren Warrows: one of the four northern strains of Warrows. Paren Warrows traditionally are field dwellers living in stone field-houses (stone dwellings and stone farmhouses situated in open fields).

(the) Path. See (the) Brega path.

Pathfinder: a name given to Cotton by Bomar.

pathfinder: a guide.

Patrel Rushlock: a buccan Warrow of the Boskydells. Hero of the Winter War. Captain of the Company of the King. A leader of the Struggles. One of Tuck's companions. Wearer of the golden armor. Bearer of the Horn of Valon. A member of Brega's squad. Also known as the Captain of the Infant Brigade, Captain Patrel, and Paddy.

Pellar: a Realm of Mithgar where dwells the High King in Caer Pendwyr. Bounded on the north by Riamon and also by Valon across the River Argon, and on the east and south by the Avagon Sea, and on the west by Jugo.

Pellarion: the common language of Mithgar. So named because it originated in Pellar. Also known as the Common Tongue. (For various words and phrases in Old Pellarion, see Appendix: Translations of Words and Phrases.)

Pendwyrian: a term meaning "of Caer Pendwyr."

Peregrin Fairhill: a buccan Warrow of the Boskydells. Ravenbook Scholar. Curator of Sir Tuckerby's Warren. Member of the Quest of Kraggen-cor. Member of the Squad of Kraggen-cor. Brega-Path guide. Wielder of Bane. Drimmendeeve Rück-fighter. Scriber of *The Fairhill Journal*. Hero of the Realm. Also known as Friend Perry, Master Perry, Mister Perry, Perry, Wee Perry, and Wee One.

Perry. See Peregrin Fairhill.

Perry's map: Perry's drawing of the Brega Path.

(the) Pitch: a great slope of land falling away to the east of the Quadran. Also known as Baralan (Châkur) and Falanith (Sylva).

Plooshgnak: a Hlōk of Gnar's Horde.

(the) Plow. See Rhone.

(the) Pony Field: a large field in Woody Hollow where ponies are kept.

(the) Pony Field stable: a common stable of Woody Hollow, situated on the southern edge of the Pony Field.

(the) Post Road: the road between Luren and Challerain Keep. Also known as the North Road, and as the South Road.

(the) Purging: the successful efforts of the Lian Guardians to drive dire creatures from Drearwood. Also known as the Great Purging.

*   *   *

(the) Quadmere: a pure lakelet on the Pitch one mile from Dawn-Gate. Also known as Châk-alon (Châkur) and as the 'Mere.

(the) Quadran: the name collectively given to four of the mountains of the Grimwall: Greytower, Loftcrag, Grimpsire, Stormhelm. Herein Kraggen-cor is delved.

Quadran Col. See Quadran Pass.

Quadran Gap. See Quadran Pass.

Quadran Pass: the pass across the Grimwall through the Quadran. Also known as the Col, the Gap, the Gap of Stormhelm, the Pass, Quadran Col, and Quadran Gap.

Quadran Road: the road from Quadran Pass down the west side of Stormhelm.

Quadran Run: the road, and the stream, from Quadran Pass down the east side of Stormhelm.

(the) Quadrill: a river flowing southeasterly from the Quadran through Darda Galion and into the Argon River.

(the) Quartzen Caves: a Dwarven mineholt of Durek's Folk, east of the Rimmen Mountains, delved in the Quartzen Hills.

(the) Quartzen Hills: a range of hills east of the Rimmen Mountains. Here are delved the Quartzen Caves.

(the) Quest of Black Mountain: the quest of Elyn and Thork to find the Kammerling.

(the) Quest of Kraggen-cor: the quest of the Dwarves and their allies to regain Kraggen-cor from Gnar's Horde.

(the) Quest of the Green Stone: the quest of Arin and of Egil One Eye to find the Green Stone of Xian.

(a) quilted down-suit: special quilted, down-filled clothing worn to withstand the bitter winter cold of the mountains.

Quiren Warrows: one of the four strains of northern Warrows. Quiren Warrows traditionally are tree dwellers living in wooden flet houses.

(a) Race. See Folk.

(the) Race: a narrow, high-walled river canyon through which the Argon River thunders at a great speed. Situated south of the Dalgor Marches.

Rach (Valur: untranslated interjection): oathword of Valon, used to express frustration.

Raech: a Man of Valon. One of the riders in Brytta's force.

Slain in the Battle of Stormhelm Defile. One of the Five Riders (q.v.).

Rael: Lian Elfess. Consort of Talarin. Mother of Gildor and Vanidor. Seeress and soothsayer.

Raffin: a Boskydell village along the Crossland Road in Eastdell.

Ragad Vale: a western Grimwall valley leading to Dusk-Door, at the base of Grimspire Mountain. Also known as Ragad Valley and as the Valley of the Door.

Ragad Valley. See Ragad Vale.

Ralo Road: the road between Luren and Gûnarring Gap.

Rand: a Man of Riamon. Prince of Riamon. Kian's younger brother. Guide to Durek's Host. Realmsman. Troll-slain in the Battle of Kraggen-cor.

Raven (Underbank-Greylock): a damman Warrow. Wife of Willen Greylock. Dam of Robin. Dammsel of Tuck and Merrilee. Raven was instrumental in the recording of *Sir Tuckerby Underbank's Unfinished Diary and His Accounting of the Winter War*. Also known as Raven the Scholar.

(The) Raven Book. See *Sir Tuckerby Underbank's Unfinished Diary and His Accounting of the Winter War*. Tuck named the journal after his dammsel, Raven; hence, it acquired the name *The Raven Book*. Also known as the *'Book*.

(the) Ravenbook Scholars: a continuing group of Warrow historians originally organized by Willen Greylock to carry on the recording of the history of Mithgar. This group continued the work started by Tuck, who had been commissioned by King Galen to record the events of the Winter War, and other history as well. Also known as the Scholars.

Rávenor (Châkur: storm hammer). See Stormhelm.

Raven the Scholar. See Raven (Underbank-Greylock).

ravers: ravagers.

(a) Reach (of Valon): one of the four quadrants into which Valon is divided (North Reach, East Reach, South Reach, West Reach). The term "Reach" translates into "Reich" in Valur.

Reachmarshal (from Reich-marshal): the Vanadurin rank below Hrosmarshal (Valur: hros = horse). Also known as Marshal and as Valanreach Marshal.

(the) Realm: generally taken to mean that part of Mithgar ruled by the High King.

(the) Realm of Death: the dwelling place of spirits in the time between death and rebirth—a Dwarven belief.

(the) Realm of the Underworld. See Hèl.

Realmsmen: agents of the High King. Defenders of the Land. Champions of Just Causes.

Realmstone: any one of the obelisks marking the boundaries of Kingdoms; e.g., there is a Realmstone on the west bank of the Quadmere marking the Realm of Kraggen-cor.

reavers. See Ghûls.

reaving-foe. See Ghûls.

(the) Red Arrow. See (the) Red Quarrel.

(the) Red Boar: an inn in New Luren.

(the) Red Caverns. See (the) Red Caves.

(the) Red Caves: the Dwarven mineholt in the Red Hills. A famous Dwarven armory. Also known as the Red Caverns.

Redguard (Mount/Mountain): a small mountain just to the west of the Quadran. Also known as Mount Redguard.

(the) Red Hills: a north-south range of mountains between Jugo and Valon.

(the) Red Quarrel: a red arrow, made of a strange, light metal (perhaps coated lithium or magnesium), found by Tuck in the tomb of Othran the Seer. A token of power loosed by Tuck in the Winter War, the Red Quarrel destroyed the Myrkenstone. Also known as the Red Arrow.

(the) Refuge. See Arden Valley.

Rell: an abandoned Land of Mithgar. Bounded on the north by Arden, on the east and south by the Grimwall, and on the west by the River Tumble along Rhone.

(the) Rest Chamber: one of the chambers in Kraggen-cor along the Brega Path.

Rhondor: a city of commerce on the shores of the Inner Sea at the outlet of the Ironwater River. Because of the scarcity of nearby forests, the city was made of tile, brick, and fireclay.

Rhone: an abandoned Land of Mithgar. Bounded on the north by the Rigga Mountains, on the east and south by Arden and the River Tumble along Rell, and on the west by the River Caire along Harth and Rian. Also known as the Plow because of its shape.

Riamon: a Realm of Mithgar, divided into two sparsely settled Kingdoms: North Riamon and its Trust, South Riamon. Bounded on the north by Aven, on the east by Garia, on the south by Pellar and Valon, and on the west by the Grimwall.

(the) riddle of Narok. See (the) Staves of Narok.

(the) Riders of Valon: Men of Valon. So named because Valon is a nation of horsemen.

(the) Rigga Mountains: a north-south chain of mountains between Rian to the west and Gron to the east, running from the Boreal Sea in the north to Grüwen Pass in the south.

(the) Rillmere: a lakelet along the southwestern side of Budgens.

(the) Rime of Narok. See (the) Staves of Narok.

(the) Rimmen Mountains: a great ring of mountains in Riamon.

(the) Ring. See (the) Châkkacyth Ryng.

Rises: the name given to the levels in Kraggen-cor higher than the entrance at Dawn-Gate. (See Gate Level.)

(the) Rissanin River: a river running southwesterly from the Rimmen Mountains to the River Argon.

Rith: the trothmate of Seventh Durek. The only female Dwarf named in either *The Raven Book* or *The Fairhill Journal*.

River Drummers: merchants who ply their trade on the rivers of Mithgar.

(the) Rivermix: a great swirl of water where the Hâth River meets the Caire River to become the Isleborne River, just north of Luren.

Riverwood (Forest): a great forest, along the Rivers Caire and Isleborne, extending into the Lands of Trellinath, Harth, and Rell.

rock-nails: pitons.

Rolf: a Baeran Man. Middle son of Baru, the Passwarden of the Crestan Pass in 5E231.

(the) Room: a term applicable to many chambers in Kraggen-cor; e.g., the Grate Room.

(The) Root: the name of Tuck's burrow in Woody Hollow. So named because it lies at the root of the coomb in which Woody Hollow is situated. After the Winter War, The Root came to be known as Sir Tuckerby's Warren and as Tuckerby's Warren.

(the) Rothro River: a river originating on the wold east of Dawn-Gate and flowing south into the Quadrill.

(the) Round Chamber: one of the chambers in Kraggen-cor along the Brega Path.

(the) Rovers of Kistan: reavers of the sea whose pirate holts are in the wild southern coastal lands of Kistan. Ancient enemies of Pellar.

Rucha (singular: Ruch) (Sylva: foul-ones): Elven name for Rücks (q.v.).

Ruchen: a term meaning "of the Rucha."

Rück-doors: hidden doors, Rück-made, along the mountain slopes, opening into the caverns of the maggot-folk. Also known as Rück-gates, Rutch-doors, Spawn-doors, and Wrg-doors.

Rücken: a term meaning "of the Rücks."

Rück-fighter: a term generally taken to mean any person of the Free Folk who has fought the maggot-folk.

Rück-gates. See Rück-doors.

Rückish: a term meaning Rück-like.

Rücks (singular: Rück): evil, goblin-like creatures from Neddra, four to five feet tall. Dark. Pointed teeth. Bat-wing ears. Skinny-armed, bandylegged. Unskilled. Also known as Rucha (Sylva), Rukha (OP), Rutcha (Valur), Úkhs (Châkur).

Rückslayer: a term used to describe any warrior who has slain several Rücks.

Rukha (singular: Rukh) (OP: filthy-ones): Pellarion name for Rücks (q.v.).

rune-jewel: a jewel inscribed with runes of power. Such a jewel was embedded in the blade of the Elven long-knife Bane.

Rûpt (Sylva: corpse-worms): the Elven name for the maggot-folk.

Rutcha (singular: Rutch) (Valur: goblins): a term used by the Men of Valon meaning Rücks (q.v.).

Rutch-doors (Valur: goblin-doors). See Rück-doors.

Rutchen: a term meaning "of the Rutcha."

Rutch-pace (Valur: goblin-pace): the running lope of the maggot-folk.

(the) Ryng. See (the) Châkkacyth Ryng.

(the) Scholars. See (the) Ravenbook Scholars.

(the) Scroll. See (the) Brega Scroll.

(the) Secret Seven: Cotton's name for the Squad of Kraggencor (q.v.).

Sentinel Falls: a waterfall of the Duskrill near the Dusk-Door. So named because of the sentinel post above the falls.

(the) Sentinel Stair: the carven stair up the bluff of Sentinel Falls and to the top of the Sentinel Stand.

(the) Sentinel Stand: a guard post atop a tall spire near the Dusk-Door where Dwarf sentries kept watch over Ragad Vale.

(the) Seven. See (the) Squad of Kraggen-cor.

(the) Seven Dells: the Boskydells (q.v.). Called the Seven Dells because the Realm is divided into seven major districts, each called a Dell: Northdell, Eastdell, Southdell, Westdell, Centerdell, Updell, Downdell.

(the) Seven Penetrators. See (the) Squad of Kraggen-cor.

Seventh Durek: the Dwarf King of Durek's Folk during the Quest of Kraggen-cor. Renowned for wresting Kraggen-cor from the maggot-folk and forging it into a mighty Realm as of old. The seventh to be named Durek (q.v.).

Shadowlight: the spectral light of the Dimmendark (q.v.).

(a) shadow-mission: a false mission or a mission of little or no hope.

Shannon. See Vanidar.

Shannon Silverleaf. See Vanidar.

(the) Shelf. See (the) Broad Shelf.

shok (Châkur: axes): a Dwarven term meaning axes.

(the) Side Hall: one of the chambers in Kraggen-cor along the Brega Path.

(the) Signal Mountains: a north-to-east-to-south arc of weatherworn, sparse, widespread mountains. Mont Challerain is the northernmost mountain, Beacontor the southernmost. So named because signal fires upon their crests were used to pass along news of import.

(the) silver armor. See silveron armor.

(The) Silver Call. See *(The) Fairhill Journal.*

(the) Silver Call: the sound of the Horn of Narok—mentioned in the Staves of Narok—which caused the fulfillment of the ancient prophecy.

(the) silver call: generally taken to mean the lure of a quest or a venture, said to fetch with a silver call. Also can mean the sound of the Horn of Valon.

silver coin. See silver penny.

(the) silver horn (of Valon). See (the) Horn of Valon.

Silverlarks. See Vani-lērihha.

Silverleaf. See Vanidar.

silveron: a rare and precious metal of Mithgar. Probably an alloy. Also known as starsilver.

(the) silveron armor: the armor worn by Tuck during the Winter War and by Perry during the Quest of Kraggen-cor. Originally made by the Dwarves of Drimmen-deeve for Princelings of the Royal House of the High King, the armor was given to Tuck by Laurelin to wear at her birthday feast. The armor was ultimately placed on display at Tuckerby's Warren, where it was to remain in possession of the Warrows until recalled by the shade of Aurion. Also known as the silver armor, the silveron mail, the starsilver armor.

(the) silveron mail. See (the) silveron armor.

silver penny: one of three types of coins used for commerce in Mithgar (gold and copper being the other two types). Also known as a silver, a silver coin, and as a silver piece.

sipar: a Rūcken shield with three strap-handles positioned such that it can be used either as a target shield or as a buckler.

Sir Tuckerby's Diary: the original diary kept by Tuckerby Underbank during the Winter War. (See *Sir Tuckerby Underbank's Unfinished Diary and His Accounting of the Winter War.*)

Sir Tuckerby's Warren. See (The) Root.

Sir Tuckerby Underbank: a title given to Tuck by Laurelin and by other members of Royalty.

Sir Tuckerby Underbank's Unfinished Diary and His Accounting of the Winter War: the chronicle compiled by Tuck and various scribes to describe the Winter War. Tuck's diary was unfinished, for he was blinded by the Myrkenstone and wrote in it no more. Yet it, plus Tuck's accounting of his memories, and the accounts of others, made up the history of the Winter War. The chronicle was commissioned by High King Galen, and funds were set aside to hire scribes to assist Tuck in this work. Raven aided immeasurably; hence, the history is also called *The Raven Book.* Also known as Tuck's chronicle.

Siven Warrows: one of the four strains of northern Warrows. Siven Warrows traditionally live in burrows dug into hillsides.

Skail: the Dragon that bore the Hèlarms to the Dark Mere at Dusk-Door.

skut (Twyll, Valur: untranslated interjection): oathword used by Warrows perhaps to mean filth. Also an oathword of Valon used to express anger.

(the) Sky Mountains: a southwesterly-northeasterly chain of mountains between Gothon to the west and Basq to the east.

(the) sleep of Elves: the manner in which Elves slumber, which is different from that of other Folk: Elves can rest their minds in gentle memories; however, after a prolonged time, even Elves must truly sleep.

Sleeth's Doom. See Elgo.

Sleeth the Orm: the Cold-drake that captured Blackstone, the Dwarvenholt in the Rigga Mountains, and took the Dwarven treasure as its hoard. Slain centuries later by Elgo.

slowcoach: sluggard.

slugabed: layabout; one who lolls in bed.

Slûk: a foul-sounding common tongue of the Spawn. First spoken by the Hlōks. Even with Slûk, however, Hlōks, Rūcks, and perhaps Ghûls and Ogrus, at times also used a debased form of Pellarion. (For various Slûk words and phrases, see Appendix: Translations of Words and Phrases.)

snap-ring: a mountain-climbing/stone-climbing device that clips onto pitons and "nuts" to fasten ropes and straps to in order to support climbers. Primarily used in Mithgar by Dwarves.

Sons of Harl: the lineal descendants of Strong Harl. Also the name given to all Men of Valon.

Southdell: one of the Seven Dells of the Boskydells.

South Riamon. See Riamon.

(the) South Route. See (the) Post Road.

Sovereign: generally taken to mean the High King, but also can mean any Lord or King.

Spaunen (Sylva: filth of the Untargarda): Elven term for Spawn (q.v.).

Spawn: the collective name given to all the Folk and other creatures of Neddra who came to live in Mithgar; e.g., Rūcks, Hlōks, Ghûls, Gargons, Ogrus, Vulgs, Hèlsteeds. Also known as maggot-folk, Wrg (Valur), Yrm (OP), *Rûpt* (Sylva), *Spaunen* (Sylva), Grg (Châkur), and Squam (Châkur). Also known as Winternight Spawn during the Winter War.

Spawn-doors. See Rūck-doors.

(a) spelldown: a spelling bee.

(the) Spindle Ford: a Boskydell ford along the Upland Way across the Spindle River.

(the) Spindle River: a river forming the northern and eastern border of the Boskydells. In the valley of the river grows much of the Spindlethorn Barrier.

Spindlethorn: an iron-hard thorn growth of great density reaching to heights of fifty feet or more. Found in nature only in the river valleys around the Boskydells. Also known as 'Thorn.

(the) Spindlethorn Barrier: a barrier of thorns shielding the Boskydells. The thorns, called Spindlethorn, grow in the river valleys surrounding the Bosky. The thorns have been cultivated to grow along the boundary in those places where formerly there were gaps in the barrier. Forty to fifty feet high, the barrier width varies from one mile at its narrowest to ten or so miles at its widest. Also known as the Barrier, the Great Barrier, the Great Thornwall, the 'Thorn, the Thornring, the Thornwall, the 'Wall.

(the) Spiral Down: one of the legendary features of Kraggen-cor.

(the) Spur. See (the) Old Rell Spur.

(the) Squad. See (the) Squad of Kraggen-cor.

(the) Squad of Kraggen-cor: those persons whose mission it was to enter the Dawn-Gate, pass secretly through Gnar's forces, and make their way undetected through the length of Kraggen-cor to the inside of Dusk-Door to repair it (if broken) and let in Durek's Army. The Squad originally consisted of Anval, Barak, Borin, Delk, Kian, Perry, and Tobin. But Barak was slain and Tobin disabled before reaching Kraggen-cor. Shannon Silverleaf and Ursor joined the Squad to bring it up to seven strong again. Also known as the Secret Seven, the Seven Penetrators, the Seven, the Squad of Seven, the Squad.

(the) Squad of Seven. See (the) Squad of Kraggen-cor.

Squam (Châkur: Underworld foul ones): Dwarven name for Spawn (q.v.).

Squam-War (Châkur: Underworld-foul-ones War): War with the Spawn.

Squire Northcolt. See Jayar Northcolt.

starsilver. See silveron.

(the) starsilver armor. See (the) silveron armor.

(the) Staves. See (the) Staves of Narok.

(the) Staves of Narok: an ancient legend, set to verse, foretelling of great sorrow to befall the Dwarven Folk during the Death-War. The Horn of Narok was intimately entwined with the fulfillment of the Doom spoken of in the Staves. Also known as the Doom of Narok, the riddle of Narok, the Rime of Narok, and the Staves.

Stel (Valur: steel): a Valonian term meaning steel, weapons.

(the) Steppes of Jord: a northern Realm of bleak, high plains in Mithgar. Bounded on the north by the Barrens, on the east and the south by the Grimwall, and on the west by the Gronfangs and the Boreal Sea.

(the) 'Stone. See (the) Myrkenstone.

(the) Stone-arches Bridge: the bridge over the River Caire along the Crossland Road.

Stone Giants: a Dwarven name for the Utruni (q.v.).

Stonehill: a village on the southern margins of the Battle Downs in the western fringes of the Wilderland between Rian and Harth. Situated at the junction of the Post Road and the Crossland Road. Also known as the 'Hill.

Stonehiller: a resident of Stonehill; the argot of Stonehill.

stone or fire: the way of a Dwarven funeral, in which the dead are placed on a fitting pyre or are buried in stone.

(the) 'Stone Slayer. See Tuckerby Underbank.

Stoog: a Hlōk of Gnar's Horde.

Stormhelm: the northwesternmost of the four mountains of the Quadran beneath which Kraggen-cor is delved. A mountain whose stone is tinged red. Said by Dwarves to be the mightiest mountain of the known ranges in Mithgar. So named because of the many storms that rage at its peak. Also known as Coron (Sylva), the Hammer, Mont Coron, and Râvenor (Châkur).

Stormhelm Defile: a steep-walled canyon on the road up the western flank of Stormhelm to Quadran Pass.

stripling (plural: striplings): the age-name given to a buccan Warrow between ten and twenty years old.

Strong Harl: The great leader of the Vanadurin in ancient times when they rode the Steppes of Jord. Also known as Harl and as Harl the Strong.

(the) Struggles: the general name given by the Warrows to the struggles to overcome Modru's forces in the Boskydells in the Winter War. Also known as the War of the Boskydells.

(the) study at The Root: one of the rooms in The Root. The study is considered a curiosity among Warrows since few, if any, other Warrow dwellings have studies.

(the) sundered causeway: the shattered causeway along the Loomwall near the Dusk-Door.

Swarm: a thousand or more maggot-folk.

swordthane (OHR: sword warrior): warrior of the sword.

Sylva (Sylva: our tongue): the language of the Elves. (For various Sylva words and phrases, see Appendix: Translations of Words and Phrases.)

tag-along: one who follows closely. In *The Fairhill Journal*, two younglings (q.v.) were called tag-alongs.

Talarin (Sylva: steel-ring): an Elf. Lian Warrior. Elf Lord. Consort of Rael. Sire of Gildor, Vanidor, and Faeon. Leader of the forces in Arden Vale during the Winter War. Fought in the Battle of Kregyn. Also known as Alor Talarin, Lord Talarin, the Warder of the Northern Reaches of Rell.

Teddy: a buccan Warrow of Budgens in the Boskydells at the time of the Quest of Kraggen-cor.

theen. See Wizard-metal.

Thief Elgo: a name given Elgo by the Dwarves after their dispute over the hoard of Sleeth. (See Elgo.)

Thimble: a Boskydell village south of the Tineway in South-dell.

Third Glain: a Dwarf King of Durek's Folk. Father of Orn, and slain with him by the Gargon shortly after it burst free of the Lost Prison.

(the) Thirsty Horse: a Boskydell inn.

Thork: a Dwarf. Companion of Elyn in the Quest of Black Mountain.

'Thorn. See Spindlethorn.

(the) Thornring. See (the) Spindlethorn Barrier.

thorn tunnel: a passage through the Spindlethorn Barrier.

(the) Thornwalkers (of the Boskydells): bands of Warrow archers set along the entry ways into the Boskydells in times of trouble to keep out all but those on legitimate business. These archers also patrol the borders of the Boskydells (i.e., the Spindlethorn Barrier), thus are said to "walk the Thorns."

(the) Thornwall. See (the) Spindlethorn Barrier.

Thuuth Uthor (Slûk: dread striker; fear lash): Gargoni words meaning dread striker or fear lash. Scrawled by the Gargon on a large stone block in the Lost Prison.

Tillok: a Boskydell village along the Crossland Road in Eastdell.

Tine Ford: the ford along the Tineway across the Spindle River.

Tineway: the northwesterly-southeasterly road between Rood in the Boskydells and the Post Road in Harth.

Tobin Forgefire: a Dwarf of Durek's Folk. Gatemaster. One of the Squad of Kraggen-cor. Tobin's leg was shattered during the Battle of the Last River Camp. Cared for by the Elves, Tobin recovered, though afterward he always limped.

Tovit (Valur: ready): a Valonian term meaning "ready" or "stand ready."

Trell: a Man of Valon. One of the riders in Brytta's force.

Trellinath: an abandoned Realm of Mithgar. Bounded on the north by Wellen and the Boskydells, on the east by Rell, on the south by the Grimwall, and on the west by Gothon.

Troll-dam of the Black Mere: a Troll-made dam blocking the Duskrill and creating the Black Mere at Dusk-Door.

Trolls. See Ogrus.

Troll's Bane: taken to mean Bane (q.v.), the Elven long-knife.

Troll War-bar: a massive iron bar borne as a weapon by an Ogru.

Tror: a Dwarf of Durek's Folk. Masterhammerer. Warrior in the Battle of Kraggen-cor. Tror and his Hammerers helped break the Troll-made dam to empty the Dark Mere during the battle with the Madûk.

trothmate (Châkur: true-pledged mate): a Dwarven term meaning "husband" or "wife."

Tuck. See Tuckerby Underbank.

Tuckerby's scribes: the scribes hired by Tuckerby Underbank to work on the History. Also known as Tuckerby's scriveners.

Tuckerby's scriveners. See Tuckerby's scribes.

Tuckerby's Warren. See (The) Root.

Tuckerby Underbank: a buccan Warrow of the Boskydells. Husband of Merrilee. Raven's sire. Hero of the Winter War. Thornwalker. Deevewalker. Bane Wielder. Wearer of the silveron armor. Arrow Bearer. Bearer of the Red Quarrel. A member of Brega's squad. Looser of the Red Quarrel. Myrkenstone Slayer. Slayer of the Myrkenstone. 'Stone Slayer.

Modru's Doom. Modru's Slayer. Died of an illness at age 97.
Also known as Friend Tuck, Master Tuck, Master Waerling,
Sir Tuck, Tuck.

Tuck's chronicle. See *Sir Tuckerby Underbank's Unfinished
Diary and His Accounting of the Winter War.*

Tuck's diary: Tuck's journal. The blank diary was given to
Tuck by his cousin Willy upon Tuck's departure from Woody
Hollow to join the Eastdell Fourth; the diary formed the basis
for *The Raven Book.*

tulwar: a curved Rūcken sword (sabre).

(the) Tumble River: a north-south river of many rapids and
falls, originating in the Grimwall Mountains and flowing
through Arden Gorge and south to join the River Caire above
Luren.

Tunnelmaster: one who has mastered the Dwarven craft of
tunnel making.

Turin Stonesplitter: a Dwarf of Durek's Folk. Minemaster
and Delfshaper. Slain by the Krakenward.

turves: squares of sod cut from turf.

(the) Twilight Path: the way of the Twilight Ride (q.v.).

(the) Twilight Ride: a way of passing from Mithgar, on the
Middle Plane, to Adonar, upon the High Plane. Elves riding
on horses can somehow pass between the Planes. Brega
observed that a ritualistic chanting and a pacing in an arcane
pattern were used to achieve passage. Other Folk know not
how or perhaps are incapable of passing between the Planes,
since only Elves and their horses, and perhaps the Vani-
lērihha, seem to make this journey. There is, however, evidence that Adon and Gyphon can open the way for others.

(the) two-mile detour: the detour taken by the Squad of
Kraggen-cor to get around the wreckage of the Hall of the
Gravenarch and back upon the Brega Path.

Twyll (Twyll: our tongue): the ancient Warrow tongue. (For
various Twyll words and phrases, see Appendix: Translations
of Words and Phrases.)

Uchan (Châkur: anvil). See Greytower.

Ūkhs (singular: Ūkh) (Châkur: stench-ones): Dwarven name
for Rūcks (q.v.).

Ūkkish: a term meaning "of the Ūkhs."

Uncle Bill: the name of a Man in the song "The Battle of

Weiunwood." Uncle Bill in fact may have been an actual participant in the battle.

(the) undead: those of Valonian legend who dwell in Hèl. Also known as Hèl's spawn.

(the) Underbanks: the Underbank lineage.

(the) Undermountain Realm of Mineholt North. See Mineholt North.

(the) Underworld. See Hèl.

(the) 'Unicorn. See (the) White Unicorn Inn (of Stonehill).

(the) Unknown Cavern: a Dwarven term meaning a place of uncertainty.

(the) Untargarda (OP: Under Worlds): all the worlds upon the Lower Plane.

(the) Upland Way: a northeasterly-southwesterly road running between the Cliffs in the Boskydells and the Post Road near the Battle Downs.

(the) Upward Way: a long, upward slope in Kraggen-cor between the Broad Hall and the Great Chamber of the Sixth Rise. A part of the Brega Path.

Ursor: a Baeran Man of enormous size and strength. Ursor's wife, Grael, and child were slain by maggot-folk. Seeking revenge, Ursor used a great black mace to slay many of the Foul Folk. Ursor became a member of Shannon Silverleaf's Elven Company and then a member of the Squad of Kraggen-cor. After the Quest of Kraggen-cor, Ursor was made Captain of Kian's Kingsguards.

Utruni (singular: Utrun) (Sylva: stone-giants): one of the Folk of Mithgar. The Utruni comprise three strains. The adults range from twelve to seventeen feet tall. Gentle. Shy. Dwellers within the stone of Mithgar (the continental bedrock itself). Keepers of the 'Stone. Jewel-like eyes. Shapers of the land. Able to move through solid stone. Also known as Giants and as Stone Giants.

Utruni eyes: jewel-like eyes. It seems that the Utruni can see through solid stone. Their eyes resemble actual jewels, and they see by a ''light'' different from that seen by other Folk. (Modern-day physicists have speculated that perhaps the Giants see by neutrino-like particles.)

Valanreach (from Valon-reich): the name generally given to the grassy plains of Valon.

Valanreach long-ride: a method of varying the gait of a horse such that a pace of forty or even fifty miles per day can be sustained over a considerable number of days.

Valanreach Marshal. See Reachmarshal.

Valki: a Dwarf of Durek's Folk. The greatest Gatemaster of the Dwarves, who in the First Era, with the Wizard Grevan, constructed the Dusk-Door.

(the) Valley of the Door. See Ragad Vale.

(the) Valley of the Five Riders: a valley of lush grass and clear water named for the five Riders of Valon slain in the Battle of Stormhelm Defile. This vale is situated on the western side of the Grimwall Mountains and is the first valley south of Ragad Vale. Here were buried the Five Riders.

Valon: a Realm of Mithgar noted for its lush, green prairies and for its fiery horses. Roughly circular and divided into four Reaches (quadrants), the Land is bounded on the north-to-east-to-south margin by the River Argon, beyond which lie Riamon and Pellar; on the south-to-west margin by the Red Hills, beyond which lies Jugo; and on the west-to-north margin by the Gûnarring and by the Great Escarpment, beyond which, respectively, lie Gûnar and Darda Galion.

Valonian: a native of Valon. Also a term meaning "of Valon."

Valonian Battle-tongue. See Valur.

Valonners: Cotton's name for the Riders of Valon in Brytta's force.

Valur (Valur: our tongue): the ancient War-tongue of Valon. Also known as the Battle-tongue of the Valanreach, the Valonian Battle-tongue, and the War-tongue of Valon. (For various Valur words and phrases, see Appendix: Translations of Words and Phrases.)

Vanadurin (Valur: bond-lasting = our lasting bond): Battle-word of Valon meaning Warriors of the Pledge.

Vanar: the capital city of Valon, central to the Realm.

Vanareich (Valur: our nation): a battleword of the Valonian War-tongue meaning Men of the Land of Valon.

Vanidar (Sylva: vani = silver, dar = leaf): an Elf. Lian warrior. One of the Squad of Kraggen-cor. Also known as Alor Vanidar, Shannon, Shannon Silverleaf, Silverleaf, Vanidar Shannon Silverleaf, and Vanidar Silverleaf.

Vanidar Shannon Silverleaf. See Vanidar.

Vaidar Silverleaf. See Vanidar.

Vanidor (Sylva: vani = silver, dor = branch): an Elf. Lian
warrior. Elf Lord. Son of Talarin and Rael. Twin brother of
Gildor, brother of Faeon. Hero. One of four Elves sent on a
mission into Gron to spy out Modru's strength at the Iron
Tower and to rescue Laurelin, if possible; Vanidor was torture-
slain by Modru at the Kinstealer's holt while on this mission.
Also known as Alor Vanidor, Lord Vanidor, Silverbranch,
and Vanidor Silverbranch.

Vani-lērihha (Sylva: silver-larks): silvery songbirds that disappeared from Darda Galion ages agone. It is told among the
Elves that when the Vani-lērihha return, dire times will be
upon Mithgar. Also known as Silverlarks.

Vanil Falls (Sylva: vanil = silvery): a cataract where the
Nith River plunges over the Great Escarpment to fall into the
Cauldron. Also known as the Falls of Vanil.

Vidron: a Man of Valon. The commander of the army of
Challerain Keep, and of the Alliance of Wellen and Arden
during the Winter War. Hrosmarshal. Reachmarshal. Field-
marshal. Kingsgeneral. General. A member of Aurion's and
then Galen's War-councils. Hero. Also known as the Whelmer
of Modru's Horde.

Vidron's Legion: the Alliance of Wellen and Arden. Also
the name given to the Wellenen who rode with Vidron to the
Boskydells, to Gûnarring Gap, and to Grūwen Pass.

(the) Vorvor (Châkur: wheel): a whirlpool on the edge of the
Pitch into which First Durek was cast by Squam. Durek was
drawn under the surface and into the caverns of Kraggen-cor.
Also known as Durek's Wheel.

V'ttacku (Valur: strike, attack): a battleword in the Valonian
War-tongue meaning attack.

Vulgs: large, black, Wolf-like creatures. Virulent bite. Suffer
the Ban. Vulgs act as scouts and trackers as well as ravers.
Also known as Modru's curs, and as Vulpen (Slûk).

Vûlks (Sylva: Vûlk = dread power): a class of evil creatures
having special powers; these powers range from those of
Gyphon (nearly equal to Adon's) to the minor effects of the
Ghûls. Another creature, the Gargon, was a major Vûlk with
power equal to that of a Wizard.

*   *   *

Waerans (singular: Waeran) (Châkur: wary-ones): Dwarven name for Warrows (q.v.).

Waerlinga (singular: Waerling) (OP; Sylva: caution-small-ones = cautious-wee-folk): Elven and Pellarion name for Warrows (q.v.).

Waldana (singular: Waldan) (Valur: wood-ones): the name used by the Men of Valon to mean Warrows (q.v.).

Waldfolc (Valur: wood-folk = folk of the woods): the name used by the Men of Valon to mean Warrow Folk.

(the) Wanderjahre (Twyll: wandering-days): the time in Warrow history when they wandered restlessly over the face of Mithgar seeking a homeland.

(the) War-banner of the House of Valon. See (the) War-banner of Valon.

(the) War-banner of Valon: the battle flag of Valon: a white horse rampant on a field of green. Also known as the green-and-white of Valon, and as the War-banner of the House of Valon.

(the) Warder (of the Dark Mere). See (the) Krakenward.

Warder of the Northern Regions of Rell. See Talarin.

(the) War Hall: one of the chambers of Kraggen-cor on the Brega Path. A vast hall, it was used to muster the Dwarven nation under Kraggen-cor when war threatened. Also known as the Mustering Chamber (of the First Neath), the Mustering Hall, the War Hall of Kraggen-cor, and the War Hall of the First Neath.

(the) War Hall of Kraggen-cor. See (the) War Hall.

(the) War Hall of the First Neath. See (the) War Hall.

(the) War Horn. See (the) golden War Horn.

(the) War of Kraggen-cor: taken to mean collectively all the skirmishes and battles fought in the Quest of Kraggen-cor.

Waroo: the Baeron name given to a mythical white Bear, bringer of winter storms. Also known as Waroo the Blizzard. Akin to the White Bear (q.v.).

Waroo the Blizzard. See Waroo.

warren: a large burrow (q.v.).

Warrows (singular: Warrow): one of the Folk of Mithgar. For a description of Warrows, see Appendix: A Word About Warrows. Also known as little uns, Waerans (Châkur), Waerlinga (OP, Sylva), Waerlings (Warrow corruption of

Waerlinga), Waldana (Valur), *Waldfolc* (Valur), Wee Folk,
Wee Ones.

(the) Wars of Vengeance: the battles fought in the millennia-
long conflict between the Dwarves and the Squam, beginning
when the Foul Folk hurled First Durek into the Vorvor, and
ending at the conclusion of the Great War.

(the) War-tongue (of Valon). See Valur.

(the) Wastes of Gron. See Gron.

(the) Watchtower: taken to mean the watchtower (now ruins)
upon the crest of Beacontor.

waugh (Slûk: untranslated cry of startlement): a maggot-folk
squall of startlement and fear.

(the) Way. See (the) Old Rell Way.

waybread: a nutritious, dense, biscuit-like bread carried by
wayfarers.

wayleader: a guide.

(the) Wee Folk. See Warrows.

Wee One: a name often given to one of the Wee Folk by
other Folk of Mithgar.

Wee Ones. See Warrows.

Wee Perry: Ursor's name for Perry.

Weiunwood (Stonehiller: Wei = wee, un = one, wood =
forest; Weiunwood = wee-one-forest): a large, shaggy forest, in the Wilderland north of Harth and south of Rian,
where Warrows live. Also known as the 'Wood.

Weiunwood Alliance: the alliance of Men (of Stonehill and
the Wilderland), Elves (of Arden), and Warrows (of Weiunwood). In the Winter War, this alliance successfully fought
one of Modru's Hordes in the Battle of Weiunwood. Also at
times known as the Alliance.

Wellen: a Realm of Mithgar bordering on the Boskydells to
the east, Dalara to the north, Trellinath to the south, and the
Ryngar Arm of the Weston Ocean to the west.

werelight: a spectral light.

(the) West Hall: one of the chambers in Kraggen-cor, just
inside the Dusk-Door, in which the Deevewalkers sought
refuge from the Krakenward. The first chamber on the Brega
Path.

(the) Wheel of Fate: usually taken to mean the inexorable
turnings of Fortune that lead toward some great, foreordained
event.

(the) Whelmer of Modru's Horde: the name given to Vidron by Talarin after the valiant stand in the Battle of Grüwen Pass.

(the) White Bear: a mythical Bear of Riamonian legend, bringer of winter storms. Akin to Waroo (q.v.).

(the) White Unicorn Inn (of Stonehill): an inn in Stonehill. Also known as the 'Unicorn.

(the) White Wolf: a mythical Wolf of Warrow legend, bringer of winter storms.

(the) Wilderland: the wilderness between Harth to the south and Rian to the north, Rhone to the east, and the western edge of the Battle Downs to the west.

(the) Wilderness Hills: a low range of inhospitable hills in the Wilderland bordering on the River Caire.

(the) Wilder River: a river between the Dellin Downs and the Wilderness Hills. Running southeasterly from the Crossland Road, the river eventually flows into the River Caire.

(the) wild kine of the south. See black oxen.

Willen Greylock: a buccan Warrow of the Boskydells. Husband of Raven (Underbank) Greylock. Sire of Robin. A scholar, historian; founder of the Ravenbook Scholars.

Willowdell: a Boskydell village along the Crossland Road in Eastdell.

Will Whitlatch, the Third: a buccan Warrow of the Boskydells. Mayor of Woody Hollow in the time of the Quest of Kraggen-cor.

Winternight: the cold darkness that grasped the land within the bounds of the Dimmendark in the time of the Winter War. Also known as 'Night.

(the) Winter War: the War between Modru and the Alliance. Fought in the Fourth Era. Called the Winter War because of the bitter coldness that gripped the land within the Dimmendark.

(the) Winter War Quest: generally taken to mean the events involving Sir Tuckerby Underbank and his friends during the Winter War.

(the) Wizard Grevan. See Grevan.

(the) Wizard Grevan's rune: a rune *G* inscribed in theen upon the Dusk-Door.

Wizard-metal: a special metal used by Wizards to form runes, sigils, glyphs, and lines that glow when evoked by words of power. Wizardmetal, like silveron, is probably an alloy, rather than an element. Also known as theen.

Wizards: persons of arcane lore and power. Said to live in, on, or near the Black Mountain of Xian.

Wizard-word: a word of power; e.g., Gaard is a Wizard-word.

Wolf Patrol: one or more patrols of Thornwalker archers guarding flocks against Wolves during times of winter famine.

woodsmen of the Argon vales. See Baeron.

Woody Hollow: a Boskydell town north of the Crossland Road and inside the western edge of Eastdell. Also known as the Hollow.

Woody Hollow Hall: the town hall of Woody Hollow. Also known as the Hall and as Hollow Hall.

Woody Hollow Road: the road between Woody Hollow and Budgens.

Word from the Beyond: a Boskydell phrase meaning news not to be trusted until confirmed.

Wrall: a Baeran Man. Youngest son of Baru, the Passwarden of the Crestan Pass in 5E231.

Wrg (Valur: foul-worms): the term used by the Men of Valon to mean maggot-folk.

Wrg-doors. See Rück-doors.

Wrg-lope: the loping run of the maggot-folk.

Wylf: a Man of Valon. One of the riders in Brytta's force. Noted for his ability to find comfort.

Xian: a Land far to the east in Mithgar where Wizards are said to dwell.

Year's End Eve: the evening before Year's End Day; December 30.

Year's Long Day: the longest day of the year; June 21. Also known as Mid-Year's Day.

young buccan (plural: young buccen): the age-name of a buccan between twenty and thirty years old.

young damman (plural: young dammen): the age-name of a damman between twenty and thirty years old.

youngling: the age-name of a buccan or damman between birth and ten years old.

Yrm (OP: worms of corruption): the term used by Men of Pellar to mean maggot-folk.

ziggurt (Châkur: shatter-rock): a Dwarven term meaning stone that is cracked and crazed.

AFTERWORD

I hope you enjoyed reading The Silver Call as much as I enjoyed writing it. For those of you who may be wondering, I have in rough outline another Mithgarian tale. I don't know how long it may take me to see if it's any good. But I'll tell you this: if I become as enraptured with this new saga as I was with The Iron Tower and The Silver Call, then it might take quite a while; for it will be a soft-blooming love, requiring much nurturing, and its many manifestations will be revealed to me only in their own true time.

D. L. McKiernan
Westerville, Ohio—1984

ABOUT THE AUTHOR

DENNIS L. MCKIERNAN was born April 4, 1932, in Moberly, Missouri, where he lived until age eighteen, when he joined the U.S. Air Force, serving four years spanning the Korean War. He received a B.S. in Electrical Engineering from the University of Missouri in 1958 and an M.S. in the same field from Duke University in 1964. Employed by a leading research and development laboratory, he lives with his family in Westerville, Ohio. His debut novel was the critically acclaimed trilogy of The Iron Tower. His second novel, The Silver Call duology, continues the Mithgarian saga.

Ø SIGNET (0451)

DISTANT REALMS

☐ **THE COPPER CROWN: The First Novel of** *The Keltiad* **by Patricia Kennealy.** When their powers of magic waned on ancient Earth, the Kelts and their allies fled the planet for the freedom of distant star realms. But the stars were home to two enemy star fleets mobilized for final, devastating war ... "A gorgeous yarn!"—Anne McCaffrey.
(143949—$3.50)

☐ **THE THRONE OF SCONE: The Second Novel of** *The Keltiad* **by Patricia Kennealy.** Aeron, Queen of the Kelts, has fled to the stars on a desperate mission to find the fabled Thirteen Treasures of King Arthur, hidden for hundreds of years. But while she pursues her destiny, all the forces of Keltia are mobilizing for war. "Brilliant!"—Anne McCaffrey.
(148215—$3.50)

☐ **GREYBEARD by Brian Aidiss.** Radiation was the executioner in a world where starvation was a way of life—where hostile armed camps, deadly diseases and mutant creatures ruled. But into this world came Greybeard—the last preserver in a world gone mad, fighting desperately to find and save the last, lost hope of humankind ... "Top-flight adventure tale ..."—August Derleth *The Capital Times*
(146611—$2.95)

☐ **GREENBRIAR QUEEN A Fantasy Novel by Sheila Gilluly.** Could they find the one true leader to stand against the Power unchained by evil wizardry? The Dark Lord's reign is about to begin, for the age of doom prophesied long ago is now upon the people of Ilyria.
(151437—$3.50)

☐ **THE MAGIC BOOKS by Andre Norton.** Three magical excursions into spells cast and enchantments broken, by a wizard of science fiction and fantasy: *Steel Magic*, three children's journey to an Avalon whose dark powers they alone can withstand, *Octagon Magic*, a young girl's voyage into times and places long gone, and *Fur Magic*, where a boy must master the magic of the ancient gods to survive.
(152328—$3.95)

Prices slightly higher in Canada

**Buy them at your local
bookstore or use coupon
on last page for ordering.**

Ø SIGNET SCIENCE FICTION   (0451)

GLIMPSE THE FUTURE . . .

☐ **WORLDSTONE by Victoria Strauss.** When parallel worlds collide, who is friend and who is foe? Alexina Taylor, a loner, has always felt different—as if she's waiting for something. Then she discovers Taryn, a young boy who has come through a passage in a nearby cave that leads to a parallel universe—one powered by telepathy. Together they journey through the other world seeking out a renegade who has stolen the Worldstone—the heart of the Mindpower world!!   (147561—$3.50)

☐ **GREYBEARD by Brian Aldiss.** Radiation was the executioner in a world where starvation was a way of life—where hostile armed camps, deadly diseases and mutant creatures ruled. But into this world came Grey-beard—the last preserver in a world gone mad, fighting desperately to find and save the last, lost hope of humankind . . . "Top-flight adventure tale . . ."—August Derleth, *The Capital Times*
                                                      (146611—$2.95)

☐ **EMILE AND THE DUTCHMAN by Joel Rosenberg.** Their mission was simple—the survival of the human race. It should have been no problem for the two toughest, cleverest mavericks in outer space... that is until they found themselves pitted against the most cunning and deadly of intergalactic aliens...   (140168—$2.95)

☐ **WULFSTON'S ODYSSEY A Fantasy Novel by Jean Lorrah and Winston A. Howlett.** Can Wulfston, the Savage Empire's greatest Adept, rescue Leonardo from an African witch-queen's war? Wulfston is ready to destroy anyone who gets in his way during this deadly contest of wills.   (150562—$2.95)

☐ **THE DARKLING HILLS by Lori Martin.** When the beautiful Princess Dalleena and the handsome nobleman Rendall fall in love, defying an ancient law, they invoke a searing prophecy of doom. Betrayed and exiled by their homeland, the couple must struggle to remain together through a brutal siege from a rival empire. "An exciting, charming, and irresistible story."—Tom Monteleone, author of LYRICA   (152840—$3.50)

Prices slightly higher in Canada

**Buy them at your local
bookstore or use coupon
on next page for ordering.**

Ⓞ SIGNET   (0451)

DEMONS AND SORCERERS

☐ **BARBARIANS II edited by Robert Adams, Martin Greenberg, and Charles G. Waugh.** Here are tales of heroes and heroines who live by the strength of their sword arms and the sharpness of their wits, warriors sworn to boldly conquer or bravely die in the attempt, whether locked in combat with mortal, demon, or god.   (151984—$3.95)

☐ **WRAITH BOARD (Book 2 of The Gaming Magi series) by David Bischoff.** When the multiverse turns topsy-turvy, then Puissant Lords of the Universe fear for their lives . . . the moon becomes a revolving die in the sky . . . a bent and ugly cobbler becomes a handsome and brave hero . . . a severed sorcerer's head speaks . . . and even the Gaming Magi becomes playing pieces on the Wraith Board of time . . .(136691—$2.95)

☐ **MORLAC: Quest for the Green Magician by Gary Alan Ruse.** Conjured from a storm-rent sea, a creature called Morlac staggers beneath a mist-shrouded sun on an alien beach. Before he can win his freedom and live as human—or return to the water, Morlac must follow the sorcerer through *all* the perils. . . .   (144473—$3.50)

Prices slightly higher in Canada

_____

Buy them at your local bookstore or use this convenient coupon for ordering.

NEW AMERICAN LIBRARY
P.O. Box 999, Bergenfield, New Jersey 07621

Please send me the books I have checked above. I am enclosing $_____
(please add $1.00 to this order to cover postage and handling). Send check or money order—no cash or C.O.D.'s. Prices and numbers are subject to change without notice.

Name_____

Address_____

City _____ State _____ Zip Code _____
Allow 4-6 weeks for delivery.
This offer is subject to withdrawal without notice.